THE RICH AND THE RIGHTEOUS
HELEN VAN SLYKE

It was the eve of his testimonial dinner, a salute to the end of an illustrious business career. And his final farewell speech to the billion dollar company he founded would end with the nomination of a new chief executive, a decision still unresolved as the dinner began.

The Rich and the Righteous is a bold and powerful novel about big business, where instinct at a Seventh Avenue fashion showing can make or break a retailer, where a vice-president negotiates the purchase of a cosmetics firm at a dinner party, where scandal runs straight down from the store president's luxurious office to an ambitious buyer's cluttered desk.

This is an honest, painful analysis of one man's life. It is about the empire he built, the family he loves, the people he trusts and the religion he turns to when he needs it most. It is a frightening look at high-level corporate politics, where a whispered word or an unsigned letter can destroy a reputation, a career or a marriage.

It is also a searching story of the four men and one woman who hope to replace Joseph Haylow, the dynamic, well-meaning chairman who had never doubted his employees' loyalty until his last year in power: the year in which he was forced to name his successor. It was a year in which Haylow discovered that he was mortal and fallible, and that some of the people closest to him were ruthless and weak. It was the year of The Rich and the Righteous.

The
Rich
and the
Righteous

HELEN VAN SLYKE

CASSELL · LONDON

CASSELL & COMPANY LTD
35 Red Lion Square, London WC1R 4SJ
Sydney, Auckland
Toronto, Johannesburg

First published in Great Britain 1972

ISBN 0 304 93866 1

Reproduced and printed in Great Britain by
Redwood Press Limited
Trowbridge & London
F.971

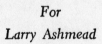

For
Larry Ashmead

The
Rich
and the
Righteous

1 ✧

In January, New York takes on the sullen aspect of a brooding empress, her massive frame wrapped in stark steel gray, her cold glass façade brittle and hurtful to the touch. Icy ruts pockmark her face, with black beauty-spots of soot emphasizing its ugliness. Like some temporarily deposed monarch, the queen of all cities has put away her crown of Christmas lights, all diamonds and rubies and emeralds. Her red-suited, white-bearded troubadours are hushed for another year, her playful courtiers and their jesters departed for the more convivial kingdoms of the Sun.

Only those subjects too rich or too poor to escape remain at her feet. The very rich bound by ropes of gold which, in turn, harness their own industrial empires; the poor chained by poverty which demands, among other hardships, the endurance of another New York winter.

At eight-thirty on this January night, the poor, muffled in scarves and earmuffs, plunged past the Lexington Avenue entrance of the Grand Excelsior hotel toward the subways which would carry the late-workers home to Queens and Brooklyn. The rich, and those whose livelihoods depended upon their association with the rich, hurried out of their rented limousines and taxis into the Park Avenue entrance of the hotel, the ladies ducking carefully coiffed heads against the biting winds which raced up the naked avenue.

1

One thousand of these formally dressed people whirling through the Grand Excelsior's revolving doors were en route to a commercial rite known as "the testimonial dinner." At least once a week, the Grand Ballroom was the scene of some larger-than-life banquet sponsored by a charity or by a major corporation honoring one of its officers.

In format, these dinners were depressingly identical. The stage at the east end of the room invariably was set up as a three-tier dais, like some elongated wedding cake designed to hold forty-eight rigidly molded, desperately bored pieces of human decoration. The highest ranking guests sat at the lowest tier which contained the fewest number of chairs and the largest and most hideous gladiola and chrysanthemum floral arrangements. The second tier, slightly elevated, duplicated the first, fanning out to accommodate more seats for slightly less important dignitaries. The botanical abortions created by the hotel florist were smaller reproductions of those on the main dais.

The third and highest tier, known to the waiters as "Has-been Heaven," grudgingly accommodated those whom protocol demanded be on stage, but whose names and faces were so little known that it didn't matter whether the audience seated at tables on the ballroom floor could identify them in the dim upper reaches. At the third tier the flowers were smaller and sadder, like the occupants whose dinner jackets had a greenish-black hue compounded of age and bad lighting.

Nevertheless, at any testimonial dinner for an important man, the mark of caste was to be seated somewhere on the stage. Caste because one's presence there denoted some degree of importance in the life of the honored guest. And there was always the consoling fact that these were free seats, as opposed to those at the tables below.

The going rate for tables of ten jammed on the ballroom floor was a thousand dollars, most of it tax deductible. Tonight the proceeds would go to the Haylow Foundation's Fund for Biblical Research, the pet project of the honored guest, Joseph Woodward Haylow, retiring Chairman of The Haylow Corporation, the world's largest and most powerful complex of retail clothing stores.

Only two visible points of difference distinguished this dinner from the thousands which had preceded it. One was the presence of the Honorable Clinton McCarthy, Governor of the State of New York, whose appearance was mute testimony of the importance of the Vermont-based Haylow Corporation to the economy of his state. The other was the enormous flag which hung behind the dais. Of pale blue silk, it was emblazoned with an enormous golden H crowned by a halo of glittering stars. Haylow flags like this one flew over the main entrance of the seven thousand Haylow clothing stores around the world. It was the proud and vulgar emblem of a billion-dollar business empire whose founder had parlayed a general store in Farmville, Vermont, into a world-wide network of fashion emporiums catering to cooks and countesses with equal success.

It was, however, the invisible and titillating aspects of this testimonial dinner which had filled the hundred-dollar-a-seat ballroom with the well-padded behinds of business leaders and members of the press. It was no secret that "The Monk of Merchandising," as *Time* once cover-captioned him, was reluctant to retire. A victim of the company policy of retirement at sixty-five, mandatory for all executives, Joe Haylow had, in the words of a homespun columnist, "raised up a crow to eat out his eyes." Nearly forty years before, when Haylow was young, vigorous, caught up in his dreams of the future, sixty-five seemed an age that other people reached. It was entirely in keeping with his advanced and progressive thinking to institute the mandatory retirement policy which forced older men to step aside and give younger ones a chance at the top jobs.

Now, as everyone in the ballroom knew, Joe Haylow would have given a great part of his millions to undo that long-ago decision. Ironically a victim of his own farsightedness, he now viewed it with the unreasonable resentment and almost uncontrollable despair of a man driven to suicide and yearning to live.

Equally fascinating to the assemblage was the fact that tonight Joe Haylow would announce the name of his own successor, the new Chairman of The Haylow Corporation. Since he was still the absolute autocrat and major stockholder, his decision would be routinely approved the next day by the Board of Directors. For once, this was no cut-and-dried, foregone conclusion, as it would be in more orthodox organizations where the President automatically moves into the Chairmanship and all other officers take one giant step forward on the corporate chart. There had been talk that Haylow might bypass Richard Cabot, Haylow's President, in favor of one of four other officers of the company. All of them were at the first dais tonight: Roger Haylow, the Chairman's brilliant thirty-seven-year-old son who was Executive Vice President; Bradford Deland III, the cool, socialite Financial Vice President; Mike Warner, the dynamic young President of Star Stores, Haylow's largest and most profitable department store chain; and Bridget Manning, the much-publicized, universally admired lady President of Bridget's, The Haylow Corporation's money-making group of specialty fashion stores. Any one of them, so the rumors ran, could be tapped by the unpredictable, daring, opinionated man who took advice from no one but God.

The press, needless to say, was out in full force for this unusual dinner whose repercussions would be felt in the business, financial, and fashion communities. Photographers crouched at the base of the stage, ready to snap Haylow and the Governor in jovial, hand-clasping mutual admiration. The news magazines were attracted by the presence of the cheru-

4

bic, elderly Methodist minister, Jimmy Jackson, whose "Pray-Ins" attracted hundreds of thousands of people and millions of dollars when they were held in the Hollywood Bowl, Wrigley Field, or Madison Square Garden. Haylow was a devout Methodist and Jimmy was not only his spiritual advisor but one of his direct lines of communication to the middle-class buying public.

A reporter and photographer from *Women's Wear Daily*, the gossipy fashion trade newspaper, were there to note what Mrs. Joseph Haylow, Bridget Manning, and Mrs. Bradford Deland were wearing. The caustic society editor of New York's most important daily would write a story for tomorrow's edition, painfully detailing how many women wore last season's marked-down evening gowns and who snubbed whom in the ladies' room. The determinedly cheeky jet-set columnist of a local tabloid would find, or invent, at least three juicy items about the evening. One would be a thinly veiled, perennial reference to the widely held belief that Bridget Manning was Joe Haylow's mistress.

Not actively working, but present in the call of duty, were the editors of *Vogue, Harper's Bazaar, Town & Country, Glamour,* and *Mademoiselle,* accompanied by the advertising managers of their magazines which depended heavily on ads run by the various Haylow divisions.

But the center of all attention, on and off the dais, was the commanding figure of Joseph Woodward Haylow, that increasingly rare and fascinating symbol of the self-made man. At sixty-five, Haylow was still young in mind, strong in body, and immovable in will. Physically, he looked ten years younger than he was. His body, always husky, was still trim and paunch-free. His dinner jacket was of a current cut, only a shade more conservative than those worn by the younger executives. The dark hair was carefully touched up so that the considerable gray showed only at the temples. The famous energy was as boundless today as it had been forty

5

years ago. And his discipline, if anything, was greater. Joe Haylow didn't drink, smoke, dance, play cards, or swear. Ostensibly, he abstained from these things because of his deep religious devotion. In fact, this was only partially true. Brought up in a strict Methodist household, where such pleasures or vices were forbidden, he had not acquired these habits in his early life. And by the time he was free to sample them, his ambitious, realistic mind advised him to reject cigarettes and liquor as monsters that dulled the brain and threatened the health. Dancing and card playing, by the same rationale, were consumers of time that could be better spent in the pursuit of knowledge, wealth, and power. Swearing was a luxury he compared to psychiatry, seeing both as crutches which weak men used to support their own conversational or emotional inadequacies.

Through all his adult life, Joe Haylow worked tirelessly, slept minimally, read prodigiously. His work was his life, and, with the church, his all-consuming passion. Since his business was selling clothes to people, he went, under the guise of business, to where the people were. Every year increased his desire to be "with it." People who did not understand Haylow, and who knew of him only as a puritan-like figure, were often surprised to see him at a theatre opening or in a new restaurant or even in one of the "singles bars" where the young went to find each other for a night or a lifetime. Such people did not understand that Haylow had to know what was happening, had to be able to stay always a step ahead of his competitors and, equally important, ahead of his own executives.

Of all cardinal sins, to Joe Haylow, one of the blackest was wasting time. He deplored the hours that most people spent sleeping and was convinced that this time-wasting practice was a matter of habit, the need for which, like the craving for tobacco or alcohol, could be mastered.

The Rich and the Righteous

At his weekly early morning staff meetings, he frequently expounded this theory. "No one needs more than four hours' sleep in every twenty-four," he'd say. "No matter what time you go to bed, just say to yourself, 'I'm going to wake up feeling rested and wonderful.' And you will."

Nearly all of Haylow's anxious-to-please executives tried the theory the following week, the night before the next meeting. Arriving bleary-eyed and exhausted, they stifled their yawns and reported to the Chairman that by-golly-Chief-you're-right-as-usual-it-works.

Haylow would straight-facedly congratulate them, knowing they were lying and secretly pleased by their failure. It reassured him that not one of them had his strength and stamina, supernatural attributes generously bestowed on men like Thomas Edison and Joe Haylow by an understanding and benevolent God.

In a man of Joe Haylow's driving and all-consuming ambition, his adoration of God seemed, to many people, incongruous and paradoxical. Haylow found it neither. He worshipped the Almighty extravagantly, blindly, unceasingly. He thought of Him as a kind of Super-Chairman, the all-wise and kindly employer who had directed Haylow's success. Like any good and faithful employee, Haylow not only served the Boss, he endlessly praised Him. He was God's Public Relations Man whose ample salary was paid in a medium of exchange called Success. If some of the business decisions he was forced to make in the interest of Haylow might seem questionable in the light of a charitable and forgiving Christian credo, Haylow was sincerely convinced that he was acting under God's advice and direction. Take the matter of firing people, a painful process for most executives. Haylow could, kindly but concisely, discharge a man with a wife, three children, and a large mortgage without feeling the pangs of remorse that so many other employers

7

suffered. When such a step had to be taken, Haylow knew that God had other, better plans for the man. He was not an unfeeling employer, simply a realistic one. Haylow employees invariably were snapped up by rival companies who knew that a man trained under the Haylow stars was, in all likelihood, an able executive and, without question, a hardworking and obedient one. Joe took this to be evidence of God's all-knowing guidance. Just as he knew that God had put the idea of a speed-reading course in Haylow's head. Since taking it, Haylow could zip through the mountains of mail, memos, and magazines which flooded his homes and offices in New York and Farmville. He also could reread the Bible cover to cover every year, a practice he had been able to maintain since taking the course ten years before. This word-devouring pace also enabled him to race through nearly every new book worth knowing about. And if the business·like scanning in a few hours of some work into which the author had put two years of agony deprived Haylow of the slow, pure, sensory savoring of the writing, he neither realized the lack nor, consequently, regretted it.

Unless he was out of the country, Haylow made it a point to spend weekends in Farmville, the quiet little New England town which remained headquarters for the giant Haylow Corporation and official home of the Haylow family. On Sunday, Joe went to church twice and taught Bible class to younger members of the Farmville Methodist Church. On Sunday evenings Joe and his wife Patricia had supper with Jimmy Jackson, the minister who had married them. Frequently the Haylows' elder son, Woodward, also a minister, Woodward's wife, Marjorie, and their two children joined the group. The church over which Jackson presided today was a far cry from the small, simple, white one in which he'd married the Haylows forty years ago. Today the town was dominated by the church, a two-million-dollar, ultra-modern architectural symbol of adulation donated by the Haylow

Foundation. The international revival meetings also were
financed by Haylow money. And though the Haylow name
was never connected with the affluence of the church, insiders knew that Farmville Methodist was one of the biggest
stockholders in The Haylow Corporation and that the stock
it owned was administered and voted by Joseph Woodward
Haylow.

Although he believed his faith to be the only right and
true one, for the sake of God and the Haylow stores Joe Haylow also enthusiastically supported other men's religions. He
was a frequent guest speaker at fund-raising dinners for
Catholic Charities and a dear friend of the Cardinals of Los
Angeles, Boston, and New York. The people of Israel were
all the better for Haylow's contributions to the United Jewish Appeal. One of the Chairman's most highly prized possessions was an ancient Hebrew Scroll presented to him by
the UJA and carefully displayed under glass in the reception
room of the Haylow offices in New York. It was a source of
great interest to the Jewish manufacturers who sold goods
to Haylow stores. It was considerably less impressive to the
rich, snobbish New York Jewish bankers who privately considered Haylow a cross between an outright con man and a
"goddamn hymn-singing hypocrite."

Joe Haylow was neither of these. Unapproachable, difficult
to know, he could have moments of compassion and something bordering on sentimentality when it involved any of
the few people he felt close to and loved. Yet he shied away
from the taking of love, from the vulnerability of it. Love
was given by habit to his wife, by duty to his children, and
by choice to God.

In the company, and behind Joe's back, the inside joke
was that The Lord was The Man Who Came to Dinner. God
lived with the Haylows in the sprawling, comfortable Vermont house when Joe was in residence, usually from Friday
night until Monday evening. When Joe moved to the Park

9

Avenue duplex, God went along, taking up residence among a priceless collection of modern paintings, antique bibles, abstract sculpture, and copies of *Fortune*.

Haylow's gratitude to his Maker had even turned His servant into a lay-preacher of sorts. Joe often managed to bring his religious fervor into the talks he made to civic and business groups. He had developed three speeches which he used over and over. The first was called "Industry and the Almighty." The second, "Heaven Is in Fashion." And the most recent was "Can Christ Be Put on the Computer?" When people asked him how he found time to compose such eloquent, timely addresses, Haylow, pleased with his little pun, answered, "God is my ghost writer." Among the Elks and the Rotarians, such modesty gave credence to the desirable legend that the Chairman had a heart as big as his business and a soul as humble as that of the lowliest stock clerk who toiled in a Haylow store at the minimum Federal wage.

Sitting on the dais at this strangely impersonal, almost funereal banquet, Joe had, as he'd had many times before, a distinct feeling of extrasensory perception. It was as though he were reading the minds of the handful of people who were closest in spirit to him. On the second tier he could imagine the sad, troubled expression of the Reverend Jimmy Jackson. He knew that the perpetually beaming face, so familiar to television audiences, would be trying to mask a look of concern. Jimmy was one of the few people who knew that Haylow's unhappiness was far deeper than the matter of his retirement, hateful as it was. The honored guest had spent too many hours in that quiet, peaceful study being the Joe Haylow that few people had ever seen. Jimmy had heard him confess his self-doubts and loneliness, recite his litany of failures as a father and a husband, his injustice and arrogance as an employer, his hypocrisy as a religious man. He'd even heard Joe strike out at God's cruelty. The Lord had tried

Haylow in this last year, not with the loss of possessions or health, as he tried Job, but with all the things he'd never been good at, like his capacity for compassion and understanding and forgiveness. I wonder how Jimmy thinks I've measured up, Haylow mused. In many ways I've betrayed him, too.

Jackson's thoughts were, as Joe felt, reaching out toward this man who'd been so good to him through the years. It seemed to Jimmy that all of Haylow's troubles had been sent in this time preceding the dreaded moment of his retirement. Perhaps if I were younger, more psychiatrist than old-fashioned parson, I could have helped him more through these past months, Jackson thought. He was awed by the strength with which Joe had faced all his problems, the threats of scandal, the demands of family, the choices which had had to be made not based on calculated business procedures but on the kind of human decisions which demanded the giving of heart and hand. He had suffered with Joe, and kept his secrets.

The only thing that Haylow had not confided to him was the name of his successor. Jackson did not know, for sure, who would be the next Chairman. It occurred to him, incredibly, that perhaps even at this last moment Haylow was still wrestling with his conscience. It seemed impossible that Joe could have come to the banquet with the matter still unresolved. A year ago Jackson would have found such an idea unsupportable. Tonight he was not certain. Help him God, he prayed silently. It is hard for a man to turn his life's work over to someone else, hard to be sure that he is making the right decision. But let it be the only just one, no matter how much he and others have to suffer for it.

Echoing Jackson's silent entreaties to the Lord was the lovely, well-dressed woman seated on Haylow's right. His wife Patricia—"my patrician Pat" as Joe sometimes called her—was an elegant, warm, and charming lady, still deeply in love with her husband. She was a wise and truly good human being who found good in everyone. No matter how unworthy or boring or absurd they were, Pat searched each person's character until she found a saving grace. It was a real thing to her, this belief that there was good in every man. Less outwardly devout than Haylow, she was inwardly a serene and intensely religious woman who found comfort in her faith, believing that God did not expect perfection in His creatures but that He realized the frailty of humanity and was appreciative of their feeble intent to be good.

With all this, Pat Haylow was also a gay and surprisingly sophisticated woman whose love was big enough not only for her family but for all the Haylow employees and acquaintances. No one had ever heard an ill word spoken of Pat Haylow. For all her gentle understanding, she was spirited and alert, with none of the saccharine, do-gooder qualities of the "professional Christians" who were her Farmville neighbors.

As Patricia Clark, she had married Joseph Haylow when he was twenty-five, she was twenty-three. Their backgrounds were as dissimilar as their personalities. Pat was San Francisco-born of a comfortable, upper middle-class family. She had made a modest debut, a bright, pretty, fun-loving young woman involved in the usual debutante round of parties and charity work, planning to marry one of the attractive young men of her group whom she had known all her life.

On her first trip east she went to visit a college classmate living in Farmville. Vermont was strange to her, provincial and dull compared to the cosmopolitan atmosphere of San Francisco. She was amazed at the pursed-lip dourness of the New England people, the narrowness of their interests, the rigidity of their moral standards. Then one night at a small dinner party she met the local boy-wonder Joe Haylow who contradicted his whole background. Energetic, enthusiastic, crackling with ambition, he was like a bolt of electricity bounding off a Vermont weather vane. That very first evening he told her of his plans for the building of an empire.

"Right now I've just got this one little store in Farmville," he explained. "But that's only the beginning. That one store is the beginning of a chain that will stretch around the world. There will be hundreds of Haylow stores. Thousands of them. Merchandising is in its infancy. There are millions of people out there just waiting to be told what to buy, only nobody's put the idea in their heads yet. That's what I'm going to do—build a big business based on new ideas."

She had been fascinated by this handsome, confident young man whose vitality and honesty were contagious. She believed that he would get everything he wanted, including, as she soon discovered, a young woman named Patricia Clark. Six months later Jimmy Jackson married them in the Farmville Methodist Church before the dubious eyes of Joe's parents and the disappointed eyes of her own.

The Clarks had serious reservations about the marriage. They had hoped for a more brilliant union for their only child, and the prospect of a son-in-law whose future might be no bigger than a single New England "dry goods store" troubled them deeply. So did the obvious willfulness of Pat's husband-to-be. There had been a violent protest from the Clarks when Pat announced her intention to be married in Farmville.

"That's unheard of," Mrs. Clark remonstrated. "A bride is married in her own church, not the bridegroom's! We'll have the wedding in San Francisco, of course."

But Patricia would not budge. The conventionality of her parents could not compete with the forcefulness of Joe's desires, then or ever.

"I'm sorry, darling," she told her mother. "I don't want to upset you, but Joe's church is so very important to him. More than mine is to me. As far as I'm concerned," she added lightly, "God is everywhere. But Joe is absolutely sure He's headquartered with Jimmy Jackson in Vermont."

There was no way to dissuade her. Just as there was no way

to convince the senior Haylows that their son was not marrying "out of his class." They loved Patricia on sight, but their New England conservatism made them worry that this pampered West Coast debutante might chafe under the stringent life that Joe offered her. Not that she had pretensions or gave any indication of being a spoiled brat. Still, without the optimism of youth to blind them, the Haylows wondered whether this golden girl could adapt to the narrowness of her new world and the domination of this loving but self-centered young man who had chosen her.

It had turned out to be a good marriage. They were completely happy. Within two years, Pat had produced two sons and Joe had given the Haylow chain two more stores in small, nearby communities.

At night, holding her in his arms in the big double bed, Joe would make warm, wonderful love to her. Then, lying back, he would talk about the future, their future.

Some of it was serious talk, most of it was about the business. Joe had a wry, mild, Yankee sense of humor when he chose.

"Tell you what, darling," he said one night. "Let's make a deal. Every time I open a new store, you have a new baby."

Pat had sat bolt upright, pretending horror. "Heaven forbid! At the rate you're going I'd have to produce quintuplets once a year!"

Those were the young, happy days when Joe's business was small and geographically arranged so that he came home every night, bubbling about the day's events, sketching plans for the next venture. They lived modestly, happily, turning whatever money Joe made back into the expansion of the Haylow stores. Through Joe's astute business sense, they even survived the Depression which put his few competitors out of the running.

How suddenly it all changed, Pat thought, sitting on the dais in her expensive evening dress, Joe's diamonds glittering on her fingers. Looking back, it seemed that overnight the Haylow empire had become a reality and Joe a beloved semi-stranger. The count on Haylow stores did rise to hundreds, then thousands. But the number of children stayed at two. There was less and less time for lovemaking, little more for conversation. On the three or four evenings that Joe was home he spent much of his time in his study with his papers and his telephone calls around the country and throughout the world. He was a firm, kind but disinterested father. Children's conversations bored him, and though he loved his sons, he was uneasy with them. Not for Joe were the camping trips, the PTA meetings, the father-son camaraderie of other Farmville parents. Woodward and Roger grew up adoring their mother and treating their father like some remote but kindly godfather entrusted with the responsibility for their formal education and their religious guidance, but unwilling, or unable, to reach them on anything approaching their own level. Woodward uncomplainingly accepted his father's absent-minded affection and unquestioningly took his suggestions and advice, even in so important a decision as choosing a career in the ministry. Roger was the rebel. More high-strung and sensitive than his older brother, Roger openly defied his father and obviously resented the lack of time and interest Joe gave to his children and his wife. From adolescence, Roger was in one scrape after another. He ran with a crowd his father disapproved of. He was known to come home in a less than sober state, particularly on the nights when Joe was there. Pat worried about her handsome, brilliant, quixotic younger son. She had been happily surprised when he agreed, indifferently, to join The Haylow Corporation after college. She was not sure that Roger would be happy in his father's business, but she knew that Joe could not tolerate the thought that one of his sons would not be his successor. He had long ago accepted the fact that Woodward was a gentle, uncommercial man, best suited for a life of religious work. Roger became the crown prince. There was no choice.

Though she made occasional visits to the New York apartment, Pat Haylow preferred to spend most of her time in Farmville. Occasionally she went with Joe on a business trip to Europe or the Orient, but she found these junkets wearing and hectic and was uncomfortable in the knowledge that she really was in the way.

She made only one demand on Joe. Every year, right after New Year's, Pat insisted that the two of them take a quiet vacation in Florida. They went every year to the same cottage on the grounds of the Lake Flamingo Hotel for two weeks of nearly uninterrupted holiday, in the middle of which they celebrated Joe's birthday. These were Pat's happiest weeks of the year. They read and swam and sunned and talked almost as easily and companionably as they had in the early years of their marriage. Occasionally, to Pat's disappointment, Joe had one of his executives fly down for the day for an important conference, and a few times in the middle of their holiday Joe had, almost with embarrassment, announced that he had to fly to New York for a meeting. But most of the time they were alone, their privacy only temporarily and happily invaded by the family and few close friends who came down for a couple of days in the birthday period.

In spite of her loneliness, Pat never doubted Joe's love or his loyalty. She had learned to live with his long absences, his intense preoccupation with business, his endless involvement with the work of God. Recognizing her place in the scheme of things, she accepted it with typical grace. The rumors of Joe's affair with Bridget troubled her so little that she had never even bothered to discuss it with him. She did not doubt that he might be tempted, for, like all men, Joe was flattered by the attention of an attractive woman. But she knew he would resist. Not only because of his marriage vows, but because Joe would not risk the wrath of his God or the disapproval of his stockholders by becoming involved in a scandal. The extracurricular marital affair had no place in the life of a Joe Haylow. Realistically, Pat knew he would dismiss the idea as sinful, inconvenient, and foolhardy.

Thinking of the past twelve months, Pat's compassionate heart went out to her husband. Almost guiltily, she had been looking forward to his retirement as eagerly as Joe had been dreading it. Pat faced the prospect of old age without fear or anxiety. Indeed, she welcomed it as a time when she would regain her husband. It made her sad that Joe fought the idea of growing old as though it were something he could conquer with drive and power and money.

Glancing at his strong profile beside her, Pat knew that this was one of the saddest nights of Haylow's life. Like Jackson, even she was not privy to Joe's decision about his successor. She knew what she hoped for, but she was not certain that her prayers would be answered.

Looking down the length of the long banquet table, Pat had a whimsical idea that the eight guests on the first tier were like the decorative mannequins constantly on display in Haylow store windows. Except, she thought, if we had been arranged by a competent display director we would be placed in more relaxed and appealing attitudes. At her right, tense and silent, sat her son Roger. On her left was an obviously introspective Joe Haylow seated next to the Governor. On the Governor's left was the eternally impassive face of Richard Cabot. Ranging down to the other end of the table, Brad Deland was making polite dinner-table talk with Bridget Manning at his left. At the far end, completing the line, was Mike Warner, a devoted, ambitious echo of Joe Haylow. The rather morbid notion struck her that they looked like a family waiting for the reading of the will, with the Governor as executor and the deceased rising to announce his own bequests. A shudder of surprise at her own gloomy analogy came over her. Joe has a long time to live, she told herself. But she knew that a part of him would die tonight, as surely as his announced successor would feel an elated surge of life.

One person at the table who felt confident of the outcome was The Haylow Corporation's current President, Richard Cabot. An orderly man, it was inconceivable to him that the second in command would not automatically become the first. After all, that was why he had been brought into the company ten years ago. At the insistence of the banks and the stockholders, Cabot had been hired as a back-up man to Haylow, against the unlikely event that illness or death would suddenly leave the vast company without a leader. Until Cabot's arrival, Joe had been President and Chief Executive Officer, with no one specifically positioned to take his place. Cabot knew that Haylow had not been too happy about the step which was an undesired reminder of his mortality. But as a businessman Joe had agreed to it, for it projected a company image of continuity of management that gave the stockholders a feeling of security and helped lull the talk in the financial community that The Haylow Corporation was a one-man organization that might well collapse with its founder's departure.

Typically, in the ten years of Cabot's Presidency, Haylow had tolerated him politely, treated him as a boring necessity, excluded him from important information and decisions. Cabot accepted his puppet role calmly, never protesting the fact that Haylow gave all the interviews, spoke publicly and internally for the corporation, presided at all executive meetings. Accepting virtual anonymity was not difficult for him, for he was at heart an introverted man more interested in profit and loss statements than in publicity and self-promotion. Haylow gave lip-service to Cabot's title, occasionally asking his advice and taking it only when it agreed with his own. Cabot was content to bide his time until the

Chairman's retirement. A decade was not too long to wait for such a prize and he had already formulated plans for his own regime. Lacking Haylow's flair for dramatics, his daring adventures into new areas, Cabot would steer the Haylow ship on a steadier, surer, less risky course. The company would go forward, not with a surge but with a profitable, even flow.

Cabot assumed that, sensibly, Roger Haylow would become President tomorrow, waiting out the next thirteen years until Cabot's own retirement. He wondered how serenely Roger would accept this. The boy was bright but hard to handle. Lately there had been some unpleasant rumors about him, but Cabot had been unable to get the facts. Joe Haylow had confided nothing, and Cabot's information was hardly more than that picked up by the secretaries at the water cooler. Soon it will be different, he thought. With Haylow gone, secrets will no longer be kept from me. Roger may become President but he will live in my shadow, just as I have lived in his father's.

The young man in Cabot's thoughts was the outward image of the rising young executive. At thirty-seven, Roger Haylow had the same dark, magnetic good looks that his father had had. From that point on, he was as unlikely a son as the Chairman could have produced. Unmarried and agnostic, Roger Haylow's god was Irreverence. He mocked the solemnity of Big Business. He was flippant about his father's religion and disinterested in his brother's pious way of life. Yet Roger had become a highly thought-of young business executive. Inheriting his father's quick mind, he was the only one in the company who could anticipate Haylow's decisions and upstage him with unexpected, invariably correct solutions to problems which Haylow presented to the executive committee.

By all modern standards, he was the shining example of the progressive young executive. People commented often on Joe's good fortune in having a son so qualified to carry on the business. So many rich men, they said, seemed to have in-effectual offspring, unable to follow in their fathers' footsteps. But Haylow, as usual, was blessed.

When these clichés were delivered in his presence, Roger smiled his sardonic smile and kept quiet. The speech he would like to have delivered played like a tape recorder inside his head.

"Idiots," he would cry silently. "Don't you know that I have no regard for the Establishment as my father sees it? Don't you know the Haylows are only rich pushcart peddlers? Look at me. I don't believe in God or fashion or the Dow Jones average. It's pure shit, all of it. But what Joe Haylow wants, Joe Haylow gets. Including me."

Roger remembered that night a year ago that now seemed to him the beginning of the end. At his father's sixty-fourth birthday party he'd been drunk enough to let the venom show, not in public but within the confines of the Haylow inner circle. His display of hatred that night had set off a chain reaction that would culminate in this evening's an-nouncement. If I believed in Joe's God, he thought, I'd think the Old Boy had worked out a Satanic script for all of us to follow.

The other Haylow executives were equally engrossed in their own thoughts. Talking easily with Bridget Manning, Brad Deland gave no sign of the inner tension that felt like a hot ball of steel in the pit of his stomach. He wanted the Chairmanship more than he wanted anything in life. At fifty, movie-star handsome, smooth, and ruthlessly ambitious, Deland had worked hard to make himself indispensable to Haylow. He had been brought into the Corporation twenty-six years before, fresh from the Harvard Business School, well equipped with a strong mind, an impeccable New York social background, and a family fortune which, though diminished, was still sufficient to support a smart town house in the sixties, membership in the right clubs, and a wife whose consuming interests were clothes, charity balls, opening nights, and the world of the Beautiful People. Doe-Doe, as everybody called Dorothy Deland, had long since lost interest in Brad as a husband. She was not one, however, to discount the entree that the Deland name provided, nor the comforts that the Deland money made possible.

Doe-Doe found Brad's business ambitions boring and incomprehensible. She knew, vaguely, that he was a financial genius who had put together deals so complicated that even Haylow didn't understand the transactions by which his company acquired other gigantic businesses without the expenditure of a penny of cash. She knew that Joe Haylow had always been impressed with Brad, perhaps even a little envious of his background and his easy, compelling personality. Her husband's career was of no interest to Doe-Doe. She never read the financial interviews with Brad in *The Wall Street Journal*. But she never missed a picture of herself in *Town & Country*. ("The beautiful Mrs. Bradford Deland III at the Heart Ball in Palm Beach, wearing a white satin gown by Givenchy and the famous Deland black pearls.") She even enjoyed a nasty squib about herself in *Women's Wear Daily*. ("Doe-Doe Deland lunching for the second time this week in Restaurant Q with her favorite hairdresser. Is the marriage of Doe-Doe a No-No?")

Chatting with Bridget, Brad's mind was completely, confidently on the announcement Haylow would make. It had not been easy this past year to take the careful steps which could eliminate Cabot and Roger, the two human hurdles who seemed most likely to stand in his way. In spite of the setbacks, he thought, I've done my work well. It will be my name that's called tonight.

No serious thought of herself as Haylow's successor was in the mind of Bridget Manning. There had been some ridiculous rumors of the possibility circulating in the fashion world in recent months, but Bridget dismissed them as she did a hundred other juicy, unfounded bits of industry speculation, including the persistent rumor about herself and Haylow. Not that she wasn't flattered by the idea of herself in the top job. She had even, for a self-deluding moment, taken half-seriously the conversation of Sally Fisher, one of the magazine editors whom she knew Haylow admired. "It would be just like Joe," her informant said, "to do the unexpected. After all, Bridget, naming a woman, especially one as qualified as you, would be the kind of daring, publicity-making gesture he'd adore. You know he thinks you're one of the most brilliant business executives he's ever known. Sex be damned. And it would be kind of a marvelous *revenge* for his forced retirement. Not, of course, that *that* would be the reason!"

No woman as successful and in love with her work as Bridget Manning could help but be intrigued by such a possibility, no matter how remote. But except for Pat Haylow, Bridget knew the Chairman better than any woman in the world. They had worked closely together for twelve years, since the day that Haylow had bought the chain of fashion shops from Stanley Manning. In making the deal, Bridget's father had insisted that his daughter, for whom the stores were named, remain as its President. At first, Joe Haylow had resisted the proviso. He had never before, or since, had a female store President or even a top woman executive in the corporation. Like some biblical patriarch, he secretly believed that women were the inferior sex to be protected and respected but never to sit in the company of men. After a dozen years he had forgotten his reluctance. Bridget had not completely changed his mind about the basic inferiority of women, for he was a man who took the Bible at its literal interpretation including the origin of Eve from Adam's rib. But she had shown him how coolly, competently, and profitably this particular woman could run a woman's business. The world called her "The First Lady of Retailing" and the press devoted millions of words to her accomplishments. As a result, Bridget's contributions to the Haylow empire were far beyond revenue. Her stores were the cherry on the corporate cake, the elegant image that rubbed off on other Haylow-owned operations. In interviews, Bridget carefully gave Joe full credit for his farsightedness and daring in naming a woman President and protested, modestly and sincerely, that she could not do it without his advice and guidance. Concrete evidence of Haylow's acceptance of this fact hung on his office wall in the form of a framed magazine article showing himself and Bridget in conference and artfully headlined "Joe Haylow—for Whom the Belle Toils."

At forty-two, Bridget was not a beautiful woman but an attractive, elegant one. Intuitive, dedicated, she was also completely feminine, capable of hiding her sharp mind when she sensed that her male associates might feel threatened by it. She loved her stores passionately, all thirty-two of them. They were beautiful little jewel-like establishments filled with expensive clothes and accessories and known to the richest women in America as The Place to buy the newest, the costliest, and the best. If Bridget was married to her job, it was a marriage of her own choice, eminently suitable and satisfying. She had tried the other kind years before, but it had ended in divorce. The successful engineer who was her husband wanted a full-time wife and a houseful of children, and Bridget did not love him enough to join the station wagon set. Or, rather, she loved her job more. In those days her father still owned the stores and Bridget was his right hand. She adored her father and had chosen him and the challenge of business over the prospect of a life as an anonymous wife and mother. After the sale of the business and her father's death, Joe Haylow had come to mean to her what Stanley Manning always had—a man with whom she could share the excitement and stimulation of a world filled with the endless thrill of accomplishment.

Tonight, at Joe's retirement dinner, Bridget found herself wondering about her future under the new regime. For many years there had been no important man in her life, no lover to provide the rapture that might replace her all-consuming passion for Haylow and her work. The few fleeting affairs she'd permitted herself since her divorce were transient things, deliberately invited for normal, momentary sexual pleasure. Her job demanded that she be seen in public almost every night, but she had fallen into the easy pattern of choosing for her escort some presentable, fortyish unattached man of the kind that abound in New York's fashion world. Latent or neatly camouflaged homosexuals, they were gay and amusing companions, beautifully attentive and completely untroublesome at her front door. Only lately had things changed.

Until now she had been reasonably content with her life. But without Joe Haylow, the business part of her life would be a mechanical thing. She tried to imagine what it would be like to report to Cabot or Roger Haylow or Deland or Mike Warner. It seemed impossible. Yet she had no choice. She was too young to retire and too high-powered to meekly accept direction from anyone weaker than Joe. Worst of all, she feared that she was too tightly tied to Haylow to offer his successor the kind of devotion and understanding she had so willingly given the Chairman. Impatiently, she opened her purse and took out a gold cigarette case. Opening it, she read for the thousandth time the inscription engraved inside, "To Bridget. Proverbs 11:16. JWH." The day Haylow gave it to her, she'd looked up the biblical quotation: "A gracious woman retaineth honour: and strong men retain riches." It would be lonely for her without him. She knew he would be lonely, too.

The last of the five possible candidates for the Chairmanship seemed to most people the least likely of all, though not on the basis of his ability. On the contrary, Mike Warner

24

skillfully directed the largest of all the Haylow chains, two thousand Star Stores spread around the world, doing a staggering combined volume of half a billion dollars in medium-priced men's, women's, and children's clothing. Mike Warner's likelihood of becoming Chairman was seriously hampered not by his lack of talent but by the one disadvantage he was not able to overcome. He was a Jew.

Overtly, as proved by Haylow's participation in Jewish charities, the Corporation was not anti-Semitic. But Haylow fought an inbred Yankee prejudice of which he was logically and consciously ashamed and emotionally incapable of discarding. Mike Warner was the first non-Christian top executive of the company and, predictably, one of its finest. He had come up, as the cliché goes, "the hard way." He was a poor boy from a close-knit Detroit family, and his first job, at the age of seventeen, was in the stock room of the Star Store in his home town. In the twenty-five years since, Mike had risen rapidly. He became an assistant buyer, buyer, merchandise manager in the Detroit store. Joe Haylow, who kept his eye on promising young talent everywhere, admired Mike's love of retailing which emulated his own. Warner had a natural flair for merchandising. Like Haylow, he thought of it as show business, compounded of promotional ideas that made sales skyrocket and inventive presentations that enhanced the desirability of the merchandise without compromising its quality.

Haylow had brought him into the New York "flagship store" as general merchandise manager fifteen years before. Three years ago he had been made President of all Star Stores and a member of the Board of The Haylow Corporation. Mike was not only grateful to Joe Haylow as an employer, he idolized him as a man. He saw a parallel in their rise from a modest beginning to positions of success and power. More gentle than Joe, and more capable of love, Mike still patterned his life as closely as possible after Haylow's. He slavishly aped the Chairman's way of dressing and imitated his interests in art and literature. He even embraced Joe's politics, a position admittedly made easier by the fact that Haylow was that almost unheard-of phenomenon, a New England Democrat.

An accidental bond between Warner and Haylow was the unswerving devotion of their wives. Rose Warner, born Rose Gottfried, was a simple, pretty, loving young woman who'd married Mike the day he was made buyer in the Detroit store. Rose had considered herself then, and still considered herself today, the most fortunate of women to have won and held the love of a man like Mike Warner. She was dazzled by his success, proud beyond measure of his rapid rise. But Rose remained what she was, a shy, insecure, moderately intelligent Jewish wife. She was incapable of keeping up with Mike on any intellectual level. Socially, her participation was sheer agony. She was awed by the Christian world of the Haylows, avoiding, whenever possible, any contact with the Cabots or the Delands. In his love, Mike was solicitous of her whenever they had to make an appearance in this group, never leaving her side at a big party, giving her a wink of understanding and encouragement across the table at the elegant dinners they were sometimes forced to attend. Joe Haylow was always kind and courteous to her, but it was Patricia Haylow with whom Rose felt most at ease. With Pat, Rose felt a kinship based on the communication of two women who lived with the conviction that their husbands could do no wrong. Rose found Pat warm and easy to talk with. And Pat gave to her the same generous affection she showed for Marjorie Haylow, her beloved daughter-in-law.

Although Mike seldom talked business at home, Rose knew that he nursed the secret hope that he might be named Chairman of Haylow. The thought of it filled Rose with alarm. Even though she knew that this would be the crowning achievement of Mike's career, she prayed with all her heart that she would never be thrust into the role of the Chairman's wife, a role she knew would be impossible for her to handle. In her sensible, realistic way, she assured herself that she was worrying about something that never could happen. She accepted Haylow's respect and affection for Mike, but she clung to the belief that even if the other contenders were somehow miraculously eliminated, Joe Haylow would never leave his precious business in the hands of a Jew.

In an effort to cushion his own probable disappointment, Mike Warner had developed a different theory. He believed that blood was thicker than water and he was prepared to accept defeat on the rationale that only family ties, never bigotry, would dictate Haylow's choice. By this same thought process, he felt that Haylow would pass over Dick Cabot and make Roger Haylow the next Chairman. Unlike Rose, he could not bear to believe that Joe Haylow was capable of religious bias. It was the kind of disillusionment too painful to accept.

The dinner was nearing its climax. Mike estimated that the Governor was more than halfway through his politically-oriented eulogy, the stickily insincere words oozing out as smoothly as the melting ice cream crawling across Mike's untouched plate of dessert. In another ten minutes, Joe Haylow would approach the microphone to make the announcement that would affect all their lives. Looking in Haylow's direction, Mike suddenly was aware of a bellboy reaching out unobtrusively from the wings to hand a folded piece of paper to Roger Haylow who sat at the other end of the table. Roger glanced at it and passed it along to his mother who, in turn, gave it to Joe Haylow. Mike imagined that all of them looked faintly surprised as they handled the note, as though they recognized the handwriting or some other mark which identified the sender.

Courteously, not wishing to distract the audience from the Governor's speech, Haylow opened the note below table level, reading it rapidly. Shock, horror, disbelief crossed his face. His skin went dead white, his hand, reaching for a glass of water, shook uncontrollably. Pat looked at him with a frightened, unspoken question. He took her hand for a moment and made a gesture of reassurance, a slight shake of his head that seemed to say, "Don't worry. It's all right."

Slipping the note into his jacket pocket, Haylow fought to regain control. The note contained a dreadful, unthinkable message that in a split second changed his decision. Methodically, discreetly, he tore up his prepared speech. With all the strength and discipline he could muster, he forced himself to look as though he was hearing every word of the Governor's seemingly endless monologue. McCarthy was a good and practiced speaker. He knew all the rules for a successful public address: Start with an attention-getting opening, extol the virtues and accomplishments of the honored guest and subtly slip in a few references to your own, and end with a memorable sentence, preferably one with a touch of humor.

Turning to face Joe, the Governor was approaching part three of the formula. "Mr. Haylow," he said, "my Irish ancestors had a saying: 'If the angels kiss a man on his hands, he will become a great pianist. If they kiss his lips, he will be a great speaker. If they kiss his shoulders, he will be a superb athlete.' Well, Joe, I don't know where the angels kissed you. But I do know that you've been a fantastic Chairman!"

The laughter was on cue, the applause loud, warm, and sustained. Joe Haylow rose heavily from his chair. Forcing a smile, he shook the Governor's hand. Flashbulbs popped. The audience, both on the dais and on the ballroom floor, was on its feet, increasing the volume of its applause.

Haylow took the Governor's place at the microphone. Chairs scraped as the guests resumed their seats. Joe waited until there was not a clink of coffee cup on saucer or a muffled cough. Finally, in the utter stillness, Haylow began to speak. The familiar voice was still strong and persuasive. It spoke calmly in the measured pace that had been heard from a thousand other platforms on a thousand other nights. Only a handful of people recognized the undercurrent of sadness. Only a few recognized, with alarm, a unique note of anguish.

"Governor McCarthy, distinguished guests, my beloved family, friends, and co-workers," Haylow began. "A French philosopher once said that a man is the sum total of his experience—minus his vanity. Tonight, in my last appearance as Chairman, I present this sum total for your reckoning.

"It is a balance sheet with both assets and deficits. There are plusses of achievement and minuses of neglect. Columns of arrogance and notations of humility. It is the ledger of a man's life, full of joy and sorrow, love and hate, unselfishness and greed. Inscribed in it are, hopefully, some words of wisdom. And, regrettably, some accounts of error.

"You, collectively, will be the auditor. I ask you to examine very carefully this final report. And then you will decide whether this employee of the Lord is spiritually sound or morally bankrupt."

Expectantly the audience waited.

Some of them had been waiting for forty years.

2 🐛

On the morning of January 10, 1968, Joe Haylow's first thought upon awakening was that this was his sixty-fourth birthday. The distasteful realization was quickly followed by another, equally unappealing: He was only one year away from his mandatory retirement as Chairman of The Haylow Corporation.

Lying for a moment in the big double bed with Pat sleeping quietly beside him, Haylow looked at the bright Florida sunshine streaming through the French doors of their bedroom. Deliberately, like a curious child inspecting some strange and forbidden object, he mentally examined the word "mandatory." It came, of course, from "mandate" meaning an order. But in today's high-powered business world, the word had come to mean "dated man." I don't feel like a man who is out of date, Joe thought. I feel more like a fella who could start all over again tomorrow and go strong for another forty years.

Quietly, so as not to awaken his wife, he slipped out of bed and pulled on a pair of swim trunks. On his way to the pool he noted with pleasure, as he did every morning, the expensive but unostentatious surroundings in which he always spent his two-week winter holiday. The well-furnished cottage on the grounds of the Lake Flamingo Hotel in Palm Beach had none of the garish, nouveau-riche appearance of the newer resort establishments. Behind a casual, almost shabby façade, it hid the fact that its rate-per-day was higher than that of the grandest suite in one of the better-known winter playpens.

Joe padded through the great living room with its comfortable groupings of deep chairs and sofas done in creamy linen and bamboo. Crossing the broad, flower-filled patio, he dove into the Olympic-sized swimming pool, easily swimming its length eight times and emerging as exhilarated and unwinded as a twenty-year-old.

In addition to the living room, the cottage had three bedrooms and baths, a spacious, airy dining room, a kitchen, and servants' quarters for Mattie and George, the black couple the Haylows always brought down from Farmville. These four were the only regular occupants. The two guest bedrooms were occupied only on the ninth and tenth of January, when "the children," as Pat called them, flew down to celebrate Joe's birthday.

Although they did not stay in the cottage, there were other guests invited from New York for those two days. All expenses paid, they were put up in the main building of the hotel. There were suites for Richard and Mildred Cabot, for Brad and Doe-Doe Deland and for Mike and Rose Warner. Large, balconied double rooms were reserved for "the singles" —Bridget Manning, the Reverend Jimmy Jackson, and Sidney Sommers, Joe Haylow's Industrial Psychologist and closest friend.

The guests had all arrived yesterday and would return to New York and Farmville tomorrow. All, that is, except Doe-Doe who was flying on to Jamaica to spend time with her rich, pleasure-loving crowd at Round Hill.

Drying himself with the big, fluffy towel monogrammed JWH, Haylow knew from years of experience exactly what the day would be like. He and Pat would have breakfast on the patio with Woodward and Marjorie. Roger would appear much later, ask for a Bloody Mary and accept, instead, a glass of orange juice and a cup of black coffee. The ritual with Roger no longer irritated Joe as it once did, but it continued to puzzle him. He wondered why Roger had to go through the motions of making a request which he knew would be tactfully ignored. In the Haylow house, drinking was not encouraged. Joe raised no objection to what people drank in restaurants or in their own houses, provided it was within the bounds of moderate "social drinking." But in his house, whether it was Farmville, New York, or the temporary residence in Palm Beach, liquor was not served during the day. Even tonight the limit, and a great exception, was one cocktail before dinner and champagne in careful quantities for toasts to his health at the birthday feast.

After breakfast the guests would drift down from the hotel to spend the day around the pool where luncheon would be served, buffet-style. Again, Joe knew with certainty how the company would divide itself during the day. Haylow, Deland, Cabot, Mike Warner, Bridget, and Sid Sommers would spend most of their time talking shop, interspersing their business conversation with frequent quick swims. Pat, Marjorie, Mildred, and Rose would sit quietly in the comfortable chaises, adjusting them frequently to escape the ferocity of the sun. They would talk of inconsequential things, as unsophisticated as four suburban housewives on a weekend in Ocean City, New Jersey. Jimmy Jackson and Woodward, casually dressed in slacks and sports shirts, would be a twosome engaged in their own kind of secular shoptalk. Doe-Doe and Roger would be the loners. Roger would wander restlessly around, sometimes diving into the pool, often disappearing for long periods. Doe-Doe would lie motionless on a mattress placed in the far side of the pool. Her almost naked body in the most minuscule of bikinis would be carefully and evenly oiled and offered invitingly, legs spread apart, to receive the rape of the sun. Between bouts of solar sex,

Doe-Doe would smoke innumerable cigarettes and lazily turn the pages of the newest, dirtiest best-seller which, Joe was certain, she always brought along to shock the other, more circumspect wives.

Though she was not the kind of young matron Joe really approved of, Doe-Doe interested and even amused Joe Haylow. A woman in her forties, married to a man of Brad Deland's professional stature, should be more conservative, he thought. Even that ridiculous nickname is unsuitable. Yet there is something so eternally young and provocative about her, like a wicked child determined to see how far she can go before some tried-to-the-limit adult turns her over his knee and whacks her bouncy little behind.

The day proceeded almost exactly as Joe had predicted. It was an unruffled day if not a stimulating one. For although this group spent a great many of its waking hours together through the year, they really had only one thing in common: the desire for Joe Haylow's approval.

By five o'clock, a day in the sun began to produce a feeling of lethargy, even in Haylow. Slowly, the gathering began to disperse, drifting to their rooms for naps before they bathed and changed into evening clothes for the dinner that Pat had so carefully planned. Joe dreaded the dinner even more than he did the day. Any outpouring of compliments or emotions embarrassed him. He felt uncomfortable with praise, even though it warmed him. Fortunately, these people who were so close to him knew how difficult it was for him to accept compliments or return any display of affection, so the flowery sentiments would be kept to a minimum. By custom, he would open his gifts before dinner and grope for the appropriate words of thanks. At table there would be only one toast, proposed by Jimmy Jackson and answered by Haylow. After a brief, polite lingering over coffee in the living room, the guests would depart. He would not see them again until the Haylows returned from Florida the following week.

Brad Deland was the first to make the move to leave the pool that afternoon. After motioning to Doe-Doe, who got lazily to her feet like some sleek, bronzed animal, Brad thanked Pat for a pleasant day.

As they started up the grassy slope, Pat called out to them.

"Don't forget, we're expecting you at seven-thirty. Now don't oversleep!"

"Not a chance," Brad called back. "If I can make the Chairman's crack-of-dawn meetings, I sure can get up in time for his dinner."

Walking beside him, out of earshot of the others, Doe-Doe laughed. "You bet your sweet bippy, you can," she said. "You could find time to kiss his ass in the window of Bridget's if you thought it would do you any good."

Brad glanced around to make sure no one had heard. Damn her rotten soul, he thought, it's going to be another one of those. She'll have three martinis in the suite and we'll have one of those screaming fights before dinner.

He had long since lost his craving for this brittle, sarcastic woman. It had been months since they'd gone to bed together. The last time was a fiasco. They had made love at Brad's insistence and with Doe-Doe's dispassionate acquiescence. Her passive, almost bored acceptance of him had instantly turned him off. His mental revulsion evidenced itself in physical impotence. Unable to complete the act, he had not dared risk such humiliation again.

Yet for a few unheeding moments this afternoon, following his wife across the green lawn, Brad felt the stirring of desire. Doe-Doe's body was like a young girl's. Diet, exercise, and lack of childbearing were the secrets of the small firm breasts and the tight, muscular belly. But these attributes were more familiar to her masseuse than they were to her husband.

In their bedroom at the hotel, Brad watched as Doe-Doe stood in front of the dressing table mirror. With detachment, as though he was not there, she unfastened the tiny bra, examining for a moment the perfect little breasts for any telltale sign of aging laxness. Satisfied, she unzipped the bikini briefs, standing for a moment naked and perfect before she reached for the thin silk robe and tied it closely around her. Then she seated herself at the dresser and began to brush the fine, silken blond hair with deliberate, self-loving strokes.

Reluctantly, Brad turned away. The momentary excitement had passed. It was as dead for him as it was for Doe-Doe. And nothing could revive it. In the bathroom he slipped out of his swim trunks and put on a dressing gown. Then he returned to the bedroom and sat down quietly in the armchair next to the dresser. He lit a cigarette and waited. His wife was oblivious to him. Finally, his voice devoid of emotion, he spoke.

"Doe-Doe, we've got to talk."

"About what?"

"About us. There's nothing between us anymore. No love. Not even physical desire."

Her laugh was brittle. "My God, you sound like a soap opera. 'Physical desire'? Brad, darling, how quaint. You're so busy being in love with Joe Haylow that sex with you would be corporate infidelity. Hell, you're mentally sleeping with Joe Haylow. And I won't be laid on that boring old bastard's time. Forget it, pet. Go get your kicks someplace else. It's a dandy little marriage. So don't make waves."

He was amazed. "A dandy little marriage? What kind of a woman are you? Oh, it's dandy all right. Two people who hate each other living together with a kind of civilized mutual agreement not to disturb the routine? Is that what you call a dandy little marriage?"

Doe-Doe's voice was amused. "Yes. What do you call it?"

"I call it obscene. And I want to talk about ending it."

For a moment, she looked frightened. Then the casual tone returned.

"You want me to divorce you, I take it."

It's incredible, Brad thought. No human being can be that cool. Sitting there in that robe, never missing a stroke of the brush, she might just as easily be talking about my suggesting a new place for dinner. Her voice brought him back to the moment.

"I said, Brad, that I assume you want a divorce."

"Yes. I think it's the best thing for both of us. I can see why you may have cause to hate me. I'm not what you might call the perfect husband for you, in any sense. I think you should be free to find a man who shares your interests. Not one, as you rightly say, who's so wrapped up in his business that he neglects his personal life."

"My, my!" Doe-Doe mocked. "Aren't we the self-sacrificing little gentleman! You do surprise me, Brad. I had no idea you cared so much about my happiness. It's a pity you're so clue-less about what really does make me happy."

"What does?"

"This may come as a great shock to you, love, but being Mrs. Bradford Deland III makes me very happy indeed. Funny, isn't it? But you see, I'm one of your more realistic types. I'm over forty. I'm not some dumb, starry-eyed kid who thinks she can go out and grab off another husband in a minute. Not me, baby. I've seen too many dames my age who stood still for divorces when their disenchanted husbands wanted out. They're noble and self-sacrificing and very, very stupid. Because the way it turns out is that they're on the nobody-gives-a-damn list. Fifth wheels. Extra women. Unattached, they have a lousy time of it. A husband, my dear Brad, even one as disinterested as you, is a very handy thing to have. It takes you to dinner parties and first nights, and it lets you get invited places as an attractive couple, not as an extra woman who may or may not be able to find herself an escort. It even looks better on your Christmas cards."

"And that's all that marriage means to you?"

"Well, that's pretty good for openers. And I'm not even discussing the matter of a standard of living. I'm sure you would be most generous about a settlement. No, thanks, a divorce is not on my list of the ten most-wanted things."

"What if it's on my list?" Brad asked.

"I'm glad you brought that up," Doe-Doe said. "Just why do you want a divorce? Unless I'm madly mistaken, you haven't had time in the last few years to find yourself some little dish that you're dying to marry."

"No," Brad said, "there's no one else. But perhaps one day there could be."

"Forget it," Doe-Doe snapped. "You're married to Joe Haylow and he's the perfect wife for you. And speaking of that, the Great Man doesn't really approve of divorces among his pet executives, does he? What would a nice juicy breakup between us do to your hopes of becoming Chairman?"

Brad hesitated. She had unerringly put her finger on the one thing that had kept them together: Deland's image in Haylow's eyes.

"Perhaps," he said, "this discussion is a trifle premature. We would not get the divorce for a year. Not until after Haylow's retirement."

Now it was Doe-Doe's turn to be astonished. "You really are too much! Not only am I supposed to agree to a divorce I don't want, but I'm also supposed to hang around for a year playing the dutiful wife for the benefit of that psalm-singing saint and his mealy-mouthed wife! You've got to be putting me on!"

Uncontrollable rage came at last. Not only fury at Doe-Doe but annoyance with himself for the tactical error he'd made in starting this conversation before he was ready to make his move.

"All right, Doe-Doe," he said, "now you listen to me. I want out of this marriage and I'll get out a year from now.

In the meantime, you'll behave yourself in front of Joe Haylow and the rest of the world. Don't get it into that stupid little head of yours that you can screw up my chances for the big job or you'll find yourself not only a middle-aged divorcee but a goddamned poor one! You make just one wrong move between now and next January and I'll give you the kind of living hell that will make a divorce seem like the answer to a maiden's prayer. Play along and I'll see that you stay up to your ass in mink. Try to double-cross me and, by Christ, you'll regret it."

Doe-Doe gave her affected little lunch-at-the-Colony laugh. "Why Brad, dear, it's a real treat to see you get so het-up. Careful, dear, your venom is showing."

Brad did not answer. Suddenly Doe-Doe became deadly serious.

"I'm telling you again. No divorce. Not a year from now. Not fifty years from now. As for Haylow, I'll be the way I always am with him, just a little flirty-wirty. Something that dirty old man vicariously enjoys. I'll be darling to the whole swarm of them, including his sainted son and that virginal Marjorie. So help me God, that one is living proof of the immaculate conception. You'll never convince me that Woodie the Woodpecker screwed those two kids out of her. Now get the hell out of here and let me rest. Not that I'll need much rest for all that high living we'll be doing tonight, dear boy."

At the door to the living room, Brad looked back at her. "Just remember this, you bloody bitch," he said. "In twelve months we're through. I don't clutter up my life with trash, no matter what boarding school wastebasket I may have fished it out of."

In the master bedroom at the cottage, Joe Haylow looked up from his book as Pat came into the room.

"Everything okay for tonight?" he asked her.

Pat smiled happily. "I think it's going to be lovely, dear. Mattie has done a beautiful job on the table and we're having everything you like."

Joe smiled, wondering, as he always did, at the basic simplicity and goodness of this serene woman he'd married. As he returned to his reading, Pat watched him for a moment, wondering whether this was the moment to bring up the problem that had been troubling her for so long. She decided that there probably would not be a better time to catch him in a relaxed and reasonable frame of mind.

"Joe," she said. "Can we talk about Roger for a minute? I'm terribly worried about him."

Reluctantly, Haylow put down his book. "For heaven's sake, Pat," he said mildly, "when are you going to stop worrying about our sons? They're not babies. Woodward is thirty-nine and Roger's thirty-seven. They're grown men with wives and families."

"A wife and a family," she corrected him.

"Is that what's worrying you? So what if Roger isn't married? Lots of men marry late. Let the boy have a little fun before he settles down. He works hard enough to deserve it."

Pat smiled her warm, understanding smile. "That's what I love about you. Occasionally you contradict yourself, Mr. Chairman. A minute ago you just pointed out that Roger isn't a boy, he's a grown man."

Haylow gave her a mock frown. "I'm glad you're not a disruptive stockholder, Mrs. Haylow," he said. "With that kind of logic you could give me trouble at the annual meetings. All right, so our Roger is some kind of a problem. What kind?"

"I don't know, exactly. I mean, he's dear and loving as he's always been, but I can't seem to get through to him lately. When we talk, I feel this kind of barrier between us. Like he's terribly unhappy and can't talk about it. And he's doing a great deal of drinking, Joe. Mattie told me today that when she turned down his bed last night she saw a full bottle of Scotch on his dresser, and this morning it's nearly empty."

Haylow's face hardened. "I won't stand for that," he said. "I can't control what he does in his own apartment, but in my house he'll live by my rules. I'll go and talk to him right now."

"No, please don't. I'm no expert at this kind of thing, Joe, but that kind of drinking must be symptomatic of some terrible inner problem. I don't want to offend you, darling. You are a good father, but Roger is in such a state that I'm not sure that either you or I are the ones who could reach him. He's a terribly complex human being."

"Oh, please, Patricia," Haylow said impatiently. "You're not going to tell me that we're the victims of the generation gap at this late date, are you? After all, I'm not dealing with a pot-smoking teen-ager, I'm merely suggesting a straight talk with a grown man who happens to be not only my son but a very valuable executive of my company. If we weren't related, I'd come straight to the point about this kind of thing. Why shouldn't I be able to do the same with a member of my own family?"

"Maybe because he is a member of your own family," Pat said slowly. "It's harder to give advice to your children than it is to talk to outsiders. And it's much harder for them to take criticism from their parents."

Subdued but not convinced, Haylow considered the wisdom of this.

"All right. What do you think we should do?"

"I'm not sure. Maybe Sid is the one to talk to Roger. He's like an uncle to him, really. He probably could be a great less emotional about it. In fact," Pat said cautiously, "I've already mentioned it to Sid."

"And?"

"Well," Pat said, weighing her words, "Sid agrees that there is something wrong. He says that Roger is doing brilliantly in the business, but he does feel that the boy needs help emotionally."

Haylow began to be exasperated. "Just what does that mean, 'emotionally'? Have you two decided that Roger needs psychiatry? Come on, Pat, there's nothing wrong with that boy that a good shaking up wouldn't take care of. He's got everything—money, a good job, a great future. Sooner or later he'll inherit the whole Haylow Corporation and he won't have to break his back for it. This whole thing is ridiculous. You've always coddled him because he's the baby. Just because he's going through a phase, you get frantic. And Sid's as bad as you are. What Roger needs is a lesson in respect. He's had too much freedom in every way, including the fact that we've let him make a mockery of God. Maybe," Haylow said, "that would be the best medicine, a little dose of faith. Maybe Jimmy Jackson's a better person to talk to him than Sid. It's about time that Roger started to count his blessings."

For one of the few times in her married life, Pat Haylow was adamant.

"Absolutely not," she said firmly. "You and I have found strength in our religion but Roger has made it very clear that he wants no part of it. You can't pour Christianity down people's throats like an instant purgative, Joe. It may make us sad that Roger doesn't believe as we do, but there's not a thing we can do about it except hope that one day he'll reach for God all by himself."

Surprised by her vehemence, Haylow did not pursue it. "All right, dear," he said. "As soon as we get back to New York, I'll talk to Sid. Perhaps you're right. Maybe he can find out what's eating Roger."

Watching him return to his book with complete absorption, Pat wondered for the thousandth time at the discipline of which Joe Haylow was capable. He was like a well-trained machine programmed to consider each problem in order of its priority, make a calculated decision, and forget it until the time came to spew out the correct answer.

This, confident, well-ordered man had no idea of how difficult it was to live with him. Some, like Woodward, retreated from him into worlds in which Haylow did not wish to compete. Others, like herself, simply went along in blind, uncomplaining adoration. But there were the Rogers of life who hammered their figurative fists against the unyielding solidity of Joe Haylow's opinionated beliefs. Roger was not the first son of a strong and dynamic man who had found himself burdened with his father's expectations. The situation was classic among the powerful, the heir to the throne trying to mold himself into the king's image and, finally, fearful of failure, taking an exact turn-about rather than continue the demanding race. Some disavowed their father's world, refusing to go into their businesses at all, preferring the indolent, unproductive life of a rich man's son to the odious comparison of a rich man's blood-line successor. Roger had, thus far, not taken this course. He had decided to come into The Haylow Corporation and prove to his father that he was the brighter, better man. But Pat feared that this obsession to outdo Joe was turning Roger into a deeply bitter, hard-drinking, unhappy human being.

Pat clung to the belief that subconsciously Roger admired his father, even loved him. If Joe had been the kind of person who could show compassion and open affection, the story might have been different. But the very fact that Roger was his son made Joe drive him harder, give him less preferential treatment than he gave any other executive in the company. Not for anything in the world would Joe Haylow be accused of favoritism in business. Instead he imposed almost impossible demands on Roger, thrust the most difficult jobs and the heaviest responsibilities upon him, as though to prove to the world that the brilliance of the first generation of Haylows

43

was, indeed, inherent in the second. But that the second would have to wait its turn.

Unfortunately, Joe did not take into consideration the difference in personalities. Joe's drive was power, no matter how pleasureless. Roger loved life and believed that success was not necessarily incompatible with pleasure. Without even realizing it, the two men had become enemies. Their struggle was philosophical, and each philosophy, curiously enough, was right for the one who espoused it. The father saw success in terms of control. The son believed that achievement could be managed with a light rein. It was too late, Pat feared, for Joe to change. Her only hope now was to somehow get Roger to see his father as he really was, an honest, undemonstrative man who did not consciously set out to hurt or destroy, and whose ambition for his son was as great as his goals for himself had been so many years before. She feared that the breach might already have become too wide. She sensed that Roger who had once thought of Joe as "a tough act to follow" might now be thinking of him as an impossible one. With a mother's instinct, she saw her child pulling away from his father with every act of defiance. Worse, she had a cold fear that Roger's resentment might turn to such deep-seated hatred that he would go to any length to hurt and humiliate Joe Haylow, even if it meant destroying his own way of life, his own brilliant future.

My Joe is a loving man, Pat thought, who is unaware of his own capacity to give or receive love. Things are so clearly black-and-white to him that he has no patience with the normal doubts and confusions that plague the rest of us. From his point of view, God gave him the brains and the strength to build this business and thoughtfully provided him with a son to carry it on. It's as simple as that. He sees Woodward as a minister and Roger as a future Chairman. He never has seen them as his children with emotional needs and human desires. And the good Lord only knows whether he ever will.

While his wife gave herself to her thoughts, Joe Haylow, having momentarily pigeonholed the whole personal matter, read on, rapidly, with complete concentration. The book was a study of the top one hundred corporations in America. It annoyed him that Haylow was only number seventy-four.

In the guest room down the hall, Marjorie Haylow was completing a telephone call to her children in Farmville. Joseph, ten, and Jennifer, seven, had been left at home with their nurse. Woodward had wanted to bring them to his father's birthday party, but Marjorie knew that little people bored Joe Haylow and imposed upon him a role he had no interest in playing—that of the jovial grandfather. So she had convinced Woodward that, in addition to the fact that there was no room for them in the cottage, it would also be wrong for them to be taken out of school so soon after the Christmas holidays. Marjorie loved her children, but secretly, almost guiltily, she was relieved to be free of them for a couple of days. She could understand Joe Haylow's attitude, in a way. At this age, small boys and girls were not the most stimulating companions, and even Marjorie, devoted mother that she was, found herself hungering, from time to time, for the interesting conversation of adults.

She had little enough worldly contact, in any case. At thirty-five, she was, to all appearances, the perfect wife of a young minister, as Woodward and Farmville considered her to be. Slender and pretty, she was a home-town girl, the daughter of a local banker. She had known Woodward all her life and their marriage, twelve years before, had seemed a perfect match which delighted both families.

Rarely, in those dozen years, had Marjorie questioned the rightness of her life. Hers was a household where voices were never raised in anger. Her children were healthy and normally well mannered. Her church duties were part of the life she accepted. So was the pattern of her sex life. Woodward was

45

as conservative as he was undemanding. His love-making was a rite accomplished with increasing infrequency but with tenderness and, to Woodward at least, with the after satisfaction he felt when he had preached a particularly uplifting sermon. In all her married life, Marjorie had never reached the sexual heights that she knew were possible. An educated and not entirely unworldly young woman, this fact occasionally troubled her. She wondered whether she was capable of rapture. She knew that many women were not. Just a few months ago, waiting for Doe-Doe in the Delands' house, she had read a *Harper's Bazaar* article called "The Erotic Life of the American Wife." It had confirmed some things she knew, including the fact that many women, like herself, had never reached a climax. It also detailed some clinical facts that surprised and shocked her. Woodward Haylow was the only man she'd ever been to bed with. The magazine article made her wonder what her capabilities might be. Not that she ever expected to find out. Like a curious schoolgirl she wondered what Doe-Doe and Brad's sex life was like. They were both such beautiful, magnetic people, so totally different from the Haylows or any of the others. The Delands lived in a different world and the two young wives had nothing in common. They lunched once or twice a year when Marjorie made one of her infrequent trips to New York. Doe-Doe flatly refused to set foot in Farmville and their only other occasional encounters were at command-performance company dinners or, as now, at the annual birthday celebration in Florida.

It was an arrangement that suited them both well. Marjorie thought Doe-Doe shallow, brittle, and selfish. She admired Doe-Doe's flair for clothes, her artfully bleached hair, but she would never forget her amazement when Doe-Doe casually confided that she had found "the most marvelous little woman who bleaches the pubic hair to match the current color of one's coiffure"! She was never sure whether Doe-Doe went out of her way to shock, or whether the supreme sophistication had been so long and carefully cultivated that now it was real.

To Doe-Doe, Marjorie was the epitome of the boring suburban matron with her almost negligible makeup, her natural shoulder-length hair, her simple tweeds which were the very essence of what Doe-Doe called "Best & Co. Basics." Describing Marjorie to her friends was always good for a laugh. "The minister's wife," Doe-Doe would explain, "is too tepid to be true! She's like a faded Bermuda watercolor." When she said such things in front of Brad, he showed his disapproval. He liked Marjorie, found her attractively unaffected, a refreshing change from the fashion-enslaved women who were his wife's constant companions. More importantly, he was angered when Doe-Doe publicly flaunted her ridicule of the Haylows. Brad knew that Joe Haylow and Pat were devoted to Marjorie. It would not sit well with them to hear Mrs. Deland making her sound ridiculous. He had tried to explain to Doe-Doe how important her conduct was in furthering his career, pointing out that in today's world of big business the wife of an executive was scrutinized almost as microscopically as the man himself. Doe-Doe, as always, had taken delight at finding another weak spot in Brad's armor. The more furious he became about her careless remarks, the more uncautiously she talked. The ability to give Brad's career a serious setback—if not a fatal blow—became her strongest weapon, a blade which she kept suspended over his anxious head.

If she knew Doe-Doe's opinion of her, Marjorie serenely ignored it. She wondered, sometimes, how a man as basically courteous and dedicated as Brad could have chosen a wife as flamboyantly vulgar as Doe-Doe, but she was not surprised that Joe Haylow seemed to find her not only tolerable but amusing. Marjorie not only truly loved her father-in-law, she understood him better than his own children did. She had always been able to reach this aloof, undemonstrative man in a way that neither Roger, who resented him, nor Woodward, who feared him, ever had managed to do. It was, of course, because she really cared about him, a fact that Joe instinctively recognized. Over and beyond that, Haylow liked women and related to them far better than he did to members of his own sex, even his own sons. He would have liked to have had a daughter, and in Marjorie he had found one made to his specifications—pretty, intelligent, loyal, and loving. Through Woodward the family had acquired the second perfect Haylow woman, as warm and charming as Pat, the First Lady to whom Marjorie was equally devoted.

Thinking of Pat, Marjorie shared the universal concern of mothers. Recently, Pat had hinted to Marjorie of her worries about Roger, never discussing it openly, but not hiding the fact that she was troubled about her younger son. With a boy of her own, Marjorie could easily associate with that concern. She knew how she would feel if her own young Joseph grew up resenting his father. It would be intolerable to stand between them with one's divided love. Fortunately, Marjorie had no such problems with Woodward. He was a devoted father, pleased to spend time with young Joe. In her heart, Marjorie was not convinced that her husband, despite his gentleness, had a true calling for the ministry. She suspected he had taken the easy way out, secure behind the protection of his collar, amenable to the plans his father had made for him. It was Haylow's intention that Woodward would one day replace Jimmy Jackson as the world-famous evangelist. Marjorie was less sure that Woodward had the drive and the personality, much less the conviction, for such a role. Even though Jackson was nearly forty years older than Woodward, his fire and energy made his soft-spoken assistant seem like the conservative member of the team. Marjorie was not certain that even with time Woodward would ever be able to project the hypnotic, zealous appeal that brought hundreds of thousands of converts to Jackson's feet. Joe Haylow seemed to have no such reservations about his son's eventual success. With a wave of his hand he dismissed the possibility that some new, fire-breathing preacher would inherit Jackson's undisputed place as leader of the world-wide Methodist flock. Marjorie recalled that the subject of Elvis Mallory, a young southern evangelist, had come up at dinner a few weeks before. Joe had brushed off the idea of Mallory as competition as decisively and quickly as he might have squelched talk of a small business threatening the giant Haylow organization.

"Elvis Mallory?" he'd said, incredulously. "Ridiculous. A Mississippi upstart who's had a few squibs in the papers. Sounds like a rock and roll singer, not a minister. So he's held a few meetings. Big deal. The day he gets Haylow kind of money behind him is the day I'll start considering him a threat to Woodward. Don't give it a second thought, Woodward. Remember, politicians can buy votes but we can buy souls. And they're a lot more worth while saving."

Marjorie knew that Joe Haylow believed that souls really were redeemable if they were reachable. And to Haylow, power and money were the way to reach everything. Including the Kingdom of Heaven.

The group that assembled promptly at seven-thirty that evening in the cottage was predictably dressed, the men in summer dinner jackets, the ladies in varying degrees of fashion from Rose Warner's not-quite-right print chiffon to Doe-Doe's skinny mini dress made of tiny pieces of flashing mirror which stopped four inches above her evenly tanned knees. Marjorie had chosen stark white linen, floor length, her only jewelry the understated diamond pin that had been her wedding present from Joe Haylow. Pat Haylow and Mildred Cabot both wore simple dresses of silk with tiny short-sleeved jackets, the careful choice of ladies over fifty whose upper arms were beginning to give away their age. Bridget

Manning was in a long, pleated pale blue skirt and a simple white shirt, open at the throat, managing, as always, to look the most casually, expensively elegant of them all.

Predictable was the key word of the evening. Predictable that Roger would arrive a little drunk. Predictable that Doe-Doe would immediately corner Joe Haylow and begin a whispered conversation with him, a move deliberately designed to worry and anger Brad. Doe-Doe, martini in hand, was perched on the arm of Haylow's chair, telling him a slightly naughty story, giving him the latest tidbits of gossip about the insane, incestuous, idiotic circles of fashion in which she moved. Predictably, Haylow was enjoying it. It was the kind of thing that he believed kept him in touch with a world that was young, daring, and very different from his own.

Watching Doe-Doe flirt with the Chairman, Brad thought that Haylow looked like a naïve child peeking through his bedroom window to watch a sex act in the apartment across the courtyard: remote but excited, learning the facts of life without the obligation to participate in them. Moving closer, Brad was relieved to hear Doe-Doe playfully scolding Haylow in a way that could only be construed as irreverent affection.

"Chief," Doe-Doe was saying, "you really are a pain in the you-know-what. Buying a present for you is like finding a bauble for Elizabeth Burton. As the saying goes, what do you give a man who has everything? Penicillin?"

Haylow chuckled. "You know how I feel about birthdays, Doe-Doe. I wish you and Brad wouldn't bother about gifts."

"Not bother!" The well-tweezed eyebrows shot up in pretended dismay. "Really, you must be quite mad! What self-respecting wife of an ambitious young executive wouldn't knock her teeny-weeny little brain out trying to find just the right thing for the boss? Brad drove me stark, raving, bananas until I found the perfect present. And if you don't adore it, I'll run screaming from this house and throw my absolutely gorgeous little body under the wheels of the nearest Rolls-Royce."

The old fool, Brad thought. He's eating this up. Too bad he couldn't have been invisible the night in New York that we talked about his precious birthday present. The Chairman's birth sign was a goat but it followed that this stupid, unaggressive animal would be the last creature with whom Joe Haylow would wish to be identified. Instead he collected lions. His office, his house, his apartment were full of them. Pictures of lions, statues of lions, leonine objects in every form. At Christmas and on his birthday the favor-seekers racked their brains for new versions of the King of Beasts. The Delands were no exception. A few nights before they came to Florida, Brad had inquired about this year's offering.

"Did you get the birthday present?" he asked Doe-Doe.

"But naturally, darling," she said. "And I had one hell of a time convincing Cartier to make a gold and lapis inkwell shaped like a lion. They thought the whole idea was really Square City. In fact, they charged us enough to buy a square in any city."

"Very funny."

"Compared to your sense of humor these days, my love, it's a veritable thigh-slapper. Anyway, it's a ridiculous waste of money. Why don't we give him a personally autographed picture of Clyde Beatty bringin' 'em back alive?"

Brad refused to rise to the bait. "I think Clyde Beatty's dead."

"What a coincidence," Doe-Doe said. "That's what I think about Haylow."

"Knock it off, Doe-Doe. If you're such a smart-ass, maybe next Christmas you can find him a nice steel engraving of Daniel-in-the-den, something he'd really enjoy."

"Gee whillikers," Doe-Doe said. "What a groovy idea. Do they put those on thousand-dollar bills?"

Watching her now, Brad had to admit that she was a good actress. She was teasing Haylow about his gift, refusing to tell him what it was, assuring him that it was far too expensive for the likes of a poor Vice President. Joe, nursing his glass of club soda, was obviously enjoying the repartee, not minding in the least that he was being monopolized by the amusing Mrs. Deland.

At eight o'clock, Pat clapped her hands to get their attention.

"My dear family and friends," she said. "Before we go into dinner, I'm going to ask Joe to open all these fascinating-looking presents you've so kindly brought. Maybe *he* can wait, but personally I can't stand it one more minute!"

"Hear, hear!" Jimmy Jackson said. "A wonderful way to start this most joyful of all evenings. Come along, Joe, and open your gifts!"

Almost reluctantly Haylow approached the mound of elaborately wrapped packages. Choosing at random, the first one he opened was Pat's, a pair of antique gold cufflinks delicately sculptured as proud, regal lions. Joe kissed her gently on the cheek.

"Thank you, Pat. They're beautiful."

"Many happy returns, dear," she said.

"Hey," Joe answered. "Cut out that 'returns' business. That's a dirty word in the retail business!"

There was dutiful laughter at the Chairman's time-worn joke. Rapidly, he opened the other boxes, admiring the obviously costly inkwell from the Delands, fascinated with the miniature set of Scriptures from Woodward and Marjorie, the little books so tiny that their perfection could be seen only under a magnifying glass. Jimmy Jackson's gift was a magnifying glass to go with them. The Cabots had selected a Cabot-like offering, an electric shoe-shiner, combining the practical with the obvious effort to find something for the man who has everything. Bridget Manning's lighthearted tribute was a handsomely worked needlepoint pillow with the words "It wasn't the lions and tigers that got us. It was the gnats"—a reference, of course, to the minor daily problems that made business more difficult than the major ones. Sid Sommers' gift was a copy of Marshall McLuhan's latest double-talk diatribe on the subject of communications. Inside, Sid had written, "To Joe Haylow—the only man who could possibly explain this to me." Rose and Mike Warner had played it gentile-safe with a lion paperweight from Steuben. The final gift was Roger's. It was a finely pleated white silk dinner shirt, the product of a women's fashion designer who had turned his effeminate talents to the production of men's wear. The Chairman would wear it with pride, feeling very young and contemporary. He would not know that it was also the current status symbol of the more discreet homosexuals, or that Roger would find a perverse pleasure in seeing his father unwittingly dressed like one of The Boys.

Joe's thanks were sincere, perfunctory, and embarrassed. He was relieved when dinner was almost instantly announced. He and Pat led the way to the festive table set with glittering silver and crystal, its centerpiece of blood-red hibiscus flowers like some great pulsating heart surrounded by a ring of sixty-four tiny white candles in silver holders shaped like lions. There would be no birthday cake. This was its replacement. Years before, Joe had announced firmly that he would endure a celebration of sorts for Pat's sake but he would not, repeat *not*, go through the maudlin business of cutting a cake, blowing out candles, and listening to a group of off-key voices self-consciously singing, "Happy Birthday, dear Joseph." Pat's compromise was the sixty-four candles burning bravely through dinner.

Woodward said grace. "Lord, we thank Thee for the bounty we are about to receive. For this glorious day and the joy of spending it with those we love. We thank Thee for Thy servant Joseph Haylow, whose devotion to Thy will is everlasting. We ask for Thy blessing upon him and for Thy help that he may continue for many fruitful years to do Thy work. In the name of Thy son, Jesus Christ, our Saviour. Amen."

As Woodward's custom-made blessing ended, Mike Warner looked across the table where Rose was seated between Jimmy Jackson and Sid Sommers. He thought, as he had so often in the past, what a considerate woman Pat Haylow was. Of all the men at the table, these two would be most kind and courteous to the shy little woman who was so insecure in this company. Mike reflected, rather ruefully, how many times he and Rose had sat at tables at which someone invoked the name of the crucified Jew who was the Christian messiah. It never failed to fill him with wonder that he was part of this WASP establishment. He could not believe Haylow's whispered reputation as an anti-Semite. Yet there was always the painful possibility that Haylow subtly used him as a propaganda weapon, unspoken repudiation of the rumor. With the sensitivity of his race, Mike knew that Joe Haylow truly liked him and admired his ability. He had succeeded in quelling the suspicion that he had reached his position in the company because he was a smart Jew boy who fortunately had a tremendous capacity for business administration.

Rose's position was, if anything, more difficult. She knew without question that her young husband was a genius. Even so, she could never get over the fact that anyone she knew—much less the man she had married—could earn a hundred thousand dollars a year. And she lived with the constant fear that Mike would outgrow her, would rise to such heights of financial, social, and intellectual loftiness that her limited capacities would be unable to follow. It was an unnecessary worry. Mike Warner loved his Rose as few other men loved their wives. Fully aware of her simplicity, he was also wise enough to know that it was part of what made her so warm and generous. Mike knew that her clothes were just a little wrong, her conversation a touch too hesitant, her interests far removed from those of the Haylow women. He knew, too, of her sadness at her inability to bear him children. Rose was made for motherhood. Denied it, she turned all her passionate affection on Mike. He was husband, lover, friend, and child to her. For him she would suffer anything. Even, Mike thought, an evening as agonizing to her as this one. Mike Warner and Joe Haylow did not share the same religion, but a nonsectarian God had given them one thing in common: sensitive wives who adored them in spite of what they might be.

Jimmy Jackson was getting to his feet now, to propose the end-of-the-dinner toast. Affection radiating from his angelic, moon-like face, Jackson tapped his water glass with a spoon to get their attention.

"Ladies and gentlemen," he said. "As you may know, I am somewhat better at speaking to larger groups whose souls are more in need of my modest services."

Under the polite laughter, Doe-Doe turned to Roger who was seated beside her. "And who are more likely to put dollars into the old bastard's collection plate," she murmured. Roger made no reply. He's really bombed, Doe-Doe thought. He must have had a helluva lot of belts in his room before he got here.

Jackson continued, "But there is no arena, no amphitheatre, no pulpit I would prefer to this warm and graceful setting so lovingly arranged by our beautiful hostess."

This time there was a light smattering of applause and smiles in the direction of Pat, who sat, radiantly happy, at the end of the table.

"Tonight," Jackson said, "our blessings surround us, embodied in the grace and charm of this loving company. Our hearts are full of thanks for the occasion which has brought us together . . . the anniversary of the birth of a man who is friend, leader, benefactor, loving husband, devoted father. My dear children, I ask you to join me in a salute to our host.

To Joseph Haylow—may his days be as numerous as his acts of kindness and his life as rich as his nature is generous. Dear friend, God bless you!"

The guests stood, raising their glasses to Joe, who responded with a smile and his own peculiar little wave of a hand which meant "thank you." But before the Chairman could get to his feet to make the customary response, Roger Haylow tapped sharply on the water glass in front of him. In surprise, every face at the table turned toward him. There was silence. With the exaggeratedly precise enunciation of the very drunk, Roger spoke.

"Having participated in these dinners since I was old enough to be allowed at the table with the grown-ups, I am well aware that I am violating a sacred and long-established ritual. This is the moment, by custom, when my father makes a small, modest speech of gratitude. As well he might. For he is truly blessed, dear friends, with all the things a man could wish for—an adoring wife, a first son who has given him a beautiful daughter-in-law and two charming grandchildren, to say nothing of a family pipeline to heaven. He has collected the finest business talent in the world—you distinguished gentlemen and one superbly qualified lady. In short, he has gathered the best that the world has to offer. And the world sees him as the most blessed of men."

Fearful of what was to come and unable to stop it, Pat Haylow sank back into her chair. Slowly, the others sat down. Around the table, their faces reflected their thoughts—curiosity on some, anxiety on others. Only Joe Haylow remained expressionless, waiting for his son to continue. Still standing, Roger plunged on.

"As I have said, my father should, indeed, recite a litany of his blessings. Because, you see, he believes that he is the image he projects to the world: kind, brave, reverent, clean, all those good Boy Scout things. Heaven has looked kindly upon Joseph Woodward Haylow. And that is the key point. What is heaven? To some it is eternal paradise. But to others, heaven is simply a collection of stars. Not the stars of stage, screen, and television. No, not even the stars that fly so proudly over the Haylow stores. The stars that rule all our heavens are those whose mysteries have been plumbed by the astrologists, that ancient cult of priests and priestesses whose art predates the kindergarten version of heaven as good Christians think of it. Never mind what blessings the world thinks God's heaven has bestowed on our Chairman. The question is, what do the stars say of him? That, dear people, is quite another zinger from the Zodiac!"

Alarmed, Bridget Manning, who sat on the other side of Roger, tugged urgently at his sleeve. In a low voice she said, "Don't, Roger, whatever you're up to, *don't!*"

Roger looked down at her with drunken amusement. "My good friend Miss Manning thinks I should stop right here. But what could she fear? I intend to quote directly from the stars. And the stars are dispassionate. The stars tell it like it is. They are as clinical as a computer which lies not, neither does it sleep.

"You know my father as a Christian businessman—a combination which some might consider anachronistic if not virtually impossible. His life is not easy. For though it is guided by God, it is directed by Dow Jones and buffeted by the fickle winds of financiers who blow hot and cold. This is why I urge him to look elsewhere for help and inspiration. His fate is not in the hands of the Securities and Exchange Commission. His destiny was ordained by the date of his birth, his character clearly delineated by the planet in ascendancy during his mother's labor pains. I say to Joseph Haylow, 'Banish the accountants and turn to the astrologers! Seek the wisdom of the all-knowing seer, the medium rare.' For here, dear friends, Joe Haylow will find his true self. And, in turn, recognize the destiny of us all."

Reaching behind him, Roger produced a small volume.

Even at a distance, Pat Haylow could read the title *Astrology —The True Word*. She tried to keep her voice light.

"Roger, dear," she called. "We all find the subject enormously interesting. Astrology, I mean. But it is your father's birthday and I do think we should hear a word from him."

From the other end of the table, Joe Haylow spoke. His voice was a cold, thin blade of steel. "No, Pat. Let him go on. I'm sure that Roger has gone to a great deal of trouble to research the subject and I, for one, would be most interested in the conclusions."

Roger made a deep bow in his father's direction. Opening the book to a marked passage, he said, "I knew that our Chairman would feel that way. His active and inquiring mind is one of his best-known virtues. It would be unthinkable that he would not wish to know more about this well-documented science, particularly as it pertains to his own character which has such a far-reaching effect on everyone in this room. Therefore, sir, with your kind permission, and with deference to Mother's request for brevity, I shall read aloud only a few of the more pertinent pieces of information concerning the natives of Capricorn, the sign of the Zodiac under which you were born. The following are excerpts from an impartial judgment of Joseph Woodward Haylow set down in a twenty-five-cent volume written by an unknown soothsayer never privileged to meet this particular subject. I quote:

" 'Capricorn, December 22 to January 19. The sign that symbolically represents sin. Significant is its animal symbol, the goat, an animal offered as atonement or sacrifice. The Child born in the stable is laid in the goat's manger in order to conquer the signs of death and thus save mankind from destruction.

" 'Capricornians are intellectuals but are among the lowest in true spirituality. Their brains are ever on the alert to seize and take advantage of circumstances. Though rarely scheming, those born under this sign have a nature directed to the attainment of selfish ends. The penetrating power of the mind is great. These people are quick as lightning to see others' weaknesses that they may work to their own advantage.

" 'The Capricornian is a pleasing personality to meet, with a neat and attractive appearance and charming manners. But when their feelings are aroused they show a strong temper and can be exceedingly critical. They can ferret out facts and knowledge where others fail. They are unusually capable of concentration and meditation. They are somewhat timid in their amours but they are loyal to the object of their affections. At times they show affection, but for the most part they appear reserved to the point of indifference. This attitude leads to misunderstanding between them and their loved ones. They have foresight and judgment about business. They should learn to do the same thing in regard to their intimate feelings. The basic nature of Capricorn is selfish. They are good providers but they are dictatorial and ultra-conservative. Those husbands born under the sign of the goat direct their homes like commanding officers with their wives as lieutenants. And as commanding officers they can be exacting, obstinate, and unreasonable in setting the laws for family routine. Such laws may be in accordance with good discipline but they are wholly unsympathetic and intolerant. Capricornians are serious-minded people who have no real understanding of life.' "

Roger threw the book on the floor and raised his glass of champagne. "Ladies and gentlemen, I give you my father, the self-engrossed goat." He finished his wine in a gulp and strode from the room looking neither right nor left.

The pause that followed seemed endless. At last, Joe Haylow rose slowly from his chair. For the first time he moved and looked like an old man.

"My dear friends," he said, "it would seem that any further remarks would be as inappropriate as they would be anticlimactic. I thank you for being here. And I bid you all good night."

He walked to the other end of the table where Pat sat unmoving, her eyes closed. The lines of humiliation and agony were etched deep on her face. Joe touched her arm and slowly she rose. The two of them left the room together.

For a moment, no one at the table moved. Then Bridget reached down and picked up the paperback. With a sad smile she handed the book to Brad Deland.

"Find out about your future."

Brad looked thoughtful. "I just did," he said.

3

On the mid-week days he spent in New York, Joe Haylow usually was the first person to arrive at the Haylow building in the morning. It was his habit to let himself into his office about eight o'clock and spend the next hour getting rid of minor matters before the interruption of telephone calls and appointments began.

Joe used this time profitably, his quiet concentration undisturbed by the commercial clatter which marked the rest of the working day. By nine-fifteen the office would come alive with the arrival of the secretaries, exchanging reports of their previous night's amours and activities as they waited for the tinkle of the bell which announced the coffee wagon bearing its life-giving cargo of bitter coffee and sticky Danish pastries. By nine-thirty the executive staff would be safely ensconced behind the mahogany doors which punctuated the forty-seventh floor corridor of the Haylow building.

Haylow's own office was, by conventional standards, a modest one for the ruler of an empire. There was only one large room with an undramatic view of the East River and, across it, a glimpse of the dreariness of Long Island City factories with their neon signs advertising bathroom hampers and Mamma Louise's Frozen Pizzas. Joe cared nothing for the breath-taking vistas of New York skyscrapers which loomed like stage settings beyond the office windows on the west side of the building. He needed no man-made props to underscore the majesty of his position, just as he needed no rich furnishings to impress visitors to the Chairman's office.

Except for the collection of lions which covered the walls and filled the chrome and glass étagère on one wall, Haylow's office was almost monk-like in its sparseness. He worked seated in a leather lounge chair in front of which was a low, modern coffee table and two canvas director's chairs for visitors. Beside him, on a small table, was a telephone and a dictating machine, a stack of yellow ruled pads and a cup shaped like a lion's head filled with sharp pencils and ballpoint pens. His decision to do away with a desk had been made years before after a conversation with Sid Sommers.

"Only the insecure executive hides behind a big desk," the psychologist told him. "It is the modern businessman's fortress that shields him from attack, like an impenetrable barricade. A big desk makes a small man feel invincible. It awes his employees and keeps outsiders at arm's length. Subconsciously, the man behind the big desk is setting up a communications barrier that reinforces his belief in his superiority."

Haylow examined the theory and found it valid. From that moment on he not only did his own work from the chair-throne but he noted with analytical interest what kind of desks his key people chose. It became a kind of game to see how the choice matched the occupants of each office. Cabot, for instance, worked at a huge, Biedermeier desk, as ponderous and heavy-handed as the man himself. Deland functioned from an elegant, leather-topped antique. Bridget Manning contained her work neatly on a small Louis XIV original. Mike Warner's desk was a modern concoction of steel and glass and Roger Haylow had chosen a parson's table lacquered in brilliant Chinese red.

All the offices except Haylow's had file cabinets and storage space. The Chairman had neither, nor did his secretary, who sat in a small, spare cubicle outside his door. Haylow boasted that there were no carbons of his endless memos and letters and bulletins, no files of the hundreds of thousands of pieces of mail he received. Unknown to him, the Board had, in secret session, overruled this unorthodox procedure. Accountants paled at the thought that no records of his dealings could be produced for the Securities and Exchange Commission or the Internal Revenue Department, or that any of the Chairman's correspondence concerning day-by-day operations would be unavailable for future review. Accordingly, Haylow's secretary made secret carbons of all his dictation and Xeroxed the memos which Haylow received from other people and which he preferred to answer with a terse handwritten notation across the top, returning the original to the sender. Surreptitiously, she filed all important incoming mail, retrieving much of it from the wastebasket where Haylow dumped it each morning. The Chairman would have been amazed to learn that there was one whole room filled with files of his prodigious business correspondence and kept under lock and key in the other end of the building.

On the first morning after his return from Florida, Haylow went quickly through the accumulated mail stacked on the coffee table, making his concise comments across most of the memos, throwing most of the routine letters and all the junk mail into the basket. Coming back on the plane, he had made four notations for this morning: (1) Dictate monthly bulletin. (2) Memo Cabot re Harrisburg store. (3) Call Bridget. (4) See Roger. Methodically, he tackled the self-given assignments in order. The first was one he particularly enjoyed. Haylow's monthly Management Letter which went out to one hundred thousand junior and senior employees was a combination of as much corporate information as he wanted them to have, plus his personal views on business conditions in general. Interspersed were words of recognition for those companies or individuals who had performed extraordinarily well in the preceding month. And always there was a dissertation, hopefully provocative, on some current subject—a discreet statement about government or politics, a recap of current fads among the young, or a fatherly suggestion about a new book which seemed worth reading or some magazine article which discussed a facet of contemporary life. These two-page bulletins also were sent to stockholders, a public-relations idea of Haylow's own, designed to foster the image of a "human" company in which investors could securely place their trust as well as their money.

Although there was a prevailing belief that Haylow opened all his meetings with a prayer, this was not true. He did, however, always include in the bulletin some home-spun adage or God-given message of inspiration, carefully selected to be nonsectarian and appealingly humble.

Picking up the microphone of the dictating machine this morning, Haylow began to compose the bulletin.

"Dear Friends of Haylow," he began. "In this first communication of the New Year, I would like to share with you a little poem that one of the company's salespeople sent to me on a Christmas card. The verse is from Raymond Wilkens of our Star Store in Memphis, and it is a heart-warming indication of the way so may of our wonderful Haylow-ites feel.

> "'Someone gave me a smile today.
> I tried my best to give it away
> To everyone I chanced to meet
> As I walked down the street.
> But everyone that I could see
> Gave my smile right back to me.
> When I got home, besides my smile,
> I had enough to reach a mile!'"

Pleased with the opening, Haylow continued to dictate a brief, well-edited report on the company's progress in the past year. It was an optimistic report, playing down the few failures and projecting a picture of rising volume and profits in the year ahead. No wonder, he said, that all of the Haylow employees and stockholders had many smiles to share with others, and many reasons to thank God for the health and vitality of the company and its dedicated, loyal workers.

Among those given special recognition in this bulletin were Mike Warner whose Star Stores had shown a seventeen percent increase, and Bridget Manning who had been awarded the fashion industry's highest honor, the Dolly, a silver dressmaker's dummy presented annually to the retailer who had made the most "conspicuous contribution to the encouragement of taste and talent in American design." It was the clothing industry's equivalent of the Oscar or the Emmy, and Haylow had been at her side, sharing the triumph, when she received it.

There were lesser paragraphs about lesser personnel, too. A word of congratulation to the best manager in the Haylow Haberdashery chain, a salute to the salesman with the highest figures in the organization. And special recognition to the ad manager of Haylowettes, the group of children's wear stores which sponsored a kiddies TV program featuring a group of precocious mini-monsters unsurprisingly called "The Littlest Haylows." Every Saturday morning, these terrifying tots sang and danced for their peers, meanwhile lisping an invitation to "get Mummie to bring you into your favorite Haylowette store for your new shoes and your very own copy of our new coloring book called 'Haylow, Everybuddy!'" Every Saturday afternoon, a hundred thousand harassed Mummies did what the kiddies ordered, to the delight of the network and the sponsor.

Haylow ended the Bulletin with his favorite subject: youth. The Chairman worshipped youth of all ages and income levels. His stores concentrated, in decor and merchandise, on young customers, being careful at the same time not to neglect those who were merely young in spirit. Haylow executives were discouraged from indulging in nostalgia or reminiscences. Though he was a believer in experienced, highly trained management, Joe Haylow frowned on references to the past as a guide to the actions of the present. And if he detested "thinking old," he abhorred "looking old." The latter subject made up his last paragraph.

"Remember," he dictated, "that styles used to be set by movie stars, royalty, and matinee idols. Today, fashion begins with the young. As merchants we must be ever alert for what young people are saying, thinking, doing. And we must be living proof that there is no such thing as a generation gap. As executives in the clothing business, you must look the part. What *you* wear is what the customer will recognize and buy. Our most effective advertising is the appearance of our people. Haylow employees have the advantage of a twenty percent discount on their clothes. Surely we can use this great company benefit to enhance our business images as well as our personal wardrobes!"

Clicking off the machine, Haylow turned to the next assignment, a memo to Dick Cabot ordering the closing of the Haylow Housedress store in Harrisburg, Pennsylvania. The Haylow Housedress chain did a thriving business in small communities. Inexplicably, this particular store, after fifteen years of operation, had succumbed to the competition of Sears Roebuck and Montgomery Ward which had opened shops nearby. Its position of dominance suddenly challenged, the Harrisburg shop had failed to respond to all the usual corporate attempts to shore up a store with sagging volume. After a year of trying, Haylow had decided to close it, a decision which Dick Cabot had, in his mild way, opposed. In fairness to the company and in token deference to the corporate President, Joe had tried to save the store. As with all faltering operations, he had sent a team from the head office. "Haylow's Hatchets," as the victims called them, had descended on Harrisburg in droves. There were Central Management Engineering experts, Electronic Data Processing professionals, Marketing and Manpower consultants. Costs were examined and slashed. Operating managers interrogated. Surveys of the competition were made and the potential of the area re-evaluated. Personnel was reviewed and realigned. In the case of Harrisburg, it had all been in vain, and despite Cabot's low-pitched plea for more time, Haylow had reached the limit of his patience. Weakness, lack of performance, improbability of growth and profit were personal affronts to the Chairman. He regretted the failure of the store from a business point of view, but, realistically, he could not permit himself the luxury of allowing one weak child to sap the strength of the parent company. Like Cabot, he disliked the idea of several hundred people losing their jobs and he privately asked God to help them through this misfortune. But, unlike the President, he believed that the good of the business precluded more time-taking, costly efforts. The well-being of a few could not take precedence over the benefits of many. His sacred duty was to the stockholders, many of whom were the little people of the Methodist Church who looked to Haylow for the comfort of a company glowing with fiscal health, basking in financial sunshine.

Dictating the memo to Cabot, ordering the closing of the store, Haylow knew that the President would offer no further resistance. He was aware that Cabot was playing a waiting game, unwilling to displease the Chairman and prejudice his own chances for the top job. It was one of the things that disturbed Haylow about Cabot, this lack of decisiveness, this overcautious, wait-and-see attitude that was so different from Haylow's. The Chairman was dedicated to the proposition that no man was his equal in business, but he felt only scorn for the opponent who would not put up a good fight. In fact, Joe loved a good argument. Intelligent opposition stimulated him and sometimes he went out of his way to provoke it, knowing full well that he intended to win the point, but enjoying the ritual of point and counterpoint that made the victory sweeter. Cabot never gave him this pleasure as a few of the less cautious, or less frightened, of his associates did. Consequently, Haylow's respect for his heir-apparent was considerably less than his admiration for Deland or Warner or Bridget. These three were fighters, a quality that Haylow understood. He wished that Dick had more of the healthy competitive spirit.

Glancing again at the list of things to do, he recalled Roger's extraordinary performance at the birthday dinner. He had discussed its implications with no one, not even Pat. The shock and hurt of Roger's sardonic, drunken, irrational speech had left Pat stunned and inarticulate. He had heard her crying softly in the night. To Haylow, Roger's defiance had been like a bitter outpouring of poison, as though a long-festering boil had come to a head, spilling its pus only over the body it infected. As a father he felt concern for Roger's inexplicable behavior. Yet Haylow also felt impatience and anger with this ungrateful child who was also his most important employee. Joe's hopes for Roger had always been high. It was his consolation that Roger would carry on the Haylow business, increase it and ultimately bequeath it to children of his own. He knew, from case histories, how difficult the life of a rich, successful man's son could be. He had read enough to be objectively aware of the awesome example men like himself set for their children. But he was determined that Roger would not retreat into drunkenness to disqualify himself from the future that had been planned for him. For one of the few times in his life, Joe Haylow had no ready answers. The idea that Roger could hate him was insupportable. He had done nothing to deserve hatred. All he wanted was what he believed best for Roger: power and success handed to him in a swift, easy gesture. Roger would reap the fruits of Joe's labors. "How sharper than a serpent's tooth," he thought. Roger must be brought into line. Quickly.

Drawing a line through the fourth item on his list, he substituted "Lunch with Sid." Before talking to Roger it would be well to explore Sommers' thoughts about the problem. He was, after all, a psychologist as well as a trusted friend.

Haylow buzzed for Miss Watson, his new secretary who had replaced Ruth Anthony, retired three months ago after thirty-five years as the Chairman's right hand. He missed Ruth's crisp efficiency, the polite and respectful but undeniable affection that he had taken for granted for all the years. The new girl was well qualified and pretty, but she performed her duties with the detached precision of a young woman marking time. Like all the "new ones," Miss Watson had no career aspirations. She would work only until her young man decided that sex is infinitely more convenient when it's home every night waiting for you with a wedding ring on its finger. Joe wondered which would come first—his retirement or Miss Watson's inevitable marriage. It was not particularly important, somehow. They were both, in their way, interim employees.

When she came in, they exchanged amenities about his holiday, reviewed the appointments she had made for him. Deftly, she removed the tape from the recording machine, gathered up the papers he had gone through, took his wastebasket ostensibly for emptying. He asked her to call Sid Sommers and arrange a luncheon appointment at twelve-thirty in the Oak Room of the Plaza.

"Even if he has another appointment, please ask him to break it," Joe said. "Tell him it's urgent I speak with him today."

When she left, Haylow used his private wire to call Bridget Manning at her unlisted number in the store. She answered immediately, made no effort to hide her delight at hearing his voice.

"Joe, how are you?" she asked. "So glad you're back! How was the rest of the vacation?"

"A little less dramatic than when you were there," he said. "How's it going at the store? Business okay?"

"Not bad for January. But I do have a problem that I need to discuss with you. Something rather unpleasant."

Haylow felt a flicker of alarm, the same feeling he always had when an employee came into his office and asked, "May I close the door?" Years of experience had taught him that those five opening words invariably meant that the man had come either to resign or to present some messy private problem for Haylow to solve. Quickly he dismissed the idea that Bridget would consider leaving the store. It must be trouble in her private life. In that brief pause, Joe felt something close to fatherly concern, a kind of protective reaching out that he lacked in his relationships with his own children.

As though she sensed his thoughts, Bridget continued.

"Don't worry," she said. "Everything is fine with me. The problem is Tom Saunders."

Saunders was Bridget's Executive Vice President and her right hand in the administration of the stores. At thirty-five, Tom was handsome, intelligent, invaluable to Bridget Manning and to the Haylow organization. They had lured him away from a Dallas store with a sizable increase in money and stock options and the almost certain prospect of one day becoming President of Bridget's. Saunders had been a great success. His strength was in the areas of finance and operations, talents which perfectly complemented Bridget's greater abilities in the areas of fashion merchandising, promotion, and public relations. The two liked and respected each other. It had been a highly satisfactory move for everyone, including Saunders' pretty little southern wife and two children who were happy with Tom's success and the benefits it provided—like private schools, country clubs, and a tastefully decorated house in Scarsdale.

All this background information went through Haylow's mind as rapidly and precisely as data being fed into a computer.

"What about Tom?" he asked. "Don't tell me he's leaving!"

Bridget sounded almost sad. "No, he's not leaving. That is, he doesn't want to leave, but I may have to ask him to resign. That's what I need to talk to you about right away, Joe."

"I have a bad day," Haylow said, "and tomorrow I have to go to Atlanta for a meeting. Be gone a few days, probably. Can you tell me about it now?"

"Are you on your private wire?"

"Of course."

"Well," Bridget said, "Tom's secretary has just been in to see me. She's pregnant and Tom is the father. No one in the store knows, but of course the situation is untenable. I don't know whether I'm more shocked or disappointed. I keep thinking about the girl. She's such a nice little thing and really hopelessly in love with Tom. And, of course, I keep worrying about Alice Saunders and what it would do to that marriage if she ever found out. And then, there's the matter of bad business judgment. I never dreamed that Tom would be foolish enough to have an affair within the store. Good Lord, Joe, if he *had* to do such a thing couldn't he at least have gone looking outside his own office? A man stupid enough to do that makes me feel as though he's not wise enough ever to have full responsibility for this business!"

"Have you discussed it with Tom?" Haylow asked.

"Yes. He just left my office. He admits it's true and is man enough not to make any excuses. He says it was stupid. Just one of those things. He doesn't love the girl and has no intention of divorcing his wife. He has offered to resign and I told him I'd let him know."

The Rich and the Righteous

Haylow thought for a moment. "Want my advice? Don't let him resign. Give him a bonus."

On the other end of the line there was silence.

"Listen, Bridget," Haylow said. "I'm as annoyed at Tom's stupidity as you are. Sorry for the girl, too. But the most important thing is that Tom is a valuable employee and maybe he's bright enough to have learned a lesson from this. It would be mighty inconvenient to have to replace him and what will you have gained?"

Bridget was thoughtful. This strange, strait-laced man, she reflected, was so utterly practical and unemotional about his business. Adultery was a sin only when it was convenient to remember the Ten Commandments. Right now it was not. Otherwise, Joe Haylow would be morally obligated to banish Saunders, a troublesome move for everyone involved.

"All right," she agreed. "I'll kick my moral questions, but you still have to resolve my financial ones. What do you mean 'give him a bonus'? Surely you don't intend to reward him for behaving like an oversexed adolescent?"

"You've got to face this like a realistic businessman," Haylow said. "The girl will obviously need an abortion. Could cost a thousand dollars which Tom probably doesn't have. And even if he does, how would he get at it without his wife finding out? So, give him a thousand-dollar bonus on the books—but make sure he knows exactly what it's for. Tell him that only you know about this. And make it plain that you'll be watching him pretty carefully from now on."

"And the girl?"

"Let Tom handle the abortion. You stay out of that. Just tell her that you'll be glad to give her a two-week paid vacation and place her in one of Mike Warner's stores when she returns. Don't give Mike any details. Just offer him a qualified employee. He'll leap at the chance to get a good secretary. She'll be safe with him. You know Mike. Sophia Loren couldn't tempt him to be unfaithful to Rose!"

"I know you're right about everything," Bridget said, "but it's all so sordid. I guess I'm square, but to me abortion is still murder."

"No," Haylow said. "In this case it's business. I know it's difficult," he added, gently, "but unfortunately you're the only one who can handle the deal. I'll try to run in and see you for a minute after lunch. Okay?"

"Okay. And Joe . . ."

"Yes?"

"God bless you."

"Bless you, too," he said.

Putting down the phone, Haylow said a silent prayer to his Friend. Forgive me if I've done wrong, but I can't believe that You would sacrifice Saunders and his family and the girl and Bridget's business for the sake of this unwanted seed. Suddenly the office seemed unbearably stuffy. Blast these new buildings with their sealed windows, he thought. It's like living in a cage. He remembered the early days and the little office in Farmville that was the original headquarters. A man could throw open the windows and breathe deep of the clean New England air, or walk down the snow-white, deep-drifted street to clear his head of his problems. J need air, he thought. Even polluted New York air. He buzzed for Miss Watson.

"Did you reach Mr. Sommers?" he asked.

"Yes, sir. He'll meet you in the Oak Room of the Plaza at twelve-thirty. I've reserved a table."

"Good. I'll be leaving now. I want to walk."

Whenever possible, Joe Haylow walked from his office to all his appointments. A car and chauffeur—the status symbol of corporate success flaunted by executives far less rich and powerful—was a pretension that Haylow's conservative Yankee outlook rejected. Aside from that, he truly enjoyed walking. It was the time that he did his best, uninterrupted thinking. Pat Haylow, half in jest, always swore that one day she would be a "pedestrian widow" because Joe, deep in

73

thought, frequently forgot to obey the "Walk" and "Don't Walk" signs and narrowly escaped being struck down by cars trying to beat the lights at the intersections.

Though he seemed thoroughly detached, loping up Park Avenue, Haylow was, in fact, very much aware of his surroundings. His trained mind noted what the women were wearing, and which costumes came out of Star or Bridget stockrooms, making mental memorandums to tell Mike and Bridget which merchandise seemed to be moving best. He also could not ignore the beggars, particularly the blind men with their patient seeing-eye dogs. Although he had heard—and believed it true—that these men were rich fakers who owned blocks of tenement houses, he was unable to pass one by without dropping a few coins into the outstretched cup. Charity was an ingrained habit with him. Remembering the biblical beggars, it seemed that this silent plea for alms ranked with prostitution as the world's oldest profession. It hurt him that any man had to beg, or any woman to whore, and the sight of either made him momentarily grateful for his own blessings.

Crossing over to Fifth Avenue toward the Plaza, Haylow remembered the very first time he had faced Sid Sommers across a restaurant table. Nearly thirty-five hard-driving, richly rewarding years separated those two meetings, and through them all Sid Sommers' cool, objective advice and support had played a major part in the Chairman's success.

Haylow recalled that first encounter as clearly as though it had taken place the day before. The scene was a grubby little coffee shop on West Forty-third Street, the kind of place where one's clothes retain the smell of greasy fried foods for hours after leaving it. The two men had sat at a bare-surfaced booth in the back of the shop talking for two hours over endless cups of terrible, overcooked coffee. They immediately had established a rare, enduring trust based on mutual understanding and admiration. Both were young and visionary. Both were starting new careers and, blessed with instinct, both men knew they would continue to be important to each other.

The meeting had been initiated by Haylow, who had come down from Farmville specifically to find Sid Sommers and, in all probability, hire him. Joe's awareness of Sommers had come about by chance. At a fund-raising dinner he was seated next to Ed Wilson, owner of Seaboard Aircraft, a still small but upcoming manufacturer of airplane engines. During the evening, Wilson had told Haylow about Sid.

"He's a brilliant young guy in a new field," Wilson had said. "They call it industrial psychology, which, as far as I can figure out, is just a fancy name for a personnel man with common sense. Anyway, I have him on a two-hundred-dollar-a-month retainer to give psychological tests to key people I'm interested in hiring. The reports he gives me are downright creepy. Amazing the way he can analyze a man's strengths and weaknesses through these damfool question-and-answer sessions. He's saved me from quite a few mistakes, I'll have to admit that. And he's steered me toward a helluva lot of good people I might have otherwise overlooked. A lot of people think I'm a nut, throwing away good money on a lot of head-shrinking crap, but I think the guy is onto something that's going to be important to big businesses in the future."

"Is he a doctor?" Haylow asked.

"Oh sure, he's got a degree. But he doesn't use the doctor handle. Says it inhibits people, scares 'em if they think they're talking to some Freudian cuckoo. Look him up next time you're in New York. But don't expect anything very fancy. He's one of those corn-fed southern types. Even whittles at things while he talks. But he's sharp as that little knife he carries. No fancy office. He's just getting started. And I guess there aren't too many damn fools like me who think that the whole motivation thing matters. As far as I know, I'm his only full-time client, but I'm really sold on this guy's approach to people. Like the other day he said to me, 'Mr.

Wilson, you can make the best airplane engines in the world, but your big asset is good people. Never forget that every night your inventory walks out the front door.' Maybe that sounds loony to you, Mr. Haylow, but it makes a lot of sense to me."

It had made sense to Joe Haylow, whose every waking moment was devoted to finding new, better, more inventive ways to do business. Within two days he was in New York, calling Sommers at nine in the morning, noting, with New England satisfaction, that the man was already answering his office phone.

Joe came right to the point with brisk, typical directness.

"This is Joe Haylow," he said. "Ed Wilson at Seaboard says you're a smart young fella with some pretty advanced ideas. When can we talk?"

Forty minutes later they met in the reeking coffee shop on the ground floor of Sommers' office building. Sid's office was too small and dingy to receive prospective clients, and Haylow had no New York office at all, just the Main Street headquarters in Farmville. Haylow did most of the talking, eagerly, convincingly.

"I have three little general stores in Vermont," he explained, "but they're only the beginning of thousands of others around the country, around the world. May sound crazy to you, but I mean to be the most important merchant that ever lived. I'm going to do things nobody's ever tried before. You see, I don't believe in rules. Except the Golden One.

"I'm willing to break my back to make The Haylow Corporation the biggest, richest, most powerful retail complex anybody's ever seen. Because I know what to sell people and how to sell 'em. But there's a lot I don't know. I'm going to need the kind of help you're giving Ed Wilson, but I think you could add a lot to it. It's all very well to screen executive personnel, but my guess is that your know-how could go way beyond that. We're coming into a new kind of business world,

Sommers. A company like mine will need an expert on labor relations, executive incentives, even that thing they call 'public image.' I want to buy that kind of talent early in the game. Think you can handle it?"

"I'm an Industrial Psychologist, Mr. Haylow," he said. "You're talking about a combination of psychologist, management counselor, and public relations expert."

Haylow laughed. "Labels," he said. "Seems to me with your kind of training, you'd have to be all those things in one anyhow."

Sommers could not dispute it. Unerringly, Joe Haylow had put his finger on the direction that Sid knew he would inevitably go. Sommers was impressed with the native intelligence, the extraordinary instinct of this vital, enthusiastic young businessman. Playing for time, he slowly cut dozens of the shop's paper napkins into small, precise squares, piling them neatly across the width of the table. It was his carefully thought-out device to project the image of the slow-thinking country boy, to disarm people while he sorted out what he heard and decided what his strategy would be. For the rest of his life, people would watch Sid Sommers whittling at pencils while he worked out complicated labor negotiations at long conference tables. Or carving up swizzle sticks in cocktail bars while he listened to a prospective executive unwittingly say the things that would reveal facts not listed on his resumé. Years later the little silver knife he carried at that first meeting with Joe Haylow would be replaced by a solid gold one engraved "To Sid, who helped hang out the stars. Gratefully, JWH." Meanwhile, in the coffee shop, Sommers played for time. Haylow interested him, inspired belief, gave out the aura of confidence that would surround every idea he embraced. He wanted to work with this man who was such an intriguing combination of drive and humility, but he sensed that Haylow would be a demanding employer and, when he so decided, a stubborn one. It was obvious that Haylow was used to having his own way, a quality that would make people confuse dedication with coldness, mistake Haylow's drive for ruthlessness. Haylow would, indeed, have trouble with his "image." He would earn little loyalty and less love. And the lack of it would always surprise and vaguely trouble him. In that first meeting, Sid Sommers sensed that only the discerning and compassionate would ever know Joe Haylow for the honest, sensitive human being he was.

The narrowing of the eyes and the slight frown that Sid was to come to know so well in the years ahead now indicated that Haylow was growing impatient with the delay. Rather coldly, Haylow spoke.

"Well, Sommers? Is it a deal? I'll pay you a hundred a week to start and you'll go up with me. 'Grow with Haylow.' How's that for a recruiting slogan, by the way?"

"Lousy," Sommers said. "But the job isn't. I don't know much about retailing or merchandising or whatever you call it, but something feels right about the job. Probably the hundred bucks a week."

Across the littered coffee table, Sommers extended his hand. "It's a deal, Mr. Haylow. I'll give you psychological lessons for money. And I'll be your friend for free."

Joe's strong hand gripped the other.

"Good," he said. "I'm glad you'll work for me. But I don't believe that anything, including friendship, comes free."

Sommers smiled his slow, Georgia-boy, scuff-the-toe-in-the-dust grin.

"You've just had your first lesson," he said.

Walking into the Oak Room, acknowledging the maître d's respectful greeting, Haylow congratulated himself for the thousandth time on his choice of Sommers. It had all come true. The Haylow Corporation had become the world's biggest clothing chain and Sid's own business had become one of the largest and most sought-after management consultant firms. Sid had even been right about friendship. He had become the brother that Joe never had. Proof, if any was needed, was that Sid was the one person in the world to whom Joe Haylow turned with a problem, be it professional or personal. Jimmy Jackson might be Haylow's spiritual crutch, but Sid Sommers was his worldly sounding board.

Today Joe needed personal help and he was delighted that a much older, definitely heavier, but equally composed Sid Sommers was already at the table waiting for him.

"Right on time," Sid greeted him. "That's one unfashionable habit that neither of us rich old coots can seem to get over, can we?"

Haylow laughed. "No, punctuality seems to be part of my middle-class background. I guess I'll never really be part of the chic set. Somehow I can't learn to be late for appointments. Very square."

They ordered lunch. Joe chose the low-calorie special, a weight-watcher's combination of broiled hamburger and cottage cheese. Sid ordered roast beef, mashed potatoes, and peas. "With plenty of gravy," he told the captain.

"Damned if I know where you get that spartan discipline about food," Sid said. "Look at you. Not a pound heavier than you were thirty-five years ago. Me, I just keep getting paunchier and uglier while you don't change a bit."

"Not true. As my closest friend, I will confide that I am uglier than I used to be."

"No," Sommers said, "blast your soul, not even that. Maybe not as youthfully handsome but a whole lot more statesman-like impressive. And," he added, "a darned sight more troubled. Let's get at it. What's on your mind?"

"I'm sure you can guess," Haylow answered. "The naming of the new Chairman in general. And my son in particular. I suppose you might say they're both part of the same problem."

"Thinking of naming Roger instead of Cabot?"

Joe shook his head. "I don't know. It's a possibility. The job is his one day, but it's a question of whether he's ready for it now. I don't have to kid you about Cabot. He's not really my style. Never has been. Oh he's solid enough, I guess. But I just can't imagine him as the Chairman. He's not a fighter, as far as I can tell."

Sid carefully turned a matchbook cover into confetti.

"Could it be," he suggested, "that Cabot knows he can't fight City Hall? No offense, Joe, but while you're around there's not too much decision-making done by anybody. Maybe Cabot is just biding his time. Like Harry Truman, he might rise to the job when he gets it."

"You mean *if* he gets it," Haylow said. "Don't overlook the other alternatives. Deland. Mike Warner. Even Bridget. Any one of them is as well qualified as Cabot. Maybe better. This is still my business, Sid. No law says I have to make the President the Chairman. With the family and the foundation I still control the stock."

"You skipped an alternative," Sommers said quietly. "Roger."

"Yes," Haylow agreed. "There's Roger. As I said a minute ago, he is the heir to this business. He's very young for such a big assignment but from an executive point of view he's as able as any of the older men. Maybe it's immodest of a man to say that his son is a genius, but mine is. When he puts his mind to it, he's sharper and quicker than any of us. Oh hell, Sid," Haylow said, in one of his rare lapses into profanity, "let's stop kidding around. I didn't ask you to have lunch to discuss my retirement, which is still a year away. I need your advice about Roger. Pat told me she'd already discussed it with you and I promised to follow up. You saw how he behaved in Florida. I know he's drinking, but you can't tell me the boy's an alcoholic. He's on the job every day and I'm not about to set myself up as a judge of what a thirty-seven-year-old man does after hours. I don't choose to drink, but I don't think I've ever imposed my set of standards on anybody else. Pat seems to think it goes deeper than just the drinking. She thinks the boy is terribly unhappy. Maybe hates the business."

Haylow stopped. Even to himself he could not add the words "Maybe even hates me." The final sentence hung, unspoken between the two men. To Haylow, the thought was impossible. Within his simple code, children did not hate their parents. They rebelled, maybe. They lost touch through a world of changing morals and values. But they did not hate a parent who had never abused or deprived them and who had, in fact, worked for their future happiness and security. Haylow had read enough layman's psychiatry to know that parents were most often held responsible for the confusion which brought adults to the couch. Trying to rationalize it, Joe could not believe that this contemporary cliché could be the root of Roger's problem, whatever it was. In Pat, Roger had a warm, loving, and undemanding mother, not the kind of stereotyped mother-image who clutched at her children, smothering them with guilt feelings and hateful obligations. Although she adored her two sons, Pat's greatest share of concern was still reserved for her husband. She was always radiantly happy to see Roger, but if weeks passed between visits or even telephone calls, hers was never the role of accuser. Inherently wise, she had no taste for martyrdom, no capacity for self-pity. She gave her children training, love, and freedom. And the affection she got in return was freely and lavishly given. Joe remembered how happy Pat had been a few years before when Roger had said to her, "You know, Mom, I don't just love you. I like you."

No, Haylow reflected, whatever Roger's problem was, it was not the usual mother-hangup which filled the psychiatrists' offices with neurotics and the gay bars with homosexuals.

It was difficult, Haylow knew, for him to analyze his own relationship with Roger. Joe was not, he admitted, the father-hero of the American dream. He had never taken his sons to ball games, or on fishing trips or tried to have those man-to-man talks with them that were supposed to be part and parcel of middle-class family life. To the boys, Pat explained this lack with the truth as she accepted it. Their father was away more than most fathers, his business was a much different and more demanding one than, say, those of the Farmville men who had nine-to-five jobs as bankers or lawyers. Joe knew this was a deception designed to protect both father and children. To be brutally honest, Joe did not care for children as people. The early conversational efforts of his sons bored him; their childish activities instilled in him a feeling of supreme disinterest. He left the formation of their personalities to the tender, sensible care of their mother. His job was materialistic. Their health and education, their ownership of the right clothes and toys and, later, cars and spending money, were his responsibility. Just as the building of a business for Roger to inherit was, he believed, the greatest contribution he could make to his son's future.

Through the years there had been no reason to question this division of parental obligation. His children had given him respect, obedience, and, he had always assumed, love. He could not remember exactly when Woodward had decided to enter the ministry or even, for that matter, whether it had been more than casually discussed. At some point, Joe had simply decided that God had once more blessed him with sons who shared, separately, their father's two great loves—business and religion. One son for each love. Each child to be dedicated, apparently willingly, to the interests closest to his father's heart. He had never doubted that the satisfaction he felt was shared by the boys. Woodward had taken to the ministry with apparent devotion and quiet enjoyment. Roger had come into the business with seeming interest and ambition. Until lately. Now some unfathomable overt disturbance was threatening the well-ordered plan of

Haylow's life. He was being jolted out of the complacent attitude created by four decades in which things proceeded exactly as he intended. He didn't like things he didn't understand. And right now he didn't understand his younger son.

Sommers' voice brought him back to the present.

"Joe," he said gently. "How can I help?"

"I guess I was hoping you could tell me," Haylow said. "I have to know what's happening to Roger. Not just because he may be the next Chairman. Because he's my son. And because his mother is fretting her heart out about it. Do you realize, Sid, that neither of us has ever seen Roger's apartment in New York? We don't know where he spends his time or who his friends are. Pat's even worrying that he's not married."

"Well, those things aren't exactly unusual these days," Sid said mildly. "It's a new world, Joe. Young people don't follow the patterns we did. It's known as defying the Establishment. Probably the same reason Roger will have nothing to do with the church. This generation wants to be as different as possible from the one before it."

"I don't think God knows about the generation gap," Haylow said bitterly. "Anyway, we're not talking about the lack of communication between parents and teen-agers. We're discussing adults who've drifted so far apart that they have nothing between them except a blood relationship. Roger can't be allowed to behave like some hippie who's out to defy his parents. He's the Executive Vice President of a billion-dollar corporation. Pat's right. He should be married, having children to carry on the business, the way we had them. He ought to care about his own future and the future of thousands of people who are going to depend on him. He hasn't an ounce of humility or reverence for anything I believe in. How can people live without believing in something, respecting something? How can they exist in a state of perpetual anger?"

Sommers let him have it. Fast. "You think Roger's homosexual?"

Haylow didn't flinch. "No. But then, does any parent ever think that of his own child?"

Suppressing his pity, Sommers moved on. "Do you think Roger hates you?"

"If I believed that, I'd have to believe that God hates me."

Time to stop, Sid thought. You can press a man too far, even a man as strong and seemingly invulnerable as Joe Haylow. He forced himself to speak lightly.

"Right now I think we're all victims of a recent wound. Roger got loaded at your birthday dinner and said a few things that hurt. It isn't always necessarily true that a drunken man speaks the truth, you know, and maybe we're all blowing this problem up out of proportion. Let's give it a little time to right itself before we push the panic button."

Almost visibly, Haylow relaxed. "It isn't like me to be so uptight about anything, is it? All right. But we've still got a problem that could affect the business. You're supposed to be the corporate problem-solver for a whale of a lot of money a year. And I'd like my money's worth—in action or advice."

"Not ready to give either right now," Sommers said. "But as I am fond of saying to your trusted employees, 'You make him rich and I'll keep him humble.' So you just keep on getting rich and let me worry about your humility."

"Meaning?"

"Meaning that I'm not yet ready to let you assume the responsibility for Roger's behavior. Nor am I ready to let you off the hook if you are the cause of it. As the kids say, when I know, I'll sock it to you, whether you like it or not. Since you've opened the door, I now feel free to thrust my everlastingly curious nose into the public and private life of Roger Haylow and anybody else who happens to be involved. I'm really a frustrated private eye, you know. Can't stand a mystery without a solution. And being a professional head doctor, people seem to think that whatever they tell me is privileged communication, like a lawyer or a priest. And speaking of the clergy, how's Jimmy Jackson's Pray-In at Madison Square? I hear it's the hottest ticket in town . . . without even a nude onstage."

Diverted, Haylow began to talk enthusiastically about the success of his minister's latest rally. Sommers half-listened. His mind already was planning the campaign to solve the riddle of Roger Haylow. And quite a few other riddles that he had carefully avoided mentioning to the Chairman.

They'd all have to be sorted out before the year was over.

4

While Haylow and Sommers were having their lunch in the Oak Room, Haylow's Financial Vice President was ruefully considering the fact that among all the people in the world he knew, there was nobody with whom he wanted to share his midday meal. Sitting in the quiet of his office, Brad Deland reflected that he was, in a peculiar way, a very lonely man. The men he'd grown up with, all now, he realized, "middle-aged," had followed different paths than his. They were a complacent, snobbish group, interested only in their Wall Street brokerage houses, their farms in Virginia, their daily lunches at the exclusive Spire Club. Even their wives were a different breed. Unlike Doe-Doe, they were poised, assured, understated women who dressed with the disregard for fashion that is the prerogative of the securely social and very rich. The Delands saw little of "Brad's crowd," as his wife called them. She found them boring and insular. And they, Brad sensed, found Doe-Doe a ridiculous and vulgar caricature of a youngish matron.

Beyond his social exile from his peers, Brad deliberately avoided the male companionship of these friends of his youth. Not only did they have different surface interests, they were far apart in their business ambitions. Most of them had inherited businesses and wealth from fathers who had made fortunes in the '20s, or from grandfathers who had been

part of the empire-building world of the Astors and Vander-
bilts. Brad's contemporaries had no need to prove anything.
None had the fierce urgency which motivated Bradford Deland, the son of a suicide.

Brad's thirst for power stemmed from the day he and his
mother had received word of his father's death at his own
hand. This was in the middle of the stock market crash of
1929. Brad was only ten years old when his father died, but
he was a precocious child with emotions far deeper than
normal for a boy of his years. From the moment he learned
the terrible news, Brad had never shed a tear, never uttered
a word of sorrow or pity for his dead father. His mother had
thought him too young to grasp what had happened. Griev-
ing for her husband, she had been grateful for his sacrifice,
understanding that the huge life insurance policy he left was
the only way that a financially ruined Senior Deland could
insure any kind of comfortable future for his wife and child.
She would willingly have accepted a new way of life rather
than have had her husband give up his own. But she knew
that Brad Deland Jr. was a proud man who could not have
borne the sight of the hardships he would have forced on the
two people he loved most in the world. He chose their
security over his own life, and a heartbroken widow revered
him for it the rest of her days.

Not so the son he left well provided for. Brad Deland III
felt nothing like sadness or respect. He did feel other things,
progressively. Shock was followed by pity, not for his father
but for himself. He cursed his own bad luck in having been
born to a man who was so stupid as to have lost his money
and his business, so spineless as to have taken the easy way
out. In Brad's eyes, his father was not a martyr; he was a
quitter. He was enraged by the gutlessness of the man who
sired him, disgusted by a father who had not fought back with
any means at hand to regain the power and position he'd
had in the first decade of Brad's life.

The Rich and the Righteous

Standing at his father's graveside, a handsome, unfathomable little boy, Brad had taken a silent oath never to be like his father. Sacrifice, he concluded, was for women and weaklings. He would prove that his father's softness was a quality he had not inherited.

In all the years that followed, Brad Deland held fast to this determination.

At prep school and college, he was best at everything—standing at the head of his class scholastically, excelling at sports and playing them with a ferocity that drove his opponents to their knees. There was an irresistible charm about him in spite of this intensity. The young men he knew felt no comradeship with Deland, but they admired his prowess in every field, including his success with young women, who were fascinated with the total arrogant masculinity of this challengingly selfish male.

Even his marriage was a nose-thumbing gesture to convention. Doe-Doe was not a girl from the other side of the tracks, but she was an unlikely choice to inherit the socially impeccable Deland name. Brad met her at a charity ball soon after he joined The Haylow Corporation and married her, over his mother's quiet protests, less than a year later. In addition to the strong physical attraction, Brad recognized in Doe-Doe the same kind of greedy self-interest that was part of his own ruthless nature. Hers was an upper middle-class family, not rich enough or powerful enough to please the ambitious Doe-Doe, whose desire for the material things of life was as violent as Brad's unquenchable thirst for success and recognition. Their lack of conscience drew them together. Their sexual compatibility made the first few years of marriage bearable. Now they cynically recognized the evil in each other. Brad was fully aware that Doe-Doe had everything she wanted, including the freedom to live her own life, and she enjoyed every moment of it. He was still unfulfilled, emotionally and professionally. On both counts he was a lonely man. The lack of love in his life disturbed him less than the fear that he might not achieve the heights of power he'd determined to reach so long ago. He would do anything, anything to prove that he was a different man than the gentle father he despised in memory.

Looking around the dark, wood-paneled office with its soft, mellowed-leather couches and chairs, Brad thought that his surroundings could well be the office of a very social downtown lawyer. The place spoke of "old money" with its deliberately faded chintz curtains, its discreetly framed autographed photographs of some of the world's richest and most influential men of politics, arts, and science. Even the paycheck that Brad received every month was evidence of his success. A man who made one hundred and twenty thousand dollars a year plus bonuses and stock options could hardly be considered a failure. But it was not money that was Brad's yardstick of success. It was control. Power was his goal, dominance his heart's desire. And it was within reach, he knew. He was tantalizingly close to the Chairmanship. He would stop at nothing to get it.

His analytical mind told him that Roger Haylow was the only stumbling block to this long-sought prize. And Roger's performance in Florida was like a gift from the gods. As a human being and a father, Joe Haylow had been wounded by his son's unconcealed contempt. But more importantly, Brad knew, Joe would be troubled by the undisciplined behavior Roger had shown. It was a show of childish emotion ill-suited to the potential head of The Haylow Corporation. Brad considered how he could foster this uneasiness in Joe Haylow. There were subtle ways to reinforce the doubts in the Chairman's mind. And, if necessary, there could be more direct and devastating steps to take. Brad felt suddenly invincible. If Roger was so uncaring, it would be a simple matter to goad him into other foolish acts and ill-considered statements. If necessary, Brad would use any weapons at hand, any guttersnipe tactics called for. The end result, the Chairmanship, was worth it.

Suddenly he felt stimulated, hungry for the moment of his triumph. Although he did not yet know what he might have to do to destroy Roger, he knew he was prepared. He recognized that this would cause unhappiness for Joe and the rest of the Haylow family. It was regrettable but unimportant. Pat would be saddened if her younger son did not take his father's place, but she would weep in private. Woodward would be vaguely troubled, saddened for his brother and his parents in a remote, uncomprehending way. Brad wondered what Marjorie Haylow's reaction would be if her brother-in-law were passed over for the coveted spot. Since Florida, he had not been able to get her out of his mind. For once he agreed with Doe-Doe. Marjorie, despite marriage and two children, seemed incredibly virginal. Brad also found her strangely exciting. He sensed in her a subdued, smoldering sexuality that surely was unaroused by the love-making of the conventional man of the cloth who was her husband. Insanely, he had a mental picture of making ferocious, abandoned love to this cool, gentle, beautiful woman. The idea was as impossible as it was erotic. Mentally he threw the cold water of reality on this flight of madness. Not only was Marjorie Haylow the world's least likely adulteress, but the quickest way to get thrown out of the Chairman's life would be to make a grab at his beloved daughter-in-law.

The idea of a liaison with Marjorie was so preposterous that Brad laughed aloud at himself. "You're really getting flaky, Deland," he thought. "Better go find yourself a little extracurricular sex. Obviously, you've been deprived too long, but the answer does not lie with the parson's wife from Farmville. Good Christ, man, of all the half-assed ideas in the world, this has got to be the screwiest."

He glanced at his watch. It was after one. Time, he decided, to grab a sandwich and maybe clean up a few details on the Elmarie Cosmetics acquisition to discuss with the Chairman. Calm now, he put on his coat and walked out into the executive corridor. By some crazy coincidence, the first person he saw was Marjorie Haylow. Brad had no idea she was in New York. But there she was, standing outside Joe Haylow's office, chatting easily with Miss Watson.

"No," Marjorie was saying in her low voice, "it's really nothing important. I wouldn't dream of having you disturb him at the Plaza. As a matter of fact, I suddenly decided to come to town for a few days of shopping and just dropped in to see if I could catch him for lunch. Please tell him I'm sorry I missed him and I hope he has a good trip."

Brad came up quietly behind her. "Since you can't have a fancy lunch with the big brass," he said, "how about settling for a hamburger with a tarnished Vice President?"

Marjorie turned, obviously delighted. "Brad, how nice to see you! Are you really free for lunch? I mean, is that a serious invitation?"

"I was never more serious. All except the part about the hamburger. As a country girl, you should know that one never trusts big-city meat markets. They sell ground-up ex-Mayors in this town and save the horses for pulling hansoms through Central Park. But I do suggest something safe and respectable, like a nice piece of sole, not to be confused with the ones your good husband is so busy saving."

"You are an utter idiot," Marjorie laughed. "And I accept with pleasure."

"Good. Let's go have somebody save us a sole."

Companionably they walked six blocks to the restaurant Brad suggested, La Seine, small, expensive, with the right combination of quiet decor, excellent food, and unobtrusive service. It was well enough known not to be considered a "hide-out," yet it was not one of the three or four "in" luncheon spots whose patrons, including Doe-Doe, gathered daily to observe one another's costumes and companions.

Brad hoped that they would not see anyone they knew in the quiet, elegant dining place he had chosen. Not because there could be anything unusual in his having lunch with the Chairman's daughter-in-law, but simply because he had, once again, this overwhelming compulsion to be alone with Marjorie, even if the privacy was only a degree of seclusion in a restaurant.

Seated at a corner banquette, they ordered their drinks. Brad took his usual vodka martini on the rocks. Marjorie asked for "a Bloody Mary with no vodka."

"They've just changed the name of that drink you ordered," Brad told her. "It used to be called a 'Virgin Mary.' Now they're calling it a 'Bloody Shame.' I suspect the influential hand of Woodward's group."

At the mention of her husband's name, Marjorie's face seemed to lose a little of her happy glow, as though she suddenly felt guilty about lunching so lightheartedly with an attractive man. The sadness was fleeting. Brad would have missed it entirely if he had not been watching her with such absorption. In an instant, the well-bred smile returned.

"I don't think you can credit Woodward with that," she said. "I doubt that he's been in a bar since his college days. We Haylows aren't much on drinking, as you very well know."

There was an awkward, momentary pause. Brad knew that both of them were remembering Roger, and he decided instantly not to pursue the scene in Florida. Marjorie was devoted to her brother-in-law and probably concerned about him. Conversation along those lines was the last thing he wanted. He was determined to make her enjoy herself, to probe, gently, for any sign that she might be interested in him. Fool, he told himself, you're doing it again. For once he couldn't fathom his own behavior. Looking at the lovely, almost innocent face, aware of the round firm breasts under the simple wool dress, Brad suddenly thought that this must be what happens to men who otherwise have good sense. He had seen a lot of them destroy their whole futures for the sake of having some woman who was out of bounds. He had always felt nothing but contempt for such stupidity and weakness. His theory about sex was that "all cats are gray in the dark." He'd been unfaithful to Doe-Doe more than once during their marriage, but always with someone far removed from his personal orbit, someone he could leave without difficulty or emotion. This woman would be something else. He could not take her to bed and forget her in the morning. If he wanted her, and God knows why but he did, he would have to manage it in a way that would let him enjoy the body of Marjorie Haylow and the crown of her father-in-law at the same time. Marjorie's voice brought him back to reality.

"As my children would say, 'A penny for your thoughts.'"

"Your children obviously have not heard about inflation. My thoughts are worth several million pennies. In fact, they were about you."

He stopped, cursing himself for his impetuous answer. He had to keep this light and easy. Otherwise, she'd run back to the sterile safety of Farmville as fast as those beautiful, little-girl legs would carry her. He needed time, too, to adjust to this madness that seemed to show signs of becoming an obsession. Quickly, he turned the conversation.

"What I mean is, I was just thinking that it's the first time in all these years I've ever really had the pleasure of talking with you alone. We're always hip-deep in Haylows or associates thereof."

"I know," she said. "I don't have to tell you how I adore Joe, but when he's around I suppose the rest of us just revolve in his orbit."

"He's the last of the greats," Brad said. "It's a shame you never see him in action in business. Sharp. Way ahead of everybody else. But always fair. It's a pleasure to watch him make a deal. And I want to tell you it's wild to see him putting us on at his Thursday meetings. There we are, a million bucks' worth of executive talent on the hoof, gathered in the board room at eight-thirty in the morning with a cup of the most god-awful weak coffee, and all trying to prove to Joe Haylow how smart we are."

Haylow's Thursday morning coffee sessions were famous in the organization and discussed with curiosity outside of it. Joe presided, as he had for thirty years, over the meetings. They were attended by all the top corporate executives and supplemented by a revolving list of lesser Haylow personnel, like buyers and store managers who received invitations three or four times a year. This was Haylow's way of "staying in touch" with members of the organization at all levels, and since the attendance was so diversified, the conversational topics were not of a top-level or policy-making nature. They were more like family get-togethers with the patriarch setting the tone.

"You really should see us, Marjorie," Brad said. "There we are, usually a couple of dozen assorted types gathered for an hour of stimulating verbal intercourse. Some stimulation! I'm sure that Joe is the only one who's really awake, and God knows that one cup of pale brown liquid they laughingly call coffee doesn't jolt the rest of us into consciousness. Joe knows everybody by name. How he does it, I'll never figure out. The only ones I can be sure of recognizing are the regulars—Bridget and Dick and Roger and Mike. The rest of them come out of the woodwork every few weeks and I never have a clue who they are. Fortunately, the first thing we do is go around the table giving our own names and affiliations. Poor Bridget, she's always so sleepy I'm not sure she'll remember who she is."

Marjorie was amused. "What about the others?"

"Well, Dick Cabot always makes me feel that Mildred has wound up the little key in his back and got him going for the day. Mike's in there participating, like a good company man. Not that I don't like him. He's just too dedicated to be true."

"And Roger?"

"Good old Rodge," Brad said laughing. "You know your brother-in-law. His specialty is irreverence. I think Joe wishes he'd take the whole thing a little more seriously, but he *is* witty. Even with a hangover."

Damn, Brad thought. I've done it again. But Marjorie let the reference pass. Brad quickly continued.

"Now I do want to make one thing perfectly clear, Mrs. Haylow," he said, with mock seriousness. "Contrary to rumors in the subversive trade press, we do not start these meetings with a biblical quotation. That's one of the things I admire about the Chairman. He takes his religion pretty big, but he never tries to force it on anybody else."

He forced it on Woodward, Marjorie thought. I'm not sure anyone knows that except me. And maybe Pat. Even Woodward doesn't realize how skillfully Joe maneuvered him away from the business and into the ministry. Joe knew that Woodward would be a terrible executive but I can't believe that was the conscious motivation. He wanted a son to give to the Lord. What will happen to him if his other son takes less easily to the role Joe has written for him? She willed herself to give her attention to Brad, who was still describing the coffee meetings in amusing detail.

". . . and the things we talk about! You wouldn't believe. One morning we play it very serious, with a lot of discussion of economic trends and the effect of the Vietnam war on the sale of civilian goods. Next week we discuss the social implications of pot. Or Joe decides to quiz us about the books we've read lately. Unfortunately, it usually turns out that nobody's read anything except Joe, who reads everything. But the best meetings are the ones where we have a guest speaker invited from outside the regular group. We've had senators and editors and bank presidents and hippies. Once we had a stripper from Forty-second Street. I regret to tell you that she remained fully clothed and was not exactly a gold mine of information about fashion trends. I'll give you three guesses who was the invited speaker at the last meeting."

"Gina Lollobrigida?"

"Alas, no."

"Albert Schweitzer?"

"Sorry. Dead, you know."

"Oh, yes," Marjorie said. "I forgot. Well, then, it must have been Jacqueline Onassis."

Brad took her hand for a moment. "I love you," he said lightly. "You're a great game player, but you lose. My dear lady, the last featured speaker was none other than Miss Minnie Forsythe."

"Forgive me," Marjorie apologized, "but you see I do live in the north woods. Who is Miss Minnie Forsythe?"

"I am appalled at your ignorance. Miss Minnie Forsythe only happens to be the lady who consistently runs the biggest sales book in the bra and girdle department in Bridget's Fifth Avenue. She does more uplifting than Jimmy Jackson, in her own modest way. And I want you to know that her talk was positively brilliant, once you got past the unadulterated Brooklynese. And provided you care deeply that the long-leg girdle shows every sign of replacing the garter belt. Her penetrating analysis of the future direction of ladies' underpinnings was absolutely breath-taking in its clarity."

"Brad, you lunatic, you're making the whole thing up!"

"Word of honor. That's the kind of marvelous thing Joe Haylow thinks up to keep us off balance. We're never sure whether he's serious about Miss Minnie Forsythe or whether he wants to see how outrageous he can be. You should have seen the faces of those guys around the table. They didn't know whether to look solemn or lecherous. And when it came time for the question and answer period, Bridget had to carry the ball. Not one of us red-blooded males could figure

97

out how to pose a question that didn't sound either stupid or dirty."

"It's absolutely fantastic," Marjorie said.

"No, what's fantastic is that wonderful guy Joe Haylow. I don't think there's another business in the world run by a man with such innate brilliance and instinct. It won't be the same when he retires."

"None of us is looking forward to that day," Marjorie said sadly. "Least of all Joe. I don't know much about such things, but it seems rather terrible to me that a man as vital and young as Joe Haylow is forced to step down when he has so much more to give."

"You're touching on a very controversial subject," Brad answered. "A mandatory age for retirement is not a fair policy for everyone, but, overall, its good points outweigh the bad. It's bad because men like Joe Haylow are sixty-five years old only on their birth certificates. They are really in their prime. Still, if there is no specified time for a man to step down, how can a company ever encourage young men to come along? A junior executive of, say, thirty-five isn't going to hang around if he thinks his superior will be there until the superior is eighty. So, for every Joe Haylow a company loses, we have to hope that we will be gaining a dozen new Joe Haylows in terms of potential executive material. Young blood is, for sure, the only hope for the future of our capitalistic system."

"And the man who is forced to retire too early? What of him?"

"Ah, well, that is the loss. Both to him and the company. But he still must be considered the sacrificial lamb. Joe knows that. He could make an exception in his own case if he chose, you know. But he won't. With him, there are no variations of company policy. Anyway, cheer up. You know Joe. He'll be into all kinds of things once he hands over the business. Probably be a consultant to a dozen firms, or write a financial newsletter, something like that. And he'll love being able to give more time to the church. He enjoys speaking at the Pray-Ins and taking the chairmanship of fund-raising drives. Now he'll have the time to make even more of a contribution in all those areas."

"I don't know," Marjorie said slowly. "The business is Joe's life. He's not a man who can take up sports or hobbies or any of the things that other retired men do. I feel so sorry for him, Brad. And for Pat, too. She is so looking forward to his retirement in the hope that she'll finally have him more to herself. But if he is miserable she will suffer for him more than he'll suffer for himself."

"Now just stop all this," Brad said. "We're not the Eskimos who put their old people out to sea to die of cold and starvation, you know. Never underestimate Joe Haylow. He's far from becoming the invisible man!"

Marjorie tried to smile. "I think you believe in miracles," she said.

Brad touched her hand lightly. "After today I'm very much hoping for one."

To Brad's delight, she did not draw back from this first, tentative approach. He could not be sure whether she regarded the touch of his hand as the friendly reassurance of a brother, but he was certain that she must have realized the implication of his last words. Just how naïve she was, Brad could only guess. Marjorie was no child. Perhaps she recognized the sterility of her life with Woodward, watching the years of dutiful boredom crawl by like some wasted life in a convent. There are moments in every woman's life, as in every man's, when the lure of the forbidden is strong enough to overcome even ingrained goodness and fidelity. Perhaps the moment of rebellion was nearing for Marjorie. How unshakable her discipline was, even she did not know. Where, Brad wondered, does the animal in her lie? And how

99

firmly will she keep it encaged behind the bars of her marriage vows?

Had he been able to read Marjorie's thoughts, Brad would have been even quicker to move toward what he wanted. His physical nearness stirred her in a thrilling, frightening way, as no man had ever done. The absolute maleness of him, the delicious sense that he could be roughly, forcefully dominant yet almost unbearably tender swept over her. And the recognition that he wanted her made her feel almost greedily alive. Her breath quickened. It had been so long since she'd felt the desire for a man, or of a man. Inhibited though they'd both been, in the early days of marriage Marjorie and Woodward had found sex an exciting new experiment. Their conventional love-making through the years had become a routine, accepted part of a well-ordered marriage. But almost from the beginning, Marjorie had known that a partner should offer her much, much more. Sometimes lying next to Woodward she woke in the night from the erotic dream of a wild sex act with a faceless lover. She would stare into the darkness, ashamed of her own subconscious desires, feeling vaguely unfaithful to the peacefully sleeping, unaware man beside her. In the reality of daylight, such thoughts had no place. She was grateful for her life, quietly and truly in love with her husband. Until now, it had been easy to subjugate this remote but undeniable urge for rapture. Perhaps, she thought ruefully, because the opportunity for unfaithfulness had presented itself only in her dreams.

But now, sitting beside Brad, feeling his hand on hers, Marjorie was engulfed by a contradictory feeling of anticipation and fear. Unreasonably, yet as surely as she knew her own name, she knew that if he wanted it she would allow Brad to take her to bed. She seemed to have no will of her own, no ability to fight this intense attraction that filled her with despair. The desire to know ecstasy was stronger than all her loyalties. She did not even try to fight it. For once in her life, she would know what it was to be a satisfied, fulfilled woman. Even a lifetime of repentance seemed a small price to pay. If God was there, all-seeing and all-knowing, He would understand. She was not just a minister's wife, she was a woman in need of physical love. If God did not choose to give her a husband capable of bringing her to life, then perhaps in His wisdom He had finally sent her a man to show her what she knew must be heaven on earth.

There it is, at last, she thought. The hypocrisy of faithfulness has succumbed to the reality of selfish desire. I want this man. And if he refuses to take me, I will beg him.

She was calm now, with a kind of detached determination. Two hours ago, she thought, these wild thoughts would never have entered my head. No, she corrected herself, that's another of my self-delusions. I've thought of Brad for months. He is the faceless man in the dream.

Quietly, she turned to him. "I really must get on with my errands," she said evenly, "and I'm sure you have a million things to do at the office."

Brad signaled for the check. Helping her into her coat, he let his hands linger for a moment on her shoulders.

"When are you going back to Farmville?" he asked.

"In two or three days, I guess. Joe's going out of town so I'll have the apartment to myself except for the servants. It seemed to be a good time to come down. Woodward's at a convention in Minneapolis and Pat is keeping the children at her house."

"Seems like we're both at loose ends," Brad said. "Doe-Doe's in Jamaica with the scuba and gimlet set. Any reason we couldn't have dinner tonight?"

Marjorie's gaze met his, openly, directly. "None," she said.

Brad forced himself to be casual. "Great. Pick you up about seven-thirty?"

"That sounds nice. Thank you again for lunch."

At the restaurant door they turned in different directions,

Marjorie toward Fifth Avenue, Brad heading back to the Haylow offices. Walking lightly, like a woman in a dream, Marjorie considered what she was about to do. Woodward had been good to her. She didn't want to hurt him. But this pull toward Brad Deland was like an urge that belonged to some other woman, some less inhibited creature to whom an occasional bedding outside of marriage was not the sin that Marjorie knew it to be. She did not even pretend to understand herself. She simply knew what would happen that night, and knew that she wanted it to happen, whatever the consequences. Like one hypnotized, she went into the Star Store, bought ski suits for the children, underwear for Woodward, a pair of white kid gloves for herself. Passing a mirror in the cosmetics department she imagined that the face that looked back at her already had changed into the face of a woman who knew the greedy delights of passion. Suddenly, fear came over her. Suppose I'm no good in bed, she thought. Maybe I can't be aroused by anyone, not even Brad. She began to laugh inwardly. What if you're just making the whole thing up, she thought. How do you know that Brad Deland has anything more wicked in mind than dinner with the Chairman's daughter-in-law? For a moment she reverted to being Mrs. Woodward Haylow, President of the Farmville Ladies Aid Society. This is nonsense, she thought, heading for a phone booth, dime in hand, ready to call Brad and break the date. The sign on the telephone read "Out of Order." It was an omen. She didn't bother to look for another booth.

Back in his office, Brad reviewed every nuance of his lunch with Marjorie. Had it been any other woman, he would have relied on his instincts and routinely prepared for an evening which would start with a good dinner and end with an uncomplicated, physically satisfying sex-filled night. Knowing Marjorie, it seemed impossible that this could be such an easy conquest. More disturbingly, even if the attraction was as mutual as it seemed, Brad knew that this would be no one-night stand. Putting practical reasons aside—and God knows the risks of playing with Haylow's daughter-in-law were frightening—Brad knew that he would feel the kind of responsibility a decent man feels when he deflowers a virgin. He suspected the feeling might even go deeper. He could love this woman for her soul as well as her body. Momentarily, he compared her with Doe-Doe. In their early years, the Delands had found each other overwhelmingly passionate. It was a marriage built on lust, an endless, selfish, uninhibited coupling in which no act was too bizarre, no invention too shocking. The thing that enthralled them had, of course, inevitably wearied them. Out of bed they shared nothing. Not mutual respect. Not even conversation. Soon, each had sought other companions, in and out of bed, accepting sexual infidelity as uncaringly as they accepted the fact that they were two people no longer sufficiently interested enough in each other to even substitute friendship.

It would not be like that with Marjorie, Brad knew. She would worship him, feed his ego, wonder at his sexual skills. And he knew himself well enough to know that she had every quality he needed in a woman, over and above the physical. If he took Marjorie to bed tonight, it would be an irrevocable step for them both. He sensed that she knew nothing of love. Just as he sensed, against all his better judgment, that she was asking for it, aware of the possible consequences, willing to accept them.

Reaching for the phone, he made a dinner reservation in the same place they'd had lunch. She'd feel more at ease there. Then he called another number. The voice that answered was that of Bill Roberts, a recently divorced friend of Brad's who had a small, attractive flat on Sutton Place.

"Bill? Brad Deland. What are you doing?"

"As a matter of fact," Roberts said, "I'm packing my black tie and Jockey shorts. One of those doddering old gold-plated Palm Beach matrons has asked me down for a week of high living and ass-kissing and I am not averse, these days, to either. Why do you ask?"

"I have a very confidential business meeting tonight," Brad said, "and I'm looking for a quiet place to hold it."

Roberts laughed. "To hold what?"

"Never mind, you dirty old man. Some of us work for a living. Is it okay if I use your apartment for a few hours this evening? In fact, two or three evenings this week if necessary?"

"You mean two or three evenings if you're *lucky*. Sure. Why the hell not. I'll leave the key with the super, in an envelope marked 'Mr. Brown will call.' You can send a messenger for it anytime after three."

"Appreciate it," Brad said. "Do you a favor some day."

"Don't mention it, pal. By the way, the sheets are clean."

Brad wondered how Marjorie would feel about going with him to a strange apartment. Would it make the whole thing seem too prearranged, too sordid? Screw it, he thought, we have no choice.

He looked at the desk clock. Five hours to go. I'm as horny as a college kid, he thought. And just about as dumb.

5 🙊

Except for the scavengers in search of marked-down, sale-priced bargains, come January customers stay out of the stores in droves. They huddle at home, licking the wounds inflicted by their cavalier Christmas spending and worrying about meeting their mid-January tax payments. For store clerks, standing like silent sentinels behind deserted counters, it is the dreariest of all periods, punctuated only with the horror known as "inventory," a counting of stock which must be done after normal working hours.

For retail executives, however, January is a high point of excitement. On New York's Seventh Avenue, the designers show their summer collections, followed almost immediately by the French and Italian Couture showings in Paris and Rome. Because the fashion business runs on a timetable all its own, the store must buy months ahead of the time the merchandise goes on sale. "Retail Roulette," Bridget Manning called it. God help the store President, merchandise manager, and buyer whose experienced eye and fashion instinct did not anticipate the upcoming trends and prepare for them at this critical time when they were entrusted with the spending of the store's money for the upcoming season.

Because of her unusual position as the beautiful youngish lady President of a great chain of specialty stores, Bridget's responsibilities and duties often exceeded those of her male Presidential counterparts. She was expected to be not only a "walking ad" for her business but she had enormous publicity value, particularly at the "upper levels." Routine publicity could be left to the store's public relations department, but certain propaganda aspects—such as lunches with important editors and publishers of magazines and newspapers—were part of Bridget's personal job. Even though she knew these lunches contributed greatly to her own image and, consequently, the store's success, Bridget dreaded most of them. She found a large part of the fashion press uninformed, pretentious, and boring, overimpressed with their own positions of power, totally lacking in the important commercial considerations of the fashion business.

Leaving her office for a one o'clock date at La Grenouille, the current fashion watering place, Bridget stopped at her secretary's desk.

"I'm lunching with Sally Fisher," she said, "and I'll go straight to Otto Van Dam's show at two-thirty. Did you arrange for the car to pick me up at the restaurant?"

"Yes, Miss Manning, he'll be there at two-fifteen."

"Good. I should be back here by about four o'clock. That's when the advertising meeting is scheduled, isn't it?"

"Right. Have a good lunch, Miss Manning."

Bridget looked pleased. "Today, I will, Margaret," she said. "Miss Fisher is one of the superior people of this dumb little planet, as you very well know."

Truer words were never spake, Bridget thought as she entered the already crowded restaurant. Sally Fisher really is one of the greats of the fashion business. Editor of *Fashion Beautiful*, the world's most influential fashion magazine, Sally was a tiny, dynamic, red-headed, tough-minded, soft-hearted pussycat. Knowledgeable, entertaining, chic in a style all her own, she looked like a Valentine and performed like a front-line general. Concise, not-to-be-disobeyed orders flowed from her New York headquarters to the seventeen foreign language editions of *F-B*, as the trade called it. There was no designer, photographer, retailer, editor, socialite—real or pseudo—who was unknown to Sally. And she treated everyone with scrupulous fairness, according to the respect or damnation he deserved.

Bridget was barely seated on a banquette in the front room of the celebrity-packed, flower-filled restaurant when Sally arrived, breezily greeting the obsequious captain, kissing a couple of her favorite designers, nodding at the manufacturers and merchandise men who reached out to attract her attention as she passed. She sank onto the seat beside Bridget and they exchanged little near-miss kisses on both cheeks, French style. For a moment they regarded each other happily with the contentment of two old friends.

"Drink?" Bridget asked.

"Um-hum. Campari and soda."

"Two, please," Bridget instructed the hovering captain. She turned to Sally expectantly.

"So what has the ringmaster done to that little pack of trained seals today?"

Sally gave her a baleful look. "As a malaprop friend of mine used to say, 'You make me sound like a terrible orgy.' What makes you think I've been rotten to those adorables I work with? Don't answer that. Happens you're right. I've been waiting for years to put Georgina Walstrom, our overbearing Society Editor, in her place and this morning she gave me a beautiful, long-awaited opportunity."

"What happened?"

"Well, would you believe that dizzy broad came into my office this morning with a cigarette holder out to *there* and in that voice that sounds like she's talking through a mouth of rhinestones brazenly suggested that I change my name?"

"She did *what*?" Bridget asked.

"Swear to God," Sally said. "Said she'd been thinking that

'Serena' had definitely more éclat than 'Sally' and perhaps I should start calling myself that in future."

Bridget began to laugh. "I'm far more interested in what *you* said."

Sally began to laugh too. "Well, in a nutshell—which is my private name for that magazine—I said to her that we did not all share her petty preoccupation with the importance of given names and that I, for one, didn't give a damn that she'd changed hers from Gertrude to Georgina. However, said I, fifty-five years ago I was born Sally Fisher. In the Bronx, yet, dahling. And if I live another fifty-five, God forbid, I shall be tucked away in my Givenchy shroud under a divine little headstone bearing the same undistinguished appellation. I then cordially requested that she get the hell out of my office and return to her effusion of editorial badinage or whatever it is with which she fills the so-called society pages of this unprepossessing publication. The whole thing made me feel just great. Shook up my liver."

Bridget was delighted. She could picture the scene. Sally had a kind of inborn imperiousness that must have sprung from some aristocratic ancestor in the old country. Some long-gone titled antecedent must have left a trace of cool, regal bearing in the Fisher strain where it had transcended generations of poverty and cropped up in this elegant offspring of immigrant parents. People who think Sally Fisher is a pain in the derrière, Bridget thought affectionately, just aren't bright enough to recognize the signs of a secure and happy woman under that veneer of outrageous sophistication. She's quite a dame. Light years ahead of the rest of us.

The captain returned with their drinks, took their luncheon order, and disappeared. Sipping her apéritif, Sally made a quick check of the room.

"My God, look at Roberta Tripwell," she said. "All in gray from hat to shoes. She looks like the sinking of the *Titanic!*"

Bridget giggled. "You're too much. What would we all do for quotes if you disappeared from the fashion business?"

"Believe me, at this season I wish I could. All these Seventh Avenue showings and then off to scenic Paris to watch the same faces and the same behinds on the same sort of torturous little gold chairs. You going over for the openings?"

"Yes," Bridget said, "leaving Saturday. Provided I live through the openings here. Incidentally, how do you like the lines we've seen so far? What did you think of Donald and Pauline and Bill's collections?"

Sally looked thoughtful. "You know, something just struck me. We kids in the rag business always refer to the American designers by their first names and the French ones by their last. You'd never ask me how I liked Mr. Brooks and Miss Trigère and Mr. Blass. But next month you'll ask what I thought about Givenchy, Cardin, and St. Laurent— even though socially you call them Hubert, Pierre, and Yves. Right?"

"Right," Bridget agreed. "So?"

"I don't know, except it might make an amusing piece for the magazine. Maybe do an article that draws a parallel between the formality of the French and the casualness of the Americans. Maybe we could call it 'Haute Couture or Chutzpah' or 'How to Do Business with the French.'"

"How do you do business with the French?" Bridget asked.

"Nervously."

Bridget shook her head. "You're about as nervous as a bottle of tranquilizers. If anything, everybody's scared of you —including the French."

"Not bad for a drop-out from the Grand Concourse, huh?"

The waiter arrived with their lunch. Casually, Sally tossed out a question.

"Speaking of nervous," she said, "you're about as jumpy as I've ever seen you. Let me guess. You're just back from Joe Haylow's birthday binge and you're uptight about his retirement. How's that for a shot in the dark?"

Bridget hesitated. She trusted Sally and she knew that Joe Haylow admired this vital, levelheaded woman. Still, she was reluctant to confide her worries about Roger and the others. Sally would see it all clearly and dispassionately because she was a clever and compassionate woman. She was also a woman who could keep a secret. Still, Bridget felt it was a "family matter," not for outsiders.

"Well, if you won't talk, I will," Sally said. "You've got a right to be nervous about Joe's retirement. Haylow is a man with a problem. It's a different world than the one he started in. When the business was all his, it was okay for him to be a one-man band. Now he has to think about all those greedy little stockholders keeping their beady eyes on him every time he goes to the john. He's got to pick Mr. Right for his job. Who is it, do you think?"

Bridget was a forthright person, incapable of evasion. "I wish I knew," she admitted. "I'd like it to be Roger, of course. But much as I'd like him to be the next Chairman, I don't know whether he's ready. Hell, I don't even know whether he wants it!"

Sally thought that over. "Whether he knows it or not, Roger probably does want it. Whether he's ready is something else. And I don't just mean his youth. I mean his current frame of mind, from what I pick up here and there. But, anyway, isn't Cabot the logical corporate choice?"

"Logical, yes."

"Well, dear heart, let's hope for once that logic doesn't prevail," Sally said. "There's something creepy about that man. I can't put my finger on it, but he's spooky. And God knows he's clue-less about fashion. You'd be reporting to an adding machine!"

"I can't argue that," Bridget sighed. "Of course, there's always Brad Deland or even Mike Warner to be considered."

"You jest," Sally said. "The Sex-Pot or the Hero-Worshipper? No way! Brad's fascinating but rotten. Besides, he's stuck with that overpriced millstone called Doe-Doe. Can you see her taking Pat Haylow's place, being darling at all those dreary charity dinners and civic sing-ins that are part and parcel of the life of the Chairman's lady? That's also part of the new executive thinking, you know. A man's wife is nearly as important to the stockholders as the man himself. With Doe-Doe's reputation, Brad's image as a solid citizen is about as secure as a mini-skirt in a high wind!"

"Even if I buy that," Bridget said, "you can't say the same about Rose Warner. A nicer, more pleasant woman never lived. She adores Mike and would do anything to please him. Besides, he's brilliant."

"He is," Sally pronounced, "a brilliant, nice, road-company version of Joe Haylow. I do loathe the word, darling, but Mike is simply adequate. Joe is pure couture, but Mike is strictly boutique. Presentable but no class. And besides, being of the same religious persuasion, I feel free to say that Joe Haylow will not bequeath his baby to one of God's chosen."

Bridget became defensive. "Sally, I will not allow you to accuse Joe Haylow of bigotry!"

"Sweetie, I'm not accusing him of bigotry. I'm giving him credit for cold, hard, business sense. We all know that the Methodists are big stockholders in Haylow. I don't believe those holy rollers would hold still for a non-WASP leader and Joe Haylow would be the first to face it."

"Then you obviously think it should be Roger?"

Sally sighed. "Do me a favor. Order me some expense-account coffee and stop putting words in my mouth. My dear Bridget, there is only one top executive in that whole gigantic rat race of a corporation with the guts and vision to make it grow the way Joe Haylow wants it to. You."

Bridget looked at her as though she'd gone mad. "Me? Oh, come off it. You've said some wild things in your life but this really does it. You know damned well there'll never be a woman Chairman of Haylow. It just isn't in the cards!"

"Stop and think for a minute," Sally said. "In addition to the fact that you know more about fashion than all those Haylow squares wrapped up together in one big blue silk flag, you've run a damned extraordinary and important division. We're in a new world of women, kiddie. I don't think you're Golda Meir or Madame Nehru but they're running countries, not just corporations. Listen, Bridget, I'm no Feminist, for Christ's sake, but Joe Haylow's no dummy. You've opened his eyes about women these last years. Think about it. Joe wants his successor to be hip and vital and gutsy. He wants Haylow to stay on the front pages as one of the seven wonders of the business world. Could any of those guys do that as well as you?"

"I still say it's fantasy," Bridget answered, sipping her coffee. "For one thing, Joe knows I'm not a financial person. Even in my own stores I have to have Tom Saunders to really handle that area."

"And as Chairman of Haylow you'd have a battery of Tom Saunders to take care of the dumb details. Maybe you've forgotten, but I haven't, that when you became President of Bridget's, it was Joe Haylow who told you to let the accountants worry about the nitty-gritty figure work. His idea, if I remember correctly, is that comptrollers and the like do all the background work and good executives just look at the important numbers to make decisions. Am I quoting him more or less accurately?"

"Yes, you are," Bridget said quietly.

Sally lit a cigarette, letting her words jog Bridget's memory, perhaps rekindle her hopes. "He's quite a guy, Joe Haylow," she said. "He doesn't trust or confide in many people the way he does in you. I know damned well, Bridget, that he tells you things he never tells any of the men. And he takes advice from you because he has more respect for your honesty and your intelligence and your instinct than he has for a dozen Cabots or Delands or Warners. Don't forget, pet, when you're in the tippy-top spot, life is really a lot easier in many ways. You can afford to surround yourself with the best people to prop up your weak areas. You could do one helluva job as Chairman of Haylow. And I think you ought to make a pitch for it."

Bridget shook her head. "I'm subdued but not convinced. Anyway, it won't be a matter of a pitch by anybody. Joe will weigh all the factors and make the right, most considered decision. You're very persuasive, dear, and for once you're also very tactful. I notice you have not referred to the well-accepted rumor that I am Joe Haylow's mistress."

"Are you?" Sally asked bluntly.

Signaling for the check and signing it, Bridget smiled. "Even to you that comes under the heading of privileged communication. In any case, as the world would say, 'Don't confuse me with the facts.' The insiders think I am, and Joe Haylow knows what they think. It seems to me that that consideration alone would refute your wishful thinking."

"If we were discussing anybody except Joe Haylow, it might," Sally agreed. "But as you just finished saying, there's one smart, tough individualist who will ultimately do what is right for the business, protocol, gossip, or even family be damned! Besides, you know what? I think he really enjoys that rumor about you two. And, incidentally, I couldn't care less, either way. Joe's got a lot of sex appeal in that courtly, respectful-to-women way of his. I wouldn't mind having an affair with him myself."

"I'm sure the feeling is mutual," Bridget laughed. "He happens to think you're one of the great personalities of our time."

"That's the story of my life," Sally said. "Always a personality, never a pin-up girl. Good Lord, don't tell anybody I said 'pin-up girl'! Those postwar babies on my staff would start putting a rocking chair and a crocheted shawl in my office! As far as they're concerned, anybody born before 1940 is Whistler's mother. Ah youth, hideous, isn't it?"

Bridget smiled. "The years do go fast, don't they? And speaking of time, we'd better get out of here. I have a car outside. If you're going to Otto's collection, I'll give you a lift to L'Avenue Sept."

"Love it," Sally said. "But look, Bridget, think about what I've said. It isn't crazy, you know. And if there's any way I can help, you know all you have to do is holler."

Bridget squeezed her friend's hand affectionately. "You sly one, you know I'm already thinking about it. Not that there's a prayer."

"Why not?" Sally asked. "That's what Joe Haylow built the whole damned business on, isn't it?"

They left the restaurant laughing. In the car, Sally let the serious matter of the Chairmanship drop. Lightly she went back to their earlier conversation.

"I've been thinking about that French vs. American designer name thing," she said. "There must be something Freudian in it."

"Will you cut it out, please?" Bridget scolded. "Think up your ding-a-ling feature ideas when you're back in that quilted padded cell you call an office. Okay, we are on our way to Van Dam's, and if the collection happens to be ho-hum we can always amuse ourselves by looking at the funny people in the audience."

Her friend snickered. "That, luv, is a career in itself."

During the hectic weeks of the collection showings, the three great buildings on Seventh Avenue which house all the great and near-great American fashion designer names are invaded several times a day by crowds of the same people. The important openings, carefully spaced not to overlap each other, are attended by a select group of retailers and press from New York and other major metropolitan centers such as Chicago, Washington, and Philadelphia. There are, in addition, a smattering of "the beautiful people," rich customers who are invited—much against the will of the retailers—to view the wholesale showings because they are friends of the designers. For the most part, the New York showrooms, even the most elegant, are small, overheated, and remarkably unimpressive. But to be absent from an important first-day showing is a distinct loss of face in the fashion world.

Although the clothes are re-presented many times in the following weeks, anything after the first day is strictly for second-echelon stores, mass-media press, and ambitious private customers still on the fringe of the best-dressed list. It is being there at the Opening that counts—the same way that first night tickets to a Broadway play separate the celebrities from the more devout and often more knowledgeable theatre-goers.

The same pecking order holds true at the Paris couture openings which take place two weeks later to allow the same American press, retailers, and customers to wing their first-class way across the Atlantic. At the Paris showings, however, the atmosphere is infinitely more dignified, almost solemn. It may be because the audience simply has to walk up a flight of carpeted stairs to their seats, rather than jam their way into the elevators of the not-too-clean American buildings. Or it may be because the clothes themselves, shown in the elegance of the couture surroundings, have a more serious air. Descriptions are seldom given, numbers rarely announced. For the most part, the French mannequins glide out, statuesque as goddesses, carrying only a discreet card to identify the model they are wearing. There is a reverence for creativity that is absent at the American showings. Part of it, of course, is due to the fact that to see a Seventh Avenue showing costs nothing, unless one decides to buy.

In Paris, no retailer or even press representative gets a glimpse until money is paid. Retailers must hand over a "caution" of anywhere from one to three thousand dollars to be applied against a purchase. Reporters pay for the privilege of publicizing the collections by means of a flat fee entitling them to attend all the showings.

But despite the difference in formality and money, first-run fashion showings on either side of the world have one distinct thing in common: everybody wants to sit in the front row. And even the most prestigious retailer or influential editor is not above clawing, scratching, and screaming to make sure that his or her bottom is firmly entrenched in a front-row status seat.

When Bridget and Sally arrived at Otto Van Dam's showroom, nearly every chair was filled, and the publicity girl was frantically trying to keep aggressive lesser personages from occupying their seats. Front row and name-tagged, the places reserved for Miss Manning and Miss Fisher were slightly separated, but with the aid of a little adroit juggling of bodies, they managed to settle down next to each other, greeting people on all sides. Neither Bridget nor Sally used the little notepads or pencils given out at the door. While the lady bosses sat empty-handed, their staffs would jot down numbers and descriptions of the clothes. Three scribbling F-B editors sat in the row behind Sally. Important possibilities for the store would be written down by Bridget's merchandise manager and better dress buyer. The lady editor and the lady President would be the last word, but they needed no notes for their final decisions. With eyes and memories trained by hundreds of such showings, they would remember every "good number," agree with or veto the choices of their employees.

Sally expertly looked over the audience, taking in the expensive, usually overdone costumes of the private custom-

ers, the generally undistinguished dress of the working reporters. She nudged Bridget.

"Have you caught Wendy Stone's outfit?" she asked, gesturing toward one of Doe-Doe's group. "My god, she looks
like a Snow Queen Hooker!"

Bridget nodded. Wendy, one of the store's best customers,
could always be counted on to appear in something outland-
ish enough to attract the newspaper cameramen who
crouched in a corner to photograph not only the models but
the more outstanding members of the audience. Wendy was
ready for them. Her obviously dyed raven hair was pulled
back in a George Washington peruke and secured with an
enormous diamond and ruby barette. Cascades of diamonds
and rubies on gold chains spilled down the front of her white
mink pants suit, and she carried the season's status handbag
of white alligator with a diamond clasp shaped like the head
of a unicorn, its horn one enormous, perfectly tapered,
flaming ruby.

"That's page one of *Women's Wear Daily* if I ever saw it,"
Bridget whispered. "Thank God, she's seen me. Even though
she's a buddy of Otto's, she'll be afraid to order wholesale
now that *she* knows that *I* know she's here. It'll break her
poor rich little heart to have to order her Van Dams through
the store and pay the retail prices."

"Serves the bitch right," Sally said. "Anyway, all she wants
is that ugly puss in the paper. That old creep she's married
to wouldn't dare question what she spends. She'd stab him
with the horn of the unicorn!"

Bridget's gaze lit on another of the public-seeking ladies.
"What on earth is Maryanna LaPorte doing in that get-up?"
she asked. "She's wearing black monkey fur all over, even the
hat!"

"Didn't you know, darling? She's in mourning!"

Bridget laughed aloud, startling the dowdy but revered

eighty-year-old deaconess of the press corps who sat on her right. Quickly Bridget turned away.

"I wish they'd start the show," she said. "I've got eight thousand things to do at the store. God knows what time I'll get out of there tonight."

"Isn't it fun-sy to be a President?" Sally answered. "Think how easy it'll be to be a Chairman."

"Oh, shut up," Bridget said affectionately. "Why do you have to make everything seem so possible when you know it isn't?"

"In the words of my sainted Jewish grandmother, 'Sez who?'"

Damn her, Bridget thought, she makes a lot of sense, but really no sense at all. I'm all mixed up. I need Joe. I hate it when he's away. Ah, well, it's only for a few days. Then we can talk. The thought was a comfort. She forced herself to give her attention to the commentator who had appeared at last, a skinny, heavily false-lashed young woman with an ill-disguised Brooklyn accent.

"Good afternoon, ladies and gentlemen," the voice grated. "Welcome to our spring-summer presentation. We believe you will find it one of the most dramatic and exciting collections ever created by Otto Van Dam."

Sally Fisher's impassive face was turned toward the doorway where the models would appear. She seemed alert, expectant, serious. As the first hideously overdone dress came into view, Sally did not move her lips. Only Bridget heard her give a one-word commentary. It summed it up.

"Merde."

In the Haylow offices, another important member of the Haylow executive staff also had reviewed his day's calendar, but with less anticipation than Bridget had glanced at hers. Roger Haylow's day was a full, if somewhat different one. His interest in business was intense, an inheritance from the father who was so deeply involved in it. But his connection with the world of clothes was a more remote one. In his role as Executive Vice President of the corporation, he functioned on a longer-range managerial level, sharing with Joe, Cabot, and Deland the operation and expansion plans of the empire his father had created and which he knew Joe Haylow wanted him to inherit.

Roger sensed, somehow, that his two-fifteen appointment with Sid Sommers had something to do with this ascension to the throne. He was fond of Sid and trusted him as he did few others. He was sure that Joe Haylow had talked to Sid about this puzzling, rebellious younger son. Sid would be the one my father would turn to, Roger thought. He understands the business in a way that Jimmy Jackson, Haylow's other sounding board, did not. And although, Roger thought, Sid has affection for me, he lacks the emotionalism which would color any conversation Joe might have with my mother on the subject of "Roger's Strange Behavior."

As always, Sommers was prompt. Seated in one of the chrome and leather chairs which flanked Roger's desk, Sid smiled easily as he squirmed to find a comfortable position for his ample bottom.

"If you're lucky," Sid said, "you'll get rid of me in a hurry. Never could stand these modern contraptions you young people call chairs. A man with a fat behind needs room to spread it, preferably on something softer than this skinny piece of cowhide. Anyway, it sure helps shorten the visit of a lot of your callers, I'll bet. Maybe that's what you had in mind."

Roger laughed. "It suits me fine if the uncomfortable perch works for some of the people who drop in here, but not you, Sid. Always glad to see you. You're like one of the family."

In the short pause that followed, Sommers fished in his side pocket for the little gold knife. Seeing nothing to whittle, he settled for bouncing it up and down in the palm of his hand. Roger lit a cigarette. He realized that he was nervous and was surprised. I've known Sid all my life, he thought. We've had a hundred conversations. I wonder why I feel so apprehensive about this one.

Sommers wasted no time getting to the point.

"Naturally you're wondering why I made a special appointment with you, Roger. Our style is usually lunch or drinks, but I wanted this talk to be as impersonal as our friendship will allow."

Roger made no answer, waiting for him to go on.

"What I have to say may not turn out to be easy on either of us," Sid said. "I can't talk to you or your father as I would to any other client. Things go too deep with us. Too personal. But I still collect a fat annual retainer as consultant to this company, so I have to butt in when it's called for. When the future of the company is involved, as well as the future of some people I care pretty deeply about."

My God, he's nervous too, Roger realized. Whatever he has to say is hard for him, so hard that he has to apologize for it.

"I've never known you to do anything that wasn't in the best interest of the Haylows—either family or company," Roger said. "Whatever is on your mind, Sid, let's have it. I think you must be aware that I respect you more than any man I know."

"Thank you for that. And thank you for giving me the opening I was looking for. It's what I want to talk about. You see, I kind of hoped that the man you respect most in the world is Joe Haylow."

Roger was silent. Expecting no reply, Sid went on. He seemed more relaxed now. Even the penknife lay still in his hand.

"What's wrong between you and your father, Roger?" he asked. "No," he went on quickly, "don't answer that just yet. Let's fill in a little background first. Some of it's real and some is just my hunch. What's real is that Joe Haylow retires next year and nothing would make him happier than to hand the

Chairmanship over to you. He knows you're brilliant. And in his own peculiar way he loves you very much. So much that you're able to hurt him deeply in a way that very damn few people can do. You don't have to be a psychology fella like me to see that you've been trying to punish him most of your life, one way or another, by doing all the little things you know would annoy him. Like drinking and running around with people he doesn't understand and refusing to give even lip service to the church. That act you put on in Florida was real. So real that Joe Haylow finally has faced the fact that you're nursing something ugly enough to be called hate."

Roger remained mute, expressionless.

"Now let's talk about my hunches," Sid went on. "My head-shrinker instinct tells me several things. First and most important, you don't hate Joe Haylow. You love and admire him so much that you're scared you can't live up to the standards he's set for you. That's classic with the sons of strong, dominant men, right?"

"So they taught me in Psych I," Roger said bitterly.

"Okay, let's accept it. At least for now, so we can get on to other things. You can live with that competitive fear because you know you're as bright—probably brighter—than your father. You've had more education, more training. So you'll do things differently, maybe, than he would. But you sure as hell will do them better. And I think you know it."

Roger's strong face hardened. "Okay, I do know it. My father's way of doing business isn't mine. He's an honest man, but he's not above some methods that, at my most charitable, I would call 'old-fashioned' . . . the kind of thing the early merchant princes did, I suppose. A kind of closing your eyes to formal procedures and substituting your own God-blessed practices, no matter how rough they are on other people. I'm no push-over in a business deal, Sid, but I'm goddamned if I can always make the end justify the means as he can."

"Fair enough," Sid said. "And when your turn comes you'll run it your way. But you don't have to fear that the way won't be as good. Once you face that—and I think you just have—we've jumped a big hurdle. Unfortunately, it doesn't explain your resentment. So let's go on to another of our classic hang-ups which at cocktail parties is called 'parental rejection.' On this I am also something of a personal as well as a professional authority. I was around most of the time you and Woodward were growing up, and I'll be the first to agree that Joe Haylow wasn't much of a father, in emotional terms, that is."

Roger snorted. "That might be the understatement of the century. Half the time he wasn't in the same city, to say nothing of the same house with us. Oh sure, he gave us all the material stuff we needed. But love? It's like all the other four-letter words he never uses. Hell, Sid. I'm bright enough to know that a lot of men put business first. Probably I will too when I get married. But most men have *some* time for their kids. How can you love a father who doesn't even know you're in the Little League much less captain of it? What affection can you have for a man who just takes it for granted that his sons will grow up to be what he wants them to be just because that's what he wants? All my life I've believed that loving is giving. My father never gave an ounce. Not to Woodward. Not to me. Not to Mother. You can spout about how he gave his life to his business and try to rationalize that he did it for his family. And I will say to you, bullshit. He did it for his own ego. The drive for power is built into some people. It has nothing to do with money. It's a pure and simple lust for control—and to hell with those who get in the way, including those whose only demands are a little of the Great Man's precious time. You may be the psychologist, Sid, but Joe Haylow's family are the victims. If he's not loved by me it's because he hasn't earned love. And you have to earn it, like you have to earn friendship."

By this time Roger was pacing the floor, his face flushed with the anger which, for the first time in his life, he had put into words. Sid sat quietly. Then he spoke in a low voice.

"So all these years you've been acting as his nemesis, not only for yourself but for your brother and your mother? Who in hell gave you the right to punish a man for being what he inherently is? Who elected you Chief Executioner? Your brother has managed to live with it happily. And so has your mother."

Roger turned on him violently. "What makes you think they're so happy? Woodward has turned into a lily-livered small-town preacher who'll never have the guts to be the Jimmy Jackson of this generation. And Mother is the closest thing I'll ever know to a saint. How lonely do you think she's been all these years? And how humiliated by . . ." Roger stopped abruptly.

"Humiliated by what?" Sid asked quickly.

"Oh, for Christ's sake," Roger said, "don't you play the game too! The whole world knows about the affair with Bridget. Ironic, isn't it? No time for a wife, but somehow he manages to find time for a mistress. Maybe she doesn't need love, just hero worship in small, definitive doses."

"Okay," Sid said. "We're finally at it. You can handle the competitive factor and even forgive him the childhood neglect because deep down you understand that kind of man. But you can't forgive him what you imagine to be the hurt he's inflicted on your mother.

"If you want to talk about irony," Sid went on, "you've just hit the right spot. You can pardon his real sins—his ambition, his neglect, his coldness. But you can't stop hating him for the one thing he's not guilty of. Listen, Roger, there's nothing between Joe Haylow and Bridget except affection and respect. Never has been. I will take any oath in the world on it. And so will your mother. Have you ever seen her shedding tears over Joe's unfaithfulness? Have you ever had the

123

slightest inkling that she gave a moment's thought to all these scurrilous rumors?"

"Sorry, Sid," Roger answered. "Your oath and Mother's lack of public display don't cut it with me. I've watched Joe and Bridget together too often not to recognize the signs. To gild an old coin, 'Where there's smoke there's a hot affair.' I suppose I should be happy that the Imperial Iceberg can work up some fire for somebody, even if it isn't his wife."

"I can't believe this," Sommers said. "You're basing a life of bitterness on a handful of rumors, a set of circumstantial evidence, and a few imagined passionate glances exchanged between people who are genuinely fond of each other? It's the worst crap I've ever heard. If you think your father is such a cold, calculating son of a bitch, how could you possibly think he'd risk a scandal by having an affair? Do you think a man like Joe Haylow—assuming he could morally justify such a thing—would be ass enough to take such a chance with one of his own employees? Be consistent, Roger, for God's sake. Is he mortal and fallible or isn't he? Make up your mind, boy. You can't have it both ways. If you really believe Joe Haylow is as selfish and ambitious as you've said, then you can't reconcile that belief with the foolhardy gambling of a philanderer!"

Sommers' vehemence reduced Roger to an uncertain silence. The logic of his argument was difficult to dispute but the conviction, nurtured over so many years, could not be dismissed in a few moments of conversation, even with so persuasive an advocate as Sid Sommers. Roger walked to the window, stood looking at the jagged skyline of Manhattan, remembering the bleakness of a view from another window. So many nights he had stood at his bedroom window in Farmville watching for the car lights that would signal the return of his father from this same demanding city. So many nights a little boy had wanted to tell a man of the triumphs of childhood. The day he hit a home run with the bases loaded. The morning he broke the high school track record for the hundred-yard dash. Even later, he would liked to have told Joe Haylow how he felt the first time he thought he was in love. There were a hundred other moments, a thousand other times when Roger needed a father to share his triumphs or heal his hurts in a way that a mother could never do. And Joe Haylow was never there. In his manliness, Roger could understand, even if he could not condone this remoteness. Sid was right. Joe Haylow was a man made differently than most men. A superior man, perhaps. But one who, in his own way, needed understanding from his wife and children. I suppose, Roger reflected, that I'm the only one who has refused to accept him for what he is. I am the one who wanted more of him and resented him for withholding it. I'm angry at myself, not at my father. It is my ego that hurts. All these years I've been raging at him for something of which he was totally unaware. But there's still Bridget.

Roger turned back to face Sommers.

"Thanks, Sid," he said. "I needed to say those things aloud. I've said them so many times to myself. And I needed somebody to let me have it as straight as you have. I buy everything you say about Father in relation to me. But I'm still not ready to take your word about Bridget. Mother doesn't deserve that and I can't forgive him for it."

Sommers looked at him with affection. "You know, Roger, you are your father's son in a way that Woodward can never be. You're so like him, it's funny. The same directness, the same humility when you realize you're wrong. I think you know that. And, I think, believing you're so much the same may be the reason why you haven't married."

"You mean you think that I'm afraid I'll cheat on my wife too?"

"If you think your father does, it might follow, mightn't it?"

Roger let this new thought sink in. His first impulse was to dismiss it as psychiatric crap. Joe's unfaithfulness had nothing to do with him. He hated it for the unhappiness he was sure it brought his mother. Now Sid Sommers was opening a whole new disturbing train of thought. Roger had known many girls, even fancied himself in love with a few of them. But something always held him back from marriage. He was no queer. He liked women, enjoyed sex. But the few times in his life he had toyed with the thought of marriage, something had turned him off. At the time he had convinced himself that there were valid reasons why he couldn't spend a lifetime with any one of them. Now he wondered whether the real reason lay deeply buried in his subconscious, neatly pigeonholed under the label "potentially unfaithful." Like his father.

Roger glanced at his watch. It was after three. He and Sid had been talking for more than an hour, yet his sensation, like that of a drowning man, was that his whole life had flashed before him in seconds. Apologetically, he gave a little laugh.

"Jesus, Sid," he said, "your rear end must be corrugated."

"Think nothing of it," Sommers answered. "Paralyzed behinds are figured into my annual fee. The important thing is, what are you going to do now?"

"What do you mean, 'what am I going to do now'?"

"Well, I think we've made a little headway about the competitive hang-up and a damn good start on your childhood, but I have an uneasy feeling that we haven't licked the big problem—your doubts about Joe and Bridget. If we don't get that one squared away, I'll have to concede that the main part of this mission is unaccomplished. While that bitterness stays in you, Roger, you and your father will be no closer than you were before I came in here today. And that will be damned unfortunate for everybody, including the family and the business."

"So now I have to find out whether the affair is real or imagined?"

"Exactly," Sommers agreed. "And obviously only two people can tell you—your father or Bridget."

"The choice is rather obvious, isn't it?"

"Would seem so to me," Sommers agreed. "With the background of mistrust you've built up, I don't quite see you walking up to Joe Haylow and asking him the question straight out. And if he denied it, you wouldn't believe him anyway."

"So I try to get the truth out of Bridget, right?"

"Listen, Roger," Sid said, "it won't be a case of trying. You'll get the truth out of Bridget. She's an extraordinary woman. Don't think all these rumors have been easy for her, but she's kept her chin up and her mouth shut. She happens to be devoted to all the Haylows and she has dignity and pride as well. How would you feel if you were a successful woman who knew that the world thought you'd made it to the top not through your ability but through your private relationship with the boss? Bridget's no casting-couch starlet. She's grade-A executive stuff."

Sommers' words cut deep. In spite of what he believed about her, Roger had never been able to dislike Bridget. His hatred had been turned completely toward Joe Haylow. And Roger agreed wholeheartedly with Sid's analysis of Bridget as a businesswoman. She could run rings around most of the men in the organization, but she was never militant about it. My God, Roger thought, her very femininity is part of the penalty she has to pay. If she were some strident, mannish female there'd be no rumors about her and my father. Suddenly he felt very ashamed, very childish.

"I won't know what to say to her, Sid," he confessed.

"Believe me, she'll make it easy for you. There's a lot about Bridget you don't know, Roger. And promise me you'll accept from her the same thing that Joe Haylow accepts. It's a rare commodity called 'truth.'"

Sid heaved himself out of his chair, rubbing his broad bottom tenderly. "After this session, I think I'll double my fee," he said. "When you get to be Chairman, the rate for instant analysis goes up unless the consultations are held in my office."

"What makes you so sure I'm going to be the next Chairman?"

"I'm not sure," Sommers answered. "That will depend on you. Lord knows the Spirit is willing if his flesh ain't too weak."

As soon as Sommers left, Roger called Bridget's secretary. Miss Manning had just returned from a showing, she told him, and would be tied up with her buyers for another hour, but would five o'clock be convenient for a meeting?"

"Ask her if she's free for dinner," Roger said. "I have a number of important matters to discuss with her."

In a minute, Bridget came on the line.

"Dinner would be lovely," she said, "and I'm as free as a bird."

For a moment the old resentment returned. I'll bet you are, Roger thought. The Old Man is out of town on business. Then he pushed the ugly suspicion aside. Be fair, he told himself. Stop jumping at conclusions the way you always have. One and one doesn't always make a twosome.

"Great," he said. "Where would you like to go?"

"I'm really pooped," Bridget said. "This is a God-awful week with the Seventh Avenue openings and I'll be here pretty late. Would you mind awfully if we had a bite at my house? I could have Thelma fix us something and we could put our feet on the coffee table and relax. I mean, if you wouldn't hate it, I'd much prefer a quiet evening."

"Have you ever known a bachelor to turn down a home-cooked meal? Especially one as good as your Thelma turns out? What time?"

"Make it about eight-thirty," Bridget said. "That will just give me time to wash my face and slip into something alluring."

Knowing that a circle of buyers and merchandise managers were listening to her end of the conversation, Roger wondered what they were thinking. Maybe they imagined she was talking to Haylow Sr. Maybe, he thought, this is the innocent fuel that keeps feeding the flames of that rumor. If Bridget was not guilty as charged, she would not think twice about the impish illusion to "something alluring." Either that or she was clever enough to use phrases so obvious that they could not be believed by a sophisticated audience. Roger hoped that Sommers' estimation of Bridget was right. He hoped that in some miraculous way he would come to know that all the suspicions he'd harbored were untrue. Regretfully he did not believe that this could happen. But it was an evening he looked forward to with mixed pleasure and pain.

"Eight-thirty it is," he confirmed. "Anything I can bring you?"

"Only yourself in a marvelous mood. I'm looking forward."

Damn her, he thought as he hung up. Am I dealing with the world's most brazen bitch or the most uncomplicated woman who ever lived? Maybe tonight he would get to know the real Bridget. As, he supposed, his father knew her. Sommers was right. Bridget Manning was the dominant, unfathomable barrier in Roger's feeling for Joe Haylow, the static in the communication between father and son. He wished for a moment that he believed in God and prayer. I want to be wrong, he told himself. If there's anybody up there listening, please whip up a revelation for Roger who really could use a good miraculous recovery from this old, festering sickness called suspicion.

If Joe's God really loves him, Roger thought, this is the moment to prove it.

6 ✾

It would have surprised nearly everybody in the world to know that for the past six months Richard Cabot had been enjoying a secret second life. To the world—which meant his co-workers, his neighbors, and his wife—Dick Cabot was the very essence of the upper middle-class businessman, the owner of a solid house with well-financed mortgage, the holder of a highly important job probably leading to a powerful one, the husband of an unattractive, opinionated woman who believed in life insurance, the Republican Party, low-cholesterol diets, and civil rights anywhere outside of her immediate environment.

The Cabots appeared to represent the typically perfect American marriage. Childless, because Mrs. Cabot was as physically barren as her husband was professionally bland, they made up for their family lack by civic participation in the building of new playgrounds and the firm support of all-white schools in their neighborhood. They divided their evenings between watching television in the "den" of their Sloane-decorated suburban house and solemn evenings of bridge with equally circumspect neighbors.

Only physically were they an offbeat pair. Dick was completely nondescript except for his under-average height. He was barely five feet, five inches tall, a dirty trick of nature that had affected his whole life. Partially to compensate for it—and

partially because attractive women were not drawn to him—
he had married Mildred, who stood five feet ten in her stock-
ing feet, a rangy, big-boned creature who satisfied his classic
Napoleonic need to dominate a female giant.

Aside from the physical difference, the Cabots were apparently well mated. They shared the same taste in food,
politics, vacations, and friends. But there was one area of enjoyment they did not share: any form of pornography. This
was Dick's secret. The fascination with erotica had begun in
his early years when "dirty pictures" were as close as a young
man of his dull personality and physical unattractiveness
could come to enjoying the exotic aspects of sex. Even after
thirty years of marriage, Mildred Cabot had no idea that her
rigidly correct husband kept a locked file filled with books
and photographs detailing every kind of unconventional
heterosexual or homosexual activity. He pored over them only
when Mildred was out of the house and kept the file cabinet
key in a secret compartment of his wallet where his wife
would never find it, even if she went looking for money or
credit cards. Mildred knew about the file, of course, but she
complacently accepted the idea that it was full of Haylow top-
secret documents in which she had no right of involvement
or, for that matter, interest.

For more than three decades, Dick Cabot kept his "hobby"
a complete secret from the world. His wife, he knew, would
have been horrified. His business associates would have been
incredulous or amused by the idea of this rabbit-like little
creature drooling over his fantasy life.

He would have kept his secret forever had it not been
for the new wave of movies.

In the summer of 1967 the Cabots saw their first "X-rated
film" for adults only. After this first and last mutual experience, Mildred swore off all movies until "the entire industry
comes to its senses." She had decided, she told Dick, that it
was people like themselves who should set the example by re-

fusing to spend their time or their money on such sordid fare misrepresented as "entertainment."

"Entertainment indeed!" she pronounced indignantly when they got home. "Why, it's nothing but filth! Smut. Trash. What is the world coming to when decent people are expected to watch naked actors doing sadistic, masochistic things that are simply unthinkable even behind closed doors? No more for me. That's the last time we'll encourage such movies by supporting them. No wonder this world is so full of drugs and promiscuity and all kinds of Communist behavior! No, indeed, no more films until they go back to making pictures that the average, respectable person can watch without feeling absolutely degraded!"

Cabot let his silence pass for agreement. Actually, he was excited by this new freedom in films. It was his hobby come to life, to be enjoyed in the presence of others, freely and voluptuously with no telltale traces to be locked away from prying eyes. He was delighted by the new avenues of enjoyment open to him for the mere price of a movie ticket. Of course, it was enjoyment to be savored without Mildred's knowledge. Which meant that somehow it would have to be relished during working hours.

The answer, of course, was to go to the movies at lunchtime. It was convenient and easy. Dick's luncheon engagements were as few as his duties in The Haylow Corporation. It would be easy, once or twice a week, to slip off to a noon-hour show. He could hardly wait.

The day after Mildred's ultimatum he went to his first twelve o'clock film. He had expected the theatre to be quite empty, its audience, he would have guessed, made up of salesmen killing time instead of making calls or housewives with nothing better to do at that hour. Instead he found the theatre nearly filled with "respectable-looking people"—men as conservatively dressed as he himself and attractive young women distinctly not of the slovenly housewife variety. And scattered throughout were a large number of smartly dressed young men, alone or in companionable pairs.

A sense of identification with this other world filled Cabot with assurance. Obviously, he was no "freak" who found pleasure in the uninvolved enjoyment of watching the uninhibited display of sexual acts. It was Mildred who was a self-righteous, purse-mouthed prude who knew nothing of his needs.

It was inevitable, of course, that the latent sex-drive in Cabot would eventually find an outlet even more stimulating than the acts that he saw portrayed in the films. In Cabot's case, the vehicle was a good-looking young man of about thirty-five who happened to sit next to him one afternoon in the smoking loge of the theatre.

As they waited for the show to begin, the stranger turned companionably to Dick.

"Excuse me, do you have a light?"

Cabot fished in his pocket and produced a package of Haylow-inscribed matches. The stranger lit his cigarette, glanced at the matchbook and returned it.

"That's a terrific company," he said. "Do you work there?"

"Yes."

"So does a friend of mine," the young man said. "My roommate, in fact. He's a buyer for Star Stores. Maybe you've heard of him—Terry White? He buys cosmetics."

Nervously, Cabot shook his head. "Sorry. Never heard of him."

"Well," the young man went on, "that's understandable in an outfit as big as Haylow, I guess. By the way, my name's Peter Johnson." He extended a well-manicured hand, the little finger encircled with a crested gold ring.

Reluctantly, Cabot shook hands. "Glad to know you," he said formally. "Mine's Richard, uh, Carswell."

As the houselights lowered, Cabot wondered why he had given Peter Johnson his middle name instead of his last one.

He had sensed, somehow, that the casual conversation was not as offhand as it seemed. Even touching Peter's hand had produced a little jolt of electricity in Cabot, triggering a response that surprised and strangely excited him. During the film, a critically acclaimed one, cited for its daring scenes of physical love between men, Peter Johnson never again glanced in Cabot's direction, gave no further indication of interest in his presence.

When the lights went on again, Johnson spoke.

"Beautifully acted, wasn't it?"

"Marvelous," Cabot agreed.

On the way up the aisle, Cabot felt an extraordinary urge not to let the encounter end.

"I suppose you're on your way back to work now?" he asked.

Johnson gave a little laugh. "Unfortunately, no," he said. "I'm an actor. 'Between engagements,' as we say in the theatre. Right now all I'm going to do is go back to the apartment and have a sandwich and a beer. I'm expecting a call from my agent, hoping to God he's doing something to start earning his ten percent."

Surprised at his own daring, Cabot heard himself saying, "Perhaps you'd like to have lunch with me instead? I've always been fascinated with the theatre. I'd like to hear more about your work."

Johnson smiled, showing beautifully white-capped teeth, the status symbol of young male actors and models.

"There's nothing an actor would rather do than talk about himself or his work, especially to someone who doesn't know how depressingly unsuccessful he is. But I do have to wait for that call. Tell you what," he said, as though it were a sudden inspiration, "I live just a couple of blocks away. Why don't you come to the apartment and have lunch with me while we talk? There's plenty for two, and it's a lot more comfortable than a crowded restaurant."

135

Cabot hesitated. The idea of spending time with this tall, handsome, friendly young man was infinitely appealing. Yet he knew it was somehow dangerous.

Amazed at his own recklessness, he heard himself agreeing with thanks. He went with Peter Johnson to the elegant little apartment. The phone call never came. And Dick Cabot did not return to his office at Haylow until half-past four that afternoon.

This was how it had begun, and how it continued twice a week thereafter. As the intimacy grew, Cabot was amazed by the lack of curiosity Peter Johnson displayed about his new friend's "other life." He knew Cabot as "Carswell" and seemed to have no interest in what position he held at Haylow. Johnson never again mentioned his roommate and Cabot almost forgot about him. Peter obviously knew that Cabot was an important man and a well-off one. He easily accepted the gifts that Dick sent him—cases of wine, new record albums that Peter happened to mention. Eventually, as Cabot's appreciation grew so did the value of the presents. Gold cuff links, cigarette cases and lighters were now the gifts of adoration offered to Johnson by his small, enraptured slave and accepted easily, graciously with value returned.

Once a month or so as winter turned into spring, Cabot began to invent excuses about "night work" which Mildred accepted unquestioningly. On these evenings, Johnson and "Carswell" dined quietly in an uptown restaurant and went back to the apartment for a nightcap. Terry White was never in evidence. Mostly, though, their meetings followed the pattern of their initial encounter. They would arrange to meet at a new movie at midday and lunch at Peter's apartment, spending a good part of the afternoon there. Dick's only demand was that Peter never call him at the office. He was to wait for Cabot's call, designating the time and place of their meeting. If Johnson had questions, they remained unasked. He was delighted with his new and undemanding source of revenue which also included modest but necessary sums of money to tide him over the prolonged period in which he continued to be "at leisure."

This was the way the unlikely liaison had continued, for six months, undetected, until the January day when Cabot, buying two tickets at the box office, suddenly heard a soft, feminine voice behind him say, incredulously, "Mr. Cabot?"

He turned, startled, to look into the surprised eyes of Joe Haylow's secretary. Speechless, his first thought was "Thank God, Peter's waiting in the lobby." Quickly, however, he recovered his composure.

"Well, hello, Miss Watson," he said cordially. "Small world, isn't it? Are you planning to see this film? It got such excellent reviews that I decided I really should have a look at it. My wife and I never seem to get to movies these days and since I had a free lunch, the thought just came to me that I'd better take a look at this picture. It's full of great clothes, I hear, and you know how Mr. Haylow likes us to keep up on exactly what's apt to influence fashion next season."

He realized that he was babbling inanely, compulsively. The girl could not fail to detect his nervousness. Idiot, he told himself, why are you acting like a schoolboy caught in a naughty act by your teacher? You're President of Haylow and this kid is just a secretary entitled to no explanations of your behavior, however unusual.

Miss Watson had considerably more presence than Cabot.

"No, I'm not going to the film, Mr. Cabot," she said. "I was just passing by on my way to Bloomingdale's. Let me know about the clothes, won't you? I'm sure that, as you say, Mr. Haylow would be interested."

"Oh, I will," Cabot assured her. "But no need for you to bother about telling Mr. Haylow yourself. I'll fill him in if it seems to have the fashion significance that *Women's Wear Daily* says it has. In fact"—Cabot's voice dropped to a conspiratorial whisper—"I'd just as soon you didn't mention to Mr. Haylow that you'd seen me here at noon. You know how the big boss is, Miss Watson. I'm not sure he'd understand this kind of research in the middle of a business day. The way *we* do, I mean. Actually, Miss Watson," he said with a little laugh, "my wife disapproves of this kind of film, which is why this is the only time I can do my business homework. But that's a secret between you and me, okay?"

The girl smiled easily. "Oh sure, Mr. Cabot. I understand. There are some things that ladies who don't work just don't understand, aren't there? I mean, like this new kind of world we're catering to at Haylow, right?"

"Precisely," Cabot agreed. "But I'll be sure to let *you* know whether it's *our* kind of picture."

Entering the theatre after Miss Watson left, Cabot felt sure that he'd made a damned fool of himself. His contrived story about the fashion influence wouldn't fool a child and his attempt to justify his presence with the true but ludicrous story about his wife had only made him look even more suspect. He wondered whether Miss Watson would tell Haylow about seeing him. Not that it could do any real harm if she did. But it might annoy the Chairman that his President had nothing more urgent to do in the middle of a business day.

For the first time he did not ecstatically enjoy his stolen afternoon. And that was surprising because the film was about two beautiful lesbians. And they were exceedingly well dressed. Some of the time.

Buying herself a blouse at Bloomingdale's, Miss Watson considered the extraordinary encounter with Dick Cabot. There was nothing wrong with the old guy taking himself to the movies at lunchtime, she thought. With the inside knowledge that secretaries enjoy she knew that for all anybody at Haylow cared he could catch two double features a day and never be missed. It was just that there was something creepy about the elaborate explanations he'd made. Like

The Rich and the Righteous

he was covering up something far more important than just going to a show in the middle of the day. Cabot's a peculiar old bastard, she reflected. Something weird about him. She was sorry she wasn't on close terms with the dreary old maid who was his secretary. It would be interesting to find out what this was all about.

She continued to think about Cabot as she walked back to the Haylow building. There was plenty of ladies' room gossip about all the male executives of the company, and the consensus was that Cabot was a dope, even though most of the girls were betting that he'd be the next Chairman. Ruth Watson wondered where that would leave her. When Joe Haylow retired, she'd certainly be transferred because Cabot would move old pickle-puss into the office of the Chairman's secretary. She knew that Mildred Cabot had picked out Dick's secretary, a severe, physical-education-teacher type, and Mildred would make sure that Cabot had no young thing like Ruth Watson around to present a daily, odious comparison to his wife. On the other hand, if Brad Deland or Roger Haylow got the Chairman's job, she might still have a chance at keeping her own lofty position. All the girls had their eye on Roger, of course. He was the eligible of eligibles. And he was nice in a cool, well-mannered way. Ruth had heard rumors that he was something of a swinger off-hours, but she was pretty sure that he had nothing to do with any of the female "hired help."

Deland, according to the cloakroom chatter, was the resident sexpot of the group. Not that he "dipped his pen in company ink" either, but he played. Even the gossip columns hinted at that. Deland would be her best bet, she thought. If he became Chairman, he'd want all the trappings—including the current secretary to the Chairman. In a professional capacity, at least.

At this point, Ruth did not know how all the pieces fit in. All she knew was that there was an internal struggle for Joe

Haylow's chair and her vote was for Deland. She had a funny idea that Brad might like to know that Cabot was nervously spending his time at dirty pictures. It was just a hunch, but worth pursuing.

She waited until late that afternoon when Deland returned from his long lunch with Mrs. Woodward Haylow. Roger was locked in with Sid Sommers. And Joe Haylow had left for the airport. On the pretext of getting him to okay a petty cash slip, Ruth knocked at Deland's door.

"Come in," he said.

She stepped into Brad's office, closing the door behind her. Deland looked up from his desk inquiringly.

"Could you okay this petty cash for me, Mr. Deland? Mr. Haylow's already left for Atlanta and Mr. Roger's in a meeting with Mr. Sommers. I'd ask Mr. Cabot but I'm not sure whether he's come back from the movies."

"I beg your pardon? The movies?"

She pretended dismay. "Oh, I'm sorry, Mr. Deland. I probably shouldn't have said that. I mean, there's nothing wrong with it, but I wouldn't want anybody to think that I'd violated a confidence!"

"What the hell are you talking about, Miss Watson?"

"Nothing, really. Honestly. I just happened to run into Mr. Cabot at lunchtime as he was going into a movie. He said he'd heard it might have some fashion significance but he asked me not to mention that I'd seen him. I feel terrible that I let it slip out."

Brad looked stern. "You know, of course, Miss Watson, that what any executive does with his time is really none of your business, don't you?"

"Of course, Mr. Deland," she said meekly. "I do apologize."

"There's nothing to apologize for," Brad said severely, "except that as an executive secretary you are out of line when you gossip about the activities of any member of this organization, whether it's our President or one of the mailroom boys. May I have the petty cash slip, please?"

Ruth stood silently as he initialed the slip and handed it back to her. Then he smiled, disarmingly.

"I didn't mean to be so rough on you, Miss Watson. Mr. Cabot was obviously following up on something for Mr. Haylow and you should respect his request for confidence, even on such an insignificant matter. By the way, what was the movie?"

"It's called *Women Defiant*."

Brad laughed. "Aren't they all? Okay, Miss Watson, that's all. And next time you run into somebody from the company, keep your very pretty little trap shut, will you? For all I know you may spot me coming out of a bar at 10 A.M. and decide it's an early morning hair-of-the-dog instead of a business breakfast!"

"I'm really sorry, Mr. Deland," she said. "I didn't mean to cause trouble."

"Now what trouble could you possibly cause? A slight, indiscreet slip of the tongue isn't exactly crashing corporate news. Just be a little more judicious in the future."

When he was alone, Brad tried to figure out what that episode was all about. Miss Watson had not accidentally let him know that Cabot had been spotted going into a film that the papers called "the frankest, most lurid exposé of the lesbian world ever released." Why did Miss Watson want him to know that Cabot had sneaked off to see it? For that matter, what in Christ's name was Mr. Milquetoast doing at such a film in the first place? The whole thing was probably totally insignificant, but these days every piece of information about Haylow executives was to be examined and mentally filed away for possible future use. If Cabot liked dirty pictures, what other questionable interests might he have?

Suddenly a phrase that Miss Watson used seemed infinitely more important. "Mr. Roger's in a meeting with Mr.

Sommers," she'd said. That piece of gratuitous information could be more significant than the ludicrous idea of Cabot sidling into a dark theatre to watch two perverted women make love to each other.

Methodically, Brad began to add up the events since Florida. Joe Haylow would certainly have discussed Roger's defiant behavior with Sid Sommers, probably asked for his help in straightening out the son who seemed hell-bent on throwing away his own chances for succession. Only something very important—as important as that—would bring Sid to the office for a special, closed-door meeting with Roger.

Brad had an uncomfortable feeling that things were closing in. Joe Haylow's retirement was still almost a year away, but anything could happen to sway the Chairman's judgment about his replacement. It was not too soon to start spreading out the pieces of this gigantic jigsaw puzzle and assembling them into the only picture that Brad would permit: that of himself sitting on a throne wearing the crown of Haylow stars, a subjugated Roger at his feet.

Promptly at eight-thirty, Roger buzzed the doorbell at Bridget's apartment. Punctuality was another trait inherited from a Yankee father, he reflected as he waited for the housekeeper to answer.

In the hours since his talk with Sommers, Roger had tried to analyze his feelings about Joe Haylow, to evaluate the possibility that Sid's belief in Joe's purity was real and that the association with Bridget was purely platonic. Roger still was unable to accept it, and less so when Thelma let him into the inviting penthouse. The living room could only belong to a sensuous woman. Done in pale beige silks punctuated with dashes of delicate color and the glitter of crystal, it was a subtly seductive room, its terrace doors left undraped to frame a romantic view of the East River and the light-festooned bridge that spanned it.

The Rich and the Righteous

Almost the same view you get from the Chairman's office, Roger thought. It must remind him of Bridget every time he looks out his window. He stopped himself. You're loading the deck again, he thought. Piling coincidence on coincidence, seeing a bogeyman under every bed like some suspicious spinster. You've come this far, he reflected. The least you can do is give them the benefit of the doubt.

"Miss Manning will be out in a minute, sir," Thelma said. "May I fix you a drink?"

"No thanks, I can find my way around. Tell Miss Manning to take her time."

I'm sure she's not used to prompt guests, Roger thought, making his way to the bar. Except for one who must always be on time. Another Haylow would also find this apartment wonderfully serene. He looked around with admiration. He had been in the room before, but always as part of a larger group invited for cocktails or dinner. Often his mother was a part of the group. She and Bridget seemed to have a deep affection for each other, a kind of adult understanding that did not exist even between Pat Haylow and Marjorie. Roger did not understand the games that women can play. If Pat believed that Bridget was Joe's mistress, it was repellent that she could be a relaxed guest in Bridget's house or that Bridget could visit Farmville with such apparent ease. Yet such polite social pretense could exist between two proud and well-bred women, he supposed. Especially if they loved the same man and wanted to protect him.

In the time it took him to make the drink, Bridget appeared, looking as fresh and unruffled as though she'd spent the whole day at home. In her tailored crepe hostess pajamas, her makeup fresh and unobtrusive, it was hard to believe that she'd put in a hard-driving eleven-hour business day. Roger realized that he'd never seen Bridget looking harried or disheveled. Her kind of crisp, clean beauty had an appeal all its own.

She hurried toward him, smiling, putting her hands on his shoulders, giving him a quick, affectionate little kiss on the cheek.

"Roger, dear, I'm so glad to see you. I can appreciate you much more at eight-thirty in the evening than I can at eight-thirty in the morning. Do you know, before I worked for Haylow, I never knew there were two seven o'clocks in every day?"

He laughed. "We Yankees are early starters. At least where business is concerned. Make you a drink?"

"Yes, please. Scotch on the rocks with a little water."

He brought both drinks to the couch where Bridget had curled up in a corner, comfortably relaxed against a little nest of needlepoint pillows. Putting the glasses on the coffee table in front of them, Roger sat uneasily at the other end of the couch. For a little while, neither of them spoke. Bridget seemed content to relax after her grueling day. Roger found her calm almost unnerving. If his call had struck her as unusual, she was not showing it.

"This is a beautiful room," he said, finally. "It looks like you."

Bridget smiled. "When people say that, I always hope it's a compliment. Anyway, good or bad, it's me, all right. When it comes to the store, I want the best professional decorators in the business. But my house has to be me, not what somebody else thinks is me. Here I don't have to please anybody but Bridget Manning, which is one of the fringe benefits of being a lone lady. I suppose it's selfish, but if people don't like my apartment, too bad. They don't have to come again."

Glancing around, Roger found it hard to believe that anyone could fault this room or the lady who put it all together. It was soothing, personal, with a kind of unstudied elegance. Simple objects collected from Bridget's travels around the world shared equally with valuable paintings. A huge, priceless Coromandel screen in one corner lived comfortably with

144

a crude but appealing child's chair which Bridget had owned all her life. One large round table was covered with framed photographs of the famous, from Presidents to polo players. In the middle was a familiar, unsmiling face: Joe Haylow's press photograph. Except that this one was signed "To Bridget Manning with admiration and devotion, JWH."

Bridget's gaze followed Roger's. He realized she'd been watching him. And he had an uneasy feeling that she was reading his thoughts.

"I wish your father would have a new publicity picture taken," she said. "That one makes him look so tycoonish, don't you think? He says I'm ridiculous, but I'd love to have one of the good fashion photographers do him, instead of one of those dreary commercial outfits. They manage to make the nicest men look like villains about to foreclose the mortgage."

"I don't know," Roger said slowly. "To me, the picture is exactly like him. Determined. Strong, humorless."

"Humorless? Oh, come on, Roger. Joe has a wild sense of humor. You know, most of the time we spend together isn't all business. We laugh a lot. There's nothing he enjoys more than a little juicy gossip or a funny story about one of those fashion editors from outer space."

Roger looked dubious. "You'd have a hard time making most people believe that. Including me. I think I could count on one hand the times I've ever really heard him laugh."

Bridget considered that for a moment. "You know, dear," she said gently, "like most of us, your father is two people. He has an on-the-job face and an off-duty one. You're right, of course. He doesn't let too many people see the relaxed, off-guard side of him. Especially men, I think. He relates better to women in business. I suppose it has something to do with a competitive feeling about his own sex that he just doesn't have with female executives. I know that most of the men who work with him are scared to death of him. And, I

145

suppose, with reason. He's tough on them, and the more fright they show, the tougher he gets. But I do get awfully mad, sometimes, with the men in the company. They lie to him because it's easier to tell him what he wants to hear than to stand up to his anger when he has to face some truth that displeases him."

"Don't you ever lie to him?"

"Honestly, no. Never. Not even when I have to tell him things I wish weren't so. I'd like him to be right all the time, but he isn't. For God's sake, he's human. He makes mistakes like the rest of us. But I've never been scared to tell him so. And I think—I hope—he likes me for it. He doesn't get much honesty from most of his associates. I owe him the truth. It's the least I can give him after all he's given me."

"Do you really think everybody else tries to fool him?"

"No. Not everybody. Not you. Or Sid. Or Mike Warner."

"What about Cabot and Deland?"

Bridget sighed. "Oh, boy. This is only my first drink, but I'll go right out on a limb and give you my off-the-record opinion. I don't think Brad Deland gives a damn about anybody or anything in the world except Brad Deland. And I don't think Dick Cabot is capable of any emotion whatsoever. Which, to me, is even worse. I like positive people, even when they're hateful. Dick is so vanilla-pudding I can't imagine him making a flap about anything. It's like he's on automatic pilot all the time. Now Brad's a schemer, but at least he's bright. I have to respect his mind, even when I don't like him. Which is all the time. No, Roger, Joe doesn't have too many people around him who act in his best interests. But there are a few he can count on to level with him. And two of them are right here in this room."

We're getting too close to the subject, Roger thought. We both want to talk about our own relationship with Joe Haylow. And I'm not ready to go on with it. Not quite yet.

"Make you another drink?" he asked.

"Thanks. Oh, lord, it's good to let down like this. Today was a real killer. But please don't let me start on that. One good thing about having been brought up in a family of re- tailers—we had a firm rule never to bring business problems into the living room. I try to remember that being a business- woman is an unnatural state for a girl. It's a bad scene to bore attractive gentlemen callers with a recitation of my petty problems in the big, cruel world of commerce. So. Tell me about your day."

Roger laughed. "Don't the same ground rules apply to men?"

"Of course not. Women are supposed to listen and sym- pathize and comfort if they can. And tonight I have a feeling that a little understanding and comfort wouldn't be amiss. Anything special go on in your life on this glorious January day?"

He handed her her drink. She'd given him the opening. No use being chicken about it any longer.

"I spent a long time with Sid Sommers this afternoon," he said directly. "It was kind of unsettling. He made me look at a lot of things I guess I didn't really want to face. About my father. And me."

He paused. Bridget waited, completely attentive.

"You know my father and I have never been close," Roger went on. "Hell, it's obvious that we don't communicate and that I resent it. You were there when I made that scene in Florida. I'm not proud of it, Bridget. I just couldn't help it. Oh, booze gave me false courage, I guess. But it wasn't just liquor talking. It's the way I've always felt about him. When you talk about him laughing and kidding, I can't believe we're discussing the same man. He's always been so remote, so disinterested in everything but the business and the church. All my life I've wanted to talk with him the way you do. And I can't. God, how I envy you! I'd give anything to know my father. I don't mean all that crap about men and their sons being pals. I can get all the pals I need. The thing that's destroying me is that I'm thirty-seven years old and I haven't got the first idea of what kind of man Joe Haylow is when he isn't being Chairman of the Board."

Bridget weighed her words carefully. She knew there was more on his mind. More that involved her in Roger's problem. He wouldn't have come to talk only about himself and his father. She had to be very gentle, very wise.

"You're a very deprived human being," she said. "No, I mean that truly, so don't look as though you're going to interrupt with a lot of protestations about the advantages you've had. There are a lot you haven't had, and you have every right to resent their loss. Maybe the reason I can be so relaxed around Joe is that I did have, for most of my life, the kind of father you've always wished for. I don't think you ever knew him well, Roger, but Stanley Manning was much more than a brilliant merchant. He was an extraordinary human being. He had warmth and sensitivity and humor. He was an ambitious man, too. But he had love. So much of it for everyone, but most of it for my mother and me. Maybe being an only child and a girl helped bring me closer to him. Maybe I was trying to make up to him for not having a son to carry on his name and his business. I know that's trite, but it's true, I think. Anyway, loving him as I did, I wanted to share his life, especially after my mother died. That's why I went into the business with him. And I really only learned to love it because I saw how much it meant to my father.

"Probably I was more than a little neurotic about my love for him. Probably a head doctor would tell me so. I don't know. But it doesn't really matter to me. And I sure haven't spent any time or money trying to find out. The only thing that counted was my father's constant and unchanging acceptance of me as I was, not as he wanted me to be. He wasn't blind to my faults, but he was very proud of my talents. I felt the same about him. And when he died, I wept for the loss of a friend as well as a parent. I was rootless, disembodied for a long time. And then, mercifully, somebody came to take his place. Somebody called Joe Haylow."

She paused to let Roger absorb the significance of this.

"Yes," she said quietly, "to answer your unspoken question, Joe Haylow has become Stanley Manning to me. People don't understand that. It's easier and more fun to assume that an attachment between a man and a woman has got to be physical. The real truth is too dull . . . or too simple. Don't misunderstand me. Joe is attractive. And I could never have the same feeling for him that I had for my father, even though chronologically he could be my father. Joe is different in many ways and very similar in others. Joe wants affection but he finds very few people determined enough to make him accept it. My father attracted affection because he was so outgoing that people responded to him without realizing it. To love Joe Haylow you have to think about it consciously. You have to reach out to him. Because he doesn't know how to hold out his hand to you. I'm not absolving him, Roger, for his neglect of you and Woodward. I'm only telling you that if you want Joe's love, go to him with yours and he'll welcome it, the same way he has accepted it from your mother because she has forced him to be aware of it every day of their lives."

Stubbornly, Roger shook his head.

"What good is a relationship that's all one-sided?"

"Ah, but that's what you don't understand," Bridget said. "It is one-sided only in the beginning. One of you has to make a start. And he doesn't know how. Love scares Joe Haylow because he's afraid it will make him vulnerable. He's cautious in the way that only people who've had to claw their way to the top understand. He's had to build a protective wall against people who would play on his affection. And it's become a habit that extends, subconsciously, even to his own children. Don't you see, Roger, he is afraid to let down that guard? He's afraid of being used, being hurt. So, it's easier to dismiss him as an unfeeling robot than to probe for the human and endearing qualities that are under that icy surface. Most people don't know or don't care to spend the time earning his love and trust. You care, Roger, but I don't think you've known this about your father. I know because I desperately needed to be close to a strong, brilliant man. He was my second chance to find Stanley Manning and relive the kind of association you've never had. You still have that chance. For God's sake, take it. Now, while there's still time for all of you to enjoy it."

She waited for his response, and there was none. But he looked somehow like a man reprieved. Bridget got to her feet.

"Well, get me," she said. "For a girl who was going to listen, I've done nothing but yak for an hour. Forgive me. You must be starved. I'll go see if Thelma's ready to feed us."

As she left the room, Roger looked after her affectionately. Wise, wise Bridget, he thought. The curbstone psychiatrists would peg her with a "father complex" and she knows it and doesn't care. Because she knows what love is all about. In its selflessness it serves selfish ends. By working to earn Joe's love, she's brought happiness to them both. No wonder he wants to be near her. She's been willing to make the down payment which I've not been bright enough to know was required. And now she's collecting the dividends that I felt I was entitled to without having to earn.

"Soup's on," Bridget called from the dining room.

As he came close to her, she put her hand lightly over his mouth.

"Before we sit down, there's one more thing. I don't blame you for thinking I was sleeping with your father. I'm glad you know I couldn't."

Through the rest of the evening they talked of inconsequential things. Bridget was gay, charming, and undeniably appealing. There was only one reference to the earlier conversation. At the door, Bridget kissed him good night, quickly, lightly, on the lips.

"Can you give a lot, temporarily, knowing how much there is to gain?"

"Thanks to you, I sure can try," Roger said.

"Then it's been a very special evening. And long overdue."

"Only because I'm a clod."

"No," Bridget answered, "because you're a sensitive, secret person. Like your father. And I love you both very much."

As he walked into the darkness of Sutton Place, the view that Bridget Manning and Joseph Haylow shared was no longer a silent insinuation. To Roger it was an outlook full of hope.

Roger could hardly wait for his father's return to the office. His dinner with Bridget had been the final turn of the key, unlocking the secrets which Sid Sommers had made him realize were behind the barrier which had stood for too long between his father and himself. With his new understanding came a mixture of emotions: gratitude to Sid and Bridget, relief and delight at the prospect of reaching out for his father's love, shame at his own willful, childish refusal, all these years, to come to grips with the real problem between himself and Joe. His new-found understanding, so painfully reached, filled him with the kind of exaltation that he supposed Jimmy Jackson's converts felt when they came forward to join the Lord. It was somehow like coming home.

Not that he expected an overnight transformation in his father or himself. Joe Haylow would not change right before his eyes just because Roger had discovered that what he thought was coldness was simply caution. Nor could Roger shed the decades of resentment in a single moment of blinding revelation. It was not as easy as that. But it was a beginning. At least now he understood and he could try to reach out for the love that he believed could exist between father and son. With understanding, the battle was half-won. He felt confident, happy, and strangely peaceful with himself. "The peace that surpasseth all understanding," he thought. He was eager to see Joe, to begin to let him know that he had the son he hoped for.

He told himself that it was not even important whether he would be the next Chairman. If Joe made the logical, expected choice of Cabot, Roger could live with that for the next dozen or so years until Cabot's retirement. But in the next breath, he admitted to himself that that was a lie. He wanted the Chairmanship now more than ever. Not as much for himself as for what he would make it mean to his father. Like Bridget, Roger felt uneasy about Dick Cabot. There was nothing one could put a finger on. Not the slightest hint of dishonesty nor even disloyalty. Cabot was an adequate man. And that in itself probably was the trouble. He was the kind of painfully methodical, unreckless man that the banks and the stockholders liked to see within a publicly held corporation. Indeed, they had chosen him, and Joe Haylow, letting the future take care of itself, had indifferently accepted him. But the "insiders" knew that Cabot would never experience the fierce joy of winning a hard-fought business battle. Even in victory, Cabot would be impassive, guarded, unemotional. In his hands, The Haylow Corporation would be a model of careful, efficient planning and a monument to boredom. Suddenly Roger knew he could not let that happen to the business that his father had so courageously and brilliantly carved out of nothing. Amused, he recognized Joe's thought processes in himself. He could be as tough and single-minded as the old man. It would be no trick to make Cabot look totally ineffectual. It would be more difficult, but not impossible, to simultaneously take Brad Deland out of the running. With no question, Roger knew that his father wanted to be able, in conscience, to give him the Chairmanship. It was up to him to prove that he was the right man for it. If he was truly his father's son, he would begin to operate with the disciplined dedication for which Joe Haylow was famous. And the Elmarie Cosmetics acquisition was the place to begin.

Joe wanted this company as intensely as he had wanted all the acquisitions he had made through the years. Perhaps even more intensely, for this one had eluded him for two years, an unusual situation which frustrated the Chairman and made his determination to buy the company all the stronger.

At the beginning, foreseeing no problems, Joe had set about buying Elmarie in his usual way—on an "eyeball-to-eyeball level." He had sought out Elwood Marina, the man who had started the cosmetics company in 1910 and who had built it into 'a nation-wide, highly successful, family-owned business. For nearly sixty years Elwood Marina had stuck to his own specialty—prestige cosmetics. Unlike Haylow, he had not gone the conglomerate route. Instead, he had kept Elmarie a privately held, enormously profitable company which had made its founder a satisfied, modest millionaire.

When Joe began his negotiations to buy Elmarie, it had looked like a routine affair. Marina was eighty-one years old and still active, but his age was the obvious factor which made him finally consider the possibility of a sale. Furthermore, he had no male heirs. There was only one child, Marie, married to Frank Boswell, Vice President of the company. Marie had no interest in the business and Marina reasoned that it was in the best interests of his daughter and his grandchildren to sell now while his own guiding hand was keeping it at the peak of profitability. Not that Boswell wasn't competent. But a family business without a son to inherit it was, in Marina's mind, a business best converted into an impressive number of Haylow shares.

He went to the first meeting with Joe Haylow determined to accept the fair offer which he was sure Haylow would make.

153

For his part, Joe went to the quiet lunch at the all-male Executives Club with the same feeling that they would reach an equitable agreement.

This was the way Haylow liked to do business. "Cracker-barrel trading" he called it, a straightforward, honest deal between two ethical businessmen. He always delayed as long as possible bringing lawyers into these matters. The Haylow Corporation retained eight overpaid legal firms and Joe basically distrusted the business ability of any of them. Grudgingly, he admitted the need for lawyers at the closing of the transaction, but until an agreement in principle was reached he did everything possible to keep them out of the picture. "Lawyers have their place," he once told Mike Warner, "but don't ever look to them for a business decision. You're a better judge in that area than the head of the U. S. Supreme Court. The best that even a Chief Justice could do would be to tell you whether the deal is air-tight, not whether it's a good idea to make it in the first place!"

Haylow's way—and it seldom failed—was to decide what he wanted to buy, have his own people check it out for reputation, inventory, net worth, and other vital statistics. If the company he desired still looked good to him, he moved in personally, using his wisdom and experience to verbally consummate the deal. Then he turned it over to others to wrap up. This was how it had worked with Stanley Manning and others. Smoothly, easily, quickly, with satisfaction on both sides. But with Elmarie he had hit an unexpected snag. Unknown to him, and even to Elwood Marina, was the fact that Marina's son-in-law, Frank Boswell, had once worked at Haylow in the accounting department and had been fired from his job. Neither man was aware of this when they reached a tentative agreement during their first lunch.

Marina, dining with Frank and Marie to tell them of the deal, learned of the complication that night. It was the first time he had discussed the contemplated sale of the company with either of them, for, like Joe Haylow's, his was a "one man business."

"He's made a good offer," Marina explained, "and I believe we should take it. There's no question in my mind that the conglomerates are eventually going to take over all good, relatively small businesses such as ours. It's the way of the future, I think, and in whatever time I have left, I'd like to make sure that you and your family are well provided for forever. Not," he added courteously, "that I don't consider you perfectly qualified to carry on, Frank. I just think that these giant corporations with their computerized facilities and their highly paid specialists have the muscle to dominate modern business. In time, I fear, the individually owned company will cease to exist. Which is a pity, of course, and I'm rather glad I won't be around to see it. But it's also, I fear, a fact of life. Haylow has a fine reputation and they've made a generous offer. Since we're a family-controlled business we can make this decision without delay or fuss. We're the only three stockholders, so we might as well have our board meeting right here at the dinner table."

Before Marie could speak, Frank Boswell slammed his napkin down on the dinner table. His face was livid. "Not on your life!" he said. "I'm qualified to run this business and I have sons to follow me. Elmarie is no candy store. It's a big, solid force in its field and I won't let you throw away its future by selling it down the river to a greedy bloodsucking giant like Haylow! I won't have it. I won't let you destroy my future just because you have none of your own."

His vehemence shocked both his wife and his father-in-law. Marina was first to recover.

"Frank," he said compassionately, "I can understand. But you will stay on in the business. One of the conditions of the sale is that you remain as President. I have made that very clear to Mr. Haylow."

"And you're going to tell me that he agreed?"

155

Marina looked surprised. "Of course he agreed. In fact, he was delighted. One of the first things any acquiring company looks for is good management. Haylow is insistent upon that. In fact, without it, they probably wouldn't touch the deal."

"And did the great Joseph Haylow say he knew me?"

"No. As a matter of fact, he said he did not, but that he was looking forward very much to meeting both you and Marie."

Boswell laughed. "Well, you're both in for a big surprise. Haylow doesn't remember me because I was much too insignificant to catch his eye. You see, I worked at Haylow years ago in the accounting department. I was just out of school, very young, very ambitious, and very idealistic. I believed all the things they told me. That I was headed for big things in the company, probably would be put in as comptroller in one of the important divisions. So I worked my ass off for peanuts. I used to be in that office Saturdays and Sundays, sweating over ways to save that bastard millions in taxes and still stay within the limits of the law. I lived on coffee, promises, and sixty-five bucks a week, legitimately screwing the government to make Joe Haylow even richer. Oh, my immediate superiors told me that I was brilliant and that the Chairman was aware and grateful. Aware? I was admitted to the august presence exactly twice in five years, for five minutes at a time. And I was thrilled. Can you beat that? I was thrilled to be standing in front of the Big Man.

"And then one day the Internal Revenue boys questioned a project that had been mine. There was nothing illegal about it. In fact it was brilliant. I'd found a tax loophole that nobody else realized existed. The whole thing was dropped when they saw that it really stood up, and I was so excited that I was waiting for a promotion and a raise in recognition of my ability. And you know what happened? Word came from the Chairman that I was fired. He appreciated my efforts, they said, and would give me excellent references, but the front office was afraid that I took too many chances, and the next one might not work out so well. So it was two weeks' severance and bye-bye Frankie baby. Oh, he's some great gentlemen your Mr. Haylow. Like hell he is. He's a ruthless, cold-blooded son of a bitch and I wouldn't let his wife buy a lipstick from us if I knew about it."

"But we sell Elmarie to his stores," Marina protested mildly.

"You bet we do. I hate that bastard but I'm willing to make money out of him. What I'm not willing to do is work for him again."

"Darling," Marie said, "I'm sorry. We didn't know."

"A man doesn't want his wife to know what a sucker he's been," Frank answered. "There's never been a reason to tell you or Dad. After all, a guy who marries the boss's daughter doesn't have to submit references to get into the firm."

There was disappointment in Elwood Marina's voice when he finally spoke. "Your being a part of my family has never had anything to do with my respect for your capabilities, Frank. I've always considered myself doubly lucky to have you as a co-worker and a son. What you've just told us makes the decision much more difficult. Obviously, it would be impossible for you to stay on if I sold Elmarie to Haylow. Feeling the way you do, it wouldn't work. But is this company so important to you? After all, you and Marie would be very rich. You could start another kind of business if you wanted. Or just live and enjoy yourselves. There's a kind of irony in the fact that you'd be doing so on Joe Haylow's money, isn't there?"

Boswell shook his head. "Not enough irony to console me for the fact that our double-dealing friend has had it his way as usual. I can't stop you from selling the company. You have the control. But I like to think that you have more concern for human feelings than for the almighty buck. Sorry, but it's as simple as that."

Marina's smile was rueful. "It may be even simpler. When I tell Joe Haylow that there's no management to buy, he may back out of the whole deal anyway. At my age, and without you, he'd be buying a shell of a company. I don't know what to say, Frank. I'll have to weigh your personal feelings against a guaranteed future for your family. I can't promise you now that I'll call off the negotiations. But I'll give it a lot of thought."

They left it at that. Next day Marina met with Joe Haylow and told him the whole story, simply and without apology for his sentimentality.

"I'm sure you will understand, Mr. Haylow," he said, "that sometimes a man has to put his children's happiness before commercial considerations. You're a father. I'm afraid that this move would destroy my daughter's marriage and alienate a man who is like a son to me. I will tell you quite candidly that I would like to sell my business, but without my children's agreement I cannot bring myself to do so. For that matter, as I told them last night, I doubt that you would want the company without management, even if Frank agreed to let you have it on those terms."

Joe was annoyed by the development. Yet he had a grudging respect for this formally polite old man. He has integrity, Haylow thought, but he's also a fool. He's letting Boswell's immature, emotional grudge stand in the way of a sound business deal. In Joe's world, such weakness was unheard of and the irrationality of it angered and frustrated him. Yet when he spoke, his tone was cool and composed.

"Naturally, I'm disappointed," he said, "and in this case I would let the offer stand because I think your company is strong enough to grow even under new management. I quite agree that Boswell's feeling about The Haylow Corporation would make it impossible for him to come as part of the package. But the package is still of interest to us, Mr. Marina, when and if you decide to sell it."

"Thank you," Marina said, "but I don't think that in my lifetime at least, Elmarie will be sold to anyone. Frank wants to run it, and I am obliged to respect his wishes and my daughter's as well."

Anxious as he was, Haylow knew when to back off. There had to be another way around this problem. He wasn't worried about the lack of management. Bridget and Mike Warner both had good cosmetics buyers and if there was no one within Haylow qualified to run Elmarie they would know where to find the talent on the outside. Blast whoever fired Frank Boswell, he thought. I never even knew about it. Not that I probably would have done differently if I had. A reckless executive in accounting can't be tolerated because one day his luck will run out. I probably would have fired him myself. Meanwhile, through some means, Boswell had to agree to the sale. But for the moment, all Haylow could do was play for time.

"Well," he said philosophically, "we can't win 'em all, can we? But I would like to make one request, Mr. Marina. If at any time Elmarie comes up for sale, you will still give us first refusal."

Marina nodded. "Of course. I promise you that I will not sell to anyone else. But that's a guarantee good only in my lifetime. Unfortunately, it's a promise that can't extend beyond the grave. I can't predict what my children might do after I'm gone. I do suspect, however," he said wryly, "that if Frank ever decided to sell you would not be offered the first option. All I can do is give you my word that while I'm still around, I will see to it that someone else does not benefit from your company's early, unfortunate mistake."

On these terms they had parted, and in the intervening years Marina had kept his word. There had been other offers, all refused. And Haylow had not lost his appetite for the acquisition. He was not used to being thwarted for any reason. And the fact that his defeat was accomplished by the unreasonable grudge of a disgruntled ex-employee made it all the less palatable. For two years he made no overt moves. But he kept his eye on Elmarie through its sales in Haylow stores. It continued to be a sweet little business, far from its potential, but tightly run and profitable. He worried that with every passing month his "guarantee," good only while Elwood Marina lived, was running out. And he knew and disliked the fact that many of his associates were aware of his failure to buy the cosmetics company. It seemed petty in view of the larger and more important deals he'd successfully put over in those two years. But to Haylow, Elmarie was a personal, provoking challenge. And in this year before his retirement he was determined to tie off this irritating loose end.

He had called a meeting of Cabot, Deland, and Roger for the morning of his return from Atlanta. The subject was Elmarie.

7 🙬

On the day of his return from his brief trip to Atlanta, Joe Haylow had three important things on his mind. Two of them could be settled in New York. The other would have to be handled in Farmville, to which Joe would return that evening.

The first order of business was his executive meeting concerning the acquisition of Elmarie Cosmetics. The second pressing matter was a visit with Bridget. She had been on his mind these past few days, primarily because Haylow realized that she had been surprisingly shocked by his swift, decisive, and apparently heartless decision about Tom Saunders' pregnant secretary. Joe couldn't bear to have Bridget disappointed in him. Her admiration and respect were exceedingly important to his self-confidence, which, as she knew, was not as unshakable as the world believed. He would spend some time with her in the afternoon, making her understand that his handling of the Saunders matter was for the eventual good of all concerned. It was important to him that Bridget agreed with the course he had dictated. They had not had enough time to talk about it before he left. He was not over-worried about convincing her of the rightness of the move, but until he was sure he had done so he would be restless and uneasy.

The third item on his agenda, the one to be completed in

Farmville, concerned Elvis Mallory. During the two days Joe had just spent in Atlanta, the young evangelist's name kept coming up with alarming regularity. Haylow's fellow Methodists told him of Mallory's following, which was growing rapidly and steadily. The young minister's eloquence was extolled by those who had attended his rallies throughout the South. There were word-of-mouth stories of near-miracles for those who came forward at his modest open-air revival meetings. And Mallory was getting an extraordinary amount of coverage in the local press. He obviously was an articulate and persuasive young religious fanatic who handled himself well with reporters and looked almost Christ-like in his photographs.

Joe Haylow didn't like it. He carefully read Mallory's interviews, many of which alluded to the young man as "A likely successor to the great Jimmy Jackson." That phrase was one that Haylow had reserved for Woodward. His ambition for the career of his elder son was as intense as his desire for the success of his younger one, and until this year he had not really anticipated an insurmountable problem with either. Now it looked as though both his boys needed help. He had already begun to lay the groundwork for Roger's reformation through his talk with Sid Sommers. Tonight he must discuss Woodward with Jimmy Jackson. Between them they would have to devise a plan to put Elvis Mallory back into the shadows from which he had so suddenly emerged, clearing the path for Woodward's not-too-distant ascension to Jackson's place of prominence in the church.

Promptly at 9 A.M., Deland, Cabot, and Roger presented themselves at Joe's office for a discussion of the Elmarie deal. He had briefed each of them through short and concise memos, outlining the problem which blocked the acquisition. "I am sure," he had said in each note, "that there is a way to overcome this hurdle which appears to be only of a personal and somewhat petty nature. However, please reserve two

hours on Thursday morning for a discussion which should
lead to a quick resolution of the matter." He had dictated
the memos over the phone from Atlanta on Tuesday. In the
intervening forty-eight hours he suspected that Dick Cabot
would have dug methodically into the personnel file of Frank
Boswell to present the Chairman with a case history of the
man's record during his five years in the accounting department. Cabot would be chagrined to discover that Joe already
had this pertinent information at hand and could recite
Boswell's statistics, performance rating, and the details of
his job termination without even referring to his notes.
Deland, on the other hand, would come to the meeting complete with a financial statement about the Elmarie Company
and its owner. Attached would be well-thought-out recommendations for the financial details of the take-over. As for
Roger, Joe did not know what to expect. Judging from his
performance in recent months, Roger's contribution to the
meeting would consist primarily of ill-concealed delight in
his father's failure to date. The recollection of Roger's increasing hostility brought a frown to Haylow's face. Sarcasm
and disrespect were qualities he would not tolerate from any
employee, even his own son. Yet this was one employee he
could not summarily dismiss.

As the three men filed in, Joe tried to read Roger's expression. It seemed relaxed and cordial, friendlier than it had
been of late. I hope Sid talked to him, Joe thought. If anyone
could help him it would be Sommers.

"Good morning, gentlemen," Haylow greeted them. "Let's
get right to work. You all know that we wish to acquire
Elmarie Cosmetics, that we have made them a fair offer and
have been refused because of the personal animosity of the
owner's son-in-law, a man called Frank Boswell. I will welcome your comments and opinions."

Predictably, Dick Cabot opened the folder he carried. "I
thought it might be useful," he said, "to first review the facts

about Frank Boswell when he was employed by The Haylow Corporation from 1949 to 1954. His personnel report shows that he—"

"I think we can dispense with that, Dick," Joe interrupted. "The man was a competent accountant specializing in tax work. His immediate superiors thought well of him but in his eagerness to please he took a dangerous, calculated risk which could have gotten us into serious trouble with Internal Revenue. Consequently, it was the recommendation of Sam Ellis, his superior at that time, to let the man go before his ambition led him to carelessness."

Cabot lapsed into silence. Closing the folder, he waited impassively for someone else to answer the Chairman. Brad Deland's smile in Haylow's direction was almost conspiratorial. Condescendingly, Brad spoke.

"Naturally, Joe," he said easily, "we're all aware of Boswell's record here. Nothing really shady in it, but the man obviously lacks judgment. Overemotional, I'd say, particularly when one considers the unjustified grudge he's held for fifteen years. Fiscally, the company he now virtually administers is sound, so he must have ability and probably feels no pressure to try short cuts since he feels his future is well assured through his father-in-law.

"The problem as I see it," Brad continued, "is how to force Boswell into agreeing to the sale. Marina, as you've told us, is willing. It's up to us to change Boswell's mind."

"And how would you suggest we make him see the light?" Haylow asked.

"Frankly, Joe, I think we might have to fall back on a phrase that is often used about politicians: 'He didn't see the light; he felt the heat.'"

The other three waited for Deland to go on.

Confidently, with his easy assurance, Brad plunged ahead.

"Like Dick, I've been doing a little research, but of a slightly different nature. I find that between Star Stores and

Bridget's, Haylow accounts for approximately fifteen percent of Elmarie's volume every year. To say nothing of the intangible benefits they reap through the well-advertised promotions they run with us. The publicity they get through our stores bolsters their position *and* their sales in hundreds of other stores that jump on any bandwagon to which Haylow hitches its stars. Therefore, we are Elmarie's single most important customer. If they lost us, it would be a crippling, perhaps a fatal blow to their sales around the country."

Haylow's eyes narrowed speculatively. "I presume you are suggesting that the way to put the heat on Boswell is to suggest that they might be dropped from all our stores, with the possible additional loss of other accounts who would discontinue Elmarie when we did?"

"Exactly," Brad agreed. "We have a strong weapon. Why not use it?"

Roger waited for his father to reject the idea. Haylow stores could well afford the loss of sales, even if the bluff didn't work and they had to carry out the threat. But Roger could not believe that Joe Haylow would destroy another man's hard-won success with such brutal tactics. To his horror, Joe seemed to be turning Deland's suggestion over in his mind. Finally, Roger exploded.

"That's about rock-bottom, Brad!" he lashed out. "It's the tactics of a bully, threatening to beat the little guy to a pulp if he doesn't knuckle under! And suppose Marina won't be bullied? Would you really have us destroy his lifework and his children's future for the sale of a lousy little acquisition? There's an ugly word for what you're proposing, and as far as I know, The Haylow Corporation has never been reduced to blackmail to get what it wants!"

Encouraged by Joe Haylow's silence, Brad kept his cool.

"Don't be such an innocent babe, Roger," he said. "What you so passionately refer to as 'blackmail' is only modern business procedure, with a little muscle skillfully applied. If you're in an acquisition battle you can't run it like a well-bred disagreement between gentlemen. This company's been in other fights before and we've won them by dealing from strength. Okay, so Elmarie is different. We've got one dumb guy with a grudge to deal with, instead of a bunch of stockholders whose proxies we have to buy with propaganda and cash. But it amounts to the same thing. Business isn't pretty. It's rough. And a company uses the tools it has at hand. If they're nice clean tools, like money, so much the better. But if they're cruder weapons—like the power to destroy—it may be regrettable but necessary to use them, but use them we must, dear boy."

Roger looked steadily at Deland.

"The power to destroy isn't a business weapon, Brad, it's a *lethal* weapon. What about the ethics and responsibility? Haylow hasn't gotten where it is by ruining other people. It's gotten there by virtue of being dedicated and determined and smart, but not at the expense of people too small to defend themselves from steamroller tactics."

Brad's tone was almost condescending. "I never knew you were such a champion of the little man, Roger. Very unlike the Chairman's attitude about the underdog. You and I have often heard him say that he fails to understand the American affection for losers—baseball teams that never win a game, fighters who are stumblebums, businessmen who are weak and indecisive. Let's stop being so carried away about a simple maneuver. We won't destroy Elmarie because Marina won't let that happen. All we'll do is let him know that we have the capability. Think of it as the nuclear arms race on a tiny scale; neither side plans to use the bomb but the one who has the most atomic power keeps the other one in line."

Reduced to speechless anger, Roger looked at his father. Joe Haylow's expression was inscrutable, neither shocked nor approving.

"Apparently you don't care for Brad's suggestion," Joe said. "Am I to assume, Roger, that you have a better one?"

"It seems to me," Roger answered, "that whether I have a better one or not isn't the most important issue at stake here. There are more important things involved. Sure, I want Elmarie for this company as much as the rest of you do, but a few things get in my way. Like decency, for one. Good Christ, what are we, the Mafia?"

"Watch your language," Haylow said sharply.

"Sorry," Roger replied automatically. "But let's go on with this. Yes, I think there's a better way. And funnily enough, I think I'm the only one in this company who can pull it off. I just have a hunch that a simple apology might work wonders with Frank Boswell. Ridiculous, isn't it? Far too easy for all the genius minds in this room. Brad may think that business isn't all pretty-pretty, but I think it isn't all that complicated if you remember that you're dealing with human beings, people with emotions. All that stands in the way of our acquisition is the wounded pride of one average guy. Why in hell—sorry—why the devil do we have to go around playing cloak and dagger before anybody's tried to reason with Frank Boswell himself? For all we know, he may be just waiting for his father-in-law to die so he can sell that business to the first bidder who isn't named Haylow. Maybe we're going to miss the boat if somebody doesn't get to him fast and hold out the peace pipe instead of the war club!"

Joe Haylow suddenly looked as though someone had given him a Christmas present.

"And you think you can pull it off, Roger?" he asked.

"Who knows? It's a gamble. But at least it's a clean gamble. You can't go to him, sir, in your position, but I can in mine. As your employee I can offer reason. And as your son, I can offer a family apology."

"Well," Joe Haylow said, "we've had two possible suggestions put forth in this meeting. Frankly, I cannot exclude the possibility that stringent methods such as Brad suggests—or some form of them—may not prove to be necessary in the long run. However, I am willing to give Roger's idea a try. Nothing to be lost, as far as I can see. Okay, Roger, try to set up a meeting with Boswell and see what you can do. If it doesn't work, we'll have to consider some alternate step. Thank you, gentlemen."

With this dismissal, the meeting was ended. The four men who attended it were left with mixed emotions. Joe Haylow had been proud to the bursting point of his son's decisiveness and integrity, yet he could not quite believe in the triumph of humility in such an important business deal. Nor could he discount the possible need to use such strong methods as Deland had suggested. He found them repellent, yet he could not help but feel an unwilling admiration for the ruthless determination Brad continually projected. A nagging fear that his son was too gentle for the tough world of business kept nibbling at his thoughts. Yet, Joe Haylow mused, maybe Roger is right. For an agnostic, he has a mighty Christian attitude. One thing is sure: it's great to be young and still idealistic. At least Roger deserves this chance.

On his way back to his office, Cabot was as unperturbed as ever. For the thousandth time in ten years, Joe Haylow had made no secret of his lack of regard for the company President. And for the same number of times, Cabot took it placidly. Let the young hotheads fight it out, he thought. When it comes up Chairmanship-time, there's no one else to whom Joe Haylow can entrust his business without having the stockholders blow their conservative tops.

Brad Deland came out of the meeting with his usual confidence shaken. The Boy Scout had come off looking pretty well for the moment. Let's hope he falls flat on his Little Lord Fauntleroy face. Deep down, Brad reassured himself, Joe Haylow knows he'll have to put the squeeze on Frank Boswell and close his eyes to the flying chips. Roger is all

White Knight in theory, but the Chairman's been around long enough to know that a bum like Frank Boswell isn't going to curl up and purr just because he gets an apology from the boss's son. Still, Deland smelled trouble. If Roger succeeded, he'd pull far ahead in the race to the chair.

For his part, Roger left the meeting feeling better than he had in years. He knew that he had grown in his father's eyes, pleased Joe Haylow with his determined stand. He had no idea whether he could make good on his plan. But it was the first step toward finding his father. And that's what really mattered.

When Joe Haylow called to ask whether she was free for lunch, Bridget lied, as she always did, and said she was. Through the years she had always made herself available, no matter how last-minute the invitation might be. It was not a matter of "pleasing the boss." Bridget knew how limited and valuable his time was, and a chance to spend an hour with him was more important than any other luncheon engagement she might have had. It was almost superhuman the way Haylow found time for everything. Scarcely a week passed that she did not meet with him, either over lunch or in her office. This in itself was extraordinary considering that she and her division were only one small facet of the glittering empire under the Chairman's highly personal supervision.

Despite the rumors, they rarely saw each other in the evening. Joe's night hours in New York were as full as his days. When Pat was not in town he usually worked very late, dined alone, and caught up on the mountain of unread books and articles that seemed to replace themselves in an endless flow. Or he attended some civic, professional, or charitable banquet, with or without his wife. He seldom dined alone with Bridget and only once or twice had he agreed to have dinner in her apartment.

The Manhattan dirt-dishers who accepted a love affair between Joe and his lady President would have been amazed to know how carefully he avoided even the appearance of wrongdoing. As his friend, Bridget understood the correctness of Joe's behavior. As a woman she sometimes propped up her own ego by thinking that perhaps he was avoiding temptation. Not that anything would have happened. She had been entirely truthful with Roger. She found Joe Haylow a surprisingly sexy man in his own contained way, but the idea of going to bed with him was as unthinkable as if he had, in fact, been Stanley Manning come back to life. She was not above a little flirting with him, which he enjoyed, safe in the knowledge that neither of them took it seriously. They had never discussed the gossip about them except in the most offhand way, laughing at the rumormongers, who were convinced that a friendship between two attractive members of the opposite sexes was an impossibility. Like Sally, Bridget was sure that in a human way Joe enjoyed the speculation that surrounded them. He had enough masculine vanity to like being linked with an attractive woman, provided his conscience was clear. Bridget admitted to herself that in some ways she liked it too. Her image as "the other woman" in the life of this powerful man enhanced her glamour. In a perverse way, it also helped her business. Her rich customers enjoyed speculating about the much-publicized lady's private life. Their husbands, like the male executives of Haylow, were quite sure that Haylow had something going for him there. Otherwise, why would he let a woman run such an important part of his business? Of course, as Sid had told Roger, this was one of the irritating parts of the rumor, a condescending male attitude that no woman could reach the top without using her bottom. Bridget remembered how angry a casual remark of Brad Deland's had once made her. "Women are like squirrels," he'd said. "They use their tails to cover their backs." Brad had not been talking about her at the time. But Bridget sensed that Deland, like most of the others, gave only grudging respect to the so-called successful career woman. He could not deny her ability; he simply looked for some additional reason why she had outstripped most women who work. Bridget's power, publicity, and the staggering amount of money she earned put her in a very select group. Few men in the country had done as well and only a dozen or so other women came near her in terms of professional and financial gains.

Bridget wore her success simply, naturally, and becomingly. She was not given to the unreasonable tantrums, the petty vindictiveness, or the unpredictable behavior of which most women executives were accused. She took her setbacks as calmly and unemotionally as she accepted her victories. Like Joe Haylow, she was firm but fair.

Watching her come into the restaurant and noting with pleasure that she was only one and a half minutes late, Joe appreciatively took in Bridget's physical attractiveness. She was a walking ad for the store, an advantage, obviously, over the male Presidents of competitive retail fashion establishments. In the current fashion she wore her red-gold hair quite long and pulled back severely, tied at the nape with a blue and white scarf. The fair, flawless complexion was subtly made up. Only an expert would recognize that it took at least ten different cosmetic preparations to achieve this artfully natural look.

She'd make a marvelous President of Elmarie when we get it, Joe thought, except we need her more where she is. In fashion, no one could touch Bridget's instinctive anticipation of the public's desires. It was not something one learned. The ability was born into those who could sense the next fashion success seasons before it actually appeared. "You have to have safecracker's fingers," she'd once told Joe. "You can keep your crazy old computers up there in Farmville. Me, I know in my bones what's going to sell. The best barometer of a woman is another woman, not some IBM machine programmed by a bunch of ninety-day wonders fresh out of Harvard Business School!"

Stubbornly, she had resisted all efforts to make her purchases and projections based on statistics supplied by the Haylow systems experts. She and Joe had had some arguments about it.

"You are working on old-fashioned methods," Joe had argued. "This is the computer age. Those machines can feed you valuable data about the buying patterns and trends across the country."

"And I can tell you more about women's reactions by walking through our stores than all your Rube Goldberg monsters can spit out in a year of mechanical gymnastics."

Invariably, believing she was blessed with a rare and magic touch, Joe would sigh and give in.

"You're the most hardheaded executive I've ever known," he'd scold.

"You know my philosophy. 'The way to succeed in business is to be wildly opinionated.' Besides, the figures don't look so bad, do they?"

He had to admit always that the figures looked very good indeed. Bridget's was a profitable part of the corporation, thanks to the fashion wisdom of its director and the careful cost control supervised by Tom Saunders. It was hard to argue with success and Joe Haylow was relieved that he didn't have to. He had too many other problems in the far-flung divisions. He only wished they all operated with as little difficulty as Bridget's.

Today they ordered their lunch quickly, both refusing a drink. Haylow, of course, was a teetotaler but he did not object if his companions drank socially and moderately. Bridget occasionally had a Bloody Mary, but today she was in no mood for a cocktail. She wanted to be perfectly clearheaded. There was the Saunders matter to be discussed, for one thing. It had hit her very hard. And there was also the recollection of her dinner with Roger. She wondered whether Joe knew it had taken place. Obviously not, she figured, unless Roger mentioned it to him this morning.

"Sorry I couldn't get back to you before I took off for Atlanta," Joe said. "Did you talk to Tom Saunders?"

"Yes. That same day."

"How did it go?"

Bridget sighed, then grinned ruefully. "About the way you said it would. You know, it's irritating the way you're usually so right. He was enormously relieved that his job was safe, and pathetically grateful for the money to pay for the abortion. As you suspected, he didn't know where to turn for that kind of cash without arousing his wife's suspicions. I really could kill him for a variety of reasons, but I couldn't help feeling sorry for him. He was so bloody contrite."

"What about the girl?"

"That was even tougher because I just couldn't be mad at her. Poor little thing, she's so scared. I tried to tell her that these operations were routine and any danger was very remote. The truth is, I don't believe a word of it. Illegal abortions are horrible things. Not only because a lot of women die, but because it is so degrading to a woman. Thank God, I've never had to go through it, but I've gone with friends of mine. It's ugly and lonely and sordid. I feel sick just thinking about it.

"Anyway," Bridget went on, "I told her that Mr. Saunders would see to it that the best possible arrangements were made and she was not to worry about the expense. Also, that her secret was safe with Tom and me, and that though we couldn't keep her on at Bridget's we'd try to find a place for her in one of the other companies. I must confess that I couldn't resist giving her a little parting lecture on the follies of an affair with a married man and a gentle reminder of the satisfactory performance of a twentieth-century invention known as the Pill. Then I called Mike and said I had a good secretary who wanted to work in a larger store and he leaped at the offer, just as you said. As soon as she's well enough, she'll go to work at Star."

"So that's that," Joe said with relief. "You handled it beautifully. As usual."

Bridget brushed off the compliment. "I don't know how well I handled it. It just got solved, for the moment at least. I really won't relax until I know that child has come through the operation okay. If, God forbid, anything happened to her, I don't think I could live with that on my conscience."

"You won't have to," Joe assured her. "A thousand dollars will get her a very good man, and I'm sure that Saunders is honest enough and remorseful enough to spend every penny of it on the operation and the aftercare. I'm still a little irritated that he was so stupid, though. We'll have to watch him carefully, Bridget. Make sure that he's learned his lesson about fooling around with employees. Maybe in a way it's a good thing this happened to Tom. Might scare him enough to teach him a lesson for life."

Bridget stared at him as though she'd never seen him before.

"Forgive me," she said quietly. "But aren't you just a little ashamed to be providing the money for this purpose?"

Joe flushed. But it was a flush of anger, not shame. He answered her in a voice that she did not recognize, a cold, righteous voice.

"No, I am not ashamed. To me, it's a good deed. Not only for the business but for all the lives involved. Perhaps you think it's strange that I can reconcile the taking of a life with my religious beliefs. But I don't believe that the Lord wants accidental bastards brought into this world any more than the people who carelessly conceive them. I agree with you about the filthiness of illegal abortions, of course. It is a highly dangerous thing for the woman. For your private information, I feel so strongly about it that I'm putting up the money for Jimmy Jackson and a group of the enlightened Protestant clergy to try to get the abortion laws repealed so that this kind of dirty business will be eliminated. I can't back the movement publicly, of course, but I can provide the wherewithal to help make it happen."

Bridget shook her head. "All these years and you still never fail to amaze me," she said. "Ah well, dear boss, these are things you never learn in Miss Richwitch's School for Young Ladies. At least *I* never learned them. And I never thought I'd have to deal with them. How come it's so hard to be a lady President?"

"Because you're a lady," Joe Haylow said gruffly. "Now eat your lunch."

Over dessert, a nonfattening fruit compote for both of them, Bridget cautiously approached the subject of Roger.

"By the way," she said casually, "did you know I had a very pleasant dinner guest a couple of nights ago? Your younger son."

Joe raised his eyebrows. "Roger came for dinner? That's interesting. Anything special on his mind?"

"Quite a lot," Bridget said. "You, mostly. He loves you very much, Joe, and he's fighting hard to find you. It's a painful process for him, but I have a hunch he's going to make it."

The morning's meeting came quickly into Haylow's mind. Somehow, in a way he did not quite understand, the pieces were beginning to fall into place. He tried to put them together: the conversation with Sid; Roger's dinner with Bridget; his son's forceful, caring words earlier in the day. It was adding up to something good. Something he'd waited for.

Flying back to Farmville late that afternoon, Joe reviewed his day and was pleased with it. He and Bridget had not gone into details about her dinner with Roger, but it was reasonable to assume that their talk had been an open and honest

one and Roger's new attitude was a healthy sign of maturity.
Joe hoped that his son would be able to convince Boswell to
change his mind about selling Elmarie to The Haylow Corporation. A feeling contrary to all his usual wariness told him
that Roger just might succeed, using a simple, direct, honest
approach to this resentful opponent. Sooner or later, Joe
thought, I will find out what has brought about this obvious
change in Roger's feelings toward me. For the moment he
was content to wait for developments, feeling grateful to Sid
Sommers and Bridget, who somehow were responsible for
what he sensed to be a new closeness between father and son.

In his orderly, methodical way, Joe carefully set these
thoughts aside and considered what he would say to Jimmy
Jackson this evening. It would be difficult, if not impossible,
for Jimmy to view the Mallory problem as if it were a business deal. But this was the way Haylow saw it: as though
Woodward was a company threatened by some unexpected
and very real competition which must be methodically eliminated. Religion, in a way, was a business too, Joe thought.
Probably mankind's most important business. It stood to reason, in his mind, that, like a giant commercial corporation,
religion should be administered by the best executive available. Whether he was called Chairman or Reverend was a
mere technicality. The important thing was that God's
earthly empire be in the hands of the strongest leader. For
years, Jimmy Jackson had displayed the qualities of leadership that had led hundreds of thousands of people to the
hope of eternal salvation. Woodward would take over this
task and make God's business grow, unless some quicker-
witted competitor like Elvis Mallory stole "God's customers"
from him.

Joe Haylow found nothing incongruous or irreverent in
this comparison of church and commerce. Both spheres had
their "stockholders," investors seeking worldly or eternal benefits. Both were entitled to top-grade management. Haylow

would not permit either of his enterprises to fall into dishonest or incompetent hands. Though he still had some reservations about the right heir for his earthly empire, he had none about the spiritual domain. Woodward was the only man to succeed Jackson. They had to make sure that his ascension to leadership was insured.

At the house, Pat Haylow greeted him warmly, happily. Returning to her, Joe felt, as he always did, blessedly cloaked in unquestioning, undemanding love. His wife represented the uncomplicated side of his life. Unlike most men, unpredictability in women did not intrigue him. His deep love for Pat was a source of strength and satisfaction for him. Had he stopped to analyze it, he would have realized that he took her for granted, safe in the knowledge that he would always find her calm and reasonable, serene and companionable. To come home and find Pat in a resentful or argumentative mood would have been as unlikely as to find her in a drunken stupor or discover her in their bed with another man. Farmville, and all it represented, including the presence of Pat, was Joe Haylow's momentary retreat from the pressures and tensions of his business life. He was as active here as he was in New York, spending long hours in the headquarters offices, but it was a different kind of pace, less hectic though no less productive. And coming home at night to his beautiful, comfortable house, where his every wish was anticipated, was a soothing change from the stark and surprisingly lonely life he led in the New York apartment. He knew he had the best of both worlds. And since Pat knew it too, there was no need to put his gratitude into trite, embarrassing words.

Tossing his briefcase onto the hall table, Joe Haylow sank gratefully into his deep, comfortable chair in front of the cheerily blazing fireplace. Opposite, Pat sat quietly. She was not the kind of wife who simulated interest in his business activities. She would have bitten out her tongue rather than utter the "How was your day, dear?" cliché. She had spoken to her husband only once on the telephone in nearly a week and she was understandably anxious to hear about his activities, particularly since she felt sure that he had, as he promised her in Florida, discussed with Sid some of the disquietude she felt about Roger. But she waited for him to settle down, readjust to this abrupt change in environment. He looks tired and troubled, she thought apprehensively. For the first time, Joe looks as though the daily battles have taken some of the strength out of him.

He twisted his head, rubbing the back of his neck hard as though he were willing the tension and fatigue out of his body. Then he smiled.

"It's been quite a week," he said in his understated way. "How has it been here?"

"Rather nice for me," Pat answered. "Marjorie spent most of the week in New York while Woodward was attending his convention. So I had the grandmotherly pleasure of entertaining two small houseguests until today. They're really enchanting children. But I guess I'm getting a little too long in the tooth to cope with small whirlwinds. I adored having them here, but I can't really say I was brokenhearted when Marjorie took them home today."

"Yes, I knew Marjorie was down while I was in Atlanta, but I missed her. She came in the office on Monday but I wasn't there. According to my secretary, Brad took her to lunch."

"It's good for her to get a break now and then," Pat said. "Even a young woman as devoted to her husband and family as Marjorie can get a little bored with conversation about third-grade arithmetic. It's stimulating to change the scene now and again. She seemed to enjoy it. I don't know when I've seen her so sparkly-eyed as she was when she came back this time. Woodward got home this afternoon too. And Jimmy called and said you'd left a message for him to drop over after dinner. He'll be here about eight-thirty."

Joe started to tell her about Elvis Mallory and then thought better of it. Like Jackson, it would be hard for Pat to understand the way he felt about this newborn threat. Better to wait until he'd talked to Jimmy. Or better still, tell her nothing until the whole matter was resolved. Besides, he knew that the child on her mind was Roger.

"I had lunch with Sid Sommers before I went to Atlanta," he said. "We discussed Roger's peculiar behavior and Sid is going to look into it. I don't know exactly what he did, but I think I saw a kind of new Roger in a meeting this morning. More decisive, less hostile, unless I'm imagining it. Anyway, he's taken on a pretty big assignment. Thinks he can swing a big deal by having a frank talk with the man who's blocking it. I have a hunch that if he can, it might make a big difference in a lot of things. I think he'll prove something that needs proving to himself and to me."

Pat looked puzzled. "I don't quite understand. But if you think things are better, Joe, that's enough for me. You know how worried I've been about Roger."

"You've had reason," Haylow said comfortingly, "and I don't mean to keep you in the dark about developments. It's just that I'm not sure of them myself. But I have a good feeling that Roger is working himself out of whatever has been bothering him. And I think we should just let him alone and await developments. Believe me, dear, I've been as concerned as you. I think you know that."

"Of course I do," Pat hastily reassured him. "I know you pretty well, Joe Haylow. You're not the big, bad wolf I keep reading about in *The Wall Street Journal*."

Rising to his feet, Joe smiled. "I know you read the *Journal*," he said, "but I'd have thought that the *Ladies' Home* rather than the *Wall Street* would be more interesting to you."

"Not at all," Pat said with feigned indignation. "*The La-*

dies' Home Journal doesn't print articles about my brilliant husband."

"Sometimes I wish *The Wall Street Journal* didn't either," Joe answered. "I'll take a quick shower before dinner. Come up to talk while I change?"

Arm in arm they entered the big bedroom. While Joe was getting out of his "New York clothes," Pat put out the more comfortable gray flannel slacks and blazer he wore in Farmville.

"How's Bridget?" she called to him.

"Fine," Haylow answered from his dressing room. "Very busy right now, of course, with the New York collections opening and Paris showing next week. Also she had a little personnel problem in the store, but it was easily taken care of. Oh, yes, she told me today that she'd had dinner with Roger this week."

"Well, that's nice," Pat said, "but isn't it unusual? I didn't think those two saw much of each other socially."

"I don't think they have up to now. But apparently from what Bridget said she enjoyed it immensely."

Pat considered this new development. "They should have a lot in common," she mused. "I mean the business and all. Bridget is a few years older than Roger, but do you suppose, Joe . . ."

Electric razor in hand, Haylow stuck his head out of the bathroom door. "You do beat all," he said. "Every woman's an incurable matchmaker. You sound like a Jewish mother. Don't tell me you're trying to build a romance out of one simple dinner between two people who've known each other for years!"

"Well, no, not really," Pat laughed. "But each of them could do worse. They are more or less of an age and their interests are similar. Besides, we both love Bridget as though she were our daughter."

"Cut it out," Joe said, "or I'll think you really *do* read *The*

The Rich and the Righteous

Ladies' Home Journal. Besides, how would the wedding announcement read in the paper? I can see it now: 'Lady President marries Vice President.' I mean, it sounds ridiculous."

"How about 'Lady President marries Chairman of the Board'?"

"Oh no you don't," Haylow said, coming over to give her a hug. "You don't trap me into revealing business secrets that way, old girl. Besides," he continued seriously, "that matter is still pending."

"But I can hope, can't I?"

Joe retreated into the bathroom. "Could I stop you?" he said.

Jimmy Jackson arrived after dinner and he and Haylow retired to the study. Joe quickly filled in the minister on the things he had read and heard about Elvis Mallory in Atlanta.

"Mallory's coming on very strong, Jimmy," Haylow said. "Too strong for my taste. What have you heard about him?"

"Quite a good deal," Jackson admitted, "some of it bordering on the incredible, I'll admit. Yet one must never question where the next voice of God may come from. I have not heard the young man speak, but those who have are convinced of his sincerity. Apparently he is a preacher with a real calling and we don't have too many of them in this world, Joe. Why should this concern you so? As a good Christian you should be grateful when God sends another dedicated speaker on His behalf."

A little ashamed but still resolute, Joe looked for the right words to express his ambitions for Woodward's future.

"Jimmy," he said at last, "we've known and loved each other for a long, long time. I have given you my elder son as a Catholic would give a child to the priesthood. To our great mutual happiness, Woodward has found his vocation in the clergy. He is a true man of God but, realistically, in the confines of this room, we know that he is no Jimmy Jackson. Not yet. He lacks your eloquence, your inspiration, your appeal to the masses. Mind you, I think these things will come if he is given time to develop them. In a few more years he will be ready to take over your crusades, ready to become the first voice of our church. But he needs those years, Jim. It's up to you and me to give them to him. We cannot permit some flamboyant backwoods actor to leap on the stage and steal the spotlight from Woodward while we are grooming him for his role as God's star!"

The aging minister looked baffled. "I agree in part with your analysis of Woodward," he said. "But I must be equally honest with you. He is a competent, dedicated servant of the Lord but I am not as sure as you are that it is in him to be the leader of the flock. That takes a certain kind of zeal which I am not sure is part of Woodward's nature. His is a more contemplative, quieter approach to religion than mine or, apparently, Elvis Mallory's. It is just possible, Joe, that we may not be able, ever, to mold Woodward into the kind of public image you would like him to become. We must be ready to accept this fact if such turns out to be the case. And because the possibility exists, we must welcome the appearance of other aspiring young movers of the masses who may be better suited to the work of God in a more overt way than your son. There will always be important work for Woodward to do, even if his sphere is only Farmville."

Joe felt frustration rising. "Are you trying to tell me that Woodward cannot replace you?" he asked angrily.

"No," Jackson said, "I am merely telling you that I am far from certain that he can. And while there is doubt, we must trust in the wisdom of the Lord. Perhaps He has sent Elvis Mallory to be my replacement. Certainly we must not take it upon ourselves to play God. We cannot make the judgment that is possible only for Him."

"I am not making a judgment," Haylow protested, "I am only asking for time. I want the brakes put on Mallory or anyone else who comes along in the next few years. As the strongest voice in our church, only you can do that. I want you to go south on a crusade with Woodward. Go to Atlanta and hear Mallory. Attend his meetings. Watch his so-called 'miracle cures.' Listen to his hellfire and brimstone meetings and then do what I know you will want to do—keep his voice quiet until Woodward is ready."

"And if I do not believe he should be stilled?" Jackson asked. "What do I do then, dear friend?"

"You'll believe it," Joe said stubbornly.

"But if I don't?" Jackson persisted.

"Then," Haylow said slowly, "we will arrive at a sad moment in our association. A sorrowful moment for me. Because I will believe that you are mistaken, Jimmy, and I will have to find my own ways to buy the one commodity that I believe Woodward needs: a little more time. It pains me to say this, Jimmy, but if you don't help Woodward now, as I ask you, I will do it alone. I will put every dollar of my financial support into a campaign to build Woodward with high-powered exposure and public relations. I would prefer not to do this because of my deep respect and affection for you, and because I know, in my heart, that Woodward is not quite ready. But if you refuse to help me, I will do it without you. It is painful beyond words for me to have to remind you that your financial support comes from the Haylow stock which I administer. I do not believe that you will, in good faith, sacrifice the ultimate good of the church for what you apparently think of as your superior judgment."

Jimmy Jackson looked at his old friend with sadness. Haylow's implied threat to withdraw his backing of the Pray-Ins and Jimmy's other activities did not anger the aging minister. He felt painfully sorry for this fiercely ambitious man.

"How dearly and blindly you love your son," Jackson said quietly.

"Yes," Haylow answered, "dearly but not blindly. It is not only ambition for Woodward that compels me. It is my conviction that it is God's will. It is His direction that leads me, as it always has. That is why, however painful, I am prepared to do anything I must, not only for my son but for my church."

"Then," Jackson said, "you are entitled to my understanding. But not to my unqualified agreement. I will make a visit to Mallory's meetings and judge them with all the objectivity and open-mindedness of which I am capable. But if, after I search my heart, I find that I cannot in conscience downgrade him, no power in this world or the next will make me do so. I can live without money and fame and power, Joe. But I could not live with the knowledge that I had helped to still a messenger of God. Not for you or for Woodward. Not even for the deprivation I might thrust upon hundreds of thousands of human beings to whom you would deny the sound of my voice."

Jackson prepared to leave. "I shall pray that I am wrong in all things, Joe, and that you are right. Pray that Woodward does have the qualities you so fiercely want him to have. Hope that I can come back and say that you were right, that Mallory is not the leader that Woodward will one day be. I shall be praying for this easy way out. But I will not turn away from the harder course if that is what my heart tells me is right. I should be a pretty poor representative of God if I did."

Haylow sat quietly for a long while after Jackson left. I must be right, he told himself. For if Jimmy does not see this as I do, God alone knows whether I have the strength to turn my back on my dear old friend. For the next few months, I shall be praying too. As hard as I've ever prayed in my life.

8 ⚜

In the summer that followed, Joe Haylow was filled with an optimism as warming as the first touch of the strengthening sun. Jimmy Jackson's tour of "Mallory country" had, at least temporarily, diverted public attention from the young preacher. He had staged a series of Pray-Ins in the South with Woodward taking a prominent and well-publicized part in the heavily attended revival meetings. Although Jackson had not accepted Joe's plans to quiet Mallory, Haylow took Jimmy's renewed efforts as tacit agreement that the crown still awaited Woodward. This was Jackson's way, Haylow decided, of solving the problem, a more constructive way than his own, Joe had to admit. In his heart, Haylow had no taste for ruthless procedure in business or in religion, and would use it only if there was no alternative. In this case, if Jackson could sublimate Mallory's influence in a kindly way, merely by turning the spotlight on himself and Woodward, Joe was content, even relieved, to live with this solution. Obviously it was working. Mallory's publicity had noticeably diminished as the press turned its attention to Jackson and Woodward's far-reaching and lengthy religious crusade in the South.

Even after Woodward returned, Marjorie continued to spend one or two days each month in New York. Sometimes she flew down from Farmville on Monday with Joe. Otherwise she drove, a pastime she enjoyed and at which she was unusually proficient. Pat was delighted to keep the grandchildren and pleased to see that Marjorie was so obviously enjoying her brief vacations from the small-town life that was doubly demanding because she was the wife of its young minister. Joe was satisfied with this new development too. He was genuinely devoted to Marjorie, who had always made her fondness for him very clear. She was like the daughter the Haylows had never had, an affectionate, considerate girl, in many ways, Joe thought, a young edition of her mother-in-law.

Though he saw little of her, Haylow was pleased to have Marjorie in the New York apartment, too. They dined together occasionally, although most of the evenings she was in New York either Joe was busy with a business engagement or Marjorie said she was meeting one of her college friends for dinner and the theatre. She would return from these evenings at midnight, looking happy and excited, stopping to chat with Joe if he were there reading or dictating his endless memos. He was glad that she was having a little innocent diversion, a break from the routine of Farmville.

Marjorie's apparent happiness and excitement, had he known it, masked her growing feelings of anxiety and guilt. Since the first night with Brad, they had met regularly, usually at his friend's apartment. Their love-making was intense and satisfying in a way that Marjorie had never known. With Brad she forgot duty and fidelity, abandoned herself completely to the accomplished sexual pleasures that Brad provided. To her delight, the enjoyment was unmistakably mutual. Brad found her response to him as exciting as though she were a virgin to whom he was introducing the joys of sex. And for Brad the affair was even more titillating because it was diabolically dangerous. The Chairman's wrath, were he to discover the liaison, would be monumental. Funny, Brad sometimes thought, that in this classic situation it is not the husband I have to fear but the father-in-law. Doe-Doe presented no problem. His unexplained evenings out, like hers, were taken by both of them as a matter of course, even of indifference. It had been a long time since either of them had bothered even to inquire what the other had done the night before.

As the months passed and the affair grew increasingly passionate, it was Marjorie who began to think, reluctantly, of breaking it off. She was desperately in love with Deland, increasingly unable to stay away from him and yet more and more shamed by the desire which was against all the obligations and virtues she believed in. The few hours in Brad's arms were ecstacy. But the sordidness of rising from a strange bed, dressing, and slipping quietly out of the Sutton Place building alone, lest someone see her and Brad together, had a cheapness that made Marjorie sick with shame. She felt like a traitor to her husband and children. And she hated herself for the apparently convincing act she was able to put on.

When she looked in the mirror, she was disgusted by the radiance that was reflected there. She knew she was more beautiful than she had ever been, a fact she found unbearable. She wondered why this terrible thing she was doing, and the torment that never stopped inside her, should not make her look as haggard and guilt-ridden as she felt. It was like a bad joke of nature that this new-found fulfillment should be so apparent in a radiance that made her eyes shine and her mouth curve into softer, more sensuous lines.

Occasionally in desperation, she entertained the idea that she might divorce Woodward. But the idea in itself made her knees tremble. She might steel herself to hurt him and his parents by a divorce, for in time they would recover. But she knew that she would lose her children, and this thought was not to be tolerated. Moreover, realistically, she and Brad had never discussed marriage. There had been oblique references to "some day," but they were part of the abandoned love-making, the tender words and whispered promises that are part of intimacy. She and Brad had never talked seriously of the future. Probably because neither of them really knew where the affair was going.

Once or twice, desperate for advice, she had come close to confiding in Bridget. Of all the women she knew, Bridget would be the most understanding, the most coolly level-headed about the problem, and the only possible ear that Marjorie could seek. For obvious reasons, Pat Haylow could not be told. And Rose Warner would be incapable of understanding, blinded by such depths of love for Mike that, though she might be compassionate, she would be as baffled as she would be helpless. There was no rapport between Marjorie and Mildred Cabot. This tall, cold, rock-bound-righteous woman was not the kind of human being one would approach on anything remotely resembling a personal level. Confused and remorseful, Marjorie pathetically needed a woman to talk to. Yet she dared not entrust her secret to anyone, not even Bridget. She lived in anticipation of her moments with Brad.

Alone in her room, she cried and prayed and tried to drive out the desire that pulled her relentlessly back to De-land. It was no good. Her lust, as she thought of it, was stronger than her loyalty. One word from her could have ended it, she knew, and she begged God for the strength to tell Brad that it could not go on, but the moment she slipped into the little apartment and felt his arms go around her, his mouth cover hers, all determination, all reason left her until her hunger was satiated. She waited, as curiously as though she were part of the audience, to see how this certain tragedy would unfold. A less emotional woman, a less honest one, would easily be able to deceive Woodward. Even now he did not question her trips to New York. The question was whether she could live with the knowledge of her deceit. And for how long.

In this period, Brad was equally caught up in the affair, but without the guilt or the problems of his more sensitive, less experienced partner. Occasionally, he speculated about the eventual outcome. For the moment, he was content to let life go on as it was. In the back of his mind, he found the idea of eventual marriage to Marjorie more than appealing. The details would be troublesome but handleable, once he had the Chairmanship. With the power in Brad's hands, Joe Haylow would be helpless to stop any action Deland chose to take, whether it was a business decision or a personal one, including marriage to the ex-Chairman's daughter-in-law.

Brad was far more concerned, at this point in time, with the threat of Roger. Since the day of the Elmarie meeting, Roger had become a different person, stronger, more dedicated, obviously growing in Joe's estimation. To Haylow's surprise and delight, Roger was making some progress in the Elmarie deal. It was a long, slow, carefully thought-out plan, worthy of Joe Haylow himself, and consequently deserving of his admiration. Roger had made his first move through Marie Boswell. With Bridget's help, it had been easy enough to find out in which crowd Marie moved. And, as that rare and desirable creature, "the extra man," it was not difficult for Roger to get himself invited to the same parties attended by Frank and Marie Boswell. In a social setting, Frank could not be openly hostile, and over a period of months Roger had a chance to carefully study the Boswells and piece together small pertinent bits of information about their interests and activities. Cautiously, carefully, like a hunter stalking the elusive prey, Roger at first kept his distance from the pair, acknowledging with polite indifference the first introduction and making sure, at subsequent gatherings, that his attention was focused not on Marie Boswell but on her closest friends.

It was a ploy that worked. Roger's undeniable charm and his designation as "a good catch" made him a prime topic of conversation among the young matrons of Marie's set. His invitations to dinner and cocktail parties which included the Boswells soon increased to the point that he became an accepted member of the group. Frank Boswell continued to ignore him, but Marie's social ambitions were stronger than her husband's hatred of the Haylows. An attractive, unattached man was too precious a prize to be ignored, and within a few weeks, over Frank's protestations, Roger was invited to his first dinner party at the Boswells.

The rules of the social game dictated that Frank, as the host, be cordial to him in a civilized, if not effusive, way. The evening, which went easily, was followed by one a month later at which Roger was the host at a small dinner party at Raffles, one of New York's more exclusive and expensive private clubs. Roger planned this evening carefully. Seated at the head of the table with Marie on his right, he filled the rest of the places with couples who were friends of the Boswells, injecting only three outsiders—two attractive, successful bachelors and Bridget Manning, who was seated, by design, next to Frank Boswell.

Bridget could be counted on to interest a man like Frank. She knew how to flatter him through her knowledge of his business, how to impress him with her offhand references to "other famous people" in the world of cosmetics and fashion. She gave no clue that she knew anything of Boswell's past or even of Haylow's desire to acquire Elmarie. Frank found her bright and interesting. Furthermore, since Bridget's stores were such important customers, it was important to Elmarie's growth for its Vice President to know the lady President.

Keeping a careful watch on these two from his end of the table, Roger simultaneously seemed to be giving his full attention to Marie. Over coffee, he carefully brought the conversation around to her father.

"I've never met Mr. Marina," he said, "but I am told that he is a remarkable man. He must have had great vision to realize the potential of the cosmetics business almost sixty years ago when he started Elmarie. In a way, your father and mine are very much alike. They both started from scratch, believing in a dream that most people didn't have the imagination to understand."

At the mention of Joe Haylow, he felt Marie stiffen suspiciously. Quickly, he pursued the subject, approaching it boldly.

"I guess that's why they have such respect for each other," Roger went on. "You know, 'Takes one to know one.' They're both men who have put personal considerations aside in their devotion to building something successful and lasting. They're above petty grievances and personal slight," he said pointedly. "It's a kind of selfless integrity that our generation doesn't seem to know much about."

Marie Boswell was far from a stupid woman. She was, in fact, far more emotionally mature than her husband. All along she had secretly agreed with her father that a sale to Haylow would be the most desirable form of insurance for her and her children. But Frank's stubborn, almost hysterical resistance to the idea had left her helpless. She could, of course, override him, voting with her father for the sale. But she loved her husband and wanted to preserve her marriage, so she had reluctantly sided with Frank in the matter. It occurred to her now that Roger might be the solution. She had no doubt that his sudden appearance in her life was no accident. She was sure that through her he meant to get to Frank and try to make him change his mind about the deal. Even now he was feeling his way, probing for her reactions, not knowing exactly where she stood on the matter. I have a pleasant shock for him, she thought. When he finds that he has two allies in the enemy's camp he'll be delirious with joy.

"Yes," she agreed, "I suppose our generation does have a kind of uptight attitude toward personal affronts, whether they're real or imagined. Maybe we are more self-involved than our parents were. I suppose they were too busy building up the fortunes that we now enjoy to waste their time on unimportant feuds."

With a surge of hope, Roger realized that the cat-and-mouse game they were playing was one that Marie thoroughly understood.

"Marie," he said earnestly, "you're a bright woman, as well as a terribly attractive one. I'm sure you know all about our offer to buy Elmarie and why your father has refused to sell. I can only admire him—and you—for your loyalty to Frank, and I wouldn't want you to play it any other way. But tell me, is there any way to get Frank to change his mind?"

She answered with simple directness. "No way that Father or I can do it, I don't think. Though, frankly, we'd both like to. We don't blame Frank for his hatred of Joe Haylow, but we're not emotionally involved in the injustice as he is, so we can take a more practical and dispassionate view of it. Look, Roger, the name Haylow is a dirty word to Frank. He's not against selling the business to anyone else, but my father has a gentleman's agreement with yours about that, so it won't happen in Dad's lifetime. When he goes, the business will go. To somebody."

"I know," Roger said. "But my father will soon be gone too, in a manner of speaking. He retires next year. So in effect, Frank wouldn't be selling to Joe Haylow in the long run. He'd really be selling to me. And I've done nothing to harm him. In 1954 I was practically an office boy in the company. I knew nothing of the matter, but if I'd been in a position of influence, I wouldn't have allowed Frank to be treated as he was."

"That wouldn't be an easy story to sell Frank," Marie said.

"Probably not, but I'd like to try. Maybe Frank and I might be able to communicate if I could only get him to talk with me. I'm sure he'd refuse if I tried to make an appointment with him. But maybe you could help me."

"How?" Marie asked.

"Well, you've managed to get him to socialize with me,

however unwillingly I suspect he's gone along. If you'll conspire with me on one last thing, maybe we'll both get what we want. And Frank, too."

Marie listened attentively.

"I thought that in a week or so," Roger said, "I'd get Bridget to invite you and Frank to dinner at her apartment. The invitation will be black tie so it will sound like a big group. But there'll be only the four of us. Frank will like that, because Bridget is an important customer. Then the two of you girls can arrange to leave us alone after dinner and I can try to persuade Frank that he shouldn't penalize all of us for a past error in judgment on the part of the Haylows."

"I wouldn't want to bet my life on your chances," Marie said.

"But you'll get him to come?"

"That I'll do," she said, "for whatever it's worth."

They set the date for ten days later, to be formally confirmed by Bridget.

The day after this conversation, Roger asked for a meeting with Joe, Cabot, and Deland.

"This is just a progress report on the Elmarie deal," he told them. "I wanted to keep you up to date. I've gotten to know the Boswells socially, a little. Frank Boswell is still openly distrustful of me, but his wife is very anxious to see the deal go through. I've enlisted Bridget's help and in the next couple of weeks I hope to have the talk with Frank that I suggested at our last meeting."

The reactions of the group had been what Roger expected. Cabot volunteered no opinion. Brad, with a sardonic smile, had wished him luck. Only Joe had responded with evident optimism and pleasure.

"Good work so far, Roger," he said. "Of course you're a long way from home but I admire the way you're going about it. We'll see how persuasive you are, now that you've been smart enough to get Marie Boswell on your side and set up the situation. I wish you luck, too."

The Chairman turned to Deland. "Maybe we won't have to use those bloodthirsty methods of yours after all, Brad," he said.

"I certainly hope not, sir," Deland said smoothly.

Roger's ability to methodically think through an unorthodox solution to a major business problem disturbed Brad as much as Joe's obvious admiration of it made him apprehensive. He was more certain than ever that Cabot would be passed over for the top job. Increasingly Haylow acted as though his second-in-command was not even in the room. But for Brad the continued weakening of Cabot's position was more than balanced by the strengthening of Roger's. Whatever had brought about the change in Roger's attitude toward his father and the business had been an effective remedy for the sick rebellion Haylow's son had shown only a few months earlier. The metamorphosis was almost incredible. Alarmed by the possibility of Roger's success, Deland began to search his mind for a suitable weapon to use against young Haylow.

Meanwhile he knew that the chairman would wait out his decision almost until the last moment. There was still hope that Roger would blow the Elmarie deal and Joe would have to accept Deland's solution. Such an eventuality would be more than a triumph for Brad; it would be a sad reaffirmation for Haylow that his son lacked the stomach for a bloody business brawl. It might even cause Roger to pull back into the shell from which he had so curiously emerged. The barriers between father and son would once again be erected by the disappointment of one and the failure of the other.

The race, he felt, was still between him and Roger. Cabot, blandly deluding himself with the belief in his automatic ascension to the throne, sensed no danger as he went calmly about his routine chores, leading his humdrum New Jersey life with his horse-faced, rawboned wife. Brad felt certain that everything would have to blow sky-high for Joe to settle for Cabot. Haylow would give him the job only as a last resort.

The Rich and the Righteous

The only ones who believed in Cabot's victory were those who did not understand Joe Haylow's intensely egocentric attitude about his business. And heading that list was Cabot himself.

In his calculations, Deland also dismissed Mike Warner and Bridget Manning, the first for his religion, the second for her sex. In addition, though both were members of the Board, neither operated strictly on a corporate level. Their day-by-day duties were in their divisions. While Brad knew that the actual buying and selling of merchandise was the facet nearest to Haylow's heart, he reasoned that it was not in the cards that operating managers, no matter how lofty their titles, nor how important their contributions, would be in line for the administration of a complex as vast and complicated as The Haylow Corporation.

Here, Brad Deland underestimated the vision and daring of Joe Haylow. In the long hours of the night when he lay awake considering each of the five possible candidates, Mike and Bridget were by no means eliminated as possibilities in the Chairman's mind. When he thought of these two, he allowed himself the rare luxury of emotional reaction. For while he was impressed by Deland's ambition and reluctantly aware of the expectations of the financial community in regard to Cabot, he felt something close to kinship with Warner and Bridget. He weighed their qualifications as carefully as the others, though on a slightly different scale. Bridget, he knew, would be a convention-defying choice which might seriously alarm the staid moguls of Wall Street, even cause Haylow stock to suffer a serious, temporary setback. Yet she was, of them all, the most intuitive and unfrightened spirit. Under her leadership, and bolstered with solid administrative aides, it was conceivable that Bridget could take the Haylow empire to expanded heights based on her certain knowledge of Haylow's primary customers: women.

On Mike Warner's scoreboard in Haylow's mind, the qualities of honesty, loyalty, and emulation stood out brilliantly and importantly. Haylow understood Mike Warner as well as he understood his own sons. Better, perhaps. Given the leadership of the company, Mike Warner would drive himself as mercilessly as Joe Haylow had always done. He knew how to be tough. Like the Chairman he had made it up the hard way. Yet despite his toughness he had the Jew's sensitivity and compassion, useful attributes in making the decisions which would be forced upon a man in his high position.

Haylow wondered how Mike would have handled the Elmarie problem. He regretted that he had not involved him in it. Mike's sensible, direct understanding of the situation would have been an interesting contrast to Cabot's pedantic approach, or Deland's ruthless suggestion or even Roger's almost naïvely forthright recommendation which Joe had accepted with hope rather than with conviction.

Joe snapped on his bedside light and made a quick notation on the pad he kept beside him. "See MW re Elmarie," he wrote. It probably was too late to involve Warner in any actual plan for the acquisition. He could only hope that Roger's hunch would prove right. Otherwise, he probably would have to go along with Deland's methods, much as he disliked them. Nonetheless, it would do no harm to fill Mike in on what was happening, since Joe was determined to effect the purchase of Elmarie, even without its present management. Mike would be very helpful in finding the right people to run the company, and he might as well start looking now.

As he drifted into sleep, Joe thanked God that he was blessed with a quintet of able replacements, each with his own peculiar assets. "It is an embarrassment of riches," Haylow thought. Better this way than if there were no one qualified to sit at the wheel when he so reluctantly gave up the driver's seat.

9 ⚬⚬⚬

At the last moment, Roger and Bridget decided to slightly enlarge the dinner party for the Boswells. On the theory that Star Stores also were one of Elmarie's biggest accounts, it seemed strategic to invite Mike and Rose Warner. And it was Mike who, in turn, suggested the addition of Terry White, cosmetics buyer for the whole Star chain.

Following his middle-of-the-night notation, Haylow had brought Mike up to date on the Elmarie acquisition problem, asking him particularly to give some thought to a possible divisional President if, as seemed likely, Frank Boswell wanted no part of the operation under Haylow.

Mike had looked thoughtful. "It's amazing how few good executives there are," he told Joe. "You'd think in a world full of bright guys there'd be a big choice for top jobs, but when you really try to sit down and pinpoint a specific person for a specific job, the pickin's are slim."

"How well I know," Haylow said wryly.

"Maybe it will seem kind of offbeat," Warner went on, "but we might be better off ignoring the men who are already Presidents of cosmetics companies and going for a bright young talent. Somebody with reasonable experience, of course. But still fresh and energetic enough to pump life into Elmarie. You know, in spite of its success, the company is almost sixty years old and has been run by one of the conservative old-timers. It might be a smart move to introduce some young blood as the leader."

"Makes sense," Joe agreed. "Have you got somebody in mind?"

"Possibly. A young guy named Terry White who buys cosmetics for all our stores. Maybe you remember him. He's been at one or two of the morning meetings. He's doing a great job for us. Knows the business and shows a real flair for merchandising and promotion. He's young. Thirtyish, I guess. I'm sure he knows a lot about Elmarie, since it's one of our good resources. In fact, I think he occasionally has lunch with Boswell."

"Sounds like a good candidate."

"I think he could be," Mike said. "Anyway, it's worth looking into. Terry might help us break through to Boswell at this stage, even if we decide he's not the one to run Elmarie when we acquire it."

Haylow was pleased by Mike's positive response, noting that he had said "*when* we acquire it," not "*if* we acquire it." Once again, he felt respect and affection for this quietly confident young executive. Mike was a very valuable addition to the Haylow stable of stars. He lacked the calculated coldness, the near cruelty of a Deland who, despite his background and breeding, had the instincts of a street brawler. He was, Haylow had to admit, decidedly more realistic and unemotional than Roger. All in all, Mike Warner was a well-rounded, nearly unflappable personality who would continue his steady climb to greater heights of corporate responsibility.

In his constant evaluation of the candidates for Chairmanship, Haylow did not discount Mike Warner. He would be a strong and dedicated leader. If only, Joe thought, he had been born a Christian. This unworthy reaction shamed Haylow but, struggle as he would, he could not overcome this deeply ingrained prejudice against minorities. Rationally he knew it was wrong. Emotionally he fought a losing battle against his bigotry. Haylow hated himself for it. Yet he was never quite able to forget that Mike Warner was one of the people that Farmville kids had always called "Christ-killers."

Once he had tried to explain this irrationality to Patricia.

"Mike Warner is one of the finest human beings I've ever known," he told her. "He's more admirable than Deland, more competent than Cabot, even more stable than Roger. Everything's right about him. I really love that boy, Pat. And still I wish he were different."

Pat Haylow understood what he meant by "different," though it simply was not in her nature to carry prejudice against Blacks and Jews. Perhaps it was her more cosmopolitan background or her innate serenity that made her a less complicated, less tortured person than her husband. She felt deeply and warmly about every living thing. She offered love in its purest, most unselfish way, rich with understanding and utterly lacking in reproach. Answering Joe's tacit plea for help, she was gentle but straightforward.

"Darling, I know how you admire Mike and trust him. I know you even feel a deep affection for him. But you don't love him, Joe. Not really. Because when you love someone you don't really want them to be different. Oh, you might like to change some little things if you could. Like wishing they didn't have some petty, irritating habit or thinking how nice it would be if they felt as strongly as you do about a minor matter. But when you truly love, my dearest, you accept the things that cannot be changed and make them part of your love. Mike can never stop being Jewish, Joe dear, even if he wanted to. If you really loved him, you would realize that and know that it's you who have to change. Because he can't."

"How lucky you are," Haylow said slowly, "to see life as such a simple acceptance of things as they really are. Even love. Such a big and elusive subject. What does it basically mean to you, Pat?"

She laughed. "After all these years you have to ask me that?" Then, seeing that he was serious, she matched his mood. "What is love to me? Well, I'm not smart enough or fluent enough to say it in all the ways that the poets and preachers have expressed it. I guess that to me love is a series of little hurts and big rewards. It's the kind of joy that needs an occasional pain to make us appreciate it that much more. I'm sure it's a special blessing available to everyone if they'll just reach out for it. But so many of us aren't grateful for it. Maybe not even aware of it. It's not martyrdom or great self-sacrifice. It's fun to give love, for the pure, selfish pleasure of what one gets in return."

She went to her dressing table and took a dog-eared little card from the drawer. Handing it to Joe, she said, almost shyly, "This is a Christmas message someone sent us years ago. I don't know whether you ever had time to read it when it arrived. But the message seemed so pure and honest that I've just hung on to it. Maybe it says in a very few words all the things I have trouble putting into long sentences."

Joe read aloud, slowly. "We give love away and it becomes the best part of us." He looked at his wife tenderly. "It's a lesson I could learn, isn't it? Being able to give love, I mean. Or at least letting people somehow know I love them even if I just can't seem to show it."

Pat put her arms around him, pressing her cheek against his.

"Oh, Joe, you do give so much love. And it's not your fault if people don't recognize it. Sometimes, most times, you don't recognize it yourself. It gets all mixed up with other emotions in you, like wanting people to be perfect because they are the people you love. Like wanting Mike not to be Jewish because to you his life would be complete if he knew the joys of Christianity. But they're *your* joys, Joe. The things that comfort you may not be the answer for the millions of Mike Warners in this world."

"Am I really that self-centered?" Haylow asked.

She hastened to reassure him from the depth of her love. "Anything but self-centered, sweetheart," she said, holding his head close to her breast. "If anything, you want the whole world to be as blessed as you feel yourself to be. I take back what I said before, darling. Of course you love Mike. It's your way of loving. And he knows it. Just as I know you love me."

Haylow held her close. "Love you? If only I could tell you how I love you! Everything I've ever done is to make you proud of me, make you love me. That's the way it's always been, Pat. Even when I haven't known how to tell you. Even when I haven't even thought about telling you. And you are right about Mike. My wanting him to be different is pure ego. I want it for my sake, not his. I guess I really want him to be like me in every way. I guess I wish he really was our son."

"He is very like you," Pat said. "And he is our son in spirit. We should be grateful for Mike, dearest. He's one of the wonderful people. There's nothing Mike Warner would not do to prove his love for you."

In his office, remembering that earlier intimate conversation, Haylow knew that everything Pat said was true. Right now, he was sure, Mike Warner was already at work on the problem of making still another of Haylow's wishes come true.

Joe's analysis was completely correct. As soon as he left the Chairman's office, Mike called Bridget and accepted the dinner invitation.

"I've just been having a talk with the Boss," he added. "He filled me in a little on the Elmarie problem and I've got an idea that might help unthicken the plot. What would you think about including our cosmetics buyer, Terry White, in your little dinner for the Boswells? He knows the whole beauty racket better than any of us so he can at least speak the language. Besides, he's a good-looking young guy, unmarried. Might be a little gay but you wouldn't know it."

"In this town, anything pretty and unmarried in pants is a hostess's dream," Bridget said. "Seriously, I think it's a marvelous idea and I'm sure Roger will think so too. God knows we're going to need all the help we can get to swing this one. I'll send Terry White a little note, but I assume you'll explain it to him? Since I don't even know him, he might think it's a touch odd if I suddenly issue a dinner invitation out of the blue."

"Of course," Mike agreed. "I'll have to clue him in on the Elmarie thing anyhow if he's going to make Brownie points. By the way, when I cleared the date with Rose she was wondering what to wear. Which means she's wondering what you're going to wear."

"Fancy pants, I guess. But tell her that anything dressy will be fine. Preferably long. Listen, Mike, why don't you be a big shot and borrow something really smashing from your custom designer shop for her to wear? No need to break the bank by buying anything when you've got a whole store full of swell clothes. And Marie Boswell is such a label-conscious snob that the whole family should look super-rich to impress her. *I'm* planning to liberate something revoltingly overpriced for the event. No reason you can't do the same for that enchanting wife of yours."

Mike knew what she was tactfully trying to say. Rose had no clothes sense. Certainly not in the way that Bridget or Marie Boswell had it. He was aware that Rose Warner's wardrobe was a far cry from what one would imagine a store President's wife would own. He simply could not talk her into buying expensive clothes, even though they could afford them. And she would never let him borrow something from stock for her to wear on a special occasion. Maybe this time, he'd just buy something for her and take it home, not telling her what it cost, knowing she'd wear it to please him.

"I don't think I can borrow a dress from the store," he said to Bridget. "It's against Warner principles."

"Yours?"

"No," he laughed. "Rose's. She'd be a nervous wreck thinking she'd spill something on a Galanos or put her heel through a Norell. Especially one that was out on loan."

Bridget's voice was understanding, affectionate. "She always looks beautiful, Mike. And you make her look radiant just being with her."

When Mike hung up, he went down to the Designer Salon and bought a dress for Rose, one she would never have picked out for herself. It was a soft violet color, the same shade as her eyes. It was cut low to show the high, beautiful bosom. And it cost six hundred dollars after his discount. He had it gift-wrapped and the price tag removed. It was a dress that Rose Warner wouldn't understand. But Marie Boswell would.

Bridget's dinner party for the Boswells was successful beyond Roger's wildest hopes. Frank Boswell, taciturn and obviously suspicious at the start of the evening, quickly relaxed under Bridget's natural skill as a hostess. Marie was obviously impressed with the understated chic of Bridget's apartment and the impeccably planned and served dinner. Even Rose Warner seemed to radiate an unusual aura of sophistication. She looked breath-takingly beautiful in her violet gown and Mike nearly laughed aloud at the casual way in which she said, "Oh, it's a Norell" to Marie's admiring question. Clothes do make the woman feel secure, Mike thought, resolving to make it a future habit to bring home other elegant, untagged clothes to his beloved wife.

The addition of Terry White has been a stroke of genius, Roger thought, watching the good-looking young man deep in shop talk with Frank Boswell. It was clear that Terry understood the cosmetics business and could talk intelligently and enthusiastically about Elmarie, paying just the right amount of deference to the man who was its second in command. Neither he nor Mike had White's knowledge about Boswell's business, Roger realized, and neither of them could do as good a job of selling the Haylow organization to Boswell. He was sure that Terry was, as Pat would have put it, "not a whole man," but he was the kind that easily could have been put in the questionable category. There was nothing flagrant or effeminate about Terry, no gesture, accent, or vulgarity of dress to mark him as "one of the boys." On the contrary, he gave the appearance of a nicely mannered, serious young executive who spoke Boswell's language and Frank was apparently impressed with his grasp of the industry and the ease with which he spoke the language of the beauty world.

According to plan, after dessert Bridget rose from the table, smiling her woman-of-the-world smile. "It may seem extraordinarily Victorian to you gentlemen," she said, "but I think that I will take Marie and Rose off into the other room and let the four of you talk awhile over your brandy. You see," she added appealingly, "I like to pretend that in my own house I'm not a businesswoman. But don't count on that, any one of you, if you come to see me at nine o'clock in the office!"

Gracefully, she led the other women from the room. The four men left at the table maintained an awkward silence for a moment. Finally, Roger addressed himself to Frank Boswell.

"Obviously you've been railroaded into an informal business meeting, Frank," he said. "We haven't even tried to be very subtle about it, as you're damned well smart enough to recognize. The simple truth is that I went out on a limb with my father about the sale you're opposed to. For all I know, it may strike you as ridiculously naïve, but all of us in this room think you have an apology coming to you, one that I am not only authorized but anxious to make on behalf of The Haylow Corporation in general and Joe Haylow in particular."

There was no mistaking the sincerity in Roger's voice. To be that simple and direct, Mike Warner thought, you've either got to be god-awful dumb or goddamned good. And Roger's good. He's got the old man's persuasiveness with less of his abrasive impatience.

"Sometimes things happen to a man when he's very young that can cloud his judgment all his life," Roger went on. "Very recently I've learned a little bit about that myself. When you're a sensitive guy, as you seem to be, Frank, it's possible to let a personal affront become more important than a sound business decision. My father can't undo the injustice that his company did to you years ago. None of us can. But neither he nor I want to see you compound our error into a decision that will deprive your wife and kids of a richer life than you can give them without us."

Boswell's face flushed. "We're not exactly hurting, Haylow," he said. "I'm not an idiot. Of course we probably could be a lot richer selling the company to you instead of running it ourselves. But as your own people, like Terry White here, will tell you, we're showing a very healthy profit at Elmarie and with more modern methods—which will come after my father-in-law leaves the business—I think I can safely assure my family of a more than adequate future. And let's get something else straight while we're at it. Sure, Haylow's made us a good offer for the business but it's not philanthropy. He wouldn't be so hot to buy the company if he didn't think it was potentially a big money-maker."

"No argument with that," Roger agreed. "We're not in the habit of making bad buys if we can help it. Although," he said lightly, "we've made one or two that haven't turned out to be what you might call world beaters. The fact is, Frank, that you probably can exist for a long while without big money and muscle behind you. But it's a changing world. In your industry, the fat sharks are gobbling up the elegant, glittering little goldfish. From what little I know of the cosmetics business, it won't be long before there will be only three or four outfits with enough money to stay in the race. The day of the small, low-budget business is just about over. I think in your heart you know that. And you also know that you're not likely to get a better offer than we've made. The longer you hold out, the greater risk you run that Haylow and all the other big-money boys will put their acquisition funds elsewhere. This is the time to sell, Frank. Not years from now when your father-in-law is dead and the few buyers who might be interested have all long since put their dough in other places. While Mr. Marina lives, you can't sell to anyone but Haylow. And when he's gone, there may not be anyone left to buy."

During all this discussion, both men had kept their voices low and carefully controlled. Terry White found himself fascinated by this methodical exchange, as formal as the deadly serious ritual of a bullfight. This is how the big boys play, he thought. This is why Mike Warner and the other Haylow brass are loaded with money and options while the rest of us piss away our lives with small-time jobs. Terry forced his attention back to the dialogue at the dining table.

"Even if I admit that your analysis of the future could conceivably be valid," Frank Boswell was saying, "what if I still refuse to sell to Haylow? Seeing the Presidents and the cosmetics buyer of two of our major accounts here tonight might suggest to a more suspicious man that you have something up your sleeve. Maybe you're thinking of dropping Elmarie from your stores if I don't go along with the sale. I'm putting it right on the line, Haylow. If my answer is no, will you try to bust me?"

There was a pregnant pause. The guy's got guts, Roger thought, to raise such a realistic question. Maybe we should have let Deland deal with him instead of me. They think alike. Boswell is anticipating exactly what Brad suggested in the meeting, on the theory that business is done only with pressure and threats. This could be my easy way out. But it would be Brad's victory not mine. And there's more at stake here than the acquisition of Elmarie. Slowly, he answered Boswell's question.

"Frank, you may believe one thing. If you still stick to your position that you do not wish to sell Elmarie to Haylow, you need have no worries about any of our stores continuing to do the best possible business with you."

Boswell looked dubious. "Why should I believe that?"

"For two reasons. First, because we are smart merchants. Unlike you, we will not allow our personal frustrations to interfere with our business judgment. Elmarie is an important and profitable line in the Star Stores and in Bridget's. We hardly are going to cut out one of our good sources of revenue just to get even with the man who won't sell it to us. Why should we reduce our volume to satisfy our wounded pride?"

"And the second reason?"

"The second reason," Roger said quietly, "is because beyond the financial considerations, and contrary to what you might think, The Haylow Corporation does not do business based on blackmail. We get what we want by making a fair, above-board offer that's advantageous to both parties. We can live without owning Elmarie. And rather than stoop to threats and dirty dealings, we'll accept our failure like the gentlemen we hope we are. You have my father's word on this. And mine."

"You know, of course, that even if I don't block the sale, I won't be part of the deal," Frank said. "Even if I reverse my position, I still would never work for Joe Haylow or even for anyone who replaces him."

"I'm not surprised by that," Roger answered. "Frankly, in

your shoes, I think I'd probably feel the same way. Naturally, we'd be sorry, Frank. There's nobody in the business who could do a better job as President of the Elmarie division. But I respect your feelings. It makes it harder for us. And, of course, we would insist on a clause in the contract that you would not go into a competitive venture. But you have laid such strong groundwork for your company that it is our hope we can find competent management to further develop the great strides you've already made."

Automatically, Roger and Mike Warner glanced briefly in Terry's direction. They were both thinking the same thing. Perhaps this capable young man could play an important part in Elmarie. Strong executives could be recruited to surround him. He was young and somewhat inexperienced, but he'd do. With the right direction and guidance, Terry White would work his tail off to succeed. And in many ways his youth would be a publicity asset, another convention-defying move that would have great appeal to the young who were heavy buyers of cosmetics.

Terry White knew he was reading their thoughts. Miraculously, the big chance was close at hand. The kind of job he'd never dared hope for might be offered to him. It seemed like a dream. Or like an old movie where the young understudy goes on for the star. The expressions on the faces of the other three men told him clearly that the acquisition was all but signed. Terry found the tension almost unbearably exciting.

They waited for Boswell to speak. Roger suddenly felt sorry for the man. He knew, all too well, how hard it was to eat one's words, to be shown that the hatred you'd carried for so long was no more than a childish self-indulgence, insignificant in the face of practical, realistic appraisal.

"All right," Frank finally said, heavily. "I'll tell my father-in-law that I no longer oppose the Haylow deal. I suppose it's time I thought of other people. No good making them suffer for my wounded vanity. What's that old saying? 'A man wrapped up in himself makes a pretty small package.' I guess I haven't really been as big as a breadbox all these years."

Roger Haylow offered his hand to Boswell. "Don't you believe it, Frank," he said. "It takes a big man to sacrifice his pride for the people he loves. In my book, you make a package as big as the Empire State. You're a hundred stories tall. And on you it looks good."

Relief was in the laughter that followed. Mike was proud of Roger Haylow, as delighted with his victory as though it had been an accomplishment of Mike's own. Roger felt his own heart beating fast. He was experiencing a kind of elation that he now realized was the way his father felt when he captured a long-desired prize. Most of all, Roger was grateful that the deal was clean. If my father had accepted Brad's way instead of mine, he thought, all the progress I've made with the help of Sid and Bridget would have washed down the drain of disillusionment. But Joe didn't accept Brad's methods, he gambled on mine. Which means he believes in me and my way of doing things. Which means, he thought with thankfulness, that he loves and trusts me. Maybe now I can return that love and trust. Wholeheartedly.

The men returned to the living room where Bridget, Marie, and Rose were chatting amiably over their coffee. Unobtrusively, Bridget raised a questioning eyebrow in Roger's direction. He responded with a quick nod and a tiny smile that was no more than a slight upturning of the corners of his mouth. Bridget's face was a study in unspoken congratulation.

"Welcome back," she said to the men. "What may I give you as an after-dinner drink?"

Frank Boswell, seated beside his wife and holding her hand tightly, was first to respond.

"If it isn't an imposition," he said, "may we have champagne? You see, it's my birthday."

Marie Boswell looked at him as though he'd lost his mind. "What on earth do you mean, 'it's your birthday'? You were born on the eighteenth of June!"

"Okay, technically you're right," Frank answered. "But to all intents and purposes 'today I am a man.' So I'm twenty-one this evening and by God I'm entitled to champagne. Okay, Bridget?"

Bridget smiled warmly at him. "Very much okay, Frank. The next sound you hear will be the popping of corks!"

It took a minute for Marie Boswell to realize what this double-talk was all about. Then, as it dawned on her what her husband had done for the sake of her and their children, her expression was suffused with tenderness. She leaned over and kissed him gently. "Papa will be very happy, darling," she said. "And so will we."

Rose Warner had no idea what all this meant, but her husband looked enormously pleased. He would explain it to her later, she knew. Meanwhile, Mike was happy about whatever they were celebrating. Rose needed no better reason for celebrating too.

Like a child with good news, Roger Haylow could hardly wait to tell his father about Frank Boswell's agreement to the acquisition. Although it was after midnight when Roger returned to his own apartment, he called Joe, knowing the Chairman would still be awake, reading or working.

"Good news, sir," he said when Haylow answered the phone. "Boswell's come around to our side. The deal will go through."

Joe Haylow made no effort to conceal his delight.

"Well, well," he said. "Congratulations, Roger. That's what I call a master stroke! Good work, boy, you've accomplished an important piece of business tonight. I sure have to hand it to you. You had a lot more faith in your methods than some of the rest of us did."

For a moment, Roger felt a twinge of the old resentment, the old unhappiness that he did not have his father's complete confidence. But the feeling now passed quickly. It's only his way, Roger told himself. I've got to stop misreading the things he says, turning what he considers a compliment into an imagined slight just because of the way he puts it.

"I can't take full credit," Roger said. "Bridget turned on a great atmosphere, and Mike Warner was smart enough to suggest we include his cosmetics buyer, that young Terry White. Everything kind of fell into place, with all of us working as a team."

"Don't be so modest," Haylow answered. "The team is only as good as its captain. You planned the strategy and I'll bet you carried the ball most of the way. What's the next step?"

He's asking *me*, Roger realized with mixed feelings of pleasure and surprise. It's taken a long time to earn my stripes, but suddenly the old man is talking to me as a colleague. His answer was firm, decisive.

"I'm calling a meeting tomorrow afternoon to announce the results of tonight's meeting. Then we can get together with Marina and Boswell to work out the details. I'll notify Cabot and Deland in the morning and I think it would be a good idea to have Mike Warner there. Oh yes, and if Sid Sommers is free, maybe he should sit in too. We'll need some management guidance because it doesn't look as though Frank Boswell will come with the package."

"Good idea," Haylow agreed. "Do you want that young Terry White in the meeting?"

"Not at this point," Roger said, "because one of the things we may want to talk about is his possible participation in Elmarie on a management level. We can't discuss that in front of him."

"Right," Joe said. "Anyone else?"

"I don't think so. Unless you have some ideas."

Haylow gave a little chuckle. "Well, I was just wondering whether you planned to include me."

"You have to be kidding," Roger said. "I just assumed the meeting would be in your office."

"Then make a new assumption," Haylow said. "This is your ball game. Play it in your home park. The meeting should be in your office, Roger, and I'll be happy to attend. As a participating member of your team."

"Thank you, sir. Two o'clock?"

"Two, it is," Haylow replied. "And Roger . . ."

"Yes?"

"I'm proud of you."

Roger felt gooseflesh on his arms. It's his way of telling me he loves me, Roger thought. Maybe as near as he can ever come to saying it.

"Thank you, Father," Roger said. "I've waited a long time."

As each man put down the receiver, he was aware that something very warm and satisfying had happened. Each had reached out to the other in an exchange that went beyond the understanding of father and son or the mutual respect of business associates. There was a tacit acceptance of each other as men, equal in strength and humility.

And each had the same self-searching thought about the other: "How could I ever have doubted him?"

It seemed strange to them all, that next afternoon, to see Roger Haylow presiding at a meeting at which his father was an invited guest. The memo summoning them to the two o'clock session had been received with varying emotions. For the first time, Dick Cabot felt a twinge of apprehension, a vague threat to his own position implicit in this new indication of leadership. Noting Joe Haylow's name as one of those carboned on the memo and seeing that the meeting was to take place in Roger's office, even Cabot's pedestrian mind grasped the implication. Unbriefed on the subject, Sid Sommers instinctively felt that something important had happened, and promptly canceled his afternoon appointments to be present. Mike was the least surprised, having been present the evening before when Roger showed his quiet, firm determination. Of them all, only Deland was acutely alarmed. He read into the summons the first concrete threat to his own standing. For a few seconds he panicked. He knew that Roger would never presume to call a meeting in this way unless he already had Joe Haylow's approval of the procedure. It must mean that Haylow already was smoothing the way for a takeover by his son, giving his implied acceptance of Roger's ability to direct the corporation. The announced subject of the meeting at the top of the memo, "Re: Elmarie Acquisition" was as good as an announcement that Roger had done the impossible, that he had somehow succeeded in bringing Frank Boswell around through the rational, softspoken methods he'd recommended. Brad knew he had to play it cool. But his mind was seething with rage, already planning counterattack.

Deland was the last to arrive at the meeting. Roger was seated at his red parson's table desk, the other men grouped around him. There was a chair between Cabot and Mike Warner and Brad took it with an easy apology for being delayed.

Simply and quickly, Roger explained the events of the evening before.

"Frank Boswell has agreed not to block the sale of Elmarie," he said. "How this was accomplished is not particularly important, except that I would like to thank Bridget Manning and Mike Warner for their help. In particular, Mike, since he introduced another voice into the discussion, his cosmetics buyer, Terry White. White turned out to be very helpful, and his future role in this division should be seriously considered."

"Very good news, young man," Cabot said pompously. "We all knew that sooner or later Boswell would have to come around. Good that we've trained a group of our younger executives to perform so capably."

You dumb, sanctimonious old bore, Brad thought. Don't be simple-minded enough to think you can put this in the light of a team effort. You're not going to kid Joe Haylow that you represent senior management which fully expected that the job would be carried out with the approval of older and wiser heads.

Roger's amused smile was evidence that he recognized Cabot's obvious ploy. But he acknowledged it gracefully.

"Thanks, Dick," he said. "Your compliments are much appreciated."

Smart bastard, Deland thought. He knows that Haylow doesn't believe that supervisory crap. This was a one-man show and Joe knows it. Cabot's just made himself look like a condescending jerk, and Roger has taken advantage of it. Score one for Junior.

"The proposal has long since been spelled out and more or less agreed to in the earlier meetings between Mr. Marina and the Chairman," Roger went on. "Now, of course, it will go into the negotiating stage with the lawyers and you, Brad. When the details are ironed out, we'll make the public announcement. I don't anticipate any government objection, but of course that will have to be carefully checked. Do you see any problem, Brad?"

"I would doubt that there'd be trouble," Deland answered. "This acquisition is out of the retail area, the only one that could give us any monopolistic jitters. Should be acceptable to the SEC and all the other boys in Washington if we handle it right. We have our contacts in the Capital, you know."

"Fine," Roger said. "Then aside from the details of the audit and the integration of Elmarie accounting and warehousing facilities into our own setup, the major problem we face at the moment is top management. Mr. Marina wishes to retire, though I'm sure he would be available to us on some sort of consultant basis if we desire it, and Frank Boswell has made his position clear. He does not wish to be associated with The Haylow Corporation, and on this matter I don't think he can be talked into changing his mind. In fact, I don't think we should even try. A man with this much inbred resentment of the organization might, even involuntarily, fail to act in the best interests of the company. Therefore, gentlemen, we will need to quickly find a divisional President for Elmarie and announce his appointment at the same time we release the news of the acquisition."

During Roger's remarks, Joe Haylow had sat quietly by, obviously well satisfied with his son's handling of the meeting. Now he spoke.

"I would like you to know, gentlemen, that I think an interesting lesson is to be learned from this whole deal. We are living in a new world, a world of people-to-people communication. It's something that the young know about and understand in a way that the previous generation does not. I admit that in our previous meeting, when Roger suggested reason and humility instead of threats and muscle, I had some doubts. I thought he was being overly idealistic, even naïve. I thought he was trying to apply to business the same hatred of force that the young evidence in peace protests and flower power. Frankly, I was surprised when he called me late last night to tell me that with Boswell reason had prevailed. I stayed awake a long time thinking about what all this meant. How it may change, in some measure, all future dealings of this company. And I reaffirmed several long-held beliefs. The most important is that honesty is not synonymous with weakness. Strength can live with sincerity. Success and forthrightness do make happy bedfellows.

"The surprising outcome of a young man's uncomplicated, undevious approach to a problem has given me a lot to chew

over in my own mind. Business is tough. That doesn't change
But there is a kind of single-minded, fair toughness that i
quite different from the old dog-eat-dog attitude of some o
us who came into the picture at an earlier time. The world i
changing. And the world is people, young people and peopl
who think young. I'm not saying that the world will be rule
by the lazy, the unwashed, the hippies. We're not going t
run Haylow with the attitude of guitar-strumming seekers
and-yearners. But if we're smart, we'll know that inherent in
tegrity is sometimes as effective as reliance on experience
We don't dress or live or amuse ourselves as we did twenty
five years ago. Why should we think we can run our busines
the way we did before the Second World War?"

Haylow turned to Roger, apologetically. "Sorry to mak
such a long speech in the middle of your meeting. But thi
seemed a good time to expose our executives to a new way o
thinking. Big business has gotten a bad name with the young
We're supposed to be corrupt, hardhearted, killers of indi
viduality. The Establishment. This is why we have troubl
recruiting bright young men and women into the world o
commerce. Every man, even in this day and age, has a yearn
ing for success and accomplishment. But more and more o
them are not willing to buy it at the expense of a humane way
of life.

"It's too bad, Roger," Haylow went on, "that the youn
people of this world can't know how the acquisition of El
marie was really made—by two intelligent men accepting eacl
other's point of view with rationality and consideration fo
others. But that's something that can't be told. However, thi
rambling dissertation of mine is not entirely off the immedi
ate subject you were about to discuss when I interrupted
namely the appointment of a divisional President for El
marie. From the little I've heard, I think some of you are
favorably impressed with Terry White. Do you think he coul
run the company for us?"

"I think he's an excellent possibility," Roger answered. "Of course, he is very young for such a responsible job, but I think that may not be bad, particularly in view of the thoughts you just expressed about the communication of which young people are capable. Certainly he knows more about the cosmetics industry than anyone within Haylow. And like you, sir, I am a big advocate of promotion from within the company. Unfortunately, I don't know him well, but I did like the way he handled himself last night. It seems to me that Mike Warner is the best person in this room to give an opinion of White's potential."

Mike looked thoughtful. "I can't deny that it would be a fairly audacious move to put anyone with as little administrative experience as Terry into such an important spot," he said. "But I think he could handle it. He's done a great job in the store. His departmental figures are among the best and he's had a lot of responsibility which he's handled well. We leave him very much alone and he shows good judgment. To tell you the truth, I'd hate to lose him from Star because I think he'd have a good future in retailing. But I wouldn't stand in his way if this opportunity were offered. And, as I said, I believe he's got the brains and the dedication to succeed."

Cabot cleared his throat. "It strikes me as an excellent thought," he said. "In line with the interesting observations made by the Chairman and with the recommendations of Mike, I believe we should use this as unmistakable evidence of our faith in young people. Needless to say, we should have to surround the boy with experienced executives who can give him sound business guidance, but I would be only too happy to work along with young White to help him master the intricacies of administration."

"What do you think, Sid?" Roger asked.

"Well, of course, I've never met him," Sommers answered, "but it'd be a very fine piece of public relations for Haylow.

As Joe says, might even convince some of the college kids that one of their own has made a dent in the solid gold Cadillac. But the main thing is, if you and Mike and Dick are all for it, I figure the lad has ability as well as news value, and that's the name of the game when you're dealing with a multimillion-dollar proposition."

Roger turned to Deland. "Brad?"

"I am unalterably opposed to such a choice." Deland's voice was icy. "Everything the Chairman has said about the young is very wise and very true, but, like all pertinent observations, should be kept within the context of sound business decisions. We are, as Sid has pointed out, dealing with millions of dollars, not only in purchase price but in future volume and profit. The administration of such an important enterprise certainly cannot be entrusted to an individual as unproven and presumably unknown as Terry White. With deference to Mike, there is a great difference between being a successful buyer and the President of a large cosmetics company. Excellent performance in one area does not qualify this young man for such vast responsibility. If you will forgive me, Roger, and you too, Dick, I have the definite impression that both of you are making recommendations based on an emotional rather than a practical point of view. Why should we do this thing the hard way when we can go out and hire a well-known name in the industry, with greater confidence that he knows what he's doing and will require less precious supervisory time from our top executives? With all due respect to this group, I am impelled to repeat that I find the suggestion nearly ludicrous!"

Brad's vehement stand caught the men off guard. There was no rational argument against Brad's views. Yet it was surprising that he would take such a strong position against something which had the virtual endorsement of the Chairman. He's up to something, Sid Sommers thought. Could be he's just trying to make Roger look like an impractical crusader, or show up Cabot as the kind of ass-kissing yes-man that Joe Haylow despises. But I've got a hunch there's more to it than that, Sommers reflected. Maybe he's putting out a feeler to see just how much weight he carries. Or maybe he's setting up a situation that could have been a long time in the planning. Like the rest, Sid waited for Joe Haylow's decision.

"You make some very good points, Brad," Haylow said. "But we took a gamble on Roger's way of getting to Boswell and it worked. No reason not to go along with him now, especially since the others think it's worth a try. We can't lose much. Elmarie could roll along on its own momentum for years, no matter who was its acting head. Let's give it a chance. As Sid says, it'll be good public relations. If our hunch is right, we'll be heroes. And if we see, in a few months, that we've made a wrong choice we can make a change. Even if that happens, it won't do White anything but good to have a divisional President's title at his age. From there he operates on a different plateau. If he left us, he could pick his next spot in the industry. I'm not dismissing your very clear exposition of the pitfalls, Brad, but I think we're big enough to take a flyer that has comparatively little risk involved. Anything else, Roger?"

"I guess that's about it for now," Roger said, keeping his tone matter-of-fact. "We all have our work to do from here on in. But I do think that in view of Brad's reservations you should have a talk with Terry White before the final decision is made. In any case, the appointment would come from you."

"Good," Haylow said, rising from his seat. Then he hesitated, smiling. "Sorry, Roger, you are chairing this meeting. Is the meeting adjourned, Mr. Chairman?"

"Meeting adjourned, Mr. Chairman," Roger said, returning his smile.

10 ❧

In the tiny basement cubicle allotted to him as buyer of cosmetics for Star Stores, Terry White almost fainted when he answered his telephone and heard the voice on the other end say, "Mr. White? This is Joseph Haylow. Could you see me in my office at two o'clock this afternoon?"

Terry took a deep breath. "Of course, sir."

"Good," Haylow said. "You're sure it won't interfere with any of your other appointments?"

Terry smiled to himself. This was this unfailing courtesy for which Joe Haylow was famous. As though he was asking for a favor, rather than issuing a command. And as though any Haylow employee would dream of telling the Chairman that an appointment was inconvenient.

"No, sir," White answered. "Two o'clock is fine."

"Thank you," Haylow said. "Look forward to meeting you, young man."

Not half as much as I'm looking forward to meeting you, Terry thought, putting down the phone. This has got to be something really big. He recalled in vivid detail every nuance of the dinner party at Bridget's. He knew he had handled himself well, in a quiet, underplayed way. He felt that Roger Haylow and Mike Warner had been impressed, and he knew that with the Elmarie deal virtually locked up, they'd waste no time setting up an organization ready to move in as soon as the cosmetics company was under Haylow control.

Terry admired the smooth, confident, efficient teamwork of the men at the top. They must have had an early morning meeting, he reasoned, to discuss the outcome of the dinner and plan the take-over of Elmarie with virtually no interruption to business. And the swiftness with which all of them, including Joe Haylow, had moved was more than a hopeful signal that their plans included Terry White.

Quickly he checked what he was wearing that morning. He knew that the well-cut gray suit was conservative, yet modish enough, to pass inspection by the Chairman. But knowing Haylow's preoccupation with the "fashion image" of his employees, Terry decided that the new brown and white striped shirt he'd bought last week would look better than the blue one he was wearing. He decided to dash home at lunchtime and change. Maybe he could work in a quick appointment at the barber, too, just for a fast trim. He reconsidered that. He'd dash up to the apartment, have a sandwich and change his clothes, even try to relax for a few minutes before his two o'clock date.

Letting himself into the foyer of the brownstone apartment he shared with Peter Johnson, Terry was surprised to hear voices in the living room. Obviously, Peter's "friend" was visiting early today. Terry had never met "Dick Carswell." All he knew about him was Peter's mocking description of the naïve little man who was so obviously enraptured by his handsome roommate. Terry had accepted, with indifference, Peter's decision that it would be better if "Carswell" felt entirely secure in his anonymity.

"He's a nervous little jerk," Peter had said callously. "This is his first time at this kind of thing and he's scared shitless that somebody will find out. Hell, I don't even know exactly what his job is. And I couldn't care less, just so he keeps paying off for the pleasure of my company."

Terry agreed. It had been a long time since he had felt any emotion for Peter. The apartment-sharing now was a matter of economy and the private lives of the two young men had drifted far apart. It was easy enough for Terry to stay out on the few evenings "Carswell" was free to be with Peter. And until today Terry had had no occasion to come to the apartment at midday. He would not have done so now had it not been for the importance of his two o'clock date with Haylow. What's more, it was unusual for Peter to be at home at this hour. Terry knew that the regular routine with "Carswell" was a movie first, then a return to the apartment.

At the doorway of the living room, Terry hesitated. For a moment he considered sneaking into the bedroom to change his clothes and creeping out. Perhaps the other two would not even know he'd been there. Then he thought, the hell with it. It's my apartment too. What's more, he was curious about Peter's unknown "patron."

Confidently, he walked into the living room.

"Hi!" he said. "Just came home to make a quick change of clothes because I have an important appoint—" Speechless, he stopped in mid-word. From his perusals of the Haylow annual reports which contained photographs of the company's chief executives, he knew he was looking directly into the distressed face of Haylow's President, Dick Cabot. Had the little man in the wing chair been Joe Haylow himself, Terry could not have been more startled.

Peter rose gracefully from the opposite chair.

"Well, surprise," he said. "Didn't expect you at this hour, Terry. This is Dick Carswell. Mr. Carswell, my roommate, Terry White."

Cabot stood up, nervously extending his small hand.

"Glad to meet you, Mr. White."

"How do you do, Mr., uh, Carswell," Terry answered. He hoped that Cabot had not noticed his hesitation. He assumed that the little man's obvious agitation was simply caused by the presence of a third, unwelcome party. Had Terry known that a good part of Dick's morning had been spent discussing him, he would have been even more appalled than Cabot. Even without this knowledge, the discovery that the mysterious Mr. Carswell was really Haylow's President was an incredible shock. In those first moments, Terry's mind was incapable of grasping the possible implications for good or bad. He had only one instinct: escape. And the sooner the better.

"Excuse me," Terry said, "have to run and change. Nice to have met you, Mr. Carswell. See you later, Peter."

In the bedroom, Terry's hands were shaking as he tried to make a knot in his new tie. Jesus, he thought, of all the guys in the world for Peter to get mixed up with! No wonder "Mr. Carswell" was so anxious to preserve his secrecy. Joe Haylow would kick Cabot out on his ass if he found out what had been going on. Terry's mind was spinning. With the El-marie deal coming up, Cabot was sure to find out, fast, who Terry White was. Or did he already know? With this connection would he find a way to queer the deal for Terry? Even in this moment of concern, he was amused at his own apt choice of words. Queer is the word, all right, he thought. Who'd have thought it of old Dicky-the-devout?

While he dressed, Terry tried to figure out what to do. In the end, the wisest course seemed to be to do nothing. Cabot might even be an ally, in the hope of Terry's keeping his mouth shut. Cabot would know that Terry's silence was a favor. He'd feel obligated to make that favor pay off.

Suddenly, Terry saw the whole encounter as a stroke of good fortune for himself. All he had to do was let Cabot sweat out the knowledge that his lover's roommate could blow the whistle on him any time he chose. If Joe Haylow was going to offer Terry the big job in Elmarie, Dick Cabot would be the last one to present any obstacles.

Almost jauntily, Terry let himself out of the apartment and

strolled toward the Haylow building, stopping en route for a sandwich and coffee. Promptly at two o'clock he announced himself to Joe Haylow's secretary and was immediately ushered into the Chairman's office.

Joe Haylow rose graciously from his chair and gripped Terry's hand firmly. The Chairman's alert eyes took in every carefully groomed aspect of the young man before him and Terry, with a rush of relief, could almost sense the first sign of approval.

"Please sit down," Joe said, indicating one of the chairs by the coffee table. "I'm glad to meet you at last. I've heard some mighty good things about you from Mr. Warner and from my son."

Terry smiled modestly. "Very kind of you, sir. And of them."

"Kindness has very little to do with it," Haylow said. "They are evaluating you on your present ability and, even more importantly, on your potential. It's obvious that you're a very likable young man, but that asset—valuable as it may be—is not the primary requirement for advancement in this company. I'm sure it's not news to you that you are being considered for an important spot in the Elmarie Company when we buy it. I presume you're interested?"

"Very much so, Mr. Haylow. I think it's a great acquisition and naturally I'd like to be part of it, because it's a business I know."

"Well, there you're one up on me," Joe Haylow said. "It's an industry I know very little about, this whole cosmetics thing. I've looked over the financial statements, of course, but all I know about the beauty business is what I see from the retail side. And of course that's a picture I like. Our cosmetics departments seem to be steady volume areas, keep increasing their figures and don't appear to have the high cost of operation that the ready-to-wear departments have. As a retailer, I like that whole set of circumstances. But if I'm going to be on the other side of the fence, I have a feeling that it's going to cost me a lot of money to do business."

"Yes, sir," Terry agreed. "You have a right to feel that way. It's a terrific industry. Just about recession-proof, because even when times are bad a woman who can't afford to buy herself a new dress or a fur coat can always find a few dollars for a new lipstick or a jar of face cream. It's a cliché, Mr. Haylow, but in my field we say we're selling 'hope in a bottle' —and that's just about what it is. Not that cosmetics aren't good. The industry has high standards of self regulation in terms of purity of product and reasonable effectiveness. And where they don't police themselves, the government sets standards to make sure that what they're selling is nonharmful in its content and nondeceptive in its claims. But the main thing is what a woman *thinks* is happening when she looks in the mirror. And if she thinks she looks better, she does look better."

Haylow was a good listener. "You make quite a case for your business," he said. "I like a man who believes in what he's doing. But let's get back to the cost of supporting these lofty ideals. How does it work from the cosmetics manufacturer's point of view?"

"Frankly," Terry said, "I think the manufacturers have been dopes. With one or two exceptions, every cosmetics firm pays through the nose for the privilege of doing business in the stores. Not many people realize this outside the industry, Mr. Haylow, but the profit on cosmetics—to the guy who makes them—is unbelievably low because his cost of doing business is so high. May I explain that?"

"Please do."

"Well," Terry said, getting wound up in his subject, "let's take Star Stores and the way we do business with our cosmetics accounts. It's typical of practically every important store and every manufacturer, with one or two exceptions. We buy at wholesale—forty percent less than the retail price.

226

That's standard. Then we require the manufacturer to pay all or part of the salary of the girl in the store who sells his line. The amount he pays depends upon his volume. If he's really big, he may be paying for two or three girls, which makes him happy because he gets that much more space in the department. He also pays a portion—or sometimes the entire cost—of any newspaper advertising or mailings we do about his products. He provides samples and gifts of his merchandise, free, for our customers. He sends special 'beauty experts' into the store for a week or two at a time to give special demonstrations. If he wants his departmental area to look super-special, he pays for the decoration. He even has his own salesman come into the store to take inventory for us. And then, as if this were not enough, he takes back anything the store decides it can't sell."

Joe Haylow was fascinated. "You mean, as a buyer, you can return as much of the inventory as you want?"

"Right. You see, cosmetics have regulated price controls. We're not allowed to reduce the prices. So, if we can't take mark-downs, the manufacturers have to take back the goods and give us full credit."

Haylow shook his head in wonderment. "I understand why you say the manufacturers are dopes. And on top of this, they have to run their own organizations, produce their products, and spend heavily on their magazine and television advertising to keep up the demand."

"Exactly," Terry agreed. "So you see, Mr. Haylow, why cosmetics is such a great area for retailers. All we give, really, is four walls in which we graciously allow the cosmetics manufacturers to sell their goods."

"Nobody would believe it!" Joe Haylow said. "How did this all happen?"

"Good old healthy competition," Terry answered. "Manufacturer A offers certain assistance to a good account, so Manufacturer B has to top him, and Manufacturer C has to come up with even more and eventually it snowballs until all the firms are trying to be the biggest Santa Claus of all—while the retailer sits back and lets them make every day like Christmas!"

The Chairman was visibly impressed. And visibly disturbed.

"With this enormous burden of expense the manufacturer carries," he said, "what are the chances of making money?"

"There are quite a few enormously rich cosmetics tycoons, Mr. Haylow. And they're rich because of several things. Know-how. They produce products women want. Cost control. They watch the cost of making their stuff. Volume. A lot of costs—like salesgirls and department space—are fixed costs. The more you sell, the less it costs you. The bigger you are, the more your percentages drop, even if the dollars you spend in advertising and promotion increase. Frankly, that's why I'm glad we're buying one of the pretty big companies. Run carefully, with Haylow facilities behind it, Elmarie can double its business in two years, without adding anything like the proportionate cost. In the cosmetics business today, the little guy can't make it. There's no way he can compete for the customer's dollar."

For a moment the two men remained silent. Terry knew he had run a risk telling Haylow the facts that few people—probably no one in the Haylow organization—knew about the problems of the cosmetics industry. There was a possibility that hearing all this might even make the Chairman change his mind about the desirability of buying Elmarie, and Terry's big chance would go down the drain, washed out by his own honesty. But sooner or later, Haylow would come face to face with these facts, and Terry sensed that his direct recital of the problems would elicit admiration from this bright, tough, powerful man who never in his life had been afraid to take on a challenge. Besides, Terry knew, Elmarie was one of those projects that had eluded Joe for so long that he would take unusual chances for the sheer satisfaction of winning a hard-fought battle.

"What's considered a good profit in this business?" Haylow asked.

"Any profit is good. Ten percent after taxes is sensational. Five percent probably is realistic."

Terry could almost see the arithmetic going on in Joe Haylow's head. Despite the insanity of its methods—an insanity self-inflicted by the cosmetics manufacturers themselves— the beauty business was a solid one. A man who could build a general store into a retail empire would be undaunted by problems as relatively insignificant as these. Terry relaxed. Elmarie was in the bag. Now, he thought, what about me?

As though he were reading Terry's mind, the Chairman spoke.

"There's very little doubt that you know how this business works. Frankly, the question is, could you run it for us? As everybody knows, I'm all for young blood, Mr. White, but yours is very young indeed. I will not lie to you. Your youth and, consequently, your limited business experience has given some of our executives pause. I will be quite candid and say that among the executive committee there is a faction that would feel more comfortable with an older, more seasoned operating head for this division. As you know, Mr. Warner thinks highly of you. So much so that he is willing to let us take you away from the fine job you're doing at Star. Roger Haylow was extremely impressed with your performance at Miss Manning's dinner. As for the other members—Mr. Sommers, Mr. Deland, and Mr. Cabot—I don't think any of them has had the opportunity to meet or talk with you. I am sure they will all want to do so before any final decision is made."

Terry could not help but be inwardly amused. He did not know how his interview with Sommers or Deland would go, but in the meeting with Cabot, Terry would hold all the cards.

"There's nothing I can do about my age, Mr. Haylow," Terry said. "That's a disease that only time can cure. But I love this business and I think I understand it. With the help of the organization, I believe I could run it in a way that would satisfy both the executives and the stockholders. I've had no experience on the manufacturing end, but my retail knowledge through Star could be an advantage that many other candidates from the industry side might not enjoy."

Haylow nodded agreement. "Tell me a little something about yourself," he said conversationally. "Are you married?"

"No, sir. To be honest with you, Mr. Haylow, on a buyer's salary, I can't afford a wife. And I've watched too many of my friends try to make a go of a marriage where both of them work. Most of those fifty-fifty arrangements end up in a divorce. I think the man's role is to be the provider and until I can take on that responsibility, I guess I'll just have to wait. Maybe that strikes you as a little old-fashioned, sir, but that's the way I was brought up."

Haylow smiled. "Some of these 'old-fashioned' principles still seem to make sense to me, too. So you live alone? Or do you have family here?"

"No, my family is in Sandusky, Ohio. My mother and father live there. Dad has a little jewelry store in town. I worked there summers when I was in high school. I think he was a little disappointed that I didn't stay there and eventually take over. I'm an only child, so I guess that even though it isn't much of a business, he wanted me to keep it going. I liked retailing—even in that one-horse town—but like most kids I wanted to be on my own, in every way."

"So you came to New York."

"Yes, sir. A friend of mine—a guy I went to school with—was dead set on being an actor so we decided to try the big town. We darned near starved to death the first year or so, but then I got my job at Star and things have been better."

"What about your friend?"

"It hasn't gone too well for him. He gets a few bit parts now and then. A TV commercial once in a while. But he's still convinced he's going to make it. And I sure hope he does. He's a nice guy. We share a walk-up in the sixties. I could afford my own place now, but, well, you know, Mr. Haylow, you hate to run out on somebody you've known so long."

Joe found himself warming to this sincere young man. There's good stuff in him, Haylow thought. Loyalty and compassion. Along with ambition and guts. A good, middle-class background, and not ashamed to admit it.

"Your parents must be proud of you. Do you see them often?"

"Only a couple of times a year," Terry said. "I spend part of my vacations at home, but there isn't anything there for me anymore, except Mom and Dad. Most of the kids I went to school with are married and we don't have much in common. I don't think I'd ever go back if it wasn't for the family. You know, it's funny, Mr. Haylow, but as you get a little older the roles of parents and child are almost reversed. I feel responsible for them and I worry about them a lot. Fortunately they can take care of themselves. Financially, I mean. But they really just live for me and it's kind of an emotional burden. It isn't easy to be the only one. I often wish I had brothers and sisters so they'd have other people to think about. I mean, Mom would just love to be a grandmother. But since all she has is an unmarried son, her whole concentration is on me. And I guess I have some of that nutty guilt thing about leaving them alone."

"You sound like a good son," Haylow said.

"Not the best, I'm sure. But I try. I really like them a lot."

The conversation had pleased Haylow. As hard-shelled as he was about business, there was a wide streak of the patriarch in him. His employees were part of his "family," although with no blood ties to bind him, he could "disinherit" any one

231

of them if they turned out to be recalcitrant children. This young Terry White promised to be "a good child."

Haylow rose, signaling the end of the interview. Terry stood, waiting.

"I've enjoyed our talk very much, Terry. We'll see what happens. Naturally, everything you know about Elmarie is strictly confidential until the deal is finalized. You do realize that?"

Terry nodded. "Of course, Mr. Haylow."

"Any personal commitment at this point would be premature," Joe said, "but I appreciate your enlightening me about the cosmetics business and I am very impressed with your sensible and knowledgeable approach to it. I think you can be assured that the executive committee will give very serious thought to the role you might play in Elmarie."

"I don't know how to thank you, Mr. Haylow. It's been a great privilege, sir."

Haylow waved off his thanks. "Just don't send me a bill for the lesson," he said. "So far, it's I who am in your debt."

As Terry departed, Joe buzzed Miss Watson on the intercom.

"Please come in and bring your book," he said.

In a moment, Miss Watson appeared with her stenographic pad. She looked so surprised that Joe laughed. "This is probably the first memo you haven't taken off the dictating machine, isn't it, Miss Watson?"

"Yes, Mr. Haylow, it is."

"Just don't want you to get too set in your ways," he said. "All right. Memo to Mr. Roger Haylow, carbons to Cabot, Deland, Warner, and Sommers. 'I have just had a very interesting interview with Terry White. He strikes me as good material for the position under discussion. Believe we should make arrangements for his replacement at Star so that he can move into new spot as soon as deal is complete. Unless any of you has valid objection, suggest Roger work out terms with White. No contract. Salary based on present compensation can be favorable to all parties.' That's all, Miss Watson. See that it goes out right away. And mark it 'confidential.' "

Roger will be pleased, Joe thought. Brad Deland will be shook up. It's one of the few times I've ever overruled him. Let's hope my son and I are right.

"Shook up" was an understatement for what Brad Deland felt when he read the terse but obviously definitive memo from the Chairman. His violent objections about the choice of Terry White, expressed in the earlier meeting, were, of course, simply a testing of his managerial muscle. The actual choice of a divisional President for Elmarie was of no importance to Brad. What counted was whether his opinion still carried the greatest weight with Joe Haylow. Obviously, now it did not. Equally obvious was the fact that some overnight change had taken place in Roger Haylow. And with it had come the unmistakable signs that the Chairman was preparing, with pleasure, to delegate full authority to his younger son. Roger's success in pulling off the Elmarie acquisition was the first step. Now the acceptance of his candidate, over Deland's vehement protests, was a clear indication of Joe Haylow's new turn of mind.

Like a general reviewing his strategy, Brad mentally ticked off his allies and his enemies. In sheer weight of numbers, Roger had all the advantages. Mike Warner, Bridget, and Sid Sommers were unquestionably pro-family. Cabot was little more than a cipher on the corporate scorecard. Yet, figurehead or not, he still held the Presidential title and was the only one of the business team who might be used to advantage. Not to be discounted, of course, was Brad's "secret weapon," Marjorie Haylow, the one "outsider" who could trigger an explosion in the Haylow organization if the need finally arose.

Disturbed by the new turn of events and annoyed that he

could not yet figure out the way to thwart Roger's rapid progress, Brad dialed Cabot's extension.

"Had time to read Joe's memo about this White kid?" he asked when Cabot came on the wire.

Cabot's voice sounded unusually strained. "Yes, I have. Why?"

"What the hell do you mean, 'Why?'" Brad almost shouted. "Because this is a damned fool move, that's why! I know you went along with the idea when it was brought up in the meeting, Dick, but *I* didn't, and I still don't. Putting an inexperienced kid into a job like that is asking for trouble. It's worse than naïve, it's downright stupid. Listen, Dick, you and I are the realistic businessmen in this outfit. We've got to stop Joe from taking a million-dollar gamble that's based on some cockamamie idealistic theories about the vigor of youth."

Cabot hesitated. "I don't know how we could do that, Brad. You know the Chairman as well as I do. When he makes up his mind, it takes some powerful piece of evidence to change it. Anyway," Cabot added mildly, "I don't see why you're so sure this is a disaster. For all we know, young White may be a brilliant chap. Perhaps just what we need."

Brad struggled to control his exasperation. How in Christ's name can this sonofabitch be so dumb? Everybody knew that Cabot was limited, but for him to fail to grasp the implications of this decision was almost impossible to believe.

Carefully, quietly, Brad tried to make his point. "Dick, I don't think you've had time to digest the meaning of this," he said. "You're being threatened, man, and you'd better realize it fast. The Chairmanship is about to be stolen right out from under you. The Chairman is going along with Roger every step of the way. If his confidence in Roger keeps growing, he'll dump you right on your fifty-two-year-old ass."

Brad waited, letting the significance of this get through to Cabot. Then he went on, gently pressing the point. "It can even go beyond that," he continued. "If Roger is named Chairman, he'll want a young President. Somebody like Mike Warner, probably. For myself," Brad said smoothly, "I'm not all that concerned. After all, I'm not in line for Haylow's job. You are. As the senior members of the executive committee, I think we'd better try to talk some sense into Joe. Convince him that Roger is well intentioned but carried away. We'll show him the numbers he's playing with, make him take a good, hard look at the bottom line. Joe's a businessman first and foremost, but if you and I don't show him what a mistake this is, he will go ahead and let Roger have his way. We're the over-fifty age group, Dick; the ones Joe Haylow has got to count on to show unemotional judgment in the interest of the company."

Brad could almost feel Cabot's confusion. It was true that he had not really believed that the Chairman's decision was anything more significant than the kind of bold, unorthodox move for which Joe Haylow was famous. He had not literally related it to Roger's rise or his own diminution of power. The Chairman's memo had unnerved him. But only because it had come so quickly on the heels of today's disclosure. Cabot knew that if he had not already done so, Terry White would soon realize that the "Mr. Carswell" who was Peter Johnson's friend was, in fact, the President of Haylow. The thought of it terrified him more than the prospect of Roger's ascension. His only hope was to win Terry's silence by supporting him for the job. Despite Brad's well-founded suggestions of what would happen if Roger continued to have his father's support, Dick Cabot knew that he had to take a stand somewhere between the devil and the deep blue sea. He was in no position to make waves about Terry's appointment. And he would simply have to hope that despite his new show of strength, Roger's youth would still keep him away from the Chairmanship for another thirteen years until Cabot's own retirement.

"I'm sorry, Brad," he said, "but I don't think I can do anything more at this point. I've already agreed that a young man in the Elmarie job could be a good thing for us. I can see no sensible basis for reversing my decision. Besides, I think you are reading more into this than actually exists. Roger is like a child. He's found a project that interests him, so he's looking very smart. But we were both in Florida, Brad. We know that Roger is unstable and Joe knows it too. I don't see this as the threat that you do. It's a momentary burst of enthusiasm. I should be greatly surprised if Joe Haylow mistook one successful deal as evidence of Roger's miraculous transformation."

Frantic with frustration, Brad struggled to sound conciliatory. "Perhaps you're right," he said, "but I do think we should talk it over a little more. What about lunch tomorrow?"

Dick looked at his calendar. At the noon hour he had penciled in "P. J. Bijou." Anyone looking at it would think it the name of his luncheon appointment for the next day. Only Dick knew that it meant "Peter Johnson, Bijou Theatre." He was looking forward to seeing a new Italian film with Peter and afterwards spending a few hours in the apartment. For a moment he wavered. It might be wise to placate Deland. On the other hand, it could be even smarter to stay clear of him in his obviously high-strung mood. Cabot decided the latter course was the better.

"Sorry, Brad," he said, "but there's something important I have to do tomorrow. It's, uh, almost impossible to break."

"After lunch, then?" Deland persisted.

Cabot, a poor liar at best, began to feel very nervous. As always, when he was upset, a small stammer crept into his speech.

"N-no, I don't think the afternoon will work either," he said. "I, uh, might not get back to the office until k-k-kind

236

of late in the day. But we'll talk some more later. Another time. I hope you don't mind."

"No, it's okay," Brad said. "We'll talk later."

Something's fishy, he thought. Cabot's jittery. He's overreacting. Dick's business responsibilities in the scheme of things were so trivial that Brad could not imagine his having any appointment so vital that it could not be broken or at least rearranged. Whatever Cabot had planned for tomorrow afternoon had to be very personally important.

Frowning, Deland methodically reviewed everything he knew about Cabot. A confirmed yes-man, an ineffectual figurehead whom Joe had accepted at the insistence of the bankers and tolerated for the sake of the stockholders. Brad was sure that Joe Haylow would welcome any excuse to replace him, but Cabot's pedestrian personality precluded any chance to legitimately remove him. He did nothing wrong. Because he did nothing. Resigned to his presence as a necessary evil, Joe was almost indifferent to him. And Brad, like the others, had shared that indifference until this moment. He could not account for the warning bell that Cabot's unusual resistance had set off in his head. But the alarm kept on ringing.

Idly, he remembered Miss Watson's gratuitous information about seeing Cabot at the movies at lunchtime. It was not possible that Dick's "unbreakable engagement" was to see a film. Yet the timing fitted. Or at least part of it did. The whole thing seemed ridiculous. But so farfetched that it might bear exploration.

Brad waited until the executive floor emptied that evening. Only a cleaning woman, idly dusting, was in Cabot's office when he walked in. Nodding pleasantly, he strolled to the desk and looked at the appointment book. The hours from twelve until four were marked out with a large X. Written across them, in Cabot's neat, spinsterish hand were the initials "P.J." followed by a dash and the single word "Bijou."

It made no sense. Who was "P.J."? And what did "Bijou" mean? The French word for "jewel"? For a moment, Brad toyed with the idea that P.J. was some woman for whom Dick meant to buy jewelry. It would be like him to construct a childish code as a private reminder of the appointment. Almost immediately he dismissed the thought. Dick Cabot buying jewelry for any woman but Mildred was an idea too incongruous to be considered. For that matter, the notion of Dick Cabot involved with another woman was ludicrous. It simply did not fit—the man did not have the imagination, not to mention the courage, for an affair.

And then it hit him. Noontime. Movies. Bijou. Of course. The Bijou was a movie house, well known for its avant-garde art films. In the reception room he found a copy of *Cue*. Running quickly through the movie listings, he found the Bijou. Its new film was announced as "a tender, convention-defying love story stronger than the obstacles of society." Interestingly, it opened tomorrow. And the first showing was at noon. It was a coincidence too absurd to be true, but too curious to be ignored.

Feeling ridiculously like a private eye in a TV series, Deland stationed himself in a luncheonette opposite the Bijou at one o'clock the next afternoon. Through the window, he had a clear view of the entrance. It was quiet now. Having checked the time of the film break, he lingered over his hamburger and coffee until the crowds began to come out at one-forty. He paid his check at the cashier and stood inside the restaurant, lighting a cigarette, watching the noontime movie-goers pouring out. He felt no particular surprise when he saw Dick Cabot among them. Cabot looked happy, excited, talking and gesturing animatedly to the tall, handsome young man who unquestionably was his companion.

Cabot and his companion turned east on Sixty-ninth Street, walking leisurely through the crowds of upper Madison Avenue shoppers. It was easy for Brad to keep them in view as he followed at a discreet distance. "Mutt and Jeff," he thought with amusement, watching Cabot's head bobbing along on a level with the taller man's shoulder. Near First Avenue, the pair turned into a brownstone house converted into apartments. Brad made sure they were safely inside before he entered the vestibule. There were ten mailbox slots, each with a name above it. Quickly Brad scanned the typed cards looking for a clue among the rows of unfamiliar names. Above the mailbox marked 3-A, he found it. The neatly lettered card bore two names: Peter Johnson and Terry White. With calm precision, Brad reread the other nine cards. Manowitz, Shapiro, John Kelly—none of the others were names he'd ever heard before. Only Terry White rang a bell. And so did the "P.J." on Cabot's calendar. They had to stand for Peter Johnson, obviously White's roommate. Things were beginning to mesh.

Letting himself out into the street, Brad was engrossed in the implications of this new development. Somehow Cabot was mixed up, directly or indirectly, with the fair-haired boy who was to be tapped for the Elmarie job. Which, of course, would explain Dick's unwillingness to protest his appointment. It would, if anything, account for his enthusiastic endorsement of White in the meeting.

Walking slowly down Third Avenue, Deland mentally double-checked his facts and his assumptions. Only some of the pieces of the jigsaw were in place. For one thing, having never met Terry White, Brad could not be sure whether he or Johnson was the man with Cabot. P.J. could be the cover for Cabot's meeting with White. There was only one way to make sure.

Unhesitatingly, he made for the Star Store on Fifth Avenue. A polite inquiry at the first cosmetics counter elicited the information that Mr. White's office was in the basement. "Right through those double doors, sir, and the first turn to your left," the salesgirl told him. He made his way through the basement aisle, cluttered with a welter of boxes and discarded display fixtures to a tiny room crammed with bottles and jars, file cabinets and stacks of inventory cards. Like all buyers' offices, it was an airless, overcrowded area, begrudgingly carved out of precious stock space. In it, behind a battered wooden desk, sat a nice-looking, thirtyish young man poring over a well-worn black notebook. Deland had never seen him before.

From the doorway, Brad spoke. "Mr. White?"

The young man looked up pleasantly. "Yes?"

"I'm Brad Deland from Haylow. We haven't met and I just thought I'd stop in and say hello."

Terry White was momentarily flustered.

"Mr. Deland? Very happy to know you, sir! Please come in. I'm afraid I can't offer you a very comfortable chair. Our offices are not exactly plush, as you can see."

Brad laughed. "That's one of the hazards of retailing, isn't it? Every precious inch a store can find is for selling or stowing away merchandise and to hell with where the poor buyer has to do his desk work. Oh, well," Brad said meaningfully, "maybe it won't always be this way for you."

Terry was quick to catch the subtle implication.

"I hope not, sir," he said.

Brad lit a cigarette. "I'm glad I found you in. I thought you'd probably be at lunch at this hour."

"I don't get out of the store much at this season," Terry said. "We're planning our Christmas season so I stay pretty close to the office."

"No time for Frank Boswell, even?"

"Oh, always time for him," Terry smiled. "But these days I think he's keeping company with more important Haylow employees."

"You were very helpful in that deal," Brad said. "In fact, I hear you had a long chat with the Chairman yesterday. You might be pleased to know that apparently you made a hell of a good impression."

"It's nice of you to tell me, Mr. Deland. I sure hope everything goes through okay with the acquisition. It's a good one for the company."

Smart kid, Deland thought. No mention of himself.

"Well," Brad said, getting to his feet, "I won't take up any more of your time. To tell you the truth, since so many of our officers have met you, I didn't want to be the last. I guess the only member of the executive team who still hasn't talked with you is our President, Dick Cabot, right? We'll have to set that up soon."

"I'd like that very much," Terry said evenly. "Everyone has been just great. I think Mr. Haylow is terrific. So's Mr. Roger Haylow and Miss Manning. And, of course, Mr. Warner is the best boss anybody could have. I consider myself very fortunate to be part of this company, Mr. Deland."

They shook hands. "As we used to say in the goddamn Navy, it's nice to have you aboard," Brad answered. "Speaking of which, were you in the service?"

"No, sir. Got a bum knee from football in high school."

"It's what you'd call a lucky break, huh? Sorry about that. It's really not up to my usual low level of humor. Anyway, Terry, it was good to meet you. We'll get together soon again."

Making his way back to the office, Brad thought, Well, one thing is sure. The man with Cabot was P.J., White's buddy. And now that I've got that pertinent little piece of information, what in hell do I do with it?

11

By early November, Joe Haylow had come as close to a feeling of contentment as it was possible for a man of his taut-wire nature to achieve. Not that he worked less. Rather, a soothing sense of well-being filled him with what he thought of as an "earthly peace." Roger's new dedication to the business was Joe's greatest new joy. Since the start of the Elmarie deal—now continuing slowly toward completion in the usual time-consuming way of acquisitions—Roger had shown anything but animosity toward his father. On the contrary, there was a new, unspoken understanding that brought Roger more often to Farmville. Sometimes he came for the weekend with Bridget, a fact that delighted Pat Haylow who, despite Joe's teasing, still entertained wistful thoughts of Bridget as a second daughter-in-law.

Unofficially, Terry White had been told of his selection as Elmarie's chief officer to take effect when the deal was completed. No announcement could be made until the final papers were signed, but Terry's assistant already was being trained to take over as Star's cosmetic buyer. To Joe's surprise, there had been no further protest from Deland. If he still opposed the choice of White he apparently had accepted it with a calmness that Joe had not expected. He had been prepared for Brad's further arguments, knowing that Deland was unaccustomed to being overruled. Haylow was thankful for this lack of resistance. At the same time, he was too shrewd not to be made uneasy by it. On the surface, Brad was the same decisive, superefficient company officer he'd always been, but Joe could almost sense a new and even more ruthless attitude in Brad as he went about solving the complicated financial problems of the company. Haylow couldn't put his finger on the problem, but the uncomfortable feeling that Deland was "buying time" persisted. He tried to dismiss it as a figment of his imagination, but the specter of Deland as a troublemaker continued to be the only cloud in these peaceful days.

That was not quite accurate. One other wisp of darkness hovered over the grateful head of the Chairman: the extraordinary behavior of his beloved Marjorie. Since their triumphant evangelical tour of the South earlier in the year, Haylow had felt considerably less alarmed about Elvis Mallory as a threat to Woodward. Even Jackson had conceded that Woodward had learned a great deal from these last months of conducting well-attended "Pray-Ins" across the country. He had gained new confidence with every successful meeting, new assurance with each flattering interview that appeared in the newspapers. Since spring, Jackson had deliberately stood back and let Woodward take the full brunt of public scutiny. And he had gone so far as to tell Joe that Woodward had done well. Jimmy was still not prepared to believe fully in Woodward's qualities of leadership for the world-wide church but he was, to Joe's satisfaction, far more confident of Woodward's potential than he had been. At the moment, this "holding action" was all that Joe Haylow hoped for. He was supremely confident that Woodward would continue to grow up to the job as Jackson's heir.

Only one thing seemed to stand in the way of that progress —Marjorie. Outwardly, she seemed as serene and gay as ever. Never had she looked more radiantly alive. But Woodward had confided to his mother that all was not well with his

The Rich and the Righteous

marriage. It had been a difficult—nearly impossible—thing for
the young minister to discuss, and only desperation enabled
him to tell Pat of his marital problems. Yet it was to her,
more as another woman than as his mother, that he finally
turned for advice. Since his return from the South, more than
seven months ago, Woodward told Pat, he and Marjorie had
not "lived together as man and wife."

Pat's distress, as Woodward haltingly made his disclosure,
was hidden behind an air of calm concern and sympathy. She
knew how difficult it was for her son to speak of such an incredible thing. She was grateful that he felt able to come to
her and she questioned him gently, the two of them sitting
quietly in the living room of the big Haylow house in Farmville.

"Does Marjorie give you any reason?" she asked.

Woodward, keeping his gaze on the horizon, shook his
head despairingly. "None that makes any sense," he said.
"She's been as wonderful as ever in every other way. Warm,
considerate, tender to me and the children. Almost more
than she was before. All she says is that she loves me as deeply
as ever, but in a different way, a nonphysical way. She says she
never again can make love to me, Mother. Never again."

Recounting the story to Joe later, Pat allowed herself the
luxury of the tears she kept hidden from Woodward.

"He told me that Marjorie had offered to divorce him. Of
course he refused. He loves her deeply and he believes that
she still loves him. She says she wants to stay with Woodward
and the children, but she accepts the fact that he is not a
celibate priest and she cannot hope that he will be able to
live under the same roof with his wife without wanting to go
to bed with her. She gives him no real explanation, Joe, except that she has lost all physical desires. Woodward doesn't
believe that, of course. He thinks she's going through some
kind of temporary mental illness."

"So do I," Joe said. "How old is Marjorie?"

"Thirty-five."

"Could she be having change of life?"

"I suppose it's possible," Pat said, "although it's unusually early. I don't think it's that, really. But it could be a number of other things."

"Such as?"

"Well, darling, she could be temporarily disturbed, as Woodward wants to believe. Or, perhaps, she is simply a frigid woman who, having borne her two children, now wants no more of an act which brings her no pleasure. However," Pat continued, "knowing Marjorie, I could not believe that of her. She is much too kind, much too caring to hurt Woodward that way. She would force herself to go through the motions if only for his sake. It might even be," Pat went on painfully, "that Woodward is a sexually brutal man, though of course I cannot accept that possibility either."

"Then what's left?" Joe asked.

Wiping her eyes, Pat Haylow faced her husband squarely. "Unthinkable as it might be, if Woodward's analysis is wrong about her mental state, then there is only one other possibility: she's having an affair with someone. A girl as honest as Marjorie could not give herself to two men."

Had the situation not been so serious, Joe's reaction would have been almost comic. His eyes widened, his mouth literally fell open.

"Marjorie in love with someone else? Marjorie an adulteress? It's the most insane idea I've ever heard! Dear Lord, Pat, we know this girl. She's like our own. No, no. I reject that completely. Besides. An affair with whom? Where? How? Absolutely not. I agree with Woodward. The child is having some kind of temporary breakdown. Woodward must get her to have professional help."

"They have discussed it. She absolutely refuses."

"Then you'll have to talk to her, Pat. She loves you. Maybe she will tell you whatever it is she refuses to tell Woodward."

Pat shook her head. "I offered, but Woodward feels it would be wrong. He says the one thing in the world Marjorie doesn't want is for us to know anything about this. He says he thinks it would drive her completely over the edge."

"Then what are we to do?"

"For the moment, nothing, I guess. Woodward believes that if he is attentive but makes no demands she will come out of this. He thinks, somehow, that all the time he's spent away from her this year might have upset her more even than she realizes. He's been traveling, on and off, for months, you know. Perhaps, in some way we don't understand, that really has upset her emotionally."

"It's my fault," Joe said slowly. "I'm the one who insisted on these crusades."

"Nonsense, darling. How could anyone anticipate this kind of thing? Besides, we don't even know the real reason. All we can do, Joe, is to act as though nothing is wrong. And pray very hard that whatever has brought her to this painful state will go away as mysteriously as it appeared. As for an affair, I can't think why I even said that. I was just looking for something tangible. It's absurd, of course."

Pat's calmness had helped to soothe his anxiety and Marjorie and Woodward seemed so relaxed and happy when he saw them that he almost forgot the problem. He wanted to believe that it was righting itself. Every couple went through these troubled-water periods, he reasoned. Even he and Pat had their little moments of tension through the years. Probably would have had more if they hadn't had the relief of his part-time residency in New York. No matter how much people love each other, they need a breather now and then, Joe thought. But a brief one. It was just too much of a separation for Woodward to have traveled almost constantly this year. Joe decided he would not allow that in the future.

He was glad that Marjorie still drove to New York for a day or two every couple of weeks. He knew that she enjoyed shopping, seeing plays, and visiting her friends. She seemed unchanged, and with relief Joe slipped into an almost-complacent illusion that all was coming right with his business and his family. Deliberately, he put the thought of his approaching retirement out of his mind. It was only two months away, a very short span of time indeed, but because of Roger it now seemed a less terrible thing. With his son's ascension, his immortality would be assured. Cabot would not like it, but Cabot's disappointment was of small concern to Joe. He would accept second place to Roger, remaining as President, because he had no choice, no place better to go. And even if the unthinkable occurred and Cabot indignantly resigned, Deland was a strong and well-prepared replacement for the Presidency.

To this day, Haylow literally did not know what had brought about the enormous change in Roger. When he tried to question Sid Sommers, that wise man told him, not in so many words, but in effect, to "shut up and count his blessings." Joe suspected that he would not have liked to hear the real story behind Roger's change of heart and was grateful to Sid for sparing him the details of whatever had been thrashed out between them. He adopted the same attitude toward Roger. What was done was done. And Joe thanked God that things were turning out as they were.

The Chairman, and those same people who cared about him, would have been considerably less placid if they'd been aware of the plan of attack that was being carefully, patiently put together by Brad Deland.

In the months following his discovery of Dick Cabot's furtive movements, Brad had, on half a dozen more occasions, confirmed the routine. It was always the same: first the X-rated movie, then the retirement to the same apartment building with the same young man, finally the late afternoon return to the office. Brad was aware that since the decision about Terry White, Cabot very obviously was avoiding any private conversation with Deland. He must be scared out of his mind that his slightly removed connection with Terry White will be discovered, Brad thought. But not scared enough to give up his sordid little afternoons with Peter Johnson. His discovery about Cabot did not, unfortunately, give Deland the ammunition he needed to win the executive war. The disclosure of Cabot's perversion would, of course, get him thrown out of the organization and, in all probability, move Brad up one step, to the Presidency. But that step was still one notch below the top, still one level below complete and autocratic control of Haylow. Roger was the only real obstacle. If only, Brad thought, it had been Roger who was involved with Peter Johnson. What a beautiful setup *that* would have been.

The idea, at first so idly entertained, had grown on Brad until he realized it would be a stroke of genius. Like a novelist outlining a plot, he let his mind carefully work out the possibilities. Johnson obviously was nothing more than a male whore, an out-of-work actor using Cabot as a source of income. What, then, if someone offered him a better income? Or threatened to cut off the present supply? Or both? Excited by the germ of the idea, Deland began to explore the idea of using Johnson, not to discredit Cabot but to convince Joe Haylow that his precious son, his beloved Roger was the homosexual in the executive suite. By God, Brad thought, it could work. If I do it right, I can make the link between Roger's sponsorship of Terry White connect with a love affair between Roger and Terry's roommate. Easy, boy, he told himself. You've got to go over it a hundred times. Make sure there's nothing to trip you up. If anything in the plot breaks down, both you and Cabot will go out on your asses. On the other hand, the way things are going there's everything to gain. At this point, Brad knew, Roger was the ninety-day wonder, a shoo-in for the Chairmanship. Only a disclosure shocking enough to make Haylow turn on his son would keep Roger from getting the nod next January. But it would take more than an accusation to convince Joe Haylow. It would take evidence. In black and white. A confession signed by Peter Johnson. Yes, that was the place to start. The rest would be strategy—the complex manipulation of emotions, the working of people like puppets, playing to their strengths and weaknesses, their fears, resentments, and pride.

The idea of substituting Roger for Cabot was brilliant, Brad thought, becoming more and more enamored of the idea. There was no end of the possibilities. Cabot, for instance, would be completely at Brad's mercy, to be used in any way Brad decided. Johnson, he had no doubt, could be threatened or bribed to go along. The only incalculables were the two Haylows. And Brad Deland knew those two personalities well enough to feel reasonably confident that in their respective outbursts of anger and pride they would crash through the thin ice on which their precarious new respect was built.

Deland found Peter Johnson's number in the phone book. As he dialed it, he realized his heart was pounding. He had never felt a greater sense of danger, nor a more exhilarating stimulus to his brilliant, Machiavellian mind. He glanced at his watch. Ten-thirty in the morning. Johnson would be alone. On the third ring, a pseudo-cultured, matinee-idol voice answered.

"Peter Johnson, please," Brad said.

"This is Peter Johnson."

"Oh, Mr. Johnson, this is Bradford Deland, Vice President of The Haylow Corporation. You've been referred to us as a possibility for a part in some TV commercials we're planning to make, and I wondered whether it would be convenient for you to come in and discuss the idea with me."

Peter took the bait quickly. "That sounds very interesting. I'd be happy to talk with you, Mr. . . ."

"Deland," Brad supplied quickly. "Bradford Deland. I hate

to impose, but I wondered if you possibly could come to the office after hours this evening? Unfortunately, I have a completely full day, but I'm free after six and we are rather in a hurry to cast this part."

"Six would be fine," Peter said.

"Good. Very cooperative of you. I suppose you know where the Haylow building is? On Park."

"Yes, I know it."

"I'll leave word downstairs with the guard. Take the elevator to the executive floor and I'll meet you at the reception desk at six. Thank you, Mr. Johnson."

So far, so good, Brad thought. I wonder whether Peter is meeting Cabot today, and whether he'll thank him for this wonderful opportunity to do a commercial for Haylow. I'd love to see Cabot's face if he does. The poor little bastard'll pee in his pants.

Brad spent the rest of the day going over in his mind the conversation he would have with Peter Johnson. Like every other step of the plan it needed careful rehearsal. By six o'clock the offices were deserted. At two minutes past, Brad took up his post by the reception desk. And at five minutes past six on a cold November day, Peter Johnson stepped confidently off the elevator, headed for a different kind of role than the one for which he thought he was auditioning.

In his office, Deland motioned Peter Johnson to a comfortable chair, part of the informal "conference area" of the room. Brad took the facing chair across the rosewood coffee table. Studying the good-looking actor opposite him, Brad summed him up as a cool customer, one of a breed indigenous to New York and Los Angeles. They lived by their wits, their "contacts," and their bodies. Doe-Doe's crowd was full of them, handsome young guys who could with equal ease romance a bored wife or subtly seduce a latent homosexual like Cabot. They always maintained a "cover." They were bit-part actors in the theatre, part-time male models, turning an occasional dollar being photographed in magazine ads or appearing on TV commercials. But their main source of income invariably was a man or woman willing to pay for their company.

Casually, Brad opened a silver cigarette box and offered it to Peter.

"Smoke?"

Peter accepted a cigarette. Reaching in his pocket, he produced a thin gold light, courteously lit Brad's cigarette and then his own.

"That's a good-looking lighter," Brad said conversationally. "Cartier, isn't it? I've always admired that model. In fact, I hinted pretty hard for one last Christmas, but Mrs. Deland said it was too expensive a toy for me to lose in a month. She probably was right. I keep leaving them in restaurants, so I guess I'm better off carrying matches."

"I guess it is a problem," Peter said. "Fortunately not for me. I've hung on to this one for six months or so. But then I'm very careful about holding on to good things."

"I'm sure you are," Brad said wryly.

Johnson shifted his long legs. Screw all this small talk, he thought. If this joker wants to talk to me about a commercial, why in hell doesn't he get on with it.

"I've brought my book," Peter said.

"Your book?" It was obvious that Brad didn't know what he was talking about.

"My model's book," Peter explained. "The one that shows you what I've done in the past. Photographs, ads, and things. I assume you do want to see how I photograph? I mean, it is customary, Mr. Deland, to look at a portfolio of pictures before hiring a guy to make a commercial."

Brad laughed. "Okay, Johnson, you've caught me with my ignorance showing. So let's get down to cases. I didn't get you up here to discuss a television commercial. We have no intention of making one. That was just the bait. The purpose of this discussion is your, let us say, 'association' with Dick Cabot."

Peter's bewilderment was unmistakably genuine.

"I don't know what you're talking about," he said. "I don't know anybody named Dick Cabot."

"Then let me refresh your mind," Brad said. "Dick Cabot is a small, nervous gentleman with whom you spend afternoons in your apartment. When he is not in your apartment, he occupies an office on this floor, the door of which is discreetly labeled 'President.' Now do you know Dick Cabot?"

"No," Johnson said slowly, "but I do know Dick Carswell. He's a small nervous gentleman available only on afternoons and infrequent evenings. He's always been extraordinarily discreet about what he does here. How smashing of him to turn out to be a big shot in business! It's rather amusing, isn't it? I mean, everybody knows about the piety of Haylow and his holier-than-thou executives. Fancy the President being a devout queen!"

Brad was momentarily startled. Not that Cabot's use of a fictitious name was surprising, nor his careful concealment of his job. What amazed Brad was the offhand way in which Peter Johnson freely admitted his involvement with "Carswell." On the other hand, Brad reasoned, why shouldn't he? He has very little to lose. At worst, there's always another Cabot in the wings waiting to hand out expensive gold lighters and, probably, even more substantial gifts. Like money.

His limited acting experience was, in fact, standing Peter Johnson in good stead. The truth about Dick Cabot had come as a distinct shock and an unpleasant one, at that. He felt nothing for the frantic, overanxious little man, but he had been generous with his gifts and his money, almost pathetic in his adoration and gratitude. Even more unsettling to Peter was the disclosure of Cabot's high position in Haylow. Remembering that it was months ago that Terry had gotten a look at Cabot, he wondered at the sudden turn of events. Terry must have recognized him then. Had he waited all this time to tell Deland that Cabot was involved in an unorthodox arrangement? If so, why? Was Terry suddenly afraid that the President of Haylow's affair with Terry's roommate would jeopardize his big, prospective job in the organization? And why hadn't Terry told Peter who Carswell was? None of it made sense, Peter thought. He knew Terry too well. He would have talked to Peter before blowing the whistle on Cabot. In all likelihood, he would have asked Peter to break off the involvement and Peter, despite his amoral credo, would have done so. Terry's friendship was the only genuine thing in Peter's life. He felt uneasy, betrayed, and completely confused. But the easy veneer of sophistication covered these emotions. Brad Deland saw only a relaxed, seemingly unconcerned man who apparently found the whole set of circumstances highly amusing.

It was Peter who finally broke the silence. "All right, Mr. Deland, for some obscure reason you've got me up here to tell me you know about Mr. Carswell-Cabot and me. So what?"

"So I'd like to talk about the interesting ramifications of the facts at hand," Brad said. "Some of them must be quite obvious to you. As you have pointed out, it would demolish Dick Cabot's career if this information reached certain executives of this company."

Johnson was flippant. "If you don't tell 'em, I won't."

"I'll buy that," Deland said. "But how do we know that your roommate won't? Terry White does know about you and Cabot, doesn't he?"

Johnson's fractional hesitation gave him away. "I swear to you, Deland, I don't think Terry knows who the man is. Any more than I did until now. The one time he did see him, for a minute, I'm sure he didn't recognize him. If he did, he sure as hell didn't enlighten me. You're not going to involve Terry in this, are you? I give you my word, it has nothing to do with him."

"You're not qualified to say that," Brad answered. "In a very curious and complex way it has a great deal to do with him. Cabot has been one of Terry's staunchest supporters for a big job the company has in mind for him. If you were Chairman of Haylow, wouldn't you find that a curious coincidence, provided you knew that the nominee's roommate was the President's lover? You see, Johnson, if Terry suddenly got the bright idea of bringing a pertinent piece of information like this to Mr. Haylow, it might make him a hero. He could denounce Cabot as he renounced you, make a clean breast of it, so to speak, and come out smelling like a rose because of his self-sacrificial dedication to the company."

"Oh for Christ's sake, Deland," Peter said, "even I'm not dumb enough to buy that! Even if Terry knows who 'Carswell' is, it's to his advantage to stay mum about it. Don't give me that hero crap. He'd be taking too big a chance, admitting his roommate was a homo involved with a Haylow big shot like Cabot."

Deland smiled. "You're far from dumb, Johnson. You may be an opportunistic bloodsucker with the morals of an alley cat, but stupid you are not. You're right. The hypothesis that Terry would breathe a word of this is ridiculous. But the importance of this matter to him—and his future—is very, very real.

"You see," Brad went on, "when the story gets out—and it will—that Terry White's roommate is involved with a high official of Haylow, that high official will be very suspect because of his support of Terry. It will, in fact, be the end of that executive. But it need not be the end of Terry White. He can plead ignorance of the whole affair and pretend righteous horror when it is revealed to him. He will be the innocent victim of circumstances. He will, in fact, not be the one hurt. His role is that of an innocent pawn."

Johnson struggled to digest what Brad was saying. Certain things were now coming clear to him. Terry had not told Deland anything about Cabot. Deland obviously was not interested in whether or not Terry was made President of that cosmetics company he was so hot for. Obviously, Deland was only out to get Cabot. And equally obviously Johnson was the key. Or so he thought.

"So you want me to authenticate the fact that Cabot's a faggot, is that what this is all about?"

"Not exactly," Brad said. "I want you to authenticate the fact that a high official of this company has a homosexual liaison with you. We will take the same given set of circumstances and make only one tiny change in the story. Instead of the name 'Richard Cabot' we will substitute the name 'Roger Haylow.' A very simple, technical bit of editing."

Johnson's eyes widened. "Roger Haylow? That's the Chairman's son, isn't it?"

"One of them."

"But I don't even know him."

"Oh, come," Deland said. "Let's not quibble about details. I have my own reasons for this, and I have no intention of going into them with you. In fact, you should be very pleased with the idea. It protects Cabot and, therefore, your meal ticket, which I am sure is not inconsiderable. We will, as I've told you, make sure that Terry is presented as an innocent victim of circumstances. And, just to make it slightly more interesting, for this simple deviation from the truth, I will personally reward you with the tax-free, undeclared sum of five thousand dollars in cash."

"And what do I do in return for all this happiness?"

Brad went to his desk and took out a sheet of paper.

"I typed it myself," he said, handing it to Peter. "Read it."

The document which bore the day's date was brief and lethal. Its intent was deadly clear. Peter read it aloud.

"I, Peter Johnson, do confirm that since 1967 I have been

and as of this date still am engaged in a homosexual relationship with Roger Haylow. I make this statement freely and of my own will. I attest that Terence White has no knowledge of this association and in return for the assurance of his continued employment in The Haylow Corporation I agree never to discuss or disclose the fact of this liaison."

"You see," Brad said, "I knew you would want to protect Terry. That's why it's all there in black and white."

Neat, Peter thought. How to be a bastard in business. So it's Roger Haylow, not Cabot, he's out to get. Somehow he's figured how to make this phony statement stick. God knows how. Roger Haylow is going to demand he prove it. Well, that's Deland's headache, I guess, the dirty blackmailing sonofabitch. I've done a lot of shitty things in my life, Peter thought, but nothing as cold-blooded as this. If this is big business, baby, they can have it. It was as calculated as a contract put out by the underworld. No matter how big they are, the tycoons can never afford to stop scheming.

Pen in hand, Peter looked up at Brad with a mixture of contempt and grudging admiration.

"Who's going to know about this?" he asked.

"For the moment, just you and me. Perhaps no one else ever will. But if it becomes necessary, of course, there will be other confrontations, during which you will stick to this story. It could get messy for you and Terry if you didn't."

Peter signed on the line indicated. Brad added his own signature as witness. Folding the paper carefully, he returned it to his desk. Then he gave Peter an envelope. Inside was five thousand dollars in cash.

Peter slipped the money in his pocket and dropped the envelope on the coffee table.

"Seems to me you could get your own ass in a sling with this kind of phony 'confession,' Mr. Deland. Aren't you taking a pretty big risk building this whole story around somebody else's name?"

Brad's confidence was supreme. "Why, Mr. Johnson, as an actor I find that an odd question coming from you. As Shakespeare once said, 'What's in a name?'"

As he rang for the elevator, Peter Johnson thought of Deland's sardonic parting remark. There were plenty of very unpretty names for conniving rats like Deland. Poor Carswell, he thought, unconsciously using the name familiar to him. No wonder the little bugger is a wreck, trying to stay alive in an organization filled with Bradford Delands. I'll be nicer to him tomorrow, Peter decided. God knows he's out of his league at the office. I wonder how tough Roger Haylow is. And why does Deland want to get something on the Chairman's son?

Peter patted the fat wad of money in his pocket. It was, after all, just another episode in his life. And he had come out of it richer and wiser. Richer, at least.

Brad Deland stayed in his office for an hour after Johnson left, taking stock of the situation as it seemed to be evolving. So far, things were going well. It had been a piece of luck to find out about Cabot, and one of those stranger-than-fiction coincidences that the man with whom Dick was involved could be so effortlessly tied into the master plan. As he had anticipated, Peter Johnson had been child's play to handle. He would not, Brad reasoned, tip off either Cabot or Terry in the fear of jeopardizing his relationship with either. Peter's genuine concern for Terry had been a somewhat surprising facet of his character. But, Brad thought with satisfaction, he had correctly anticipated that possibility by using the protection of Terry's job as a convincing reason for Peter to sign the "confession." It had been an instinctively perfect touch.

On the whole, Brad was satisfied with the progress of his plot. But realistically, he knew that the trickiest parts were still to come. There had to be a way to alert Haylow to the confession without making Deland himself look like the unwelcome bearer of bad tidings. Of all the pieces of information in the world that Haylow would least wish to hear, the evidence of his son's sexual deviation would be first on the list. Brad knew that Joe Haylow would strike out in anger against the man who brought him news of this unthinkable flaw in Roger's image, particularly now that father and son had achieved a closeness and a mutual respect that was obvious even to outsiders. In these days of pride in his son's business ability, Joe Haylow would be less quick to believe the story than he would have been a year earlier. He would also, Brad realized, be more ready to accept Roger's denial.

But these were later steps. The next step was to get the information in the hands of Joe Haylow. Suddenly Brad knew the way. He remembered one of the famous Haylow breakfast meetings two or three years back. The subject of anonymous letters had come up. As Brad recalled it, they had started talking about it because Joe Haylow had received an unsigned crank letter accusing him of being a Jew who had changed his name from Halsinzky to Haylow. Some of the executives had laughed. Others were outraged by the warped, bigoted mind of the writer. One in particular, Brad recalled, a fashion buyer from Star, had been vehement in her condemnation of anyone who was cowardly enough to send an anonymous letter of any kind.

Joe Haylow, to everyone's surprise, had disagreed with the young woman.

"It may surprise you, Miss Westly," he'd said, "in fact it may surprise everyone here to know that I think the anonymous letter not only can often have great value but is sometimes the only possible course of action for the writer. Naturally, I do not mean this kind of warped, senseless accusation. I am talking about the kind of information that the writer could not, perhaps, admit to giving. Yet it can be very valuable to the person to whom it is addressed."

It had been Bridget Manning, Brad recalled, who, as usual, had courage to disagree with the Chairman.

"I don't understand what you mean, Mr. Haylow," Bridget had said. "I must agree with Miss Westly. If the person is too cowardly to sign his name, then I consider the information unworthy of consideration. If he is speaking the truth, why shouldn't he be straightforward about it?"

"Very simple," Joe answered. "Sometimes people have to protect themselves from those who can harm them. For example, suppose a buyer in one of your stores knows that another buyer is stealing from the company. It is information that honest Buyer A believes we should have about dishonest Buyer B. Now, if Buyer A makes a flat accusation, she may end up in all kinds of internal upheaval. She can lose friends. Maybe even unfairly lose her job. She believes she is making a contribution to the company but she does not want to be, as the saying goes, 'directly involved.' By sending the information anonymously, she alerts management without risk to herself."

"But can you honestly give credence to an unsigned letter?" Bridget asked.

"I don't give credence to anything unless I have proof," Joe said. "I didn't say I *believed* anonymous letters, but I have every one of them followed up to see whether there is anything to the content. If there is not, I forget it. But you would be amazed if you knew how much correct information this company has been given anonymously . . . information it might otherwise have taken us years to discover and which might have cost us hundreds of thousands of dollars in the interim."

Stubbornly, Bridget persisted. "I still think the place for an unsigned letter is in the wastebasket. You can't go around encouraging every disgruntled employee with a grudge to send in an anonymous complaint."

"Possibly not," Haylow had said quietly. "But I do encourage honest, well-meaning members of this organization to adopt the method if they feel that otherwise they would have to suppress vital information. Remember, the key here is that we do not accept these letters as fact. But it can harm no one to quietly check them out."

Brad had not forgotten the incident. It was another one of the Chairman's surprising reactions, unconventional yet based on realism. In the past, Haylow had sent one or two such letters to Brad to follow through. They had proved to be groundless accusations but they could as easily have been tip-offs from a reliable grapevine, just as the Chairman had explained.

Now Brad realized, this was the way to get the "information" about Roger to his father. Quickly he put a plain piece of paper into his portable typewriter.

"Dear Mr. Haylow," he wrote. "Mr. Bradford Deland has in his possession certain information concerning your son which has been concealed from you. Being a loyal employee, I think you should have this information for the good of the Company, but being your friend I don't think Mr. Deland will ever let you see it. Why don't you ask him about it?"

Brad reread the note. It sounded right. Literate enough to come from someone in the executive area. Not too smooth. More like something a secretary would type. He made sure there were no typing errors. Then, leaving it unsigned, he put it into a plain envelope and addressed it formally to Mr. Joseph Haylow, adding PERSONAL AND CONFIDENTIAL in the lower left-hand corner. He stamped it and dropped it in the corner mailbox on his way home.

That should start things moving, he thought. And soon. It had to be soon. Time was running out.

12 🙠

The letter lay, unopened, on the top of the neat pile of mail Miss Watson had arranged on Haylow's coffee table. The sight of it did not particularly alert Joe to trouble. He was used to receiving letters marked "Personal and Confidential" which, as a good secretary, Ruth Watson did not open when she sorted the rest of his correspondence. Usually, such letters were applications for jobs, written by people who wanted to make sure that their qualifications reached the eye of the Chairman himself. Occasionally, they were crank letters. And frequently, to Joe's irritation, they were advertising solicitations, a practice which Haylow considered fraudulent and which invariably caused him to send a stinging reply to the publication, reminding it that all such communications should be directed to Haylow's advertising department.

In his own way, the Chairman believed in delegating responsibility and authority to his divisional and departmental heads. Not that he hesitated to interfere if the progress of any area did not come up to his standards or expectations. But on the surface at least—and in all minor matters—he prided himself on giving his executives a free hand to run their own bailiwicks. He also encouraged them to do the same for their subordinates. In line with this, every executive was required to take an annual vacation of at least two continuous weeks. Joe did not believe in vacations taken a few days at a time or spread, as some would have preferred it, over long weekends throughout the summer. "If you don't stay out of the office for at least two weeks at a time," he told his managers, "no one who works for you ever learns to make a decision. Any problem can be postponed if your people know you'll be back in a few days. But if they know you won't be around for a couple of weeks, they'll be forced to use their own judgment. It's good training for people who, we hope, will be our future administrators."

In accordance with this policy, Dick Cabot was on holiday with Mildred, dutifully spending his two weeks at a middle-class New England resort hotel where they had gone for every vacation since their marriage. His "subordinate," Roger Haylow, was technically standing by to make decisions in Cabot's absence. Bridget was visiting the branch stores before the Christmas rush. Brad Deland, Mike Warner, and Sid Sommers were all in town on this cold, clear day which was to mark the beginning of one of the most terrible periods in Joe Haylow's life.

Matter-of-factly, noting there was no return address, Haylow slit open the innocent-looking envelope. The terse communiqué seemed, at first, to have all the earmarks of a bad joke. But with the second rapid reading, Joe felt a twinge of apprehension. His breath quickened and the perfectly fitting collar of his tailor-made shirt suddenly seemed unbearably tight. He looked at his calendar watch. The time was 8:40 A.M. and the date was Monday, November 9, which meant that the letter probably had arrived while he was in Farmville. Ruth Watson would have put it on his table on Friday, awaiting his return to the office this morning.

At this hour, Joe was alone in the executive wing. It would be nine o'clock at the very earliest before Brad Deland would get in. He read the ominous words for the third time. "Certain information concerning your son," it said. The logical assumption was that the son referred to was Roger and that the

The Rich and the Righteous

information was connected with business. On the other hand, Joe thought, it conceivably could have to do with Woodward —his disturbed marriage or even his still-threatened position of leadership in the church. Whichever, if the warning was valid it had to be bad news. Otherwise, why would Brad withhold it "as a friend"?

Impatiently, he watched the minute hand crawl toward nine. Almost on the stroke of the hour, he heard Miss Watson moving around in the outer office. As he touched it, he imagined that even the interoffice buzzer had a staccato note of alarm.

"Yes, Mr. Haylow?"

"Please see if Mr. Deland is in his office."

In a moment, Miss Watson signaled him. "Mr. Deland is on his way in, sir. His secretary expects him in about fifteen minutes. Shall I leave word for him to see you when he gets here?"

"Yes," Haylow said. "Immediately."

Another quarter hour to sweat it out, Joe thought. His own uneasiness amazed him. It was inconsistent with his nature to push the panic button under almost any circumstances. It was incredible that he was doing it now based on nothing more than an anonymous note which actually revealed nothing except the possible existence of some information which was being kept from him.

As he waited for Brad, Haylow tried to read through the rest of his mail. Even his extraordinarily disciplined mind could not thrust aside the threat which, by now, had become real to him. Finally, pushing the papers aside he went to the window and stood looking out across the bleak rooftops. Deliberately, he tried to make his mind a blank, tried to clear it to receive whatever it was Deland could tell him.

A light tap on the door announced Brad's arrival.

"Morning, Joe," he said. "You wanted to see me?"

Wordlessly, Haylow handed him the letter. Brad read it, scowling. In anger, he threw it back on the coffee table.

"Goddamn whoever did this!" Deland exploded. "Rotten, snooping, prying busybodies! When I find out who wrote this, I'll kill him!"

"So it's true?" Haylow asked. "You do have some information you've been keeping from me?"

Brad sat down heavily, clenching his hands so tightly that the knuckles showed white. "Yes," he said grimly, "it's true. And I wish I could have kept it from you forever."

"All right, Brad, since it can't be kept from me, let's have it. All of it. I assume the son referred to is Roger?"

Brad nodded.

"And the facts?" Joe was calm now, as calm as a patient who has diagnosed and accepted his own terminal illness and pities the doctor who has to put the terrible fact into words. It was Brad who seemed to be in agony. Perspiration dotted his forehead. Compulsively, he pulled at his fingers until loud cracking of the knuckles was the only sound in the room. It was a convincing act, made truly convincing by his real fear that something would go wrong in this conversation.

Deland kept his eyes away from Haylow's narrowed gaze. Looking at the carpet, he spoke slowly, almost inaudibly.

"Roger's involved, emotionally, with another man."

At first, there was no response from the powerful figure on the sofa. The Chairman's face was impassive, but when he spoke his voice was hard-edged and disbelieving.

"I think you'd better explain that," he said flatly.

Deland sighed heavily. "All right, Joe. You want to hear the word? The word is homosexual. Roger is homosexual."

Haylow's reaction was instinctive. His fist clenched as though he wanted to smash the mouth that had spoken the devastating words, as though by silencing Deland he could deny the charge that had been so reluctantly extracted. He felt the sweat in his armpits, recognized the clammy chill of distaste that followed it like an ugly sickness enveloping his whole body. No, he thought. No, not Roger. Not now when everything I've hoped for is bound up in him and his future. Slowly, he fought for control. With effort, he kept his voice icy-cold.

"I don't believe it. How dare you come in here with this insane piece of gossip—this malicious accusation?"

Suddenly it was Brad who assumed the attitude of anger.

"Hold it," he said roughly. "I didn't come to you, remember? It was you and your calculated theories about anonymous letters that started all this. Whether you believe it or not, you'd never have heard this from me. What the hell do I care about Roger's private life?"

When Joe answered it was in the normal tones of the Chairman, composed, unemotional, boring in for the facts.

"I apologize, Brad. You're right, of course. You didn't start this. But I don't understand. How can you be so sure that what you're saying is anything more than a rumor started by somebody who hates me or envies Roger?"

Deland felt something like pity for the old man. Simultaneously, he felt a surge of triumph. Haylow was going to buy it. He knew that.

"Joe, I have written proof."

Haylow's eyes widened. "Written proof? How is that possible?"

"The only way to tell you the whole story is to begin at the beginning. But before I do, I want you to believe that I had no idea what I was getting into. I swear to you that if I'd had any inkling I'd have killed the whole plan before it got this far."

"Go on," Joe said. "Tell me what happened."

"Well, it started in a routine way. When the Elmarie deal began to look good a few months ago, I did what I always do when we're looking at an acquisition—started getting a run-down on all the people involved, as well as the financial stand-

267

ing and good-will value of the company itself. Everything checked out okay on the company's worth, and the private investigating company we use dug into Marina's background and Boswell's and they seemed okay too. They came up with that thing about Boswell's dismissal from Haylow, but we already knew about that. Otherwise, the Elmarie people, including the daughter, seemed to have good character references."

Deland stopped. A little more composed now, he lit a cigarette. Then, reluctantly, he went on.

"That's where I normally would have stopped. But then Roger and Mike and Dick Cabot came on so strong for an unknown kid named Terry White that I thought it couldn't do any harm to find out a little more about him too, since we were obviously going to give him such a responsible job. I probably wouldn't have done it, if it hadn't been for that mess a couple of years ago. Remember how Sid Sommers told us we were idiots not to get a thorough run-down on key executives before we put them in important spots?"

Joe did remember. The trouble had come with a highly paid merchandise manager in one of the Star Stores. The man had been caught taking expensive gifts and money from the suppliers he dealt with. They had checked his record, after the fact, and found that he had been dismissed from two other jobs for accepting bribes. Sid Sommers had been furious when he found out.

"For a giant corporation, you all operate like a billion-dollar button shop," Sid had told Haylow and the executive group. "You think nothing of giving a man twenty-five thousand dollars a year in salary, plus bonuses and stock options, but you wouldn't spend a couple of hundred bucks to check him out before he's hired! Don't you know by now that the references a man gives aren't worth the paper they're written on? Only an idiot would give the name of somebody who'd say a bad word against him. And only a jackass company

would entrust a responsible job to some joker whose background they hadn't investigated on their own!"

Recalling the incident, Haylow nodded. "Go on," he said.

"We'd already run the routine checks on Terry White,"
Brad continued. "In the company, I mean. His record with
Haylow was good and, as you know, both Roger and Mike
were very impressed with the way he handled himself. But I
figured we'd better take Sommers' advice and have an outside
agency do a confidential search for anything that we might
have missed. That's when they turned up the thing about
Roger."

Haylow sat deathly still. Waiting.

"It seems that Terry White shares an apartment with an
unsuccessful actor named Peter Johnson. They used to be
emotionally involved, but that ended years ago, with Terry
White doing the breaking-off. White got ambitious and decided it was bad for his career to hang around with Johnson
and his group of faggot friends. But Johnson was still crazy
about Terry and persuaded him to stay on in the apartment,
even though they led separate lives, so to speak.

"Our people, of course, were keeping an eye on White and
the comings and goings at his apartment. All the reports
seemed innocuous until last week. Then they fed me a report
that said Terry White had gone home at lunchtime, entering
the building a few minutes after his roommate had gone inside in the company of another man.

"The other man, Joe, was Roger.

"The report went on to say that Terry had left almost
immediately, but Roger and Peter Johnson were in the apartment for over two hours. Then Roger left alone."

Brad sighed deeply. "I should have quit there, but I didn't
like the looks of it. I was afraid that Terry White or his roommate was blackmailing Roger somehow. I don't know what I
thought, except that it was strange to find out that the three
of them would meet at such an odd hour in any place as out

of the way as that crumby apartment. It seemed odd to me that Terry White had come up so fast, out of left field, and figured so prominently both in the acquisition of Elmarie and in our future plans for it. I just had a crazy gut-feeling that somebody was putting pressure on. So help me God it never entered my mind that Roger was anything but a naïve tool in some lousy scheme those two had cooked up.

"Anyway," Brad went on, "I got Peter Johnson into my office on the pretext of hiring him to do a television commercial. I pulled a big bluff, told him we'd had Terry followed and that we knew that Terry was blackmailing one of our executives. He got very excited and said that Terry didn't know anything about it, that it was he, Peter Johnson, who'd made up his mind to help Terry's career by getting someone high up in Haylow to help him. He said that—God forgive me, Joe—he was Roger's lover and because of that Roger had pushed Terry for Peter's sake. Johnson said he did it because he hoped that Terry would be so grateful he'd learn to love Peter again."

Haylow looked like a man who had gone into shock. His eyes were glazed, his normally ruddy face as white as the envelope he had opened only minutes—or was it hours?—before. Compulsively, now, Brad continued to talk.

"When I heard this, my first thought, of course, was to protect Roger and you. I told that conniving queer that if he ever breathed a word of this to anybody we'd make damn certain that neither he nor his beloved Terry White ever got any kind of a job, anywhere again. I even typed up a statement for him to sign, swearing that he would never reveal his association with Roger and promising, in return, that we would not change our minds about Terry White. I know we don't give employment guarantees, Joe, but I took it on myself to do so. White is the innocent victim here, I believe, and it was the one way I could make sure that Johnson would not decide to expose Roger."

The irony of Deland's referring to Johnson's confession as an "employment guarantee" suddenly struck Haylow. He began to laugh. Not mirthfully, but hysterically and then, to Deland's horror, the laughter turned to tears. For a few seconds, turning his back to an amazed Deland, the unshakable, unemotional Joe Haylow wept. Brad's instinct was to leave him alone with his grief, but Haylow, with obvious effort, quickly recovered himself. Removing his glasses, he wiped his eyes.

"Forgive me," he said. "That must have been terribly embarrassing for you."

Brad shook his head, saying nothing.

"You mustn't blame yourself for what you did, Brad," Haylow told him. "You set out to protect the company's interests, and that's what you're paid to do. As for the rest, I don't know what anyone would have done. You tried to be fair to everybody and to spare me. But it wasn't to be. I can't deny that I wish I didn't know. It could alter so many things. I have to have time to think about them. Meanwhile, we will keep this entirely between ourselves, of course. I will want to see that signed statement, right away. Bring it in, will you, please?"

"Wouldn't you rather just forget it?" Brad asked. "If it hadn't been for that anonymous letter, you'd never have known. Why don't we just leave it alone?"

Haylow shook his head. "Even if I could forget it, I must not," he said. "I must face Roger's problem in two ways—as my son and as an executive of this company whose judgmental decisions must not be based on emotional involvement. Besides, someone else knows our secret. The person who wrote the anonymous letter."

"And I won't rest until I find out who that is!"

"It's not important," Haylow said. "If this is true, it was bound to come out sooner or later. Now let me see the statement, please."

As he made his way to his office, Brad congratulated himself on the way the meeting had gone. Haylow had been pathetic and his unexpected tears had given Brad a momentary pang of remorse but essentially the tower of strength that was Joe Haylow had revealed himself, in Deland's eyes, as nothing more than a sloppy, sentimental old fool. Perhaps, Brad thought suddenly, he may have even harbored an uneasy feeling about Roger before this. Unmarried at thirty-seven, maintaining his own apartment which Brad knew the Haylows had never seen. Perhaps the old man wasn't as unsophisticated as he appeared. What a twist it would be if the idea born in Deland's devious mind should turn out, in fact, to be the truth. Suppose Roger and Cabot were both queers! Jesus Christ, he thought, wouldn't that be the breathing end! Out of nowhere, one of Doe-Doe's smart-ass quips occurred to him. "Tutti-frutti," she'd once said. "That's the Italian translation for 'All the world is queer.'"

Putting Johnson's confession in an envelope marked "Confidential," he walked back up the hall and gave it to Miss Watson.

"Please give this to Mr. Haylow right away," he said. Suddenly, he didn't want to look at the Chairman again.

Like his father, Roger Haylow could not remember a happier year. Unaware of Woodward and Marjorie's problems, he did not even have that worry to cloud his days. It seemed that everything he touched went right. The Elmarie deal should be closed within a few weeks and he was delighted that Joe Haylow had reinforced his faith in him by going along with Roger's recommendation of Terry White.

The weekends he'd been spending at Farmville were happy, relaxed ones—a far cry from the painful "family reunions" of the past. Once he had looked forward only to seeing Pat. Now he could honestly say that he anxiously awaited the time he could spend with his father. He even had taken to going to church with Joe occasionally, a fact that gave Haylow obvious, undisguised pleasure.

I owe it all to Sid and Bridget, he thought. If they hadn't cared enough to level with me after that terrible fiasco in Florida, I might never have faced my own resentments or learned how to offer affection to a man who really wanted it all the time.

He found his fondness for Bridget growing constantly and wondered if it was approaching love. She was, by far, the gayest and most stimulating woman he'd ever known. And though she teased him gently about being seen with "an older woman," Roger knew that the slight difference in their ages did not concern Bridget any more than it bothered him. They found themselves sharing the same interests, professionally and socially, and more and more they drifted into a kind of easy companionship that so far was no more serious than a lighthearted good-night kiss at Bridget's door. Roger was acutely aware of her physical attractiveness and roused by it, but thus far he had made no romantic gesture toward her. He was not sure how it would be received. At least this was his conscious rationalization. He did not want to admit that deep in his subconscious he might still retain a lingering, unwelcome doubt about Bridget's relationship with Joe.

On the surface, at least, it was a companionable, satisfying relationship that suited them both. Then, one night shortly before she left for a trip, Bridget had been almost provocative in her conversation during dinner. They had been agreeing with each heartily over some political viewpoint when Bridget abruptly reached out and took Roger's hand.

"Have you noticed that we're turning into a monotonous mutual-admiration society?" she asked. "Why don't we have a good, healthy, knock-down, drag-out fight just to prove we love each other?"

273

Roger held her hand tightly. "Okay," he said amiably, "what do you want to fight about?"

"Oh, I don't care. The color of your tie? The way I eat an artichoke?"

"No good. I like the color of my tie. And I'm crazy about the way you eat an artichoke. So neat. Not messy like some girls."

Bridget laughed. "Then how about having a good character-assassination session? We could chew up the reputation of some poor, unsuspecting soul. Make mincemeat of him."

"Negative. We couldn't work up an argument that way. We both like the same people, and dislike the same ones. It's only fun to commit verbal murder when the victim has somebody on his side for you to convince."

Bridget pretended to think about a subject. "We could always play Haylow horse-race," she said finally.

"Don't think I know that one."

"Why, my dear Mr. Haylow, it's played in all the best fashion circles these days. Wherever have you been? The object of the game is to pick an entry, place your bet, and wait to see who rides into the winner's circle as the next Chairman. Want to know the odds around town?"

"Sure. But I'm not a gamblin' man."

"Well, now, I'm right glad to hear that," Bridget clowned. "Don't want no man of mine spending his hard-earned money on crap games and fast women. But seriously," she said, "you do know that the odds have changed, don't you? Six months ago, Cabot was the all-out favorite, with you a doubtful second. Now it's exactly the opposite way."

"What about Deland?"

"Still a dark horse."

"What about Mike? Or you?"

"No way," Bridget said. "Darling Mike just isn't at the right level. Neither am I, for that matter. Nope, unless the roof falls in, it's got to be one of you three."

Roger didn't answer. He knew that he wanted the Chairmanship. Not in the way that Cabot wanted it, as though it was his due. Nor the way Brad would want it because it represented complete, autocratic control. Roger wanted the job not only for himself but for his father.

"Lightning could always hit the roof, you know."

"If it does," Bridget said pertly, "I hope it strikes Cabot and Deland."

They changed the subject, but these days it was with all of them, constantly. Roger had made up his mind that he was not going to take advantage of his position, that newly secure spot so close to the throne. It's Joe Haylow's decision, he told himself, and he'll make it on merit. If Cabot's a better man, or Brad, then the job should be his. The only glimmer of hope Roger allowed himself these days was the honest knowledge that he was doing a good job, and the firm belief that his father's dependency on him was growing as his pride and confidence increased.

So when Joe Haylow sent for him on that November morning, Roger was totally unprepared for the scene that followed.

For a long while after he had read Peter Johnson's confession, the Chairman paced his office. Almost as though they had human form, his emotions strode beside him. Outrage, disbelief, suspicion, and bitter disappointment were the quartet of devils which accompanied him as he walked restlessly from one end of the room to the other.

The father in him, which had found new joy in a son miraculously remade in his own image, refused to accept the seemingly unassailable evidence of deceit. But the business-leader part of his nature—which had, over forty years, seen far more surprising disclosures than this one—forced him to face the possibility that Roger could be using his position of power to further his personal interests.

Unwillingly, he forced himself to remember some of the things that Roger had said on that shattering evening in

Florida. One phrase, impossible to forget, kept returning to Joe. "Capricornians are serious-minded people who have no real understanding of life," Roger had said. Was the boy even then trying to tell him something too foreign for him to grasp? Haylow had to admit to himself that until these last months Roger had seemed like someone else's child. Sardonic, private, unapproachable. So different from Woodward, who had fallen in easily with Joe's view of a proper life, its acceptance of home and family and religion. Had he, Joe wondered, been lulled into a false sense of security about Roger? Had he too easily, too readily, too hopefully accepted the "new Roger" because it was the one he had so long prayed for?

There was only one way to find out. Face Roger with these accusations which were too well documented to be ignored yet too incredible to be believed.

"Ask Mr. Roger Haylow to come in," he told Miss Watson. "And hold my calls until I tell you."

The moment he stepped into his father's office, Roger had a sense of foreboding. Joe Haylow looked a hundred years old, like some craggy biblical patriarch ready to unleash a thunderbolt of wrath. At the same time, Roger realized, he was a study in wretchedness, a man visibly wrestling with some terrible problem. Joe motioned his son silently to a chair. In his hand, the Chairman held two pieces of paper. Roger waited. The usually voluble Joe Haylow was uncharacteristically groping for a way to start the conversation.

"Something very serious has come up," he said, finally. "It concerns you and the Elmarie deal. There have been some accusations made regarding the extent of your personal interest in the matter, interests which go beyond the bounds of normal business procedure."

Completely at a loss, Roger said nothing. But, as he had in the old days, he began to feel a chilling reaction to the cold, flat, steely voice which addressed him as though he were an office boy.

"These accusations," Joe continued, "have come to light quite by chance, as such things often do. And unfortunately, since they involve an element of business judgment, I must present them to you not as my son but as a highly placed member of the Haylow organization."

Whatever it is, Roger thought, I'm not going to let him send me into an emotional tailspin. We're playing employer-employee, the man says. Okay. So be it.

"And what are the accusations?" Roger asked.

Joe handed him the first paper, the anonymous note. "I received this this morning."

Roger read it quickly. "So, of course, you immediately called in Deland."

"Yes."

"Well? What is this mysterious information? Obviously I'm the son referred to since I'm here."

"First let me tell you, Roger, that what Brad did was strictly in line with his duty. The information he stumbled onto cropped up simply in a routine investigation of the private life of Terry White. He tried to keep it from me. And I think he would have, if our anonymous writer had not interfered."

"For God's sake, Father, what is this all about?"

In answer, Joe silently held out Peter Johnson's statement.

Reading it, Roger's first impulse was to laugh. For a fleeting moment, the whole thing struck him as so farcical that he was sure his father was waiting to join in. Then, just as rapidly, the realization came over him that Joe Haylow was giving more than a little credence to the preposterous "confession." Incredulously, it was apparent that the Chairman was waiting for a denial. Or, Roger wondered, was he expecting an admission?

"Obviously," Roger said, "I'd like the whole story."

The Chairman's expression was unreadable. Matter-of-factly, he presented the case as Deland had outlined it to him, but with the kind of legalistic or journalistic loopholes that left room for denials. His recital was sprinkled with words like "alleged" or "supposed," as though, Roger thought, he is the prosecuting attorney being careful not to provoke objections from the defense.

Listening to the whole story unfold, Haylow's son felt as though he were living through some kind of hideous nightmare. His first reaction was, literally, to kill Brad Deland who, he felt absolutely certain, had invented this intricate plot. "A dark horse," Bridget had called him. "The Prince of Darkness" would have been a more apt description.

As his father continued, Roger could almost physically feel his own reactions changing. Deland was a conniving, clever sonofabitch who would stop at nothing. Roger could accept, even if he could not understand, the lust for power that would drive Brad to such desperate measures. He could not even hate him for concocting a story so intricate that a man like Haylow would not be able to ignore it. It was a web of circumstances so meticulously woven that the average man would not be able to invent it. Only a brilliant mind could put all the pieces together to make a picture so bold that its very audacity gave it the ring of truth.

In an amazed way, Roger almost admired Deland for his daring. Surely Brad must know that Roger could squash this whole thing right on the spot by an outraged denial, a demand to confront Peter Johnson and Terry White. These, of course, were the things Roger would not stoop to do. And they were the very things that Deland would count on. Oh, he is a clever man, Bradford Deland III, Roger thought. He knows how his subjects will react. He had found a way to play on all of Joe's old unspoken reservations about his son. And the Chairman was ready to buy it, lock, stock, and barrel.

Suddenly, all the old hatred and resentments returned to Roger. He tasted his bitterness, savored it. I've let Sommers and Bridget con me into thinking this cold-blooded, distrustful old man was not what I believed him to be all these years. And I was right all the time. He doesn't know the meaning of faith in anyone. I've let two people I respect convince me that this man has been waiting for me to offer him my love. That he was only anxious to return it. Well, screw him. And screw his business, his phony religion, and his convenient paternalism. He's waiting for me to deny an allegation that a normal father would tear up and throw in the face of the bastard who made it.

Let him sweat, Roger thought. No power in heaven or hell will make me dignify this with an answer. For once, let Joe Haylow be the loser. For a while he thought he had a son. I thought I had a father. We were both wrong. But at least, I've always known the truth about *him*. His punishment will be that he'll never really know about *me*. Let him wonder the rest of his life, the goddamn unfeeling bastard.

As he waited for Roger to answer the accusation, Joe found himself praying for the vehement denial that he was eager to accept with thanks to God. Instead, he could almost feel the hatred pouring out of his son.

"So you think I'm a queen," Roger said quietly.

"Now just a minute. I've made no accusations. I have simply given you a chance to present your version of this ugly story."

"Given me a chance!" Roger echoed. "What the hell kind of man are you? What kind of ice water runs in your veins? I'm your son, remember? How do you weigh your flesh and blood against an anonymous letter and the sworn statement of a man you've never met? What gives you the right to question me like I'm some kind of accused criminal? Well, hear this, Father, you can go to your grave wondering where the truth lies. You can forget you have a son named Roger. You can take your suspicions and your doubts and your questions and shove 'em up your sanctimonious ass. You're not going to get an answer out of me. *Any* answer. If this is what you want to believe, believe it, and revel in your righteousness! Oh you're a big man when it comes to faith, aren't you? A very special kind of Christian who writes his own ten commandments. And the first one is 'Thou shalt not trust thy own son.'"

"Roger, wait!" Joe said. "I've not said I believe this. All I want is your assurance that none of it's true. Then we'll find out how all this started and why."

Roger gave a bitter laugh. "If you have to have that kind of assurance from me, who the hell needs you? I've needed you all my life. To believe in me. To be proud of me. God help me, even to love me. But not you. You're the facts and figures boy. If it's in black and white, it's true to you. Like your goddamn fairy-tale Bible. As far as you're concerned, they did make Eve out of Adam's rib. And the whale swallowed Jonah. These things you believe in. This crap you accept as facts built on faith. But your own son's behavior is fair game for every rumormongering shit-head who reinforces the doubts you've probably had for years. You're a phony, Father. A power-mad, coldhearted money machine who'd sell his own kid down the river rather than take a chance on doing something wrong for his precious empire! You've never been a father to me. You're some kind of programmed machine that makes noises like one. What if I am queer? Does that make me less your son—or less able to run this business? And what if I'm not? Are you ready to push me out of your life because I won't give you the satisfaction of an answer? Think about it, Mr. Chairman. Think about all your fucking Christian principles and be damned!"

Roger was trembling with anger as he made for the door.

"I wish I could say it's been nice knowing you," he said. "But as a matter of cold, hard fact it's been thirty-seven years of pure hell."

As Roger slammed out of his office, his last words stayed with Joe. "Thirty-seven years of pure hell," he'd said. Dear God, he prayed silently, if this is what it's been like for him, what of the others? Has living with me been unbearable for Pat too? Surely not. Surely hers was a devotion built on happiness, fulfillment. Or was it? Had he neglected his wife, taken her love for granted, demanded her steadfastness and offered nothing but superficial affection in return?

It did not seem eccentric to Joe to have these silent conversations with his Maker. All his life he had been incapable of the easy confidences that others gave to their earthly companions. Even to those nearest to him, he could not express the doubts and fears that he could present nakedly to God. Despite the image of self-assurance he projected to the world, Haylow was an introvert. Self-revelation was nearly impossible for him. Articulate in his business, he was virtually tongue-tied when it came to expressing his personal problems or his private joys. The world would have been amazed to know that he was a shy man. Only a discerning few realized it. Only a handful of people used their love of him to cut through the protective shell that kept most of the world at arm's length.

Joe loved the people who knew him. But even to them his responses were limited, his display of affection guarded. Only to God could he bare his soul, give voice to his failings, accept His final judgment. Inside his head he talked to God now, never doubting that He listened.

"Were all these things that Roger said true? Should I have faced him with the facts I wanted him to deny? How could I have done otherwise? Because he is born of me, is that reason enough to believe in him blindly? Wouldn't that be, in truth, the greatest ego of all—this refusal to believe that because he is mine he could be imperfect?

"You have given me the responsibility of a great business. One that affects the lives of thousands of Your people. How could I entrust their future, heedlessly, to hands that might be too weak, too vulnerable to hold the reins? Yet how dare I ask for such reassurance?

"Are we so proud, so puffed up with arrogance, my son and I, that we deny each other the comfort of compassion? What strange values we put on the surface things of life. I was wrong, Lord, to question my son. His weaknesses are meaningless. True or false, they are totally, stupidly unimportant. How dare I judge what is right for another man? But in my self-righteousness, my misguided idea of duty, I have driven away my only hope for the future. Roger. A child who has allowed me to use my vanity as the weapon of his destruction."

The sound of gentle tapping at the office door made him start as violently as if it had been an explosion. For a wildly hopeful moment, he thought it might be Roger returning. But in answer to his response, Miss Watson opened the door.

"Excuse me, sir," she said, "but I saw Mr. Roger leave and I thought you'd want these telephone messages now."

"Thanks. Just leave them. I'll take care of them later."

Alone again, he tried to sort out his thoughts. How would he explain this new development to Pat? She must not know, must not even guess the reason why Roger would leave the business, as Joe knew he would. He would have to invent some excuses for what Joe knew would be Roger's withdrawal from the whole family scene as well. There would be no more of the happy, affectionate weekends at home, days filled with Roger's obvious affection and Bridget's lighthearted presence.

And what of his retirement? Since the Elmarie deal, Joe had privately decided to bypass Cabot and turn over the Chairmanship to Roger. He had told no one, not even Sid, of his decision. Now everything was changed. Cabot might have to move up as the man himself expected, with Deland made President. But Joe was uneasy with this thought. Cabot, the weakling, lacked the capability needed by the vital, dynamic Haylow Corporation. Perhaps it should be Deland. He had the ambition, the strength, the organizational turn of mind to push the business forward. Damn his efficiency, Joe thought suddenly. If it were not for his conscientiousness, the terrible, irreparable rift with Roger would never have happened. But it was not fair to blame Deland. He had planned to keep this wounding knowledge to himself. And even though that, perhaps, would have been wrong, Haylow wished with all his heart that Brad had been able to do so.

For the first time in years, Joe Haylow felt helpless, unable to cope with a situation. Even more frighteningly, he did not know where to turn for help. He would have talked to Bridget, but she was out of town. The matter could not, as he'd already decided, be discussed with Pat. And Jimmy Jackson's world was far removed from the complex machinations of commerce. To be honest, Jackson was the last person in the world Joe Haylow wanted to see at this moment. He did not want to hear what he feared Jimmy would tell him: that he'd been uncharitable and un-Christian, the victim of his materialistic ambitions.

There was, of course, only one person, in the final analysis, to whom he could go for advice and counsel. But he wasn't ready to face the terrible honest appraisal Sid Sommers would also make.

It would have to wait a bit. Perhaps God in His infinite wisdom would produce a miracle. It would not be the first time He had done just that for Joe Haylow.

13 🙠

On a crisp clear day late in November, Marjorie Haylow was driving fast but skillfully to New York. Comfortable in the isolation of her sedate and powerful car, she looked like an attractive well-organized, respectable young matron on her way to the city for a couple of days of routine shopping. The casual observer would have been startled to know that she was, in fact, en route to two highly improbable engagements. One was a rendezvous with her married lover. The other was a secretly arranged appointment with a reputable obstetrician.

It had been many months since Marjorie had been to bed with her husband. Her relationship with Brad, more sporadic since Woodward came home, still continued, its lure as sensuously irresistible as it was morally loathsome. Her self-torment was so great, her guilt so enormous, that to compound it by a sexual act with Woodward was unthinkable. It had not been difficult to invent the pretext of extreme emotional instability, to give every evidence of a woman going through a period of nervous tension, unable to give herself in love to her husband. Because it was all true, though not for the reasons she gave Woodward, nor for those he had concluded for himself. Marjorie was simply overwhelmed with disgust at her own uncontrollable lust. She

The Rich and the Righteous

would have felt doubly dirty to give her body to two men. And she felt, in her heart, that she would in some odd way be sullying Woodward who loved her deeply and who accepted so patiently this long withdrawal from the physical aspects of their marriage.

She rejected his suggestion that she seek psychiatric help, stalling for time, hoping that her own will would be strong enough to overcome her seemingly insatiable desire for Brad. As she knew he would, Woodward had been patient, undemanding. He was so confident of her fidelity, her goodness that he waited quietly for her to become, once again, his dependable, acquiescent Marjorie. In return, she had gone out of her way to be almost sisterly affectionate, seeing to his comfort, conscientiously acting out her roles as dutiful daughter-in-law and charming wife of the minister.

There was no telling how long this strange marital relationship could have continued. After her first, distressed offer, they had never again discussed the possibility of divorce, an idea which Woodward had totally rejected and which even Marjorie, despite her infatuation with Brad, could not really visualize. The situation might have gone on for years if it had not been for the fact that Marjorie had good reason to suspect that she was pregnant.

At first, she put the idea out of her mind, attributing the lateness of her period to her own, very real emotional distress. But when the second cycle was missed, her fears became a horrifying certainty. She had not told Brad of her suspicions, and her relationship with Woodward had been so remote that no explanations were necessary. Instead, she had telephoned for an appointment to a doctor in New York whose name she had heard and was on her way now to have her self-diagnosis confirmed.

At the doctor's office, a competent, disinterested middle-aged nurse at the appointment desk filled out a card for this new patient.

"Name?"

"Mrs. Robert Lewis," Marjorie said.

"Your first name, Mrs. Lewis?"

"Patricia."

"Address and telephone?"

Marjorie supplied a fictitious address and telephone number. "That's in San Francisco," she explained. "I'm just visiting in the East for a few weeks, so I'll be paying in cash for this appointment. It won't be necessary to bill me."

The nurse nodded agreement. "Have you any children, Mrs. Lewis?"

"Yes. Two."

"All right," the nurse said pleasantly. "Just have a seat. Doctor will be with you shortly."

As she waited, Marjorie leafed idly through a magazine, seeing nothing on the printed page. Sadly she remembered the other two times she had waited, like this, in the front parlor of her doctor's house in Farmville. She had been so happy then, eager for official word that she was carrying Woodward's child, pleased as a child herself when her pregnancy was confirmed. Now the thought of the tiny spark of life that was growing inside her filled her with despair and shame. It gave her guilt a finality, made her commitment to Brad irrevocable. She looked at the other patients in the waiting room, noting their varying degrees of pregnancy, wondering whether they were excited or apprehensive. She tried to imagine what their husbands were like, and how they reacted to the announcement of impending fatherhood.

She remembered Woodward's delight when she had told him their news. His joy had matched her own. The only person who outdid their happiness was Pat Haylow, who was deliriously excited by the prospect of her first grandchild. Even Joe had hugged her warmly and advised her to take very good care of the newest Haylow.

How different this would be, Marjorie thought sadly. This poor, unwanted baby would be wished away, if such a thing were possible. She wondered how Brad would take the news. She was determined to tell him tonight. Whatever their future course, there were plans to be made.

The doctor had been kind and matter of fact. He examined her, made notes of her responses to his questions, and requested the usual specimen. After the examination she dressed and returned to his office.

"I don't think there's much doubt about your pregnancy, Mrs. Lewis," he said. "You're about six weeks along, I think. Right? We'll run the usual tests and I'll give you final word in three or four days, but I think you can count on having a nice, new baby in July. You're in good health. There should be no problem."

You don't know how funny you are, Doctor, Marjorie thought. Instead, she said, tentatively, "What about my age? I'm thirty-five, you know."

The doctor smiled reassuringly. "That's not exactly ancient, Mrs. Lewis. Besides, it's not your first baby. I deliver women much older than you, though I haven't yet had one on Medicare. Don't worry about it. Just go about your usual business and check with me in a few days. Then we'll set up your future appointments."

"But I live in San Francisco."

"Oh," he said, glancing at the typed card in front of him. "So you do. Well, in that case, you probably have an obstetrician there. I'll forward the report to him, if you like."

"Thank you, but I'll come back for it in a couple of days and take it to him. You've been very kind, Doctor."

"Not at all, Mrs. Lewis. I wish all my patients were as physically fit and emotionally uncomplicated as you!"

On her way out, Marjorie paid for the visit and accepted a receipt. "Come back in about three days," the nurse advised her, "and we'll have the final results of your test."

On the sidewalk, Marjorie glanced at her watch. Four o'clock. She had three hours to kill before meeting Brad at the restaurant. "Their restaurant," they called it. The same one in which they'd had their first luncheon together. Was it only last January that this affair began? It seemed years that she had lived with this delicious, forbidden sense of fulfillment. Always when she knew she was going to meet Brad, her excitement was overwhelming, her anticipation so intense that she could think of nothing except his love-making. But today, with her new knowledge, she had an impulse to run. To get back into her car and drive home to the conventional, reassuring safety of Farmville. For a wild moment she considered doing just that. She would confess everything to Woodward, beg his forgiveness, plead with him to accept her and her illegitimate child in Christ's name.

Woodward, the man of God, probably would be able to do that, she thought. He is so good, so charitable, so lacking in malice that he could accept what other men would reject in outrage and disgust. But simply because he was so good, Marjorie could not do this to him.

For three hours she walked, blind to her surroundings, tortured by her loathing for herself, frightened for her future, filled with sadness for the helpless, innocent victim she carried within her.

At seven o'clock she walked into the restaurant. Brad was already at the bar, quietly sipping his martini. He came forward to meet her.

"I'll have my drink sent to the table, darling," he said. "What shall I order for you—tomato juice?"

"As a matter of fact, I think I'll have what you're having."

Brad raised an eyebrow. "A martini? Well, now that's a conspicuous first! I've never seen you take a drink in your life!"

Marjorie smiled. "There's never been a day like this in my life."

Brad made no comment. "Another martini," he told the waiter. "And send mine over." Settling on the banquette, he picked up her hand and kissed the palm of it. "Have I told you you're exceptionally beautiful today, Mrs. Haylow? Though I detect a trace of sadness that perhaps contributes to the Mona Lisa quality. Something wrong?"

"I don't know," Marjorie said. "Anyway, let's discuss it later."

"Okay. Anyway, how are things in dear old Farmville?"

"About the same in my household. But I'm sure there's something wrong at the big house. Pat seems very distraught. Neither she nor Joe has mentioned Roger in a couple of weeks and there's been no sign of him."

Brad looked at her sharply. "Here's your drink, love," he said. "I don't know what your original reason for ordering it was, but you're going to need it now. Take a very small sip, darling. That's what we call liquid ambush. Cheers."

Marjorie took a small taste and made a face. "It's terrible. Like bad medicine."

"Which automatically means it must be good for you," Brad said.

Obediently, Marjorie took another small swallow. She could feel the liquor burning deep in her stomach and wondered insanely whether the child was recoiling from the harsh bitterness. You must be drunk on two sips of a martini, she told herself, though that has to be impossible even for a person who's never had a drink in her life. I really want to be drunk, she thought. Now I understand why people drink. To forget, even momentarily. To run away from their problems. Like I want to run away from mine. Abruptly, she realized that Brad had said something very strange. "You're going to need it now," he said. He had no idea about the baby. It must be something else.

Alarmed, she turned to look at the handsome, sensuous face.

"Brad. What did you mean, I'm going to need the drink?"

"Sweetheart, you don't know about Roger?"

"No. What about Roger?"

"He left the company two weeks ago. And God help me, it's all my fault."

"Left the company! Brad, that's impossible. When? Why?"

"I think I need another drink," Deland said. "What about you? You've hardly touched that one."

"No. Nothing."

"Just one more," Brad told the waiter. "All right, baby, you have to know sometime. While I was checking out a routine investigation, I turned up some disturbing evidence. Roger is homosexual. And Joe knows it."

Marjorie looked stunned. "You told him?"

"No, of course not," Brad said impatiently. "On the contrary, I tried to hush it up. But somebody found out and sent Joe an anonymous letter."

Marjorie's face was a study in bewilderment. "Then, surely," she said, "Joe questioned Roger about it."

"You bet he did. He made me give him the evidence and he and Roger went behind closed doors. Nobody knows exactly what happened, but the next scene was Roger flying out in a rage. He left the office and never came back. Two days later, Joe called me in and said that Roger had left the organization and I was to say nothing about it to anyone. He indicated that for the time being, anyone who asked would be told that Roger was on a business trip. Jesus, Marjorie, you can't imagine how I feel. If it hadn't been for me, Joe would never have known."

Still trying to grasp the full implications of what she had heard, Marjorie held tightly to Brad's arm. "But there must be some terrible mistake," she said. "Nothing could make me believe that of Roger. Dear God, didn't he deny it?"

"It is true, dearest," Brad said gently. "As I told you, I don't know what was said between the two of them, but Joe had signed proof in front of him. A confession from the guy Roger's involved with."

"But that could be a lie!" Marjorie protested. "He could be lying for some reason."

"Darling, please. No. I witnessed the confession."

In disbelief, Marjorie had no answer. The revelation was too much to bear. She thought of Roger, of the happiness he had radiated since spring. It's not possible, she told herself. It's some kind of awful joke. But why didn't Roger prove to his father that it was a lie, if it was a lie? And what must this be doing to Joe Haylow, whose whole dream of the future rested with this younger son? And Pat. Does she know? Dear Lord, if she does, her heart must be breaking. Even Brad, Marjorie thought with pity, must be cursing himself for being the one to uncover this horror story. For a few moments, Marjorie forgot her own troubles in her sympathy for the lives that had been so terribly affected by this undreamed-of turn of events.

Gently, Brad touched her hand. "Sweetheart, you must not say anything about this to anyone. I don't think Joe has told a soul except me. I imagine he told Pat that Roger was away on a trip. It's possible he's not told Woodward anything at all. So you must keep quiet about it until Joe figures out what he's going to do."

"Do about what?"

"Eventually, he will have to account for the sudden disappearance of his son from the business. Right now, nobody even knows where Roger is. And then there's the matter of the Chairmanship. This puts a different light on the choice of Joe's successor, you know."

"Poor Joe," Marjorie said sadly. "It's worse than if Roger had died."

"You don't really mean that."

"Yes, I do. Death isn't so bad. At least there's a finality, an inevitability that one is forced to accept as the will of God. But this . . ."

"Okay," Brad said briskly. "Enough of this. Our evenings are so few and far between these days that I'm not willing to waste a precious one doing anything but enjoying you. And if you'll pardon my leer, that's exactly what I have in mind for later. I love you very much, darling."

"Do you, Brad? Truly?" A note of anxiety had crept into Marjorie's voice.

"Have you some reason to doubt it?"

Her answer was a small, wistful smile. Later when she told him her news she would know whether there was reason to doubt it. Meanwhile, over dinner she would force herself to play her usual games with him, laughing at his nonsense, feeding his ego with her admiration of his talents, exciting him with the sexual attraction that was so strong between them. Already, Brad had launched into one of the light-hearted anecdotes that he told so well.

"I had the world's nuttiest lunch with Sally Fisher last week," he said. "You've met her, Marjorie, haven't you? She's the heap-big head editor of *Fashion Beautiful*. Well, she started telling me stories about that wacky magazine of hers. Honest to God, you'd never believe what those fashion types are like! How they manage to get out a magazine once a month is beyond me. And a damned good one, at that."

"I didn't know you ever lunched with the magazine people," Marjorie said. "I thought they only saw Bridget and occasionally Joe."

"Normally, they do. But with things likely to come on a little sticky with Haylow in the future, I decided it wouldn't be a bad idea to have as much of the press on our side as we could manage. So I called her and asked her to have lunch. Frankly, I was surprised when she accepted. I never felt she liked me very much. But she couldn't have been more charming. Or, as I said, more amusing. She told me one story that really broke me up. Seems that last winter one of her elegant fashion editors went to the theatre, dressed fit to kill. When this woman and her escort came out of the show it was snowing like crazy and they couldn't get a cab, so they decided to take the subway to the Plaza. Well, they got on, and this dame, all dolled up, was hanging onto a strap and pretending to find it all very amusing. So the train is barreling uptown and the editor says in a loud voice, 'Isn't this mahvelous? I haven't been on a subway in *years!*' At which point a guy sitting behind a copy of the *Daily News* puts down his paper and gives her a look. 'And how we've missed you, lady,' he says, 'how we've *missed* you!'"

All through dinner, Brad kept up a stream of diverting chatter. Almost, Marjorie thought, as though he's trying to keep me from saying something he doesn't want to hear. But it must be said. And tonight.

As he had done so many times before, Brad unlocked the door of his friend's apartment and let Marjorie precede him into the now-familiar hideaway. Closing the door, he took her into his arms.

"Love," he whispered, "dearest little love. It's been too long. I've missed you so much."

Instinctively, Marjorie responded. Their kiss was deep, long, and passionate. Then Marjorie stepped away from him. "Let's sit for a minute, Brad. There's something I've got to tell you."

He joined her on the sofa. "All right, little one. I know you've had something on your mind all evening. What's wrong?"

"Brad, I'm pregnant."

For a moment, the words hung in the stillness between them.

"You're sure?"

"Completely."

Brad went to the little bar in the corner of the living room and began to mix a drink. With his back to her, he spoke. "Have you seen a doctor?"

"This afternoon. He's running the final tests, but there's no doubt in his mind. Nor in mine."

She wished she could see his face. She felt very alone, very frightened. He seemed to be taking an extraordinarily long time to make the drink. She heard the ice cubes clink into the glass, the sound of scotch and water splashing over them.

"The baby's mine, of course?"

Disbelief stunned her. Disillusionment was like a hand tightly gripping her throat, choking off the impulse to scream. Vacantly, unwilling to accept what she had heard, Marjorie made no answer.

Brad came to her quickly, kneeling in front of her as she sat on the couch, rigid as a statue, all the hurt reflected in her eyes. He buried his head in her lap, his arms pressed tight against her thighs.

"Oh, God, forgive me, my darling," he said. "Forgive me."

Still Marjorie made no move. She seemed to be scarcely breathing.

Raising his head to look into her eyes, Brad cupped the deathly still face between his hands.

"Marjorie. Angel. Love. I adore you. God in heaven only knows why I would even ask such a question!"

"Then why did you?" She spoke woodenly, automatically. "Have you had to face this kind of situation so often that it's the normal thing to ask?"

Slowly Brad dropped his hands. "I deserved that," he said quietly. "Even though you know in your heart it isn't true."

"Do I?"

He rose to his feet. Leaving the untouched drink on the floor, he sat beside her on the couch, not touching her, not looking at her. He began to speak, staring straight ahead as though an invisible jury sat on the other side of the room.

"No, you don't know it isn't true. For all you know, I may

295

have paid for a dozen abortions. I may have asked a hundred promiscuous women whether I was the father of their unwanted babies. You can't even know, for certain, whether or not I'll just walk out of here saying, 'Sorry, sweetie, but that's the breaks.' You can't know these things, Marjorie, unless you unquestioningly believe the truth—that you are the only woman I have ever loved. That I love you now. And that I love the child inside of you which is the living proof of that love."

At last the tears came. Like a wounded child, Marjorie crept into his arms. He held her gently, stroking her hair, lightly kissing the top of her head until her sobs subsided.

"Now," he said, "let's talk."

In control of herself, Marjorie dried her tears and even managed the vestige of a grim little smile.

"My darling," Brad said, "the choice is up to you. None of our options are very pretty, but we have to look at them realistically. And whichever one you choose is the one I will agree to."

She nodded mutely.

Brad hesitated. "You have three choices, dear heart. The first and most obvious is, of course, an abortion."

Marjorie sat up, withdrawing from the circle of his arm.

"No," she said. "I have no fear for myself. Not physically. But I would fear for my sanity. If I destroy our child, the only child I've ever borne out of love, I would live with that guilt the rest of my life. I would go out of my mind. Literally, Brad. I know I would."

"All right, sweetheart," he said soothingly. "Then you must consider the second possibility. You're what—two months pregnant?"

"About six weeks."

"Then it is still possible for you to resume your relations with Woodward and produce a premature but unquestioned baby that everyone, including Woodward, will think is his."

Before she could answer, Brad went on. "Remember, my darling, we are talking about *practical* possibilities. I think I know very well what you are going to say, but you must think about it. You would have your child, to grow up safely and securely with the other two you adore. You would spare Woodward a scandal which might ruin his future in the church. You would save Pat and Joe Haylow unspeakable anguish."

"And what of our anguish?" Marjorie asked. "Could you bear to think that your child was never to know you as its father? Do you think I could ever look at Woodward without remembering that I had made a fool of him? Do you think we have strength never to be together again? I belong to you, Brad, now more than ever. I can't pretend this all never happened. Since we met, I have never let Woodward touch me. Do you think I could do it now, knowing that your child is inside me?"

"Darling," Brad said, "please try to be calm. I told you I knew what your answer would be. But you must take as objective a view as you can. My God, Marjorie, I know what that would be like for you. What do you think it would be like for me, knowing I've lost you forever, picturing you back with Woodward, imagining your torment? Don't you know how much I want this child? I've never had a child. Never wanted one by Doe-Doe. I'm fifty years old. Pretty old to start being a father. But I want this baby because it's born of you, because it's my last feeble grasp at immortality. But goddamn it, Marjorie, we have to look at the facts!"

It was she who was the one in control now. It was her turn to comfort and counsel.

"It's a very practical, very sensible, very cold-blooded solution," she said. "And you know I can't accept it. Even if we sacrificed our own desires, even if I steeled myself to being a wife to Woodward again, I would feel cheap and dirty. I've been unfaithful and I pray that God will forgive me for that.

But I'd already reached the point, even before I knew about the baby, where I knew I couldn't go on this way. I had made up my mind to give up my one and only love. To try to make it up to my husband. Now all that's changed, Brad. The child would make it a never-ending deceit."

For a long moment, neither of them spoke.

Finally, Brad sighed heavily. "Then we're left with the third possibility. We'll both have to get free to marry. Is that what you want? Remember, my darling, that too is a mixed bag of curses and blessings. We'll be free to love each other, openly and publicly. To have our child. For me, it's a prospect wonderful beyond belief. But we'll pay for it, too. I know you so well, my little Marjorie. You will still feel your terrible guilt for the hurt you've inflicted on Woodward and your children. It's even possible, you know, that Woodward will not let you have your children. You'll be gossiped about in a way you've never dreamed of. You'll have to face the disappointment of Pat Haylow, a woman you love dearly. And the rejection of another person you care for—Joe Haylow. Think about it, my love. Am I worth it? Is the price too high?"

In answer, Marjorie put her arms around him, touching the strongly chiseled features, gently stroking with her fingertips the worry lines which creased his brow.

"Before I knew we were going to have a child," she said, "I thought about all those things and knew I couldn't face them. The loss of my children, the terrible sadness and disappointment in me that Woodward and Pat and Joe would feel. That's when I made up my mind to break off with you, even if it broke my own heart. But it's somehow different now. These same people who will be so hurt will give all their love and care to my children if Woodward won't let me have them. My husband one day will find someone better and more decent than I. And until he does, he will have the church to sustain him. With your love, I can make it, Brad.

From my point of view, the last choice is the only honorable one. But what about you? Is this what you want?"

"Sweetheart, I want you and our child. But the choice had to be yours."

"Will Doe-Doe divorce you?"

"Strangely enough," Brad said, "the last time we discussed it was when all of us were in Florida for Joe's birthday. She flatly refused. But there are ways to get anything you want. I found that out long ago. Off the top of my head, I'd say the way to get Doe-Doe's agreement is with money. Probably all I have. But who the hell cares? Anyway, my love, that is not your problem. Believe me, it will be arranged."

A sudden, disturbing thought crossed Marjorie's mind.

"There's something else we haven't discussed," she said. "What about your future in Haylow? Joe may be bitterly disappointed in me, but what will he do to you?"

"I don't know. Get rid of me, probably. Hell hath no fury like the Chairman scorned . . . or words to that effect."

"But with Roger gone, and now you . . ."

"Dearest, this is like the Doe-Doe problem. Mine. Not yours. There's no need for you to worry. I'm highly employable, you know. Haylow-trained, and all that. We'll always have 'eating money.'"

"Brad, you know that kind of thing never would cross my mind."

"I know, honey, I was only making a bad joke. The least of our problems is my business future. The thing I hate most is the thought of your having to tell Woodward. Everything else can be handled, but I want to help you figure out a way to do this with the least possible pain to you, my darling. I think you should say nothing for a little while. Meantime, I'll start quietly lining up things with my lawyer. In a month or so from now, with any luck at all, we'll be on our way to Mexico."

He put his hand under her chin and raised her mouth close to his.

"Stop looking so forlorn, my angel," he said. "There's a wonderful life ahead. Trust me. You'll see."

"I trust you."

Brad's hands began to move slowly over her body. "You're my wife already," he said. "Just keep that in mind."

As always, Marjorie's senses began to swim. She made no protest as he picked her up lightly and started for the bedroom. Soon, soon, she thought dreamily, there'll be no more secret apartments, no more stolen rapturous moments. It's worth it. All of it. Now and forever.

14

For the first time in nearly half a century, Joe Haylow faced his inability to cope with a problem. Remembering every nuance of his last conversation with Roger, he had the peculiar feeling that he had been watching some other man in action. Had the "accused" been anyone but his son, the Chairman would have proceeded in a deliberate, unemotional way to verify or disprove the story put forth in the anonymous letter and confirmed by Brad Deland. He would have done the obvious: called in the mysterious Peter Johnson and provoked a nose-to-nose confrontation with Roger Haylow. Instead, almost as though he had been waiting for it, he had taken Roger's outraged refusal to confirm or deny the charge as a tacit admission of his guilt.

There had been no word of Roger since the day he slammed out of his father's office two weeks before. Joe had not tried to find him. He had invented a business trip for Roger. Pat had accepted the story, though she expressed understandable surprise that her son had not even called to say goodbye. Joe had tossed it off lightly. "You know how Roger is, darling," he'd said. "He sent you his love and said not to worry if you didn't hear."

Only two people knew the real story—Deland and now, though Haylow was unaware of it, Marjorie. Since the awful moment of his break with Roger, Joe had not been able to speak of it to anyone. It was totally unlike him to accept, without argument, a fact that came close to destroying his whole world. He had not even felt capable of anger. He had been, for the second time in life, nearly speechless in the face of Roger's outpouring of bitterness and hatred. It was as though he was reliving the birthday dinner. He remembered that he had made no answer then, either. He had been overwhelmed, stunned by the depth of his son's resentment, struck dumb by the realization of Roger's long-harbored, agonized feeling of rejection.

Finally, as he had in January, Joe turned once more to the one man whose advice and counsel he respected. Sid Sommers came immediately in response to Haylow's call. As the world outside Joe Haylow's office drowned in tears of cold November rain, Sid sat quietly beside the Chairman listening to the story as his old friend slowly, painfully outlined it. The account ended, as it had, with Roger's furious departure. Taking in every word, reading into each one shades of meaning that eluded the narrator, Sid Sommers felt a terrible pity for the Haylows. He understood them both better than they understood themselves. But even stronger than his pity was his revulsion for Brad Deland. The story, Sid felt sure, was so obviously a well-conceived scheme drawn up by an evil man who knew how to manipulate the emotions of his victims. Yet, Sid was sure that such a story could not be made up out of whole cloth. More likely it was a fabrication built on some elusive vestige of reality, a half-truth used as the basis of an almost plausible lie.

When Joe had come to the end of it, Sid asked the obvious question. "You've made no effort to find this Peter Johnson?"

"None."

"That's so strange, it must even strike you as odd," Sid said. "I've watched you in operation for too many years, Joe, to accept that as your normal way of business. You're not the kind of man who listens to one side of a story and accepts it without digging into the background."

Joe felt provoked. "In the name of heaven, don't you think I know that? I can't even believe my own behavior! Why do you think I've called you—to confess? This thing has floored me, Sid. What has happened to me? The fight's gone out of me. Right or wrong, I've always been a decisive man, an opinionated man. You know that. And yet here I am, frightened as a woman!"

Sommers let him have it without pity. "What are you afraid of, Joe? Afraid that if you investigate this matter your worst suspicions will be confirmed? Scared you'll find out that your son is a homosexual? You couldn't stand that, could you? You couldn't bear to know for sure because it would be such a reflection—not on Roger, but on you. That's what you're really scared of, isn't it? That you, the great Joe Haylow, could produce a less than perfect specimen. Does your ego know no bounds? Is it so great that you'll sacrifice a good man like Roger Haylow and let a sonofabitch like Brad Deland maneuver you and a lot of other innocent people into the very spot he wants them? What are you saying to yourself, Joe—'What I don't know for sure won't hurt me?' Well, forget it, friend, it won't work. If you don't find out right now what's at the bottom of this, you'll never have an untroubled day the rest of your life. God isn't going to pop up with a miracle, though I'm sure you've asked Him to!"

As Sid hoped he would, Haylow struck back. It was the old Haylow speaking, the tough, self-willed, indomitable Haylow.

"That's enough!" Joe shouted. "Not even all these years of friendship gives you the right to accuse me of such weakness! I'm a proud man, Sid, but I've never been a vain one!"

"Haven't you? Where does one draw the line between confidence and ego? How do you tell the difference between pride and vanity? Are you such a superior human being that you are without faults and weaknesses?" Sid's voice softened, compassionately. "Dear friend," he said, "we are all mortal and fallible. We all have our share of inner fears and self-doubts. Sometimes we can't bear to admit to ourselves that we have failed. Because the best of us, like you, are not without flaws which we keep hidden behind a dazzling façade of success or righteousness. In many ways, Joe, you are an exceedingly humble man. You fear your God as you adore Him. You are grateful for your good fortune and you try to repay it with overt acts of charity and good will. But you are as emotionally blind as you are logically perceptive."

Haylow said nothing. His anger subsided, he knew that Sommers had put his finger on the fear that gnawed at Haylow's heart and mind. It was true. He did not want to pursue the accusation against Roger because he could not bear to have it proved out. It was, in a strange way, easier to accept the doubt than live with what Joe despairingly felt was the truth.

With an uncharacteristic gesture of defenselessness, Haylow held out both hands. "Help me," he said. "In God's name, Sid, what am I to do?"

All the love he felt for Joe Haylow was in Sid Sommer's voice, though his words were brisk, unemotional, objective.

"All you can do now is let me go to work," Sid said. "You're too personally involved in this problem to see it through. That's my kind of job. And I've got a few ideas where to begin."

Hopefully, Joe felt as though a burden had been lifted. He had needed the therapy of this conversation, needed the calm, direct reaction of Sid Sommers whose love for him made it possible for Joe to articulate his problems and accept, almost with humility, the criticism he knew he deserved. Yet one nagging question remained.

"I still don't understand something," Haylow said. "If Roger is innocent of this accusation, why didn't he deny it?

Why didn't he insist upon my getting hold of Johnson and Deland and making them prove these charges? Why did he refuse to answer?"

Sommers sighed. "Until you understand that, Joe," he said, "you will understand nothing. I don't think this is the time or place to go into it. Perhaps when we get more answers, you will have no need to ask the question. But there's one thing you must promise me."

"Anything I can," Haylow said.

"Whatever we find out about this matter, you will continue to love your son."

Haylow smiled. A sad, almost wistful smile. "You don't need my promise for that," he said. "I may suspect him, denounce him, even revile him, but I could never stop loving him. He's a part of me." Then Haylow laughed ruefully at his own words. "I guess that's ego too, isn't it?"

"You're beginning to get the message," Sid said. "It's going to be all right, Joe. I promise you."

"Yes," Haylow answered, "I believe it is."

Sommers' first stop after his disquieting talk with Haylow was the office of Bridget Manning. Her secretary showed him in immediately, and Bridget greeted him with a warm hug.

"Well," she said, "this is a nice surprise. To what do I owe the honor?"

"You know I never pass up a chance to talk to a pretty lady," he said, "but actually I'm here in my official capacity as the resident Company Snoop. Bridget, I need some information and I hope you can help. First of all, have you seen Roger lately?"

Bridget looked troubled. "No. Not seen him nor even heard from him in a couple of weeks. His secretary tells me he's on a trip, but it certainly was a precipitous and mysterious departure. And not even a call, which is kind of odd, considering."

Sommers lifted his eyebrows.

"Not that he has to account to me or anybody else for his comings and goings," Bridget said, "but Roger and I have been pretty close these last few months—a lot of it thanks to you, really. Anyway, what I mean is that I was surprised that he'd just suddenly disappear without mentioning the fact that he was going away."

"I'm not trying to pry into your personal life, Bridget," Sid said, choosing his words with care, "but I have a reason for asking and I hope you won't be offended. Is there anything between you and Roger?"

"You mean an affair? No. I think I'd have one with him if he made a move toward it, but he never has. No, Sid, I'm very attracted to Roger. In these past months, since I've really come to know him a little, I find him enormously appealing. Hell, I don't even care that I'm a few years older. But it's never gotten beyond the hand-holding stage, and that's the truth."

"I'm almost as sorry about that as you are."

Bridget looked puzzled. "Don't tell me you're playing matchmaker, too! Between you and me, I can see that look in Pat's eyes every time I go to Farmville. But I don't think it's going to happen."

"Why not?" Sid asked.

"Just call it woman's intuition. Now, look, Sid, what's this all about? I know you didn't come here to find out whether Roger has honorable intentions toward me—or vice versa."

"In a way I did," he said. "To be perfectly honest, I was really hoping that you'd tell me you and Roger were having a wild thing together. I know this whole thing sounds insane, Bridget, but I'm just not at liberty to tell you what's behind it."

"Then I won't ask," she replied. "But I will ask something else. Is Roger in some kind of trouble? Is that why he took off so suddenly?"

"Yes, he's in trouble," Sid answered. "At least, he will be if I can't get to the bottom of a mystery. Listen, I do apologize for being so cloak-and-dagger, honey. There's nothing more irritating, I know, than for somebody to bring up a subject and leave you wondering what it's all about. But for now that's what I have to do. You'll know the whole story eventually. And I hope it has a happy ending."

"But you are telling me that Roger's really vanished, aren't you?"

"Yes," Sid admitted, "I am telling you that something pretty sad happened between him and his father. It was bad enough to make Roger chuck the whole thing and run. Right now, all the missionary work that you and I have done this last year seems to have gone to hell in a handbasket."

"Somehow, I just knew it was something like that," Bridget said sadly. "Whatever it is, Sid, please fix it. For both their sakes. And if there's anything, anything at all that I can do, you'll tell me, won't you?"

"Of course. Meantime, don't mention any of this to anybody, including Joe. And if you do hear from Roger, let me know. I think you might be the only one he'll feel able to talk to in time."

Ambling along, looking like a stupid, fat man without a care in the world, a deeply troubled Sid Sommers headed for his next interview, a talk with Mike Warner. Sid admitted to himself that knowledge of an affair between Roger and Bridget would have considerably eased his mind. Not that he believed for a moment this crap about Roger's homosexuality. Nor would it have proved anything if Roger had been sleeping with Bridget. Lots of guys swing both ways. Still, it was strange that with Bridget so obviously willing to go to bed with Roger, nothing had come of it. Did he still think she was Joe's mistress? Circumstantial evidence, he told himself. But disturbing.

This is a crazy kind of jigsaw, Sid thought, going up in the elevator to Mike's office. All the pieces of the plot are here, but somebody's tampered with the edges of the puzzle to make them damned near impossible to put together.

"It's my lucky day," he said to Mike when he was shown into the Star President's office. "First I make an unannounced call on Bridget and find her in, and now I barge in and find you minding the store."

Mike laughed. "Obviously you don't know much about the retail business. This time of year we all stay close to home. 'Tis the season to be jolly. It may only be November to you, but it's the onslaught of Christmas to us merchants and this is the time we make it or drop dead."

"Seems to me we didn't used to worry about Christmas till December," Sid said. "Now you vultures start pushing us right after Halloween."

"You're right," Mike agreed. "We get greedier and greedier. The only trouble is that most of the public is just like you. Even if we put up the decorations in July, nobody would start their shopping until Christmas Eve. Anyway, we try. God knows we try! The things we do for Joe Haylow surpasseth human understanding."

"Amen," Sommers said. "But he's worth it."

"Worth it and then some," Mike said. "There's nothing we wouldn't do for the Chairman. Like now. Whenever I see you, Sid, I figure you're on some mission for Joe. Right?"

"One of the toughest I've ever had," Sid answered. "Can you spare a little time?"

"All you want."

"Okay. Needless to say, everything I'm going to tell you is classified information, but I hope through you we can unravel a pretty dirty deal."

For the next half hour, Mike Warner listened as Sid detailed the story of Roger as Joe had told it to him. To the facts Joe had given him, he added Bridget's small, probably insignificant contribution and filled Mike in on the events

The Rich and the Righteous

which had followed the Florida birthday party, explaining Roger's new-found understanding of his father, and the happiness Roger's changed attitude had brought everyone.

"And now," Sid concluded, "this goddamn thing has happened."

Mike Warner was aghast. "Jesus, Sid, it's a setup. That bastard Deland has rigged it!"

Sid nodded. "That's what I believe. The question is, how are we going to prove it? Joe can't face making an investigation. And Roger, assuming we could find him, is so insulted by the allegation that he won't even stoop to deny it."

"What do you want me to do?"

"Well," Sommers said, "the way I figure it is that the key to the puzzle is sitting twelve stories underneath us right now."

Mike thought for a moment. "Of course," he said, "Terry White! The guy who signed the so-called confession is his roommate. And you say that this Johnson character supposedly did it to protect Terry?"

"That's Deland's story."

Mike buzzed his secretary. "Call Mr. White in cosmetics," he told her, "and ask him to come to my office immediately." Mike turned back to Sid. "What do we do when he gets here?" he asked. "Play it straight or do we set a trap?"

Sommers looked grim. "We'll do anything we have to. Joe would call it 'fighting fire with fire.' But in the newspaper business, they have another expression. They say, 'It takes a dirty mind to put out a clean newspaper.' We're up against some rough players, Mike. Blackmailers, liars, opportunists. If Terry White is one of them, we'll try to beat him at his own game."

"And if he isn't?"

"Then we'll find out even faster what's behind all this."

Each engrossed in his own thoughts, Joe Haylow's two friends awaited Terry White. Sommers was quietly planning

309

his approach. Mike Warner was thinking of his wife. It was not an irrelevant wandering of the mind. In times of deepest trouble, the vision of Rose was like a link with that part of the world that was sane, uncomplicated, and trusting. And Mike invariably imagined himself trying to explain to her the ethically dubious machinations of the world of big business. By so doing, he was really trying to rationalize them to himself. Usually, as now, it was an impossible task.

The young man who was unwittingly the cause of the upheaval within The Haylow Corporation came innocently to Mike Warner's office like, he later thought, the proverbial lamb. Peter Johnson had told no one, not even Terry, of his strange meeting with Brad Deland. Like Brad, Peter was waiting until the appropriate time to collect his reward. In his case, he hoped it would be the gratitude of Terry White.

Terry had almost forgotten his one brief encounter with Dick Cabot. Subconsciously, he had put it out of his thoughts, instinctively classifying it as dangerous knowledge. As a result, the sexual deviation of Haylow's President was the farthest thing from his mind when he responded to a not-unusual call to come up to see Mr. Warner.

He did not know the heavy-set man who lounged in the chair beside Mike's desk. Hesitantly, Terry lingered in the doorway.

"Come in," Mike called. "There's someone here I want you to meet. Mr. Sommers, this is Terry White who, as you know, is slated to be President of Elmarie. Terry, Mr. Sommers is the Corporate Public Relations Consultant for our company and the Chairman's personal advisor."

The two men, one so young and eager, the other so seasoned and deliberate, acknowledged the introduction.

"Sit down, Terry," Mike said. "Mr. Sommers has a few questions for you."

Sid gave an easy chuckle. "Good Lord, Mike," he drawled,

"you'll scare this young fella to death. You make me sound like the Lord High Executioner with all those high-flown titles. Mr. White will think he's going to undergo some kind of Perry Mason cross-examination. Shucks, all I'm looking for is a little background information."

In spite of the deadly seriousness of the situation, Mike had to smile at Sid's imitation of a slow-thinking Southern backwoodsman. It was a good act. The only thing missing was a piece of straw sticking out of the corner of Sid's mouth. He could almost see Terry relaxing, lulled into the momentary delusion that he was dealing with a kindly old Haylow retainer. His first words confirmed Mike's analysis. Terry's tone was respectfully courteous.

"Certainly, sir," he said pleasantly. "Anything you want to know."

Plucking a paper match folder from Mike's desk, Sid began to slice the cover into small pieces with the famous little gold knife.

"Just one or two little things," he said casually. "I've heard some mighty nice things about you from Roger Haylow. You two good friends?"

"Well, I hope we're friends," Terry said earnestly. "I admire Mr. Haylow very much and I'm grateful for the way he's supported me for the job at Elmarie."

"I'm sure his trust is well placed," Sommers said easily. "Tell me, Terry, does your friend Peter Johnson share your high regard for Roger Haylow?"

It was a quick thrust. Terry felt a sudden twinge of alarm. Why was Sommers bringing Peter into this conversation? Obviously Sommers knew, from Joe Haylow, that Terry shared an apartment with Peter Johnson, but what did that have to do with Roger Haylow? Terry's hesitation was only fractional but, to Sommers' practiced ear, it was a revealing pause.

"I don't think I understand your question, sir," Terry said.

"I have spoken of Mr. Haylow to Peter, of course. But they've never met."

"Funny," Sommers said. "That's not what Mr. Johnson allows."

Terry looked quizzically at Mike Warner, who sat quietly at his desk, saying nothing. Sommers made a deep slash in the match folder.

"In fact," Sommers went on, "Mr. Johnson says that he's much friendlier with Roger Haylow than you are. Much friendlier." He underlined the last phrase meaningfully.

Terry's bewilderment was unmistakable to the other two men in the room. Still no words came from the young buyer.

"Mr. Peter Johnson," Sid said, drawing out the name as though it was some kind of ugly disease, "Mr. Peter Johnson claims to be involved in a homosexual liaison with Roger Haylow. Mr. Peter Johnson has sworn to that fact in a signed statement."

Terry's reaction was violent. "That's insane!" There was no mistaking his incredulity. "Mr. Sommers, that's a lie! I swear to you, Peter has never even met Roger. Why would he make such a statement?"

"He was found out by one of our executives," Sid explained. "And his confession was accompanied by his promise of secrecy. In return for which, he was given assurance that your future in The Haylow Corporation would be in no way jeopardized. It seems that Mr. Johnson is very fond of you and afraid that his corruption of the Chairman's son would, understandably, reflect on your advancement in this company."

Terry's face was ashen. Desperately, he tried to figure out the purpose of all this. He assumed that Sommers was telling the truth in this shorthand version of what must be a long and complicated story. But, Terry wondered, what was behind it? Why would Peter confess to a lie that implicated the innocent Roger Haylow? What would be the purpose? And who

The Rich and the Righteous

was the executive who "discovered" the story and made the deal with Peter?

Terry's head was swimming. Speechless with confusion and a sense of foreboding, he groped for words. Helplessly, he looked from Mike to Sid. Both men were impassive, waiting motionless. Piteously, Terry appealed to Mike.

"Mr. Warner, what can I say? None of this is true. I swear before God. I don't understand it."

Mike felt sympathy for him. But they could not let up. Somewhere, Terry had the answer to Deland's treachery. They had to find it, even though Terry himself might not know what it was.

"Terry, we believe you're telling the truth." Mike looked to Sid for confirmation and was answered by a slight nod of agreement. "But we must find out why your roommate was party to this vicious story. Tell us a little about him. Maybe we'll get a clue."

With effort, Terry sketched in the background of his life with Peter Johnson, embellishing it with details which he had carefully omitted from his conversation with Joe Haylow.

"It is true," Terry admitted, "that Peter and I once were involved with each other, but that ended long ago. I've been straight for years, but Peter has been so down on his luck that I couldn't move out and let him starve. I was relieved when he found someone else who was fond of him and who was willing to supply him with money and . . ." Terry stopped short. The recollection of Cabot suddenly came back with all its possible significance. Horrified, he faced his inquisitors. Both men realized, instantly, that they were on the trail of something important. Sid Sommers jumped in quickly.

"Yes? Go on, Terry. Who came into Peter's life?"

Terry wavered uncertainly. "I can't. I mean, I'm not sure. I only saw him once for a minute . . ."

"Goddamn you," Mike Warner shouted, "give us that name!"

Physically frightened now, Terry blurted out the truth. "All right, the man is Mr. Cabot."

If White had said Jimmy Jackson, Terry's audience could not have been more stunned. Mike and Sommers looked at each other in pure amazement.

Finally, Sid spoke quietly. "Okay, Terry, let's get this straight. You're now telling us that Richard Cabot is the man with whom your roommate is involved? Richard Cabot, the President of Haylow?"

Terry nodded mutely.

"Yes," Terry answered. "But I don't think Peter knows who he is. Peter told me about him, but he always refers to him as Carswell. They meet in the afternoons at our apartment. I had never seen him until one day, months ago, when I went home unexpectedly at lunchtime. Carswell was there with Peter and I recognized him from his photographs in the annual report. It was Richard Cabot."

Mike Warner gave a low whistle. "Wow," he said. It was Sid Sommers who took charge.

"As you can see, Terry," he said, "you've given us quite a surprise. Not a very happy one, I must say, but at least a lot of things are coming clear. And perhaps, thanks to you, a terrible wrong can be righted. We appreciate your honesty, son. You've done a great service for a couple of damned wonderful people named Haylow, and we won't forget it."

Mike Warner came around the desk and put his hand on Terry's shoulder. "I second those words," he said. "That wasn't an easy story to tell. But we are grateful. There's just one thing more for now, Terry. No word of this must leak out. To anyone. Mr. Sommers and I can't even tell you some of the things you must be anxious to know. Like the name of the man to whom Peter made his so-called confession. Or why he did it. We're not free to give you these details, but some day you'll know the whole story. And when you're sit-

314

ting in the President's chair at Elmarie, you'll understand even better the need for this kind of executive discretion."

What a nice man you are, Terry thought, looking up into the gentle, compassionate face of Mike Warner. He realized that Mike's humane qualities went far deeper than any condemnation of Terry's unconventional life. He had also managed to tell him, obliquely, that his cherished dream was still alive; he would be President of Elmarie, despite the cloak of suspicion that Peter Johnson and some unknown devil had managed to draw around Roger Haylow and, indirectly, around Terry himself.

"I promise you, Mr. Warner, that I'll say nothing. You can depend on it. You too, Mr. Sommers."

Sid nodded. "We feel confident of that, Terry."

Hesitatingly, Terry rose. "That's it for now?" he asked.

"As far as you're concerned," Sommers agreed. He hoisted his bulk out of the chair. "As for me, I've got a few more odds and ends to tidy up. By golly, you'd think an old crock like me would be sittin' on his front porch whittlin' at a stick instead of runnin' around trying to untangle a lot of confounded, city-slicker complicated plots."

Sid had reverted, almost with a touch of comic relief, to the exaggerated drawl he had used when Terry White first came in. Relieved, both of the other men smiled at the deliberate parody of a rube. No wonder they call him "the velvet knife," Mike thought. He's an accomplished actor. That terrific old boy can handle the best of them—or the worst. And they never know their throats have been cut until they try to turn their heads.

When Terry had gone, Mike turned to Sommers.

"Can you believe it?" he asked in amazement. "Dick Cabot, that meek little undersized hunk of vanilla pudding involved with a fag actor?"

"Mike, my boy, nothing surprises me any longer," Sid said. "It's only the obvious that's really obscure. When you think about Cabot—admittedly in the light of what we now know—it's not hard to accept. The poor little devil. Pint-sized, insecure in a world of mental and financial giants. Married to that domineering Amazon. Where could he go to find love? Where could he even buy it except from an amoral alley cat like this Peter Johnson?"

"I suppose you're right," Mike admitted. "But I'd never have suspected in a thousand years."

"Tell you the truth," Sid answered, "I don't think anybody would. Including me, the great big hot-shot psychologist. Hell, he even fooled that battery of psychological tests we put him through when he joined the company. Maybe his homosexuality was so latent even he had no idea about it until he ran into this cheap chiseler Johnson. Can't help feeling sorry for him. It's likely to be the end of him with Haylow, for one thing."

"What are you going to do now?" Mike asked.

"Well, we haven't put all the parts of the puzzle together even yet," Sid admitted. "But if I were going to make a wild guess, I'd say that Mr. Bradford Deland III is going to have a lot of explaining to do to Mr. Joseph Woodward Haylow."

"You're going to see Brad?"

"Nope," Sommers said, "that's Joe Haylow's job. My next step is to give a big, scared Chairman a piece of very good news about his son. And a piece of unfortunate information about his President. Not that the latter will upset him very much, I guess. His opinion of Dick Cabot has never been very high. Maybe he subconsciously sensed something that none of the rest of us did. Anyway, he's never given two hoots for Cabot. You know that, Mike. But Deland will be something else."

"Yes," Mike agreed. "Joe admires Brad. I hate to think how he'll react to this kind of double-dealing on Brad's part."

Sommers frowned. "I hate to think that this kind of thing can go on in the big, respected world of commerce. My God, if people knew what petty, conniving minds were functioning at the top level of industry, they'd all sell their stocks and keep their money in their mattresses!"

"Not as long as they knew guys like you were still on the scene," Mike said admiringly.

Sid shrugged off the compliment. "All in a day's work," he said. "But by God I feel sorry for Joe Haylow when he realizes how unfair he's been to Roger."

"I take it," Mike said wryly, "that you don't have much sympathy for Brad Deland."

"You know," Sommers said slowly, "in a strange way I do have sympathy for Deland. Oh, he's a no-good, destructive animal, that's for sure. But did you ever think, Mike, how terrible it must be to be so obsessed with ambition that there's nothing too rotten to do if it will further your ends? You have to feel pity for that kind of compulsive drive because it controls a man, makes him the slave instead of the master. God knows, I don't condone what Brad did. Or tried to do. I just feel sorry for any poor bastard who's eaten up with avarice. It must tear at his guts. The lust for power can be more consuming than the urge for a woman. Because it's insatiable."

Slowly, almost sadly, Sid Sommers lumbered toward the door. "Well," he said, "now I go see my good friend Joe Haylow. Wish me luck."

In fifteen minutes, Sid was facing the Chairman.

"Lean back and relax, Joe," he said. "I've got a very interesting story to tell you."

15

Cheats, liars, and thieves were no strangers to Joe Haylow. In decades of dealing in the retail business, with forays into Wall Street, the Chairman had met all kinds, professional and petty. Some of them had been rough customers, but Haylow, secure in the knowledge of his own strength and ability, had taken a certain pleasure in outmaneuvering them. He had never lost a business battle. Never met a man —or a company—who could not be brought around, however reluctantly, to Haylow's view of things.

Yet, as he listened to Sid Sommers' calm recital of the facts he had learned that day, Haylow felt physically ill. Sid had been right. Joe's reaction to Cabot's part in the story was almost negligible. He felt nothing for the man, personally or professionally. What sickened him was the realization of Deland's filthy deception, for he, too, felt certain that Deland had, with diabolical calculation, rearranged the facts of the story to suit his own ends. Far worse still was the shame Joe Haylow felt for the injustice he had done his son. He knew now what Sommers had meant when he told Joe that until he understood Roger's refusal to deny the charge, he would understand nothing. Roger was a sensitive man, but he was truly a man. To have his integrity questioned by his own father was insupportable, too insulting to be worthy of a reply. Disgust for his own iron-fisted, thick-skinned mishandling of the situation weighed heavily on Joe Haylow. The realization of his own arrogance and lack of faith was a crushing admission of his own selfishness.

When Sid had finished his story, Haylow's quick mind filled in the gaps. He turned to Sommers for confirmation.

"It seems obvious what he did, doesn't it?"

"The facts look pretty clear," Sid said. "There's no doubt that somehow Deland got wind of what was going on with Cabot and Johnson. Then he conveniently decided to make it look like Roger was the one involved instead of Dick. He played on Johnson's attachment for Terry White and probably threw in a wad of hush money as extra insurance that Johnson would stick to his story."

Haylow shook his head in amazement. "That's the way I figure it too. Do you think Cabot knows about it?"

"Frankly, I doubt it," Sid said. "I don't think Cabot has the guts to go along with a deal as risky as this one. I'm sure he'd sell his soul to keep this thing quiet, no doubt about that. But I don't think Cabot's a vicious man. Misguided and pathetic, all right. But not ruthless."

"I agree," Haylow said. "Deland is the villain of this piece, and Roger was the intended victim. Imagine a man's mind working that way, Sid! For all its disgusting aspects, it's fiendishly brilliant. Brad knew that I was coming closer every day to deciding on Roger as the next Chairman. I've made no bones about my admiration for the way he's functioned this last year. So," Haylow went on, thinking aloud, "Deland had to get rid of Roger who stood in the way of his own Chairmanship. He was counting on the fact that I'd never name Cabot. My God," Haylow said wonderingly, "he's been diabolically clever. Think how skillfully he anticipated everybody's reactions, especially Roger's and mine. And how close he came to getting away with it! Probably would have, if it hadn't been for you."

Sommers frowned. "It isn't quite solved yet, you know.

Even when you face Deland with your knowledge of the facts, you have a few problems left. You'll get rid of him, of course. And I don't think he's in any position to make trouble about that, now that we have Terry White's information. I suppose you'll also want Cabot out, too. But that means unless you can make peace with Roger, you'll be left with no one ready to step into your shoes in January."

"I have to make peace with Roger," Joe said. "Not only for the sake of the business. That's secondary. I have to try to make amends for my lack of faith in him. I only hope it isn't too late."

Sid tried to console him. "Roger's a decent, understanding man," he said.

"Much more than I am," Joe replied bitterly. "In his place, I don't know whether I could find it in my heart to forgive my father for the things I've done to him. Not only in this case but, I guess, all through the years. I haven't tried to be very close to him ever, Sid. I was always too busy, too ambitious, too intolerant of his needs. He's told me that. Twice. Can I overcome it all at this late date?"

"We'll just have to wait and see. But before you can apologize, we have to find Roger. Nobody's heard from him. I'm hoping he'll get in touch with Bridget."

"You've told her the whole story?"

"No. Just that there's trouble between the two of you. But I've asked her to let me know if Roger turns up. Then we'll take it from there."

"Meanwhile," Joe Haylow said heavily, "I have to see Cabot and Deland."

"Okay if I make a suggestion?" Sid asked. "I see no reason to involve Cabot in this at the moment. We know about him, and the fewer hysterical people we have running around right now, the better our chances for keeping this whole thing quiet. What the hell, Joe, you never tell him anything anyhow. Why start now?"

Despite his unhappiness, Haylow had to laugh. "All right, I won't talk to Cabot, at least not until everything's ironed out. But you do agree," Joe said seriously, "that I've got to thrash this out with Deland immediately?"

"Of course. And as my grandson says, 'Keep your cool.' This is a barracuda we're dealing with. I don't think he can cause a public scandal, but with that kind of a warped and twisted mind you can't be sure whether he won't go off the deep end when he finds out his plan has backfired. I'm counting on the fact that it's power, not paranoia, that drove him to this, but you can't ever be sure."

"You think he's unbalanced?"

"No," Sommers said, "not in the true medical sense. But I think he's proved what a driven, desperate man he is. With this frustration, he might go to any lengths for revenge, including his own destruction if he thinks he can destroy you and the company with him."

Haylow looked doubtful. "Sounds a little farfetched to me."

Sommers gave his own knee a resounding smack. "You do beat all, Joe Haylow! I've just outlined one of the most cunningly contrived plans in the history of big business, and you have the nerve to sit there and tell me that it's farfetched to think the guy who made the plot isn't capable of even more deadly complications!"

"You're right," Joe agreed. "I'm just having a hard time grasping this whole thing, I guess. Okay, Sid, you have my word. I'll try to stay calm. And Sid . . ."

"Yes?"

"How can I ever thank you?"

"Why don't you shut up and go to work?" Sommers asked affectionately. "Remember me? I do my job. Let me know what happens."

It was late in the afternoon when Sid left and, as he often did, Joe decided to "sleep on the problem" before talking to

Brad. He realized that Sommers' warning about Brad's behavior could have more than a little validity. He needed time to think about the shocking things he'd heard, the terrible injustice that had been done. Realistically, he also needed to consider the future of his business in the unthinkable event that Roger would never return to it.

Haylow spent a sleepless night. For once he could not lose himself in his reading. Even the Bible gave him no comfort. Every passage he turned to seemed to confirm the wickedness, the godlessness of man. From his bedroom window he watched the feeble morning light of winter appear, saw the early dog-walkers hurrying their shivering pets into the gutters where little patches of ice had formed overnight. A few sleepy doormen, already bundled into their winter overcoats, took up reluctant posts at apartment entrances nearby, preparing for the frustrating task of whistling for rush-hour taxis.

Joe wished that Pat or even Marjorie had spent the night at the apartment. He had never felt so alone, so unsure of his next move. He dreaded the interview with Deland but to his surprise he felt more sorrow than anger. He supposed this was good. It would help him to follow the unemotional course that Sommers had advised.

Shortly before eight o'clock, Haylow was in his office. In the next hour he made three trips to the men's room, unlocking the door with the key awarded, like some status symbol, only to the company's top brass. On the third trip, he thought about the meaning of "a key to the Executive John." We're all so high and mighty, he thought, that we even have to have a special place to perform the natural functions. Every move we make is a subtle reflection of our need for reassurance: the personalized office, the first-class airplane seat, the meaningless awards and trophies, the friendships with people in high places, the ego-swelling publicity interviews. We use them to bolster our conviction that we have power and prestige, that our success has made us invulnerable. Brad Deland

323

is guilty of this false pride. And so, thought Haylow, am I.

As though to mark the uniqueness of this meeting, Joe decided to have the talk in Deland's office rather than his own. A few minutes after nine, Haylow's Financial Vice President was startled to enter his quarters and find the Chairman sitting there, waiting for him.

"Well," Brad said. "Good morning, Joe."

Haylow's expression was blank, unreadable. "Morning," he said.

"Tough morning," Deland said, "looks like we're going to get a lot of snow."

The very fact of the Chairman's presence in his office alerted Brad to trouble. Except for a quick word on his way out, Haylow never spent time in the offices of other executives. It was, Brad remembered, the very fact that the significant Elmarie meeting had taken place in Roger's office that had rung the alarm bell in Deland's own mind. He sensed, intuitively, that the Elmarie meeting and this one were ominously related.

Haylow came right to the point. "I've come to ask for two things," he said. "The first is a written retraction of the story about my son and this Peter Johnson."

Brad's eyes narrowed. "And the second?"

"Your resignation."

Brad studied the Chairman carefully for a long moment. With certainty, he knew that somehow Haylow had found out the whole truth. Which meant that he also knew about Cabot. Deland weighed his words carefully.

"Two very large favors," he said coolly. "On what basis do you make them, may I ask?"

"First of all, they're not favors," Joe said. "They're demands. I have irrefutable proof that you forced Peter Johnson into signing a false statement implicating an innocent man. I have a witness to this fact. And I can produce additional witnesses if you make such a step necessary."

The Rich and the Righteous

It was a bluff, but Deland could not know that. So far Haylow had only Terry White's word that the man involved was Cabot, but it would be easy enough to prove. Joe knew that Cabot, unmasked, would cry like a baby and Johnson, under pressure, would repudiate his "confession." For all Deland knew, these things had already happened. Or if they had not, Brad was smart enough to know that they could.

"On the basis of these facts," Haylow continued, "I could dismiss you. For the harm you have done, I would like to take my revenge. I would enjoy nothing more than making sure that you were exposed to the world as a blackmailer. God forgive me, it would give me great pleasure to see to it that you could never be anything better than a clerk for the rest of your life. I'd like to ruin you, Deland. But I will not be so self-indulgent. You have your orders. I will prepare a statement of retraction and you will submit your resignation effective immediately, for reasons of health or whatever acceptable excuse you wish to provide."

Haylow himself was surprised by his own control. His impulse was to roar with rage and anguish, to strike out physically at the handsome, expressionless face before him. The Chairman's outbursts of anger were rare but notoriously monumental, and those who were unfortunate enough to experience them never forgot the tongue-lashing that this articulate man could deliver when driven to heights of fury. He had never, of course, leaned towards physical violence. But now, trembling inwardly, he knew what it was like to want to kill another human being. It took all his discipline to maintain the calm manner in which he delivered his ultimatum to Brad Deland.

Brad's composure was equally astonishing. His matter-of-fact tone matched Haylow's.

"Sorry," he said. "But I can't oblige. I must compliment you, Joe, or whoever did your work for you, on your ingeniousness in unraveling my little plot. I really thought it

325

was foolproof. You're quite right. The confession is a fake. Peter Johnson doesn't even know Roger. He is, shall we say, 'intimate' with Richard Cabot. It was pure accident that I found out about it. Even Cabot doesn't know he's been discovered. But I'm sure you and your sleuths know all that."

Joe waited, sensing that some terrible further treachery was forthcoming.

In the manner of a poker player who held the winning hand, Brad went on. "But you see, Joe, there's something else you obviously don't know. Something that will make you withdraw your request for my resignation. Oh, you've been very clever in clearing your son Roger. But have you forgotten that you have another son?"

Sid's right, Joe thought. The man is mad.

"You're not making any sense, Deland," Haylow said harshly. "What does Woodward have to do with all this?"

Brad was apparently savoring this moment. His tone was almost condescending.

"Woodward has very little to do with it," he said easily. "But Woodward's wife figures very importantly indeed."

There was no mistaking Haylow's astonishment. "Marjorie?"

"I believe that's the only wife he has," Deland mocked. "Yes, Marjorie. We have been having an affair for nearly a year."

"Why you dirty, filthy, rotten—"

"Just a moment," Brad interrupted. "That's only part of it. The rest is even more interesting. Marjorie is pregnant. And the child is mine."

Haylow felt the room begin to swim. His hands clutched the chair arms for support. His mind rejected what he had just heard, but his reflexes did not.

"You are a madman!" Haylow thundered. "My God, Deland, you're sick with your lies and your fantasies! First you thought you could weasel your way into my chair by causing a breach between me and my son. And I nearly bought it! Now you've invented another depraved story in the insane delusion that you can brainwash me into believing it! You're crazy! God help you, you really are out of your mind!"

"On the contrary," Brad said, "I fear it is you who are out of your mind. With fright. Think about it. This is a story I couldn't invent, as I did the other. This time the witness is all mine. And the evidence is unimpeachable."

The truth of this struck Joe Haylow with terrible force. It was true. Unless Deland was really insane, he could not hope to get away with a story so easily disproved. And the hard knot in the pit of his stomach told Haylow that it was really true. Marjorie unfaithful? Marjorie involved with this amoral, despicable excuse for a man? With terror, he remembered what Pat had told him about the worrisome situation between Woodward and Marjorie. Dear God, he thought, this explains her unwillingness to sleep with her husband, her unusual tenderness toward him which Joe now recognized as repentance for her guilt. Pat was right. There was another man. Mutely, he waited for Deland to go on.

"I'm afraid," Brad said, "you will not only have to withdraw your request for my resignation, but I will now demand from you a commitment that I will be named the next Chairman of The Haylow Corporation. I am, of course, prepared to be generous. I will disclaim the confession which implicates Roger and will be perfectly agreeable to his replacing Richard Cabot as President. Marjorie and I will get quiet divorces and be married as soon as possible."

This man will stop at nothing, Haylow thought. He fought for control.

"And if I do not agree to this blackmail?"

"Blackmail is such an ugly word," Brad said. "I seem to remember Roger using it too. Let's just call it sensible procedure. If you don't agree? Then, of course, I will have to meet your original demands. Since you can expose me as the perpetrator of a fraud, I will have to resign gracefully from the company. But there will be some exceedingly messy loose ends. For one thing, Marjorie happens to be in love with me, strange as that may seem to you. But without the Chairmanship, I will refuse to marry her. And it will be painfully obvious to Woodward that her pregnancy was conceived elsewhere. That's for openers. In such an eventuality, I would not vouch for Marjorie's sanity. Right now, she's half-crazy with guilt. Even if Woodward forgives her, she will never forgive herself for what she has done to him and to you. I think—though I hate to say it—that she might be desperate enough to contemplate suicide.

"But let's say," Brad went on reasonably, "that Woodward forgave her and she managed to live with herself. It would be ridiculously easy for me to let the truth leak to a few sharp-eared gossip columnists. Hell, I'd have nothing to lose. In fact, it might work to my benefit to say that the great Joe Haylow fired me for knocking up his daughter-in-law. And wouldn't this kind of immoral goings-on be the end of Woodward's aspirations to succeed Jimmy Jackson as leader of the Great Unwashed? Of course, you may not care about all that as much as you care about your precious business, but you can't really relish the kind of scandal that the whole Methodist world would never forget. So take your choice, Mr. Chairman. Boot me out, make it up with Roger, and to hell with the rest of the family. Or settle for Brad Deland, quietly and discreetly married to your ex-daughter-in-law and doing one helluva good job as Chairman of the Corporation. Of course, there's one other alternative."

"And what," Joe said bitterly, "is that?"

Deland laughed. "Well," he said, "you could kill me."

Haylow made no reply. When he tried to rise, he felt as though he could barely move his legs. Finally he got to his feet. There was one final, mundane question he had to ask.

"How far along is Marjorie?"

"Not quite two months. If we move fast, there's still time for us to marry right after my appointment is announced. We'll be dubiously but acceptably under the wire when we have a premature baby."

Haylow looked at him with undisguised disgust.

"Is it possible that this wonderful girl loves a creature like you?"

Brad smiled. "You wouldn't understand," he said.

Haylow found his dignity. Once more he looked like the indomitable lion the world knew.

"You'll have your answer within a week," he said. Then, like a judge pronouncing the death sentence, he looked Deland squarely in the eye. "And may God have mercy on your soul."

The middle-class, unsophisticated atmosphere of Farmville did not soothe Joe Haylow as it usually did when he returned to it after a tension-filled week in New York. Driving from the airport, he idly noted the small shops decorated with their simple, amateurish Christmas trimmings, so different from the determinedly clever, avant-garde symbolism affected by the jaded Manhattan stores.

The thought of Christmas filled Joe with a sense of sadness this year. Usually he welcomed its approach, delighting in the pleasure of his grandchildren as they opened their gifts under the huge tree that Pat lovingly decorated with sentimental ornaments, some of them dating from Joe's own childhood. The deep religious significance of the season was an even greater source of joy to Haylow. Of all church holidays, he had always found this the most hopeful, the most miraculous. The Holy Infant, His little hands reaching out to a lost world, represented to Joe the purity and innocence that he had always believed triumphed over the wickedness of the earth. In later years, he had been happy that his own parents had named him for Mary's husband. It made him feel part of an unbroken chain leading back to the cradle of the Blessed Babe.

This year, the sweetness of Christmas would be tinged with bitterness. Another child was on the way. But this one was conceived in sin and deception, anticipated not with exaltation but rather with its mother's guilt and its father's self-seeking exploitation.

As he neared his own brightly lighted, welcoming house, Haylow could literally feel the heaviness of his heart. The decision he had to make drove everything else from his mind. And it was a decision he had to make alone. He was determined, at this point, to keep the story from Pat until it was resolved. She was already troubled enough by the unexplained disappearance of Roger, the worrisome difficulties of Woodward's marriage. Whichever path he chose, Joe knew, there would be heartbreak for Pat. No need at this moment to torment her with his own anguished search for the solution which in any case would deeply affect the lives of both their sons.

Forcing himself into a semblance of naturalness, Joe let himself into the house. "Anybody home?" he called. In answer, Pat came quickly down the stairs, smiling with happiness to have him back. She was startled at the intensity of his hug, the extra warmth of his welcoming kiss.

"Goodness," she said, "you must have had a terrible week! You seem terribly pleased to see your old, timeworn spouse!"

"You'll never be old," Joe said. "Nor timeworn. You look prettier to me today than you did forty years ago. And you cook a lot better, too!"

Arms around each other, they went into the living room. Joe settled himself comfortably near the fire. For a moment, looking around the room which was so sweetly familiar to him, he was able to pretend that this was a normal homecoming, complicated with nothing more serious than a recital of Pat's activities while he'd been away. The content he felt was momentary. Like a time bomb in his head, the need for a decision kept pace with the ticking of the mantel clock. Before long, this placid, conventional world would explode around them all, destroying some, maiming others. Unaware that he was frowning, he heard Pat's concerned voice.

"Something wrong, dear?" she asked.

With effort, he tried to resume his normal attitude. "No, not particularly," he lied. "Just been a kind of rough week, that's all."

"Have you heard from Roger?"

"Now, Pat, you know that boy. When he's on a trip he's much too busy to waste time on postcards. He'll be turning up in a few days, full of bounce."

"I know," she said. "It isn't the first time he's gone away without letting us hear from him, but I just have an uneasy feeling about him. In fact, I called Bridget this evening to see whether she'd had any word."

Joe stiffened. Sommers had assured him that Bridget did not know the whole story. Still, she was a perceptive woman. Pat's call must have reinforced her own suspicions that there was trouble.

"What did Bridget have to report?"

"Nothing," Pat said. "She hasn't heard from Roger either. But she didn't seem particularly concerned. I guess I'm just making a noise like a fussy old mother hen. But when one of my chicks is missing, it starts me clucking."

"Roger's not a baby," Joe said. "He can take care of himself."

Pat laughed at herself. "As you would say, logically I know that, but emotionally I guess I still think of him as that shy, closed-in little boy who always seemed to be tugging at my skirt, begging for affection."

Unwittingly, she had painted a picture that intensified Joe's newly discovered remorse.

"What about Woodward?" he asked. "Do you have the same protective instincts about him?"

Pat thought for a moment. "I guess not," she said. "I love the boys equally, but Woodward has always seemed so much more—what shall I say—phlegmatic? He never seemed as defenseless or as sensitive as Roger. That's strange, isn't it? When you think about it, you'd think that Woodward would be even more high-strung than Roger, with his vocation for religion rather than business, I mean."

"Perhaps his religion has given him greater peace of mind."

"I'm sure you're right," Pat agreed. "I'm sure that Roger's marvelous new outlook in this last year has been partly due to the fact that he's begun to accept the church. Aren't you delighted, Joe, with the change in Roger? He's so responsive, so much warmer and happier than he's ever been."

The irony of this did not escape Joe Haylow.

"I suppose that's why I find it so odd that he hasn't been in touch with us this time," Pat went on. "Once the lone wolf has rejoined the pack, his next absence is that much more noticeable."

Suddenly Joe couldn't bear to talk about his younger son any longer.

"What's planned for this evening?" he asked.

"Nothing special. I thought you might be tired, dear, so I didn't make any engagements."

"Marjorie and Woodward coming by?"

"No. Woodward's attending a board meeting at the church. Marjorie's at home with the children. I asked her if she'd like to drop over for a while after dinner, but she said she thought she'd catch up on a few chores since Woodward will be out all evening."

Through the evening meal, Haylow relaxed companionably, talking of inconsequential things. Pat chattered animatedly of the coming holidays. Christmas was always a gala celebration at the senior Haylows'. Pat was full of plans.

"Let's make it a special Christmas," she said. "Not just family. I'd like to have the same group we had at your birthday in Florida last year—Bridget and the Cabots and the Delands. Sid too, if he'd like to come, though I suppose he'll want to be with his grandchildren."

Sid's wife had died years before, but he had two daughters and five grandchildren with whom he liked to spend his holidays.

"Oh," Pat went on, "and the Warners too, if they'd like it." She hesitated. "I suppose they celebrate Christmas?"

"I'm sure they do," Joe said. My poor, darling Pat, he thought. By next Christmas there will be little for any of us to celebrate. The cheerful gathering his wife was mentally picturing would be the last. Next year the Haylow "family" would be scattered by the winds of misery, drowned in a sea of disillusionment.

After dinner, Joe was restless. Instead of losing himself in one of his endless unread books, he kept walking to the window, looking out at the cold, crisp, starlit expanse of the garden. Attuned to his moods, Pat said nothing, but she sensed, as she had from his arrival, that he was struggling with some ferocious problem. Finally, he spoke.

"I just can't seem to settle down tonight. Guess I've been cooped up in the office too much this week. Maybe I'll take a little walk before bedtime. Want to come?"

· Whatever he needs to work out, he needs to be alone, Pat thought.

"If you don't mind, darling," she said, "I think I'll pass. It's too darned cold out there. I'll just keep fighting this needlepoint, nice and cozy by the fire. But you go ahead. A little exercise will do you good. Probably make you sleep like a baby."

Bundling himself into his sheep-lined car coat, Joe Haylow reflected that the word "baby" had seemed to come up in every other sentence tonight. Of course it hadn't. He realized that his awareness of it was like something he'd heard women say: when you suspect you're pregnant, every woman you see on the street seems to be wearing a maternity dress. The thought of Marjorie's child was so much on his mind that the word "baby" only seemed to permeate the conversation.

As he left the house, he knew exactly where he was going. With Woodward out for the evening, this was the ideal time —if there could be an ideal time—to talk frankly with Marjorie. He had no idea what he was going to say. All he knew was that until he heard the story from her own lips it would remain untrue. And until he heard it, no decision was possible.

At her doorway, Marjorie greeted him warmly. This gruff, well-intentioned bear of a man who thought he kept his deep affections so carefully hidden did not fool Marjorie. She knew how deeply he cared for the people nearest to him and how difficult it was for him to let the caring spill out.

Helping him out of his coat, she led him into the living room.

"Make you some coffee?" she offered.

Joe noticed that she had shown no surprise at his arrival, asked no questions about his unusual and unexpected visit alone.

"No thanks, dear," he said. "I won't stay long."

They sat in silence for a long moment. Somehow, she knows why I'm here, Joe thought. Perhaps it's a sixth sense, a moment she has been waiting for. But her words dispelled that eerie speculation.

"Brad called me this afternoon," Marjorie said quietly. "He said he had told you about us. And about the baby. I'm sorry. I wanted to do that myself. I wanted to tell you that it's not Brad's fault. I fell in love with him, and I deliberately led him on to make love to me."

Marjorie's tone was sad but her manner was one of great

The Rich and the Righteous

dignity. She was all woman. The regret she felt for the hurt she had inflicted was apparent in her eyes. But this was no sniveling, frightened creature begging for mercy. She was offering no excuses, making no accusations of guilt toward anyone except herself. She carried her burden unflinchingly, and Joe, suffused with tenderness and love, suddenly wanted to take her in his arms and comfort her. My God, he thought, how this child has suffered. Yet she has prepared herself to pay the price.

When he spoke, Joe's voice was barely audible.

"What else did Brad tell you when he called?"

"Only that he had also spoken to you about our plans to marry as quickly as possible so that we could be together with our child."

"Nothing about the business?"

Marjorie looked surprised. "No. Why would he talk about the business? We both knew he'll have to leave it. He is willing to make his sacrifices, just as I have to make mine." Suddenly her voice broke. "And mine are greater by far. The crushing blow to Woodward. The pain I know I'll cause you and Pat. And, for me, the most unthinkable of all, the fear that you will not let me have my children. Dear God, Joe, what is a job compared to those terrible things?"

Joe felt as though he was suffocating. Deland, that miserable excuse for a human being, had told her nothing of his devious plot involving Roger. And thank God she was ignorant of the callous way in which he was willing to trade marriage to Marjorie in return for the only thing he really wanted, the power of the Chair. The greatest revulsion yet swept through Haylow. This beautiful, honest, brave woman knew nothing of the man she fancied herself in love with. Of course, Deland would have told her nothing of all his tortuous double-dealings. Marjorie would have turned away in disgust and horror, leaving Deland weaponless and defeated. I could tell her the whole story, Joe thought. But the words

335

would kill her as surely as though each one was a bullet aimed at her unsuspecting heart. No, one thing was certain: she must not know how she has been used.

"My dear," Joe said gently, "it is not my province to judge your actions nor to condemn you for them. I know you have done that yourself, over and over again. But I have a stake in this too. I want your happiness because I love you as though you were my own daughter. I want the happiness of my wife and my grandchildren. And I care very deeply for my son, the man who took you as his wife and who has never stopped loving you and believing in you."

Marjorie was crying softly now, her face turned away from Joe.

"And there's one thing more," Haylow said. "You are married to a man of God. Have you thought what this could do to him, to his future, to the respect with which the community—and perhaps someday the whole world—will regard him? Are you willing to take this responsibility, Marjorie? You hold the fate of more than just a few lives in the palm of your hand. You could be affecting the salvation of thousands, maybe millions of people in all the years to come. A divorced minister is suspect, my dear. Forget Woodward's personal sorrow. Can you live with the fact that you might deprive the world of a great Christian leader—a messenger of our Lord?"

Marjorie had stopped crying. Transfixed, she stared at Joe Haylow. For a moment, he felt her waver.

"Please," she said, "don't make it harder for me than it already is. You're right. I had not thought beyond the sadness of the people who are near and dear to me. But it alters nothing. Even if I give up Brad, I am carrying his child. It's too late, Joe. May God forgive me for the harm I've done, but it's too late."

"No," Haylow said, "it isn't. There is still time for you to make the greatest sacrifice of all. You can give up both Brad Deland and the child."

Marjorie's eyes widened. "I don't understand."

"Sweetheart," Joe said gently, "let me arrange it for you. An abortion. A complete break with Deland, as far as all of us are concerned. And my personal assurance that he will be offered a position in another company as good as, if not better than, the one he holds in Haylow."

The shock on Marjorie Haylow's face turned slowly into something akin to disgust.

"So this is the great Joe Haylow in action," she said bitterly. "All nice and neat and tidy. 'Oh, don't worry about it, sweetheart,'" she mocked. "'Just give up the only man you've ever loved. Go out and murder your child. And for heaven's sake never let your husband know anything ever happened.' What a harlot you must think I am! People aren't people to you. They're little bits of flesh and bone to be shoved around by the almighty Chairman. Hunks of humanity to be dealt with from the lofty heights of Haylow wisdom! You pretend to be a man who loves the world so much that he sends his first-begotten son to save it. Well, let me tell you something. You're not God and Woodward is not Jesus Christ. The world will survive without both of you. And so will I. I want my life and I want it with Brad Deland and his child. Don't come into my living room and try to conduct a prayer meeting while you are suggesting murder and deception. You don't give a damn about all those people you're so piously pretending to care for—those millions of souls in need of salvation. All you care about is the precious name of Haylow. Protect it at all costs. Insure its immortality in the history books and the annals of the church. Well, to hell with you and your phony Christianity! I only wish I could take back all the tears I've shed, thinking of the way I'll hurt you. You can't hurt a dead man. And that's what you are—dead to the needs and the feelings of the people you're supposed to love!"

Hysterically, Marjorie fled from the room. Like a sleep-walker, Joe Haylow found his coat and let himself out the door. Halfway back to his house, sobs racked him, tears ran unchecked down his cheeks. For the rest of the way home, the Chairman cried. Like a baby.

16 🙖

On the morning after his talk with Marjorie, Joe Haylow sought out the man to whom he could bare his soul, pour out his misery and hope to find consolation. Without calling for an appointment, he knocked at the door of the manse, knowing that Jimmy Jackson would be there on this cold Saturday morning preparing his next day's sermon.

The old minister was, as expected, working in his study. But he put down his glasses and pushed aside his papers when his housekeeper ushered Joe Haylow into the room. Jackson was shocked at Haylow's appearance. Joe looked haggard. He seemed to have aged twenty years in the week since Jimmy had last seen him. Even the proud, erect carriage had become the round-shouldered, drooping posture of a man weighed down with problems. The only thing familiar to Jackson was Joe Haylow's automatic courtesy, expressed in his opening words.

"I'm sorry to trouble you on a Saturday morning," Joe said. "I know what it's like to be interrupted when you're working on a speech. Can you spare a few minutes?"

In spite of his concern, Jimmy felt a trace of amusement. To Haylow, every public utterance, even from the pulpit, was a "speech." Perhaps he's right at that, Jackson thought. One shouldn't preach to people; one should speak to them. Or with them. Today's world was not the place for a Sermon

339

on the Mount. It was the time for humanitarian exchange, for communication. Hellfire and brimstone have been replaced by rationality and the voice of experience. Reality, Jimmy thought, has reached the church audience as certainly as it has infiltrated the rest of people's lives. And the weary man seated beside his desk obviously had come up against some terrible realities. Jimmy knew that Joe Haylow was not here for psalm-quoting. He was here for help, in a very real sense.

"You have all the time you want," Jackson said.

Haylow nodded his thanks. "I came because I need to talk," Joe said. "I don't think you can help me. I don't think anyone can. But I have to hear myself say aloud the things I cannot believe when the words are bottled up in my head."

Jimmy made no answer. He sensed that Joe was figuratively in the confessional, filled with the need to give voice to his sins. Perhaps he was also hoping for some kind of absolution, but Jackson doubted it. The deeply troubled man who spoke in an unnatural, halting voice had already judged himself and found himself unpardonable.

Slowly at first, then with more speed and clarity, Joe Haylow told his minister everything. Even Jackson, used to the recital of problems of his congregation, found himself stunned by the magnitude of the sorrows and disappointments that had beset his old friend. Though he knew that Joe was using him merely as a sounding board, Jimmy could not help comparing Haylow with the biblical Job. Here, too, was a man wondering why God had turned his back on him, why he had heaped such trials upon His faithful servant. As Joe related the bitterness of Roger, the defiance of Marjorie, the deceit of Deland, Jimmy heard the voice of Job as he had so often read it: "Oh that I were as in months past, as in the days when God preserved me; When His candle shined upon my head and when by His light I walked through darkness;

The Rich and the Righteous

As I was in the days of my youth, when the secret of God was upon my tabernacle; When the Almighty was yet with me, when my children were about me."

Haylow was, however, unaware of the comparison which crossed the mind of his minister. He was there, as Jimmy had suspected, to revile himself for his own failures as a man, a father, a Christian. As he continued to speak, without interruption, his self-vilification was the keynote.

"I have been so shamefully self-involved that my conceit has blinded me as surely as though it were some terrible disease which destroyed my sight. I haven't seen the people I love as people. I have not seen them as human beings at all. To me, they have been like stockholders whose lives I could vote by proxy.

"Well, it's come home to me at last, Jimmy," Haylow said. "God has let me live a life of blissful ignorance. And now God has decided to punish me. I don't question His wrath toward me. I am ready to suffer for my wickedness. But why does the Lord see fit to destroy the innocent ones who already have been bruised and burdened by my disregard, my single-mindedness? Why should my own terrible self-revelation be the cause of so much unhappiness? I welcome my own pain. But how can I continue to worship a God who uses my punishment to destroy those who don't deserve destruction?"

"You are wrong, Joe," Jackson said quietly. "God does not strike down the wicked nor cause the innocent to suffer. Any form of Divine punishment is the withholding of God's help. God is not punishing you for what you have done. He is refusing to help you and those nearest to you. There is a great difference, dear friend. You have been the most fortunate, the most blessed of men. For though you have served God all your life, you have never truly, until now, needed His help. This is your revelation, Joe. This is why you would prefer God to punish you rather than ignore you. But he will not strike

341

you down with wrath and anger. He will forgive you. But only when you have tasted humility. Only then will God once again offer his loving hand."

"How can God forgive me?" Joe asked. "How can I forgive myself for my blindness, my arrogance, my ambition which made all these things possible? I have been filled with my own ego, impressed with my own importance, deaf to the people who were crying out to me for love and understanding. I deserve this agony. But what of the others, Jimmy? What of Pat and Roger and Woodward? What of Marjorie and her unborn child? What of the lives that will be smashed by my heedlessness, my lack of faith? My needs are no longer important. I know that now. But whom shall I sacrifice? How can I choose which shall be destroyed and which saved? In business, I have had a sanctimonious, self-righteous rule of thumb: everything has a priority. But there are no priorities here, are there? No one human being is more important than the next. If I give in to Deland, I sacrifice Roger while protecting Woodward's future. And I allow Marjorie to marry a man who isn't worthy of touching her. If I tell Deland to go to hell, I can, hopefully, beg Roger's forgiveness and implore him to come back into my life. But I will destroy Woodward's lifework, ruin his marriage, perhaps drive Marjorie to some irrational act. And whatever course I choose, there is my beloved Pat. The happiness and fulfillment of her whole life revolves around her family. Her agony for her children may be matched by her hatred for me. Dear God in heaven, what have I done with my selfish indifference to those I love most in all this world?"

Jimmy Jackson had never felt such pity. But pity was not what Joe Haylow needed. In a calm, dispassionate voice, more friend than minister, Jackson answered.

"To you this is a nightmare," he said. "And indeed it must seem like a terrible dream. But it is real, Joe. Except that you are not seeing it with reality. As you have done all your life, you are underestimating the strength of others. You are disregarding the ability of these very people you love to make their own judgments and decisions. I fear you are still arrogant. Still playing God. Still convinced that you are the only one who can manipulate lives and make decisions."

The unexpected words were like a dash of cold water in Joe Haylow's face. For a moment he was resentful. Had he not just finished humbly confessing that he and only he was to blame for the chain of events that led up to this moment? Had he not willingly, nakedly revealed his blindness, his conceit? He stared in surprise at Jimmy Jackson. Unflinchingly, the old minister returned his gaze. Then Jackson continued.

"In all you've told me," he said, "one thing comes forth with clarity: your determination to solve all the problems. Have you thought of giving the others a chance to choose their own destinies?"

"I don't understand," Joe said.

"Let us take it one by one, Joe. Have you told Roger what you now know—that he is innocent?"

"No. I've not seen him since the day he left the office."

"Have you discussed any of this with Pat? With Woodward?"

"Of course not," Haylow said. "How could I?"

"What about Marjorie? Does she know how Brad is using her?"

"Don't be ridiculous," Joe said. "I'd cut out my tongue before I'd let that poor girl find out what a no-good piece of scum Deland is!"

"Yet," Jimmy said wryly, "you are considering making it possible for her to marry that piece of scum."

Haylow considered this in silence. It was true. Yet what choice did he have?

"All right," Joe said finally, "I see what you're trying to get at. But I still don't see the way."

"Well, you might start by really respecting those other people instead of wallowing in the luxury of self-condemnation. Let's begin with Woodward. If you think he is such a fine man of God—as indeed he is—why do you presuppose that he would lack charity and compassion? He has already shown great evidence of it in his trusting belief that Marjorie is just going through some sort of strange nervous condition. He has been patient and undemanding. What makes you think he would not wish to be forgiving? Woodward is a good human being, Joe. And more importantly, he is of a different generation than yours and mine, less given to condemnation, perhaps. I think if Woodward knew the truth, he would beg Marjorie to stay with him and that he would love her child as tenderly and truly as he loves his own. Why not let him make his own decision, based on the facts?"

"I know what a fine person my son is," Joe agreed, "but how can you be so sure of his reaction?"

"Because I have faith," Jimmy said quietly.

Joe recognized the reproach. "All right," he said, "but assuming he took the attitude you suggest, what of Marjorie? She fancies herself in love with Deland. I don't believe she'd be willing to stay with Woodward in any case. And what about his chances to succeed you? The scandal will ruin him unless we can get Marjorie quietly and quickly out of his life."

"But," Jimmy persisted, "hasn't Marjorie the right to make her choice based on the knowledge of Woodward's willingness to accept what she has done and forgive her for it? Perhaps, the evidence of his true understanding might bring back her love for her husband. In any case, she deserves the right to choose with that knowledge. And," Jimmy went on reluctantly, "there's something else I must tell you, Joe."

Haylow flinched as though he expected still another blow.

"It is something else you have not wanted to hear," Jackson said, "but you might as well know it now. Whether Woodward stays married to Marjorie or not, he does not have the calling we both hoped for. With or without her, his role is destined to be one of a more modest nature. We have both prayed that Woodward could be the leader of millions. But it will not happen that way, Joe. You in your ambition, and I in my desire for your happiness, have both tried to mold Woodward into the kind of inspirational preacher who could convert lost souls. It is not in him. He is a wonderful minister and he will do work equally important to God. But he will do it right here in Farmville or some community like it, where he can be close to his people, guiding and counseling his small flock. And that he can do with or without Marjorie. So the decision about their lives must be a personal one only."

"I don't believe that," Haylow said angrily. "For some reason you don't want Woodward to take over after you're gone. Perhaps, Jimmy, you don't ever want to *be* gone!"

Jackson smiled. "Is that what you're really saying, Joe? Or do you mean it is *you* who doesn't wish to go from your position of power and control? Which of us is really reluctant to name a successor—*any* successor?"

Joe stood up, his face red with anger. "So I can't even talk to you," he said. "Even you have your axe to grind, your vanity to sustain."

Jackson put out his hand. "Sit down, dear friend," he said. "You do not believe those things. And I know you don't believe them. You are in a torment of indecision, Joe. Please let me help if I can. Let us both forget our personal considerations, if indeed they exist. You are a student of the Bible. Remember one of your favorite quotations from the Book of Job? 'Surely God will not hear vanity, neither will the Almighty regard it.' Let neither of us confuse this discussion with our all too human failings."

Slowly, Haylow sat down. "I apologize," he said. "It was unpardonable of me to say those things to you. But Jimmy, I can't do what you ask. I can't tell Woodward the truth about Marjorie, nor Marjorie the truth about Deland. Perhaps in some miraculous way things could come right if they both knew everything, but this is a gamble I am not strong enough to take."

"I understand," Jackson said. "And in a kind of strange inverted way it must seem that I am still asking you to play God. But what of Roger? Isn't he, too, entitled to know that you are aware of your mistake? And that you so deeply regret your lack of faith in him? Isn't he entitled to fight for the Chairmanship if he wants it? Unless you tell him about Brad and Marjorie you deprive him of weapons that are rightfully his."

"Yes," Joe answered slowly. "That is something I can do. I can try to find Roger and go down on my knees to him, to beg his forgiveness. And I can," Joe continued reluctantly, "give him the privilege of using the rest of the information if he so chooses."

"Will you?"

"I don't know," Haylow said. He thought for a moment. "Yes," he said, "I will. I'll find him and tell him the whole story. He is my son. To do less would be to continue on the path I've pursued all my life—the conviction of my own superior judgment, the plain downright arrogance that has made me believe I know better than anyone else what should be done with everybody's life. But Jimmy, I can't tell Woodward or Marjorie or Pat. Maybe I'm a coward. Afraid of what I'd have to live with forever. But that I can't do."

Jackson's voice was understanding. "God has never tested you so terribly, Joe," he said. "But remember He has never failed you, either. Don't lose faith in Him now. Or, for that matter, in yourself."

Jackson walked Haylow to the door. "It's pointless to say how sorry I am, Joe," he said. "You don't deserve this."

"Don't I?" Haylow echoed. "Maybe yes, maybe no. I'm an old man, Jimmy. Oh, sixty-four isn't old by today's standards, but I've always behaved like a bearded patriarch. Those things that Roger said about me in Florida were true. An old goat. Domineering and demanding. Now it's come full circle. What good is my poor, little inflated ego on this last lap of the race, Jimmy? Ironic, isn't it? The great Joe Haylow shot down by the kind of human emotions that can't be computerized and programmed. The dominant is dominated. And too ashamed to fight back."

Jackson watched him make his slow way down the path in front of the manse. Sadly, the old minister returned to his sermon. His "speech," Joe Haylow had unconsciously called it. Well, tomorrow he would speak to his people. He tore up the nearly completed text. He would choose a new quotation as the basis for this Sunday's talk. For a moment he thought. Then, very carefully, he wrote across the top of the yellow pad:

"Today, we take our thoughts from Proverbs 27. 'Boast not thyself of tomorrow; for thou knowest not what a day may bring forth.'"

Joe will know, Jimmy thought, that the speech in church tomorrow comes from what this day has brought forth. Earnestly, Jackson went to work. Perhaps he could, from the pulpit, give comfort and strength to the friend who needed it so very much.

At midnight, Bridget Manning let herself wearily into her apartment. At her door, she had said a cheerfully quick good night to the neuter fashion designer who had been her escort at the black-tie gala they'd just left. At this season, there were two or three such dinner-dances every week. "Charity Ball blackmail" was Sally Fisher's apt and scornful description of these events. They were always benefits to raise money for some worthy cause, with the guest of honor picked not necessarily for his merit, but for his ability to insure a good attendance at the function. Store Presidents, important editors, leading manufacturers were chosen over and over again as the recipients of "awards" for outstanding service to some civic or charitable enterprise. In most cases, the honoree had done nothing more than lend his name to the invitation. But that was enough to guarantee that everyone who did business with the guest of honor would buy tickets to the event. In Bridget's business, attendance at these gatherings was a tribal law. For the sake of the store, she could not afford to be absent at a ball in honor of a magazine publisher who gave her important publicity. Nor could she ignore the manufacturer who made sure that Bridget's got his exclusive, expensive designs each season ahead of other stores.

It was an inane and wearying business, attending these evenings. Bridget would much have preferred to make a donation and stay home, but her physical presence was nearly as important as the money she and her buyers raised through the sale of tickets.

In her bedroom, she kicked off her shoes and, almost too tired to undress, flopped on the comfortable chaise near the window. Lighting a cigarette, she glanced idly at the photograph of her father which stood on the table beside the chaise. In his day, business was still a thing mercifully apart from one's social life. One went to work and put in a long, full, hard day. But the evenings were for family and friends, for the loving surroundings of a world that had nothing to do with public relations and customer good will. Lost in thought, Bridget could almost hear her gentle father speaking to her, urging her to be a good girl, a charitable and honest girl. "You will want to go far in this business," he'd once said to her, "and you will go far. But never be anyone but yourself, my little Bridget. Build. Grow. Achieve. But be sure the foundation of that growth is as solid as the basic virtues your mother and I have tried to teach you. Remember Isaiah: 'Enlarge the place of thy tent, and let them stretch forth the curtains of thine habitations: spare not, lengthen thy cords, and strengthen thy stakes.'"

Remembering the words she'd so often heard her father use, Bridget realized that she did not know exactly what the biblical quotation meant. She supposed that the prophet had been advising his listeners to grow, work hard, expand and be strong—just as Stanley Manning had said. Some day, she thought, I must ask Joe Haylow for his interpretation.

The ringing of the telephone brought her back to reality. Apprehensive because of the lateness of the hour, she picked it up quickly. On the other end was a voice she'd not heard in two weeks.

"Hi," Roger Haylow said, "you're out pretty late for a school night. I've been calling you all evening."

Suddenly Bridget was alert. "Roger? You're back! I'm so glad! *How* are you? And *where* are you?"

"I'm okay," he said. "But I'm not back because I haven't been anywhere. I mean, I've been staying in Brooklyn at a friend's. But I haven't wanted to see anyone. Not even you."

He sounded tired, depressed, like a man coming home from a long, frustrating journey.

"Well, I'm delighted you finally decided to surface," Bridget said. She hoped her tone did not betray her anxiety. "We were beginning to think we had another Judge Crater on our hands."

"We?"

"Pat and I, particularly."

"How is she?" Roger asked.

No questions about Joe, Bridget mentally noted. "Oh, she's fine, dear. And I'm sure she'll be even better when she sees you."

The silence on the other end of the wire spoke for itself.

"Roger, where are you now?"

"Just a couple of blocks away," he said. "In a bar on First Avenue. Bridget, can I come and see you?"

"Of course, dear. Just give me ten minutes to get out of my Charity Ball ceremonial robes and into something comfortable."

"Thanks," he said. "See you shortly."

Rapidly, Bridget slipped out of her evening dress and zipped herself into a long robe. In two minutes she had Sid Sommers on the phone.

"Sorry to wake you," she said to the sleepy voice, "but you asked me to let you know if I heard from Roger. He just called. He wants to see me, and he'll be here in about ten minutes."

"How did he sound?"

"I'm not sure," Bridget said. "Maybe I was reading into his voice something that wasn't there, but he sounded sad. He hasn't been far away, Sid. He's been hiding, hasn't he?"

"I guess that's what you might call it. Anyway, he's back, thank God, and at least that gives us some place to start. Now listen, Bridget, I'm going to do something you might not approve of, but please go along with me. I'm going to call Joe and tell him to come over to your place."

"All right," Bridget said, "if that's what you think best."

Thank heaven for a sensible woman who doesn't stop to ask a million questions, Sid thought. "Whatever you do, keep Roger there," Sommers told her. "And above all, don't tell him his father is on the way."

"Will you be coming too?"

"No. These two have something to straighten out between them. I'm sorry to put you in this spot, Bridget, but it's our only hope. I don't know how to tell you to play it, but if you can disappear and leave them alone, maybe they can come to grips with their problem. I'm afraid you'll just have to wing it, old girl."

"Lucky Pierrette," Bridget said ruefully, "in the middle again."

"I know," Sid said. "It's a tough situation, but it means

everything to these two. And to a lot of other people besides."

"I'll do my best."

"Good enough. I'll get Joe on the phone now. Hope he isn't out at one of his bloody business dinners."

"No, he'll be home now," Bridget said. "I just saw him an hour ago leaving the same bloody business dinner I was dragged to."

"Okay. He should be there in twenty minutes, then. Thanks, Bridget. And good luck, my dear."

Sensitivity is not necessarily at odds with masculinity. Roger Haylow was male to the roots of his being—but he was an aware man, conscious always of the reactions of those around him, careful to avoid the accidental insult, the unwitting slight. When he set out to hurt, as he had on the night of Joe Haylow's birthday party, the intent was deliberate and the remorse inevitable. In the months following his outburst in Florida, Roger's search for his father's approval had been, at first, a kind of penance for a life of resentment which culminated in that unkind performance. Then, to his surprise, as well as to Joe's, the reparation had turned into an honest interest in the business. He had been happy, strangely fulfilled, almost visibly glowing in the warmth of his father's delighted acceptance of him as an executive. Then Joe had blown the whole relationship with his questioning of Roger's sex life, his implied doubt of Roger's motives in sponsoring Terry.

Perhaps, Roger thought, walking slowly toward Sutton Place, I have been sulking like a child. He tried to imagine what he would have done in his father's place, how he would have acted in that dual role of parent and Chairman. But no amount of rationalization could make the rejection palatable. Roger would have done it differently. He would have reassured his son that he took no stock in the story. Had Roger been Joe Haylow, he would have unquestionably chosen the thicker ties of blood over the watery content of an accusation by strangers. As he had dozens of times in the last two weeks, Roger reviewed the whole ugly affair and, admitting his own sensitivity, still felt that his father had been a cold-blooded, devastatingly impersonal inquisitor. He hasn't changed, Roger told himself sadly. I only seduced myself into thinking he had, because I wanted him to. God, how I wanted him to!

The front door of Bridget's penthouse was ajar, welcoming him. It was a subtle piece of symbolism that did not escape Roger. He felt a rush of warmth, knowing that there was someone inside eager to see him.

In the foyer, he gave a low whistle. The dearly familiar voice answered, burlesquing the famous *To Have and Have Not* line.

"If you want me," it said, "all you have to do is whistle."

Roger laughed. For the first time in many miserable, soul-searching days and nights, he felt almost cheerful. It was the happiness he always felt in Bridget's presence. At least that had not changed.

She was waiting for him in the living room, arms outstretched. For the first time, he held her closely to him, feeling the fast beat of her heart. Then he kissed her deeply, hungrily, and, with joy, felt her response.

The moment left them both silent, surprised at the intensity of their reunion, confused by the unexpectedness of it. Bridget was the first to break away. Stepping back, she looked at him carefully.

"You're thinner," she said. "You look like you haven't eaten for weeks, you idiot."

"Well, Brooklyn isn't exactly a gourmet tour of southern France, but I haven't exactly gone into a decline. Besides, booze is loaded with calories and all those good, healthful things."

She had made up her mind to ask no questions. Not where he had been, nor why he had gone. It was enough that he had come to her before anyone else. It was a good sign that he had emerged from this self-imposed exile. Bridget said nothing. Instead, she curled up in her favorite corner of the big couch, letting Roger decide where he would sit. He chose, as she had hoped, to sit close beside her, not touching her, but communicating intensely, all the same.

For a long moment, only the French clock on the mantel ticked through the quiet. Even the barges glided silently up the East River at this early morning hour. It was as though the whole world was holding its breath.

Finally, Roger spoke. "You were wrong about my father."

Bridget raised her eyebrows. "Wrong? In what way?"

"About the kind of man he is. You and Sid. Both of you. Wrong. You convinced me that he was capable of love if I would reach out for it. Well, I reached. And got my hand chopped off at the wrist."

Bridget waited.

"Would you like to know the whole story?" Roger asked.

"If you want to tell me."

He told her. About Brad and the fake confession. About the anonymous letter. About the last time he and Joe Haylow had faced each other. As he talked, Bridget struggled to hold back her tears. The devilish cleverness of Deland did not surprise her, though she was aghast at the depths to which even he would sink. Her anger at Brad was insignificant compared to her compassion for the two men she loved most in the world. With more objectivity than either of them could manage, she saw clearly the working of both Haylow minds, so alike and yet so far apart in their outward manifestations. Unerringly, she analyzed each. The father believing it his duty to get to the bottom of the story. The son deeply wounded at the implicit doubt expressed by the man whom he unknowingly adored. In a few months, they had almost

353

built a bridge across a chasm carved by thirty-seven years of misunderstanding. Then, together, in a single moment, they had unwittingly destroyed it. Soon, Bridget thought, we'll find out if the rift is irrevocable. Joe Haylow will ring the doorbell and the two men will once again face each other across this gorge of misunderstanding.

She was aware, suddenly, that Roger had stopped talking. It was her moment to speak. Carefully, almost fearfully, she groped for words.

"Darling," she said, "what do you want me to say? That you were right all the time and Sid and I were wrong? That your father is an unfeeling bastard who never has loved you? That you had every reason to storm out of his office in righteous indignation and worry all of us—including Joe Haylow—half out of our minds? No, dear heart, I can't say these things because they are not true. I understand you. I feel for you. I love you. But I love the man, not the child in a pique who picks up his tin dishes and runs when the game isn't played his way. Sure, you were wounded by Joe Haylow's questioning of you. But Roger, what else could he do? Don't you know he was hoping for an outraged denial—praying for it, if I know your father? Can't you see that it's simply not possible for such a man to gloss over any serious accusation like some fatuous, permissive parent who thinks 'my child can do no wrong'? You accuse him of ego. The real ego would have been if he'd assumed you innocent because no child of his could be guilty of wrongdoing. It was because he loved you so much, Roger, that he was begging for a manly denial. Instead, you gave him silence—your own form of revenge. You used the one weapon you knew could kill him: doubt. So who is it that hasn't changed, my love, you or Joe Haylow?"

As she paused, Bridget was trembling. She had taken a terrifying calculated risk. It would not have surprised her if Roger had walked out the door, out of her life forever. She knew he had come to her expecting agreement and sympathy. Instead, she had thrown his own childishness in his teeth. Dared him to admit his petulance. Implored him to be a man, a bigger man than his father. And it was not only for Roger and Joe Haylow that she was fighting. Since his kiss, she knew it was also a battle for the life she wanted for herself. A life with Roger. I'm in love with him, she thought wonderingly. I've known it for a long time and I was afraid to admit it, even to myself.

Scarcely breathing, she waited for his answer. Every second counted now. The confrontation with Joe Haylow could be only minutes away. Looking at Roger's face, she was relieved to see no anger. Only a thoughtful frown. How much pride can one man swallow? And if Roger can admit his failings, what will be Joe's attitude when he arrives? Or, for that matter, will he arrive at all? Perhaps he had refused when Sid asked him to come for a meeting with Roger. God knows, they have pride, these Haylow men. Stubborn, unyielding, yet strangely thin-skinned creatures they are, mirrored in one another and hell-bent on shattering the reflected image.

Her answer to one question came in the peal of the doorbell. Startled, Roger looked at her questioningly.

"It's Joe," she said. "I called him. Or, rather, Sid did."

Roger's smile was derisive. "Still on his side, you two, is that it?"

Bridget lost her temper. "Damn you, Roger, you're not worth it! There are no sides here. You and Joe Haylow are both bloody damned lucky to have people care enough about the two of you to stick their necks out just in the hope of getting you back to some kind of mature relationship! Hell, I wish I'd never gotten into it! No good deed goes unpunished!"

The bell rang again. More insistently. Bridget looked at Roger.

"Well?"

"You'd better answer the door," he said.

In the corridor, Joe Haylow was nervous about the meeting. And the delay following his first ring made him more so. Perhaps Roger had never arrived and Bridget had gone to bed. Or, worse still, Roger might be there now, refusing to see his father, forbidding Bridget to let him in. Haylow thanked God when Bridget opened the door. But one look at her flushed face told him that all was not well. Wordlessly, he quickly walked past her into the living room. Roger stood looking out at the river. Joe looked at Bridget, who simply shrugged her shoulders. Haylow came up behind his son, not touching him. His voice was tentative. Almost humble.

"Roger," he said. "Son. Please. I've got to talk to you."

When he turned to face his father, Roger's face was composed, unfathomable, as distantly courteous as though he had swung round to be introduced to some stranger.

"I've come to ask your forgiveness," Joe said simply.

"Better late than never?" Roger's voice was cold, even cruel. But Joe Haylow appeared to take no notice.

"I suppose you could say that," he answered.

Bridget made a move as though to leave the room, but Haylow held out his hand.

"No, Bridget, please stay," Joe said. "I don't know how much of the story you know, but you have as much a stake in this as the rest of us. I want you to listen. As I'm hoping my son will."

Bridget looked imploringly at Roger. Surely he could not be unaffected by this repentant man who spoke so simply yet so desperately. As if in answer, Roger took a chair beside the coffee table. Bridget and Joe took their places on the sofa. Haylow did not take his eyes off Roger as he began to speak.

"If you hate me," he began in a low voice, "I cannot blame you. Because your hatred of me is nothing compared to my loathing for myself. I have always professed to be a man of faith, of Christian spirit. I have always done what I thought was right. And the only thing I have to offer in my own defense is that I mistook good fortune for some kind of extraordinary patronage from God. I have been terribly, terribly wrong. Willfully arrogant. Blindly unheeding of the rights of others.

"There has been no charity in me, no compassion. Nothing but the absurd delusion that my judgments were superior to all others. Perhaps even to the Lord's."

Bridget desperately wanted to escape. It was unbearable to hear this strong, forceful man humiliating himself. She felt as though she were eavesdropping in a confessional. But she stayed, knowing that this self-flagellation before two people he loved was part of Joe Haylow's therapy, perhaps even, for him, a way of clutching at sanity.

"Had I been a man of faith," Haylow continued, "I would have torn up Deland's false evidence, both pieces of it, and thrown it into his evil face. But the fear in me took over. The mercenary part of my nature that protects the business I love was, momentarily, stronger than the belief in my own child. For this lack of devotion, I can never compensate, never atone. I can only beg for understanding, for forgiveness. It is your right, Roger, to withhold both, if you choose."

No word came from Roger's lips, but the hard lines of his face grew softer. Still, he would not make it easy for his father. He waited.

"After you left me, that terrible day, I was like a drowning man," Joe said. "In my heart, I knew Deland's accusations were lies. But you had not denied them. I know now that to do so would have been to compound the insult I unwittingly thrust upon you. But I did not understand that then.

"Thank God, I went to Sid. And through him, I found the truth. Peter Johnson has been having an affair with a high official of our company. But of course it was not you. The other man involved is Richard Cabot."

Involuntarily, Bridget gasped. Roger looked stunned.

Joe Haylow nodded. "I know. Incredible, isn't it? But true, though Cabot still does not know he's been discovered. In any case, when I learned the truth, I directed Deland to hand in his resignation."

"Thank God," Bridget breathed. "So it's all over."

Joe Haylow shook his head sadly. "Unfortunately, he declined."

Now it was Roger's turn to speak. "Declined! How could he decline when you'd caught him red-handed rigging a phony story? You mean he denied it?"

"No," Joe said, "he admitted it freely. He'd found out about Cabot and Johnson and simply juggled the names to involve you. Johnson agreed in order to protect his roommate, young Terry White. Deland made it all sound very plausible. But Sid and Mike got the whole story out of Terry."

"Then why wouldn't Brad resign?" Bridget asked.

"Because," Joe said heavily, "he has a much stronger weapon." Slowly, reluctantly, Haylow went on. "Deland has been having an affair with Marjorie. She is deeply in love with him. What's more, she's pregnant with his child."

The impact of these sparse, dreadful words hit Roger and Bridget with the force of a car crash. The full realization of all the repercussions slowly reached them. Roger found his voice first. He gave vent to his anger in profanity.

"That dirty, goddamn, rotten sonofabitch! That stinking, lousy, conniving bastard! I'll kill him. I swear to God I'll kill him!"

The eternal female in Bridget reacted differently. Her first concern was for Marjorie. She quickly grasped what this would mean to Woodward, to Pat, even to Joe's hopes for his elder son's future, as well as Haylow's dreams of glory about the transfer of power in his business. Gently, she touched Joe's arm.

"You've talked with Marjorie?"

"Yes. She loves Deland and wants to have his child. Of course she has no idea what kind of man he is. She knows nothing of the business with Roger. She thinks I am simply, once more, trying to run her life. As I've tried to run everyone else's."

There are times in life when values demand reassessment. The three people sitting in a room which represented all that was secure and successful by the world's standards, were, at that moment, poorer than the occupants of a rat-ridden ghetto. A poverty of spirit, a sense of futility gripped them. Their money, their success, their power were meaningless in the face of human tragedy. In his own way, each of the three searched for the meaning of life. Fear was in the room. And sorrow. And, above all, a terrible realization of how far the soul can stray from the earthly happiness that has nothing to do with the possession of material things.

For a long while, no one spoke. Words were suddenly meaningless, no more than a combination of sounds. Angry or soothing or sensible, words were only the human equivalent of an animal's cry of pain or roar of rage, anguished and inadequate to its needs.

Roger was the first to find his voice. "There's an expression horse-players use when they're in a losing streak," he said. "When you try to get even, you get even worse."

The other two looked at him in surprise. Incongruous words for such a solemn moment. But Roger meant them solemnly.

"I'm not being facetious," he said. "Revenge has no place here. If we destroy Deland, we destroy Marjorie. And we also destroy the good that Woodward can do for other frightened people."

"Not quite," Joe Haylow interrupted. "There's one other

thing I've been unwilling to admit. Woodward is never going to be the world's messenger of God. Oh, that's what I'd planned for him, of course. But that, like many other things, was a headstrong, selfish delusion of my own making. Jimmy Jackson has finally made me see that, too. He has made me realize that I have glorified Woodward out of all sensible and reasonable proportion. Not for God's sake. For my own."

"So whether Marjorie leaves him or not isn't significant as far as his future in the ministry is concerned?" The question was Bridget's.

"No, it's not significant," Joe said. "Not in terms of his success—or what I have always thought of as success—in the church. But his personal happiness—that's something else again."

"And Marjorie's," Roger added.

"Yes," Joe agreed, "Marjorie's too. At least her momentary happiness. I suppose, in a strange way, she is the one about whom I feel most guilty. If my ambitions for Woodward had not been fierce, if I had not sent him away for so long on those foolish witch-hunts, none of this would ever have happened."

"I don't believe that's true," Bridget said. "No amount of separation can destroy a marriage that's solid to begin with. The opportunity may have been handed to her, but somewhere inside the desire for a different kind of love was already there. If she had been completely happy with Woodward, it would not have been possible for her to fall in love with another man. No, there is a Marjorie none of us ever knew. Nothing you could have done—or not done—would have kept that other Marjorie hidden forever. She would have found another way out of her prison. Or, even worse, she would have lived only half a life, the quiet-desperation kind."

Haylow thanked her with his eyes. "I hope you are right," he said. "I have to believe, somehow, that you are, for the sake of my sanity."

Roger, who had been pacing the room during this exchange, suddenly came to a halt directly in front of his father. He was calm, composed, very much in charge of the situation.

"Father," he said, "all my life I hoped you'd find me. Then, in this last year, I thought I'd found you, only to lose you again. Now we have one more chance and I'm going to take it. I love the business and I want to run it. But I love you more. I'm not going to throw away the meaningful things of life just to keep the superficial ones. And I'm not going to let you do that, either.

"You haven't said it in so many words, but what you're doing is asking me to make the decision, isn't it?" Roger's question was direct.

Slowly, Joe Haylow nodded. "Yes. It is your right, your privilege. It can be your triumph. Or your sacrifice."

"Those are just words," Roger said kindly. "If I demand that you throw out Deland, what is my triumph? A job. At the expense of so much heartbreak for so many people that every moment in the Chairman's seat would be like ruling from a bed of nails. I don't call that triumph. I call it torture. And if I tell you to name Deland the new Chairman, what is my sacrifice? Still only a job. And a temporarily postponed one, at that. Because if it will make you happier, you must remember that the job will be mine in any case one day. When Deland retires in fifteen years, I will be only fifty-two years old. What's fifteen years in return for the love that you and I can share in those years?"

Haylow looked at him in amazement, seeing his son through new eyes. Pride in this young man filled him until he felt as though he would burst with it. Bridget was deathly still.

In one last effort, Joe offered an avenue of retreat.

"Are you sure, Roger? Can you swallow the bitter gall of seeing this unprincipled man put in such a position of power while you take second place? Fifteen years is a long time, son. And every day will remind you that it is your voice that should be making the decisions, your name that should be on the Chairman's door. Can you take it, Roger—knowing that this man who is beneath contempt is there because you have allowed him to ride roughshod over you and me?"

"I can take it, Father. Can you?"

"Yes," Joe Haylow said. "I can take it. For the same reasons you can. It's a small price to pay in exchange for the return of my son."

"Prodigal son?" Roger asked kindly.

"No," said Haylow with a wry flash of humor. "Prodigal father."

For the first time in Roger's memory, Joe Haylow kissed him. The two men stood quietly, holding onto each other. Unobtrusively, Bridget left the room. In the kitchen she busied herself making coffee. There was much more to talk about and it would be a long night.

17 ❧

On the night of their reconciliation, Roger and Joe talked until nearly dawn. New York was at its best in the first breaking light of day before the angry population was abroad, making its snarling, thoughtless, discourteous way through another day of the big city survival. In the hush of the first dawn of wintry light, they parted, having made several painful yet joyous decisions.

They agreed that with the decision to name Deland Chairman, Cabot's resignation would be required in order for Roger to assume the Presidency. No word of their knowledge about Cabot would reach him until after the dinner because secrecy, at all costs, must be maintained.

Later, he would be told the truth and a generous retirement arranged. He would be no loss to the company, and Roger's appointment would more than satisfy the bankers' demands for a "line of succession." For the moment, Woodward would have to remain ignorant of his wife's plan to divorce him and marry Brad. Both men felt sure that Marjorie would agree to live her lie for another couple of weeks. Brad, damn his soul, would be the one to convince her that he needed just this little more time to arrange matters with Doe-Doe. To make the business transition look as logical as possible and to keep the personal aspects away from the gossipmongers, those who knew everything would have to remain silent until after the retirement dinner. Those who knew nothing, like Pat and Woodward, would be left in blissful ignorance. Those who knew most of the story, like Sommers, Jackson, and Mike Warner, would simply be told by the Chairman that he had made his decision and would announce it at the banquet.

It was all a terribly complex and possibly unfair way to go about it. Pain and suffering were inevitable but they could be postponed for a little period of grace, and hopefully softened by the realization of a fait accompli. With Roger as President, Mike Warner would be made Executive Vice President. A new Financial VP to replace Deland would be found, hopefully within the vast account and auditing department of The Haylow Corporation.

Ridiculously, in view of the terrible giant steps he had had to take in January, the one thing Joe Haylow dreaded almost more than any other was the prospect of simulating a joyful Christmas. To cancel Pat's plans for a big gathering in Farmville would only arouse suspicions. It was unthinkable that the deceivers and the deceived would have to gather under one roof to play out the little game of togetherness. But there was no other way. Some of them would have to be very skillful actors. Others would be innocent pawns in this intricate game.

Following his all-night session with Roger, Haylow called Deland into his office the next morning and tersely outlined the plan. Struggling to control his loathing, irritated by Deland's superior smile of victory, Joe spelled out the terms in a matter-of-fact voice: Brad was to arrange Doe-Doe's departure for Mexico the day after the retirement dinner. Meanwhile, no one was to have a hint of his future plans and it was up to Brad to explain to Marjorie the necessity for a further short period of silence.

"You may tell Marjorie," Haylow said, "that I will do everything in my power to convince Woodward to let her have custody of their children. I cannot speak for my son, but I am sure he will agree to let them be with their mother. With the usual visiting rights, of course."

"She'll do anything I tell her," Brad said confidently. "As for Doe-Doe, I may need a substantial sum of cash quickly. More than I can get hold of right now."

Insult upon insult, Joe thought bitterly. But all he said was, "That can be arranged."

"Good enough. And don't worry about your business, Joe. I've learned a lot from you."

Haylow laughed mirthlessly. "And I from you, Deland."

"Touché," Deland said. "Anyway, Roger will be around to keep an eye on me, won't he? Not that he'll have the power to do much about it."

"Yes, Roger will be around. And you're right; he won't have the power. But you've overlooked one thing."

"What's that?"

"You'll have the title," Joe Haylow said. "But I'll still have the power. It's called 'control of the stock.' You'll make a good chief executive in your own way, Deland, but you'll still be only an employee while I'm the principal stockholder. I can block every unethical move you might try to make. And I will. I dreamed this business, created it, wrung it out of my guts. And I meant it for my son. Until he has it, I'll hold you accountable. And you'll sweat to prove the rightness of every decision you take. You'll justify every action to the Board of Directors and the stockholders of Haylow."

Deland's hatred was obvious. "Always the stubborn old goat, aren't you, Haylow? And the master of the cliché. So you intend to be 'the power behind the throne,' as the saying goes?"

For a moment Joe felt the old thrilling emotion of victory. He narrowed his eyes in the familiar Haylow scowl.

"Clichés? Perhaps. But there's one I like better. And I

intend to live it: 'A man is known by the company he keeps.' I'll still keep mine."

"We'll see," Deland said. "Is that all?"

"For now, yes."

"Okay," Brad said. "See you at our Christmas reunion in Farmville."

Haylow was shocked. "You're coming?"

"But of course. Doe-Doe and I wouldn't miss it. After all, Pat invited us. And, what's more, our absence might cause talk."

He is Satan, Joe thought helplessly. As black and evil and diabolical as sin. God help me. God help us all.

Oblivious in her goodness, Pat Haylow went happily about her preparations for Christmas in Farmville. Everyone except Sid Sommers and the Cabots had accepted. As she had anticipated, Sid had begged off to be with his grandchildren and their families. And Mildred Cabot had called to regret because, she said, she and Richard had planned to have one of Dick's old friends at their house for the holiday. Pat knew that the real reason was that Mildred was terrified of traveling in bad weather and it promised to be a very white Christmas in Vermont. The real old-fashioned kind, Pat thought with pleasure. The kind that's worth braving the icy roads and the hours-late train for, because it's so beautifully, virginally untouched, so much the way Christmas ought to be.

Like an impatient child, she awaited the day. The enormous tree begged to be decorated, the elegant but unpretentious dinner table waited to be set. And all around her would be her own people. There was room in the Haylow house for the Warners and Delands to stay overnight. Marjorie and Woodward would put up Bridget at their house. And, most blessed of all, Roger would be there. He had called her to say he was back from his trip and would bring Bridget up for the holiday. He sounded warm and loving, and hearing his voice made her realize how much she had missed him.

Since Woodward's revelation of his problems with Marjorie, they had had no further talks about it. Woodward volunteered nothing more, and Pat was not the kind of woman to pry into the lives of her children. Outwardly, all seemed serene with Marjorie, and Pat prayed that whatever had been troubling her had receded into the mysterious recesses of her mind from which it had sprung.

At noon on Christmas Eve, the "New Yorkers," as Pat thought of them, began to arrive. Roger and Bridget drove up with the Warners, arriving in high spirits and with reassurances that the drive hadn't been all that bad.

Bridget made a face when Roger nonchalantly dismissed the trip as nothing. "A piece of cake," he said.

"Maybe it's a piece of cake to a racing car driver," she said, "but I wouldn't have ventured it with anybody but you. Those roads are slicker than the glass in our Fifth Avenue windows!"

"And cleaner, too," Mike Warner teased.

Bridget pretended indignation. "Speak for your own," she said.

Pat was delighted with their nonsense. Even Joe who had come home the night before seemed to relax. Pat had been troubled by his quiet air when he arrived. He'd tried to reassure her that he was just tired. "The weather's too bad for flying," he explained, "and you know how I hate that blasted train. It always makes me testy. I'll be okay when I have a good night's sleep next to you."

Seeing him smiling now, joking with Mike, putting his arm affectionately around Rose, Pat felt relieved. It was going to be a happy Christmas.

"When do the Delands arrive?" she asked Joe.

"I think they're taking the morning train," he said. "Should be here by suppertime." For a moment, Pat saw the grimness return to his face. It made her uneasy.

"I'll go pick them up at the station later," Roger said. "Meantime, why don't I take Bridget over to Marjorie's and let her get settled in?"

"Fine," Pat agreed. "And I'll take Rose and Mike upstairs to unpack. I hope Brad and Doe-Doe's train isn't too late. I thought we'd have dinner about eight and I hate to rush them."

I wish the train would run off the track, Bridget thought. I wish I never had to see that Judas face again as long as I live. She glanced at Roger and Joe. They're better at this acting business than I am, she told herself. My God, how are we going to get through the next day and a half?

The New York train did not run off the track. Miraculously, it was only half an hour late, and by half-past seven everyone, including Jimmy Jackson, was gathered in front of the fireplace. There were the usual compliments for the tree, which stood ceiling-tall in the corner, its base covered with packages of all sizes and shapes.

"When do we open?" Roger said, looking at the mound of gifts.

"Are you kidding?" Woodward asked. "You forget that we have two very small Haylows reluctantly tucked into bed nearby. They'll be over here at dawn waiting for the moment, I warn you. Marjorie and I will try to keep them home by brute force until eight o'clock in the morning, but after that get ready for the onslaught!"

"I know it's awful to rout you all out so early tomorrow," Pat apologized, "but it's a favor for a very fatuous pair of grandparents. Joe and I just can't bear not being around when the children open their presents. None of the rest of you has to get up, really, if you can sleep through the din."

"I wouldn't miss it," Rose Warner said wistfully. Mike gave her a warm, understanding look.

"Well, frankly, folks, I can bring myself to live without it," Doe-Doe said. "Not that I have anything against the happy chirp of little voices, but at eight in the morning I'm a road-company Lady Macbeth. I'd walk in, arms outstretched, muttering, 'Out, damned spots!' Besides, Brad got me up with the birds to make that milk train this morning. So if you'll forgive me, I'll go to bed tonight with earplugs and you can tell me later what a great season F.A.O. Schwartz had, thanks to the Haylows."

She really is such a superficial bitch, Bridget thought. If her husband was anybody but Brad Deland I'd feel sorry for him. She looked to see where Brad and Marjorie were. They were almost studiedly oblivious to each other. Brad, lounging, drink in hand, near the fire seemed unaware of Marjorie's presence. And Marjorie, looking beautiful but deathly pale, made no effort to go near either of the Delands.

When Bridget was settling into the guest room at the Woodward Haylows', Marjorie had come in for a moment, full of friendly, hostessy concern for her comfort. But there had been no indication on Marjorie's part that she wanted to talk to another woman. Of course, she had no idea that Bridget knew of her troubles. Undoubtedly she would have been horrified if she had guessed that anyone but Brad and Joe knew the truth.

If Marjorie's attitude toward Brad was one of careful avoidance, it was one of strained cordiality toward her father-in-law. Both tried to act as though nothing was wrong between them and, to a surprising degree, succeeded. Only those who knew what had transpired could guess at the effort it must be taking to maintain the guise of normalcy.

Looking around the room, imagining what must be going on in the minds of so many of its occupants, Bridget gave a little shiver. It was an eerie feeling to realize that some of these people were happily unaware of how close at hand personal tragedy was. And it was almost indecent to watch the

369

carefully controlled good manners of those who despised and
feared and pitied and loved. Hateful to see the truth carefully masked by the outward trappings of civilized behavior.
Good breeding, Bridget thought, can be a terrible burden.
"Our kind of people" don't yell and accuse, much less murder.
We accept, as gracefully as we can, the patterns of behavior
most becoming to ladies and gentlemen. We are disciplined
and considerate. And most of us live with ulcers and die with
heart attacks.

Of all the people there, Joe Haylow's thoughts most closely
paralleled Bridget's. How can we do it? he wondered. Brad
and Marjorie, Roger, Bridget and I—how can we make the
small talk, the polite responses when we are so filled with
guilt and lust and loathing? From his big chair, he watched
these people he knew so well moving through their decorous
dance, saw the give-and-take of their conversation, the precise patterns of their behavior, and felt as though he were
watching some ritualistic ceremony which would culminate
in solemn, terrible ceremonial rites. It was morbid, this
"last Christmas," as he thought of it. It would be the last
in which even a pretense of harmony existed. Certainly it was
the last in which these same human beings would all be
gathered under one roof.

Somehow they got through dinner. Only Woodward's
gaiety seemed unforced. Of them all, only he seemed oblivious of the tension which lay like an invisible blanket of gloom
over the cold reality beneath. Pat and Rose, completely unaware of the reasons, were, at the same time, sensitive enough
to feel an unexplained tautness of the atmosphere. Jimmy
Jackson's face was full of unspoken questions. Doe-Doe had
managed, somehow, to get slightly drunk. Probably, Bridget
thought, she'd had a head start from a carefully packed flask
while she was dressing for dinner.

As they moved back into the living room after the meal,

Marjorie excused herself, obviously on her way upstairs toward the master bath.

"Hey, wait for me," Doe-Doe called. "I'll go with you."

Marjorie stiffened, then managed a smile. Together the present and future Mrs. Delands left the room. Chummily, Doe-Doe slipped her arm through Marjorie's. Inside the senior Haylows' bedroom, she closed the door. Her voice, which had been a little thick all through dinner, was completely clear and commanding.

"Grab a chair, Marjorie," she said. "We have a little talking to do."

Obediently, as though hypnotized, Marjorie did as she was told. She had always disliked Doe-Doe, but now she also felt fear of her. Or was it only guilt that made her incapable of looking directly at the hard, almost sadistic face of the woman who sat in the chair opposite her?

Doe-Doe took a cigarette out of her evening bag and lit it slowly, deliberately as though she savored this moment.

"Well, well," she said at last. "Who would have thought it? Of all the broads in the world that Brad Deland has laid, who'd have thought he'd end up with little Miss Good Ship Lollipop?"

Marjorie winced. Of course she knew that Brad had other women during his marriage to this horrible creature, but like a foolish schoolgirl she tried not to think of them, tried to tell herself that he had been involved but never in love. She clung to the belief that this was different.

"Oh, for Christ's sake," Doe-Doe snapped, "stop looking like a wounded dove. So you screwed around with my husband. You're not the first. And I daresay you won't be the last. As I recall, he's very good at it. And God knows that must be a revelation to you after what you've been living with."

"Doe-Doe," Marjorie said, "Brad and I love each other. We want to be married. Hasn't he told you?"

"Oh, yes, indeedy, he's told me all right. And I'm sure you'll be overjoyed to hear that I've agreed to let him go . . . poorer but wiser. I suppose he's told *you* that I get everything, including the kind of cash settlement that will put him in hock up to his ass for the rest of his life?"

"He hasn't discussed that part of it with me," Marjorie said with dignity. "But thank you, Doe-Doe. Thank you for letting us be together. It's not important about the money. All we both want is a life with each other."

"And with the darling little new baby, of course."

Marjorie was aghast. "You know about the baby?"

"Yes, I know about the baby," Doe-Doe mimicked. "You think I'm a rotten bitch, and you're right. But believe it or not, next to the fact that I'm going to be a filthy rich lady while I'm still young enough to enjoy it, the fact that you're pregnant was one of the reasons I decided to go for the divorce. Hard to believe, isn't it?"

"Yes," Marjorie said quietly, "it is."

"And I'll tell you something else that'll flip you out. I understand Brad Deland better than you or anybody else in this world will ever understand him. The only thing in this world he wants is power. And somewhere still inside of me is the stupid desire to see that he gets what he wants. Maybe I still even love him a little. Or else I'm getting soft in the head. But what the hell, if marrying you can get him the Chairmanship, who am I to be a dog in the manger about hanging on to him?"

Marjorie's bewilderment was unmistakable. "I don't understand," she said. "Marrying me will get Brad the Chairmanship? What are you talking about? If anything, it's just the opposite. I'm Joe Haylow's daughter-in-law. If anything, Brad's love for me is going to cost him his chance at that job he wants so much! That's one of the things that's so wonderful—that he will risk his whole future because of his love for me!"

Jesus, she doesn't know about him, Doe-Doe thought. She doesn't know that Brad has blackmailed Joe Haylow into swapping the big job for shushing up a big scandal. She doesn't know that Brad has used her as the weapon. And that he'd drop her like a hot canapé if Haylow backed down on the deal. She really, honest to God, doesn't know!

For a moment, Doe-Doe was tempted to shut up and let Marjorie live with her fantasy as long as she could. Then fury at Brad took over. That son of a bitch, she fumed. I thought Marjorie was in on the deal with him. The poor, dumb kid—throwing away everything she's got for my stinking husband. Okay, so Woodward's a drag, but he's honest and he loves her. Brad will use her and then, some drunken, bored-out-of-his-skull night, he'll tell her the truth. And she'll wish she were dead.

"Listen, Marjorie. I'm sorry. I thought you knew that the Chairmanship went along with the package. To tell you the truth, I figured that because you were so mesmerized by Brad, you'd agreed to force Haylow's hand. I really believed you knew the score and were willing to pay the price. To me, it made sense. Like he gets the job and you get him. I should have had better sense, knowing both of you."

The full significance of what Doe-Doe was saying began to reach Marjorie. But even as she absorbed it, she denied it. It wasn't true, she told herself. Brad loved her beyond all other considerations. He wanted her for herself, and for the child Doe-Doe had never given him. The job, the ridiculous, meaningless job, was of no importance to him. I mustn't listen, she thought. I mustn't let this vengeful woman put these terrible doubts in my mind. Not now. Not ever.

"You're lying," she said. "You've never wanted to divorce Brad, not even for money. This is your way of holding on to him now."

"Oh, Marjorie, don't be an ass," Doe-Doe said impatiently. "If I really wanted to stop this thing I could. Or at least I could drag my feet so long that your kid would be in kindergarten before you could legalize it. What I told you before was true. I agreed to the divorce because I've still got some kind of crazy love-hate feeling for that louse. I wanted him to have what he wanted—that goddamn job that's such an obsession with him. And I figured the only way he could get it was through you. I knew that Joe Haylow would make the sacrifice for you and for Woodward. There was no other way for Brad to make it—not with Roger right there waiting to slip into the old man's chair."

Doe-Doe laughed bitterly. "Bradford Deland III," she went on. "Con man par excellence. What an operator! My God, it's funny. He even found a way to get to me, after all these years, with that pathetic story about his one great chance for success. And I bought it. Imagine that. I bought it. Tough, cynical, selfish little Dorothy Deland got all emotional and decided to make the big sacrifice for a guy she once loved. Now ain't that a kick in the head!"

A numbness had come over Marjorie. Reluctantly, she began to face the truth. This was why Brad had insisted, over her protests, that she tell Woodward nothing until after Joe Haylow's retirement dinner. This was why Joe had begged her to give up Brad and his unborn child. They both knew that her naïveté had been her undoing. But one wanted her to retain it for his own selfish ends. The other did not have the heart to tell her the truth. She began to laugh, hysterically. She laughed uncontrollably until Doe-Doe came over and shook her roughly by the shoulders.

"Stop it!" Doe-Doe commanded. "Stop it, Marjorie. They'll hear you downstairs!"

Her laughter turned now to a whimper, little moaning sounds of pain. Unaware of her actions, she put her hands protectively on her belly where the victim of her innocence lay.

When she spoke, her voice was a whisper. "Dear God," she breathed, "what have I done to us all?"

Doe-Doe's voice had returned to its usual crisp flippancy. "Whatever you've done to us all, it's too late now. No use standing there like the kid with the match, wishing you hadn't burned the house down. Even if you threw yourself on your husband's mercy, you won't get Joe Haylow off the hook. That won't stop Brad from destroying everybody in sight. There's a madness in him. If he loses you, the only weapon he has, he'll let the world know that your baby is a bastard and your husband cuckolded. He'll make such a stink about the Haylows that none of you—not Roger, not Pat, not Woodward— will ever be able to look at each other again. Oh, the Haylow dynasty will continue, all right. The business will go on. But no longer as the model of the empire administered under God. Brad will make sure that the world knows he was purged for impregnating the minister's wife while the minister was out trying to destroy his nearest competitor. Believe me, Marjorie, I know him. Jesus Christ, do I know him! Nobody denies Brad what he wants. Ever. Look at me. It took him years to find my Achilles heel, but he managed. I can't back out of the divorce now and save you that way. It wouldn't do any good. Because it wouldn't stop Brad's vicious smear campaign. Nothing can."

The anguish in Marjorie's eyes reminded Doe-Doe of the face she used to see in her own mirror years ago when she still loved Brad deeply and when he could still wound her beyond endurance.

"Look, kid," Doe-Doe said. "It isn't the end of the world. You'll be the right kind of wife for the new Chairman. Woodward will get over it. And if we're lucky, only a handful of people will ever know the truth. I don't promise you'll live happily ever after with Brad, but you'll have some happiness. Enough, maybe, to compensate for the guilt and the tears.

"We're strange creatures, we women, aren't we?" Doe-Doe

went on. "Once we've found the guy for us, no matter how rotten he is, no matter how selfishly and dishonestly he uses us, we can't just brush him aside, can we? In spite of all this, you still want Brad. And you still want his baby. Right?"

"I don't know," Marjorie said miserably.

"The hell you don't. You want him. Maybe not right this second. But you'll want him in the middle of the night when you wake up next to Woodward and wish it was Brad there waiting to make love to you. I know. I've thought the same about a lot of guys on the other pillow. After Brad it's never the same. I've always wanted him too, even when I pretended I didn't."

For the first time, Marjorie looked at this woman with new respect. This was the Doe-Doe kept hidden from the world, protected by an armor reluctantly donned for self-preservation. Her flippancy, her shallow self-indulgence, her studied irreverence were deliberate cover-ups for a sensitivity that had been bruised once too often.

"I never knew you before," Marjorie said wonderingly. "If I had, things might have been different."

The voice that answered was the old, cynical one of an hour before.

"Sure," Doe-Doe said. "And if my aunt had balls she'd be my uncle."

The two women, so different yet so closely tied by their bondage to one man, looked at each other with sympathy and understanding. It would never happen again, this precious communication, this defenseless honesty, this professed love for a common enemy. They spanned a thousand years, spoke a million words in one single, unflinching gaze.

Then they went back to the party.

The group broke up early, grateful for the pretext of the impatient children whose curiosity would not be contained past eight o'clock on Christmas morning. A subdued Marjorie and an ebullient Woodward took Bridget off with them. Jimmy Jackson gripped Joe Haylow's hand firmly as they said good night at the door. Reassuringly, the Chairman smiled. The Warners, the Delands, and Roger went up to their rooms. Pat wandered around turning off lights, talking over her shoulder to Joe, who waited for her.

"I think it was a nice evening, don't you, dear?" she asked.

"Perfect. As always."

"Woodward seemed in awfully good spirits, didn't you think? I do hope he and Marjorie have set things right between them."

She did not seem to notice Joe's lack of response.

"And isn't it wonderful to have Roger home again? He seems thin to me, though. I don't think he eats enough." She laughed. "Listen to me. You're right. I do carry on about him like he's still a baby. It's hard to remember that he's thirty-seven. Joe?"

"Hmmm?"

"Wouldn't it be wonderful if Roger and Bridget got married?"

"Yes, darling, wonderful. But wouldn't you rather see him choose someone a little younger? You know how much I love Bridget, but to be practical, it might be late for her to start a family."

"Oh, pooh," Pat scoffed. "These days lots of women in their early forties have children. Anyway, Joe, as much as I'd like more grandchildren, that's not as important as their happiness. Maybe children don't mean that much to them. Or they could adopt. Anyway, we have Woodward's two little ones to spoil rotten!"

My beloved Pat, Joe Haylow thought, how soon your bubble will burst. Are you really as lighthearted and oblivious as you seem? Or are you pretending for me, as you've done so often in all these years? He had no way of knowing whether the undercurrents of the evening had reached her. It seemed impossible that they had not. Yet his own awareness might have been less acute if he, like Pat, had no knowledge of the next act of the drama they were living.

Undressing in their own room, Pat continued to chatter away.

"The Warners are such darlings, aren't they? Mike's been wonderful about that cosmetics company you plan to buy, hasn't he?"

"He's been invaluable," Haylow said.

Climbing into bed, Pat gave a little sigh of contentment. "I missed Sid tonight," she said. "Dear, old friend. Whatever would we do without him?"

Joe slipped under the covers on his side. Gently, he took her hand.

"I suppose it's wicked of me," Pat said, "but I didn't really miss the Cabots. Oh, they're nice enough people, but they don't really contribute much. Dick is so, I don't know, unfathomable. And Mildred just overpowers me with all that competence!"

Haylow chuckled. "You have an extraordinary way of pinpointing people. And if you're wicked, then we're a pair of lost sinners. I didn't miss the Cabots for a minute, either."

"That's nice," Pat said comfortably. "Makes me feel less guilty."

They lay quietly in the darkness. Outside, the world was white and still and deceptively remote from the dark problems that surrounded them. Then Pat spoke softly.

"Joe?"

"Yes, my love?"

"Did you notice how long Marjorie and Doe-Doe were gone when they came upstairs this evening?"

Yellow light. Caution. Joe was instantly alert to danger. He tried to keep his voice noncommittal.

"Well, yes, they did seem to stay awhile. What of it?"

"I don't know. Except that those two have never been very

close. If it had been Marjorie and Bridget upstairs gossiping, I wouldn't have thought anything of it. And they both looked so unhappy when they came back."

Joe had noticed the prolonged absence too, and worried about it. Brad must have discussed the divorce with Doe-Doe, but what else had he told her? It was not possible that he had revealed Marjorie's pregnancy nor his own guarantee of the Chairmanship. Yet it was possible, if those were weapons he needed to get Doe-Doe's agreement. Suppose money had not been enough? Suppose he had had to play on Doe-Doe's sympathy? He might even have used the Chairmanship as a threat. The last thing in the world that Doe-Doe wanted was the obligations and restrictions which throttled the life of the Chairman's wife. Perhaps she had agreed to the divorce just to avoid them. And, most unbearable of all, what if she had told the whole story to Marjorie? Despite the cold night, Joe began to sweat profusely. What if Marjorie knew, right now, how she had been used by Deland? What if, at this very moment, she was telling it all to Woodward? Calling on all his discipline he put these thoughts out of his mind. The answer he gave Pat was the one he made himself believe.

"Darling, I don't see anything so unusual about a couple of ladies spending time in the powder room. Maybe you didn't notice, but Doe-Doe was a little drunk. Marjorie probably stayed with her while she was pulling herself together."

Please buy it, Joe willed silently. Please let me give you just a little more time before the heavy weight of sadness descends.

"I'm sure you're right," Pat said. "Silly of me, but I never think about people getting drunk in this house. She must have brought something with her. She only had one cocktail before dinner and a little wine."

Joe breathed a sigh of relief. "Get some sleep, sweetheart. Your grandchildren will be beating on the doors before you know it."

In the darkness, he could imagine her smiling with anticipation at the thought.

"All right, dear," she said. "But I have one more sin to confess before I say good night."

"And what's that, you fallen woman?"

"I really don't like the Delands."

"If it's any comfort," Joe said lightly, "you have just joined a very large segment of the population. Now shut up, love, and go to sleep."

She nestled her head on his shoulder and followed his orders.

Haylow could not close his eyes all night.

18 ❧

A howl of protest awakened Joe Haylow on the morning of his last day as Chairman. For a moment, it seemed like a scream from deep within himself. Then, feeling foolish, he recognized it as the shrieking of the gale outside his window. Somehow it was fitting that he would make his exit in a raging blizzard. The weather matched his mood—angry, rebellious, almost violent. The gigantic storm gnashing its teeth in fury was a menacing omen of the day to come, the day that would end in an agonizing announcement.

In the Park Avenue apartment, Pat slept fitfully beside him. Through the night, they had been a restless pair. Joe had managed to keep the full knowledge of the recent events from her. But she was too sensitive, too delicately attuned to his feelings to be unaware that for the last two months she had been living with a tormented man. She asked no questions and he volunteered no details. But the anguish that encompassed Haylow left its uneasy mark on his wife.

Because of the blizzard—*The New York Times* called it the worst in twenty years—Pat had come down from Farmville the day before, insurance that she would be beside him on the dais that night of his retirement dinner. Jimmy Jackson came on the train with her and was safely ensconced in the Grand Excelsior. Woodward and Marjorie had planned to drive down together, leaving very early this morning. But two days before, Woodward was summoned to the White House for a meeting of Clergymen for Drug Rehabilitation, a group which had been petitioning the President for an audience. Unfortunately, the leader of the Nation had chosen this unfortunate moment in time to see them. It was a command performance, an invitation impossible to decline. It was also a new area of work in which Woodward was intensely interested. He would come up from Washington on the train this afternoon, meeting Marjorie in New York.

For her part, Marjorie had reluctantly agreed to take the morning train from Farmville to New York. She loathed the train and had suggested that she drive down alone. On the phone the evening before, both Pat and Joe firmly vetoed the idea.

"Absolutely not," Haylow had said. "The storm is getting worse by the minute. You take the train."

On the extension, Pat echoed his decision. "We know you're a wonderful driver, Marjorie dear, but you simply have no idea how awful the weather is here. They say the storm is moving north, too. It really would be too dangerous."

"Honestly, it isn't," Marjorie protested. "The roads are still clear here and traffic is moving nicely. That train will take absolutely forever. Besides, you know how I enjoy driving. And I'm as careful as a little old lady."

"Well, I want you to live to be one," Joe said gruffly. "Now let's have no more arguments. I'll send a car to the station for you. The train doesn't get into New York until six-thirty so Pat and I won't be able to meet you. There's a reception before the banquet. But you come straight here, change your clothes and have the car wait to bring you and Woodward to the hotel. We'll all meet outside the Main Ballroom a little after eight. You're sitting on the dais next to Woodward, you know," he said meaningfully. "And we're having a little family get-together here later. A final, unofficial farewell."

"I know," she said. "I suppose you're right about the drive.

I might miss the whole thing if I tried it. Okay. See you later."

Poor Marjorie, Joe thought now, remembering last night's call. These last months have been hell for her, and it's only the beginning of her agony. After tonight, after I announce Brad's appointment, every meeting with the Haylows will be a nightmare. When she is divorced and married to Deland there still will be no escape for her. As the wife of the new Chairman, she'll be more involved than ever in the family business. Logically, his thoughts turned to Woodward. From his son's attitude, Joe was sure that Marjorie had kept her promise of silence about everything. It suddenly occurred to him with horror that Woodward might hear it all tonight, for the first time, at the "family get-together." Surely, Marjorie would have prepared him for the terrible news, figured some way to prevent his humiliation before Deland and the others. Yet how could she without breaking her word? In a lesser way, Joe was equally guilty. He had kept Pat in the dark, too. Mother and son would innocently come to the "celebration" after the dinner, not dreaming what revelations were in store for them.

Joe shuddered at what lay ahead. He wished now that both Pat and Woodward had been let in on the terrible secret, but looking at his sleeping wife he knew that he could not tell her before the dinner. He considered calling Woodward in Washington and immediately dismissed the thought. This news could not come to a man impersonally, over the telephone. Dear God, what cowards we are, he thought. We masquerade our weaknesses under the pretense of sparing our loved ones as long as we can. He now realized that the conference to discuss the sordid details of divorces and the disposition of goods both human and inanimate should have been done before this day. There should have been a family meeting right after Christmas. He hadn't been able to face it. He couldn't face it now, even if it had been possible to get them all together before the banquet.

The banquet. A feast of fools. He shuddered at the thought of play-acting his way through the interminable dinner. Only Roger, Bridget, and Deland were, to his knowledge, aware of what his decision would be. The first two had accepted it with compassion and understanding. The "winner" had cared only for the victory, nothing for the unfairness of it. Haylow did not know what had transpired between Marjorie and Doe-Doe on Christmas Eve. The next day they had maintained their usual attitudes, Marjorie sweetly involved in the children's excitement, Doe-Doe unmistakably bored and restless, anxious to get away from the stifling ritual of a family Christmas.

In the week between Christmas and New Year, Deland had matter-of-factly confirmed to Haylow that Doe-Doe would leave for Mexico the morning after the banquet. Too disturbed to ask for details, Joe assumed that Marjorie would follow a few days later and that Brad would join her. The two would be married in Mexico. Even as quietly as they could manage it, the whole affair would be splashed all over the press. The ugliness of it, the sadness of it, was like a hidden cancer in Haylow. Perversely, he almost welcomed the operation which would be an open admission of the disease. He was coming to the breaking point, weighed down with his awful knowledge, unable much longer to maintain the pose of invincibility. Let it be over, he prayed. No matter how terrible, let it be over.

He had even accepted what he rejected in anger a few months before—the conviction that Woodward was not meant to be a world figure in the work of Christianity. Leafing through a news magazine the week before, he had read a story about Elvis Mallory, the young southern evangelist. Seeing it there in black and white, Joe at last believed what Jimmy Jackson had been trying to show him for a year.

"Religious rap," the news story was headlined. Joe read it carefully. "Twenty-two-year-old, bearded, blue-jeaned Elvis Mallory is representative of the new wave of Christianity which many believe is the way of the future. In artists' lofts, Mallory's religious services are held against a background of abstract paintings. The burning smell is not incense but pot. The 'choir boys' are long-haired and barefooted. The 'congregation' wears Indian headbands and love in its eyes. Mallory is a new kind of 'preacher' who tells his flock to 'turn on with love,' to 'rap with Christ.' His followers, mostly young, now number in the thousands, finding hope and truth and consolation in this unorthodox leader who tells a two-thousand-year-old story like it is."

Looking at the photographs of the rapt young face of Mallory and the ecstacy of his listeners, Joe Haylow accepted what Jackson had told him earlier.

"This is the way of religion in the future," Jimmy said quietly. "It will not replace churches or formal rites for many people, but it lets a new generation identify with the Almighty. They can relate to the subject in a way their parents could not. By touching each other, they touch God. Mallory understands this. He talks about things they understand. Things *he* understands. War and peace, discrimination, poverty, drugs, and brotherhood. Christ-like things, Joe, when you think about them."

In a last protest, Haylow had looked thoughtful. "But this is a passing phase. It's youth forever trying to find itself and always coming back to the verities. Woodward's kind of teaching, like yours, is built on centuries of truth, the Bible, the Written Word."

"Yes," Jimmy agreed, "and it will endure for much of the world. But our kind of preaching is equivalent to a politician of the old school, whistle-stopping from the back of a train while his opponent sells his campaign on television. The young believe in themselves. Their spiritual leader must know life the way they do, must want the same kind of forceful, rational changes that they want. To this generation, God isn't a white-bearded old man who threatens. He's a beautiful piece of electric energy that revitalizes them."

"And Woodward's role in all this?"

"It will be a smaller one," Jackson said, "but no less an important one. He will guide his flock as he knows how to do, to the accompaniment of a gentle voice, not to the strains of a rock group. Let him be, Joe. Let him find his own place in the scheme of things. This is what God wants, I think. And Woodward will do it well. Don't pressure him. Let him live his own dreams. Not yours."

Watching the snow press against the sides of the window, Joe felt comforted. Woodward was strong. He would survive the loss of Marjorie. Perhaps he would feel relief, freed of the demands of an ambitious father. The hope of world recognition had never been Woodward's at all. Jackson was right. The power drive was Joe's.

It would be all right with both his boys. They were better men than he, stronger in their own ways. He had wanted power for them and they had wanted only love. They had tried to match his ambitions, coddle his vanity, insure his immortality. And God had stepped in and said No.

Beside him, Pat wakened, smiling uncertainly. For a moment she watched him wordlessly. Her only concern was that this was the day he would give up the business he loved so much. Today she had beaten her rival. But she felt no joy in the winning. Only pity for the man who seemed terribly far away, deeply engrossed in his own thoughts. He lay motionless, arms behind his head, a terrible resignation in his eyes yet, Pat thought, with a certain fatalistic acceptance as well.

She put her head on his shoulder. One still-beautiful arm rested lightly across his chest.

"Are you terribly sad, darling?" she asked.

"Sad? That isn't sadness you see. It's hunger. I'm waiting for my lazy wife to get up and fix my breakfast."

She was not deceived.

"I know how you feel about leaving the company, dearest, and this is the day. Dare I say, my love, 'Happy Birthday'?"

Joe hugged her very hard. "Dare you *not* say it! Come on, Mrs. Haylow. Up you go. Relinquish me, woman, I have work to do!"

His bravado broke her heart. But she tried to match his cheerfulness. Slipping into her robe, she quickly ran to close the window.

"Brrrrrr," she shivered. "Not much like Florida! When can we leave for the sunny South?"

"Would twenty minutes be too soon?"

"Not for me. But you see, I have this famous husband who has to get honored tonight. The Governor of New York will be there, and lots of important personalities, and a whole raft of what we call the Beautiful People. So I just have to stick around—at least until tomorrow. But then I'm free as a bird. And so is my famous husband."

Some bird, Haylow thought as he stepped into the shower. Once I thought of myself as a young eagle who would become a wise old owl. And what did I become? An ostrich with my head buried in the sands of imagined glory. Haylow, he told himself, Roger was right. You're a phony. Tonight you're going to make a phony speech, ending with a fraudulent endorsement. It's a very pretty ending, isn't it? Expedient and very, very sensible. The sorry solution of Joe Haylow—the Gutless Wonder.

In this mood of deep depression, the Chairman made his way down Park Avenue through the heavily falling snow, past the army of doormen who were fighting a losing battle to keep the entrances of their apartment buildings cleared of the sleety downpour.

As he entered his office on this last official day, it already seemed a strangely impersonal place. Irrelevantly, he wondered whether Deland would move his "early Wall Street" furnishings into this room or whether Haylow's quarters would remain intact and empty, like some gloomy monument to the founder who was dead though still living.

Suddenly he couldn't bear to leave it all. For a reckless moment, he thought of announcing tonight that he had decided to remain as Chairman, overturning his own rule for the benefit of his company. But of course he couldn't. Any more than he could hand over the business he'd built to the one who rightfully deserved it.

Determinedly, he began to draft his speech for tonight. Bitterly, he wrote: "I, Joseph Woodward Haylow, being of sound mind and body . . ." Angrily, he tore the yellow page off the pad and threw it, wadded, into the wastebasket.

Then, in his precise, constricted handwriting, he began to compose the last message he intended to deliver as Chairman.

They were all there on the dais as the Governor trod his patent, political way deftly toward the introduction of Joe Haylow. All, that is, except Woodward and Marjorie. Neither had arrived shortly after eight o'clock when the guests of honor gathered to march in, like some ridiculous procession of royalty, to take their places on the platform. A few minutes after the hour, Joe had sent Roger to phone the apartment. He had returned saying that no one answered. Pat had looked troubled. She drew Haylow aside.

"Joe, dear, you don't think anything has happened to them, do you?" she asked. "They should be here by now."

"Darling, they're probably stuck in traffic," he'd reassured her, "and there'd be no way to let us know. Don't worry. They'll be here, even if they have to walk."

Secretly, Haylow was apprehensive. But for a different reason. He was suddenly convinced that Marjorie had decided to tell Woodward about herself and Brad. He was sure that they were still in the apartment, talking, refusing to answer the insistent demands of the telephone. He felt that neither of them would appear at the dinner. And he was grateful and relieved that Marjorie was sparing Woodward the cruelty of hearing her news in the presence of others. Of course, that's what it was. How could he have thought for a moment that any woman, least of all Marjorie, would permit an innocent man to be so publicly humiliated, so flagrantly emasculated? He thought with sadness of the scene that must be taking place between them. But it was better. By the time the group assembled at the apartment later, Woodward would have had time to compose himself, to accept the dreadful finality of it all.

When the folded note addressed to him in Woodward's handwriting was passed to him during the Governor's talk, he was not surprised to see his son's familiar script. As he prepared to open it discreetly beneath the table level, Joe knew what it would say. Woodward would explain that he and Marjorie would not be coming to the dinner because of a personal problem. Instead, he read, with horror, a dreadfully different message written in a shaky scrawl.

"Father," the note said, "there has been an accident. The police called to say that Marjorie's car went off the road an hour ago. I am on my way there now. She is dead, father. Marjorie has left me. Pray for us. Woodward."

Shock and agonizing disbelief overcame Joe Haylow. Vacantly, he patted his wife's hand in an automatic gesture of reassurance. Marjorie was dead. By accident or by her own design? Only God would ever know. Like a well-programmed robot, his next reactions were conditioned. Methodically, discreetly he tore up his prepared speech. The hand of God had cruelly cleared the way to the only just decision. Or, Joe thought, tasting the bitterness of his own sorrow, was it the hand of a woman who had deliberately determined the destiny of the good and the evil?

Dimly, Joe Haylow heard the applause which signaled the end of the Governor's introduction and the beginning of his own remarks. For a terrifying moment he was certain that no words would come. That there was, indeed, nothing to say. Nothing that mattered anymore. Then discipline returned. Life goes on, he thought. The sacrifice of one is the salvation of many.

Not knowing how he got there, he found himself at the microphone. He had, he supposed, shaken the Governor's hand, probably even smiled for the benefit of the popping flashbulbs. He waited for the silence. Then he began.

"Governor McCarthy, distinguished guests, my beloved family, friends, and co-workers. A French philosopher once said that a man is the sum total of his experience—minus his vanity. Tonight, in my last appearance as Chairman, I present this sum total for your reckoning.

"It is a balance sheet with both assets and deficits. There are plusses of achievement and minuses of neglect. Columns of arrogance and notations of humility. It is the ledger of a man's life, full of joy and sorrow, love and hate, unselfishness and greed. Inscribed in it are, hopefully, some words of wisdom. And, regrettably, some accounts of error.

"You, collectively, will be the auditor. I ask you to examine very carefully this final report. And then you will decide whether this employee of the Lord is spiritually sound or morally bankrupt.

"Come back with me to another world. A world of forty years ago. A world into which many of you here tonight had not even come. A world in which others of you were happy children or eager young people teetering expectantly on the edge of adulthood . . . reaching out for the moments of ecstacy which you knew lay just ahead.

"We think of it now as a different world, a naïvely simple, uncomplicated place compared to the one in which we live today. We had lived through a big war—to keep the world safe for democracy, they said. We were riding high in our possession of material riches. For in January 1929 we did not

know that we were mere months away from the greatest
financial disaster our nation had ever known. We had our
dreams, our ambitions. We kept them in the rumble seats of
our cars and the pockets of our raccoon coats. We flaunted
our self-confidence for all the world to see, like carefree
students waving their college banners at a football game. We
paid our dues to the world in small-change tokens of respect
for motherhood, apple pie, the American flag, and God. We
sought success, power, riches. And, of course, we expected
that mirage called happiness. Man-made, with the benevolent approval of an all-wise and protective God who asked
only fidelity in return.

"Forty years ago I thought I knew how to get all those
things. And for thirty-nine years I thought I had them.

"Success? Today the Haylow flag flies in nearly as many
places as the American emblem. In Japan they make it of rice
paper. In Paris they stitch it up in peau de soie. Is it any
more than a symbol of one man's ego?

"Power? I have held in the palm of my hand the lives and
destinies of hundreds of thousands of people. Some have
found shelter in that palm. Others have felt it open relentlessly and drop them cruelly into oblivion. Many have
profited by the soft touch of Haylow's hand. Others have
been crippled or slain by the relentless karate chop of the
executive decision. In the name of power I have provided joy
and provoked despair. And for thirty-nine years I was untouched by either emotion.

"Riches? All these years I thought the word meant money.
Money to compensate for compassion, money to divert those
nearest and dearest to me from making demands upon Joe
Haylow the man, the husband, the father, the friend. Money
to work for God. Money to help the poor. Money to buy the
future safety of the people I love. That's what I thought
money was for. I traded it for time. Time to make more

money, grasp more power, swallow more and more heady gulps of success.

"And what of happiness? In my vanity, I thought I had it all. I thought God had prepared some kind of special blessing for me. I thought he had immunized me against the disease of failure with some miraculous heavenly serum. God continued to smile. And I mistook his kindness for approval, his benevolence as a just reward for the service I gave him."

In the audience, Joe was aware of an embarrassed shifting of bodies. His trained ear detected a tiny murmur of conversation, voices wondering almost inaudibly at this unorthodox and untypical display of emotion. Like the trained public speaker he was, Haylow knew when to switch his tone. An uncomfortable audience was an inattentive and unreceptive one. And he meant them to remember this speech.

"I am very proud," he said quietly, "of what The Haylow Corporation has become. It is a sound and solid business built on integrity, hard work, and skill. Not mine. I was only its sire. For forty years, the growth of Haylow has been nurtured by the ability of its employees, the honesty of its policies, the appreciation and support of its public. We have grown as a company because of the only thing that counts —the unselfish giving of themselves by people who have gently and compassionately allowed the Chairman to indulge his fantasy of omnipotence.

"This is why I say that for thirty-nine years I lived in blissful ignorance of the real reasons for my success, my power, my riches, and my happiness. In one year—one short, stunning year of upheaval and trial—my fantasies have been revealed to me for what they truly are. I have seen my wife as she really exists. Not merely a beautiful, wonderful companion, but a steady source of faith and comfort, a wellspring of unquestioning faith and true Christian love. I have come to know my sons as men of character and strength, willing to sacrifice their own desires for the peace and protection of others. And for the fulfillment of my own foolish, shallow dreams. I have seen, with grateful new eyes, the depth of tolerance and understanding of which my dearest friends are capable. I have tried their patience, doubted their wisdom, closed my ears to their gentle offers of help, arrogantly disdainful of the pitfalls they warned me to avoid."

Deliberately, Joe Haylow paused. Turning his head slowly from right to left, he looked down the length of the front tier. Roger was a study in intensity. Pat's eyes welled with tears. Cabot seemed politely disinterested. Brad's jaw had tensed, as though he knew something had gone wrong. Bridget and Mike Warner seemed to be sending him silent messages of love and encouragement. Steadily, Joe went on.

"Until this year, I could see none of these things, none of these people. Because my eyes were fastened on the only goal I really wanted: unending power. It is no secret to most of you that I have dreaded this retirement day. My confidence in anyone but myself was so frail that in my heart I believed this great corporation would snap like some fragile thread unless I alone held the string. In my fear for its safety I was ready to compromise its future.

"I came here tonight prepared to name a man unworthy of the sacred trust I was about to give him. Not unworthy in a business sense. Far from it. A skilled executive, a dedicated one. A strong, single-minded, hard-driving tyrant who would have run this business well but who would have changed it from the thing it started out to be . . . the thing of which I, too, lost sight in thirty-nine years of cold-blooded conceit and reckless ambition.

"Perhaps," Joe Haylow said quietly, "I saw in that man a reflection of myself. Obsessed with power, lusting for control, heedless of consequences. Rich and righteous. I rationalized my choice in the name of kindness to others, in the self-induced delusion that by sacrificing his principles a man can still maintain his honor.

"What nonsense. What an unforgivable sin I was about to commit. Under the cloak of common sense I was hiding a frightened, intimidated spirit. I was prepared to be unjust, unpardonable, and un-Christian. No one on earth was going to stop me. But someone above mortal pettiness could. And He did.

"God knew I lacked courage. So God did my job for me. He ripped the thin veil of cowardice from these eyes and forced me to look at the most terrible truth of all. And the truth is that when a man fancies himself above his Maker, he will be punished for his impertinence.

"A few moments ago, God forced his help upon me. In the cruelest fashion He showed me the right way. His strong hand reached out and struck a blow that brought me to my knees. The way a loving parent strikes a willful child, not in anger but in love.

"Tomorrow you will know terrible facts of that blow. You will, I know, grieve with me for the terribleness of God's wrath. But I alone will atone to God and ask for His forgiveness. All the while thanking Him for sparing so many the penalty of my arrogant concern with a few.

"Tonight, despite its moments of pain, has mercifully turned into an occasion of thanksgiving. For in the most heartless of ways, God has acted not only for the good of His servant Joe Haylow but, much more importantly, He has seen fit to protect the lives and well-being of hundreds of thousands of people whose lives and well-being depend upon this company and the man who will lead it. This is right. This is just. This is God's will.

"My friends, with the humility of a mortal, the confidence of a businessman, and the pride of a father, I give you the next Chairman—my beloved son Roger Haylow."

For a fraction of a second, Roger did not believe what he'd heard. He saw the happy face of his mother, the stricken look of Dick Cabot, the disbelief of Brad Deland. With a surge of joy he recognized the love of Bridget Manning and the surprised delight of Mike Warner. But above all, he saw his father, a man proud in his admission of frailty, strong in his confession of error.

Like a man in a dream, Roger rose slowly to join Joe Haylow at the microphone. Once again the ballroom was a sea of rhythmically applauding hands and craning necks, all eager to see and approve Haylow's choice. When the ovation ended, Joe, his arm around his son, spoke once again.

"There is no one to whom I can more fittingly bequeath this great company, this demanding mistress who was born in an age of youthful optimism, who survived the years of abuse, and who will continue to live and grow even more beautiful in the hands of one who will understand and cherish her. I have no parting words for my son. No advice. No caution. Only confidence. He is my offspring but not my image. He sees hope where I have seen duplicity, reality where I have clouded my eyes with self-serving visions. I give him only my faith, my pride, and a tribute he will understand:

"'Two men look out through the same bars:
One sees the mud, and one the stars.'"

Quietly Joe Haylow stepped aside. In the center of the stage Roger Haylow stood tall, powerful, and beautiful. Filled with love.